To Valerie

Hope you enjoy the

Story

Best Wishes

THE CALL OF THE HUNTSMAN

NINA WHITEHOUSE

The Derwent Press
Derbyshire

www.derwentpress.com

The Call of the Huntsman
By
Nina Whitehouse

ISBN: 1-84667-015-2

Cover art and book design by:
Pam Marin-Kingsley
www.far-angel.com

Published in 2006 by
The Derwent Press
Derbyshire, England

www.derwentpress.com

Dedication

*I dedicate this book to the memory of
my dearly loved sister Eileen.
Her life shines like a beacon to women.
This is how mothers should bring up their children.
Her capacity to go to work everyday and never
complain or say a bad word was saintly.
She supported each and every one of us
when we ran to her with our problems.
She dedicated her life to achieving
the best possible life for her children.
Her great epitaph will always be
their success in life.*

Acknowledgements

Without the constant tech support of David Artschan I could not have finished this book. He recovered the files many times over the ten years of writing. He constantly rebuilt my computer and found lost files when I had made some stupid mistake and given up. Thank you David!

My thanks to David and Michaela Smith who always provided me with the latest technology and taught me how to use it!

My thanks to Caroline Artschan for correcting my English!

My apologies to my grandchildren Rebecca Artschan, Charlotte Longdon, Sebastian and Oliver Smith for locking myself away and not answering the phone for weeks at a time and threatening to turn them into frogs if they spoke to me when I was writing.

My thanks to the following people who read the manuscript throughout the work in progress always encouraging me to write the next chapter:

Dean Lindley, Craig Lindley, Rebecca Cavagnari, Alan Mitchell, Janet White, and Sarah Roberts, Margaret Longdon, Irene Munday, Gloria Quarmby and Sue Baillie for taking a good picture of me at the Christmas party.

And an added extra thanks to Coralie Hughes Jensen for her advice and services in putting the final polish on this manuscript.

Chapter 1

Nottingham, April 1999

After taking a rather long lunch, Alex Campbell was running late. He rushed into the estate agent office, which he managed in the centre of Nottingham.

"Did the Lambecote Grange client ring?" he called to his secretary as he ran through the reception area.

"No, Mr. Campbell, but the Bank called regarding Lambecote. They have an offer to split the house from the land and asked you to call the manager as soon as possible."

"Good, Kim, put me through to him." Alex sat at his desk and began to look through the paperwork awaiting his attention.

The telephone rang.

"Mr. White from Henderson's bank is on line one, Mr. Campbell," Kim said.

"Peter, how the devil are you?" Alex greeted Peter White, the manager of The Henderson Bank Group.

"Hi, Alex," Peter White replied. "I need a meeting with your surveyor regarding Lambecote Grange—tomorrow, if that's possible."

"Sure. I am about to show the place this afternoon. This is the first viewing for some time. I was contacted online and asked to find all the relevant information regarding the past owners, going back at least two hundred years. If you have any details on hand from the deeds, I would be grateful. They were very insistent that I have them today and are due here in thirty minutes."

"You are cutting it a bit fine, Alex," White said, irritated. "You could have given me a little more time, but I shall see what I can do."

Peter White had his promotion on the line over the bankruptcy of Lambecote Grange. He had authorised the deal to use the land as collat-

1

eral for the one million pound loan the previous farmer had taken out, hoping to turn the farm into a golf course.

The previous owner, Edwin Sutton, had decided to leave farming when his herd of cattle were slaughtered after contracting BSE, known as mad cow disease. The farm had been in the same family for several generations. Plans to change the land into a golf course had hit one difficulty after another, and the business got deeper and deeper into debt as time went by.

Eventually, Edwin Sutton, who was well into his nineties, died. The death duties owed by his heirs, Andrew and Robert Sutton, put the farm into bankruptcy, and they were devastated when the bank refused any more time to repay the loan. They were declared bankrupt and the receivers had asked Campbell to value the land and farm as a working business and hopefully to return some of the creditor's money.

A consortium of businessmen interested only in purchasing the land but not the house had approached the receiver with a much reduced offer. An attempt to remove the land from the green belt was being considered by the local council. But this had to be handled delicately. Building large housing estates in this beautiful English countryside would bring opposition from neighbouring parish councils.

The deeds were brought out of the bank vaults, and Peter White read the back copies. He rang Campbell. "Hi, Alex. I have the details regarding Lambecote Grange. How far back do you want to go?"

"How far back *do* they go?"

"They go back quite a long way, probably four hundred years or more. Bingham was the family name before the Suttons. Why do they want them, do you know?" White was not happy with this viewing. There had been no interest in the last eighteen months. Farming was not a popular business venture these days. Prices had dropped through the floor as foreign imports flooded the markets. Selling land for development was the only real option if local councils could be persuaded not to object. With that information to take to the creditors meeting next month, he could get their permission to sell to developers at a reduced price. He had been promised a chance to buy a block of C shares if he could pull it off.

Campbell was very suspicious of White, regarding the sale of Lambecote Grange. He hoped this client was a bona fide buyer, if only to give Peter White a run for his money. White claimed the land was overgrown, and the house needed modernising. Campbell's gut feeling told him it would be best all round if the whole lot was knocked down and redeveloped. Someone would make a killing if that did happen, and Peter

White would not be a million miles away when the shares were allocated if he could get the price reduced.

Backing for more than eight million pounds would have to be shown to the creditors if a bid were to be accepted. A consortium of businessmen had decided they would not let the green belt law, ensuring the land remain agricultural, stop them. They could always offer the argument to the planning department that affordable housing was paramount in their minds. Councillors would surely bow to pressure for housing on the outskirts of a major city.

His phone rang. "Mrs. Wiseman is in reception, Mr. Campbell," Kim said.

Campbell eventually came from his office, and holding out his hand in greeting, said, "I am sorry to keep you waiting, Mrs. Wiseman."

Frances Wiseman shook his hand and walked with him toward the door.

Outside in the car park, Campbell asked, "Would you like to take your own car, Mrs. Wiseman, or would you like me to drive? We have to travel almost fifteen miles to Lambecote."

"Oh, we can take your car. Did you manage to get the history of Lambecote Grange, Mr. Campbell?"

"Yes, indeed I did."

"How far back does it go?' Frances asked.

"Four hundred years I believe. I have not had the opportunity to read it myself. It has just arrived by fax this afternoon. Do you wish to browse through it whilst we are travelling?"

"No thank you. Before I make any decision on the previous owners, I would like to see the property," she said firmly.

Campbell thought she was a crackpot. He had a sneaky feeling this woman was just playing some kind of game. There were some pathetic people who liked to live in an imaginary world, and viewing expensive houses was their way of spending a day out in the country. There were a growing number of people trying to trace the family tree, and viewing property like this was a definite possibility for them to find information regarding ancestors who had lived and worked in service in houses in the Lambecote Grange category. This property was on the market in excess of eight million pounds, and this woman would have to have some hell of a backing to beat off the business men who wanted to buy it for as little as possible. Still, he had to show the property to everyone who asked to view it.

After some ten minutes of complete silence driving through the villages and hamlets, Campbell said, "We are just about to enter the Lambecote Grange land area, Mrs. Wiseman."

Frances looked around for something to jolt her memory. The stories her mother had told her as a child had haunted her for so long and could be based on happenings that occurred on this very land. Excitement rose in her chest. Her heart was beating fast, and she began to perspire.

"Would you open the window a little, Mr. Campbell?" she asked.

"Certainly," he answered. "Are you familiar with these parts, Mrs. Wiseman?"

"No, not at all," she said, moving her face closer to the open window. She was so hot. "How far is it to Lambecote?" she asked.

"We should be able to see it when we get to the top of this incline."

The car reached the top of the hill with Frances strained to look out of the window. The sun was so bright she screwed up her eyes to focus. And then the vision appeared. There was Lambecote Grange in all its glory, just as she had pictured it in her mind. She gasped.

"Yes, it is a beautiful sight, isn't it? I believe the place was quite something in its heyday," Campbell said.

Frances was silent. She was sure this was the place.

They left the car in an overgrown area at the back of the house. As they walked around the west side of the property, which would probably have been the vegetable garden in the past, a twelve foot high wall built around the garden triggered a memory—the story of picking gooseberries with the housekeeper and bottling fruit grown in the garden. This was surely the place. She could not wait to get inside because she knew the interior of this house as certain as if she had lived here herself. "Could we enter through the front door, Mr. Campbell?" Frances asked.

"Of course," Campbell replied, looking puzzled. This woman *did* seem to know just where to go. She was walking around these grounds with great authority. *Perhaps Mrs. Wiseman is a relative come to stake a claim*, he thought. Well, she would not be getting much from this legacy. The bank would take every penny they could squeeze out of any buyer. He opened the front doors and they went inside.

Frances remembered her mother telling her about the scenes on the front doors, heavily carved with equestrian motifs.

Once inside the most magnificent hall, she remembered the story of the huge Christmas tree standing beside the green Italian marble fireplace. She walked over to the fireplace and lovingly ran her fingers along it. Her eyes moved to the floor and the memory of the Italian marble tiles came flooding into her mind. As a child, Frances had no idea of the significance of Italian marble, but here in this perfect setting, the tiles looked wonderful. Walking through to the dining room, she thought this must be where her grandmother worked when she first came to Lambecote Grange in 1890.

She ran around looking for the drawing room, and opening the door, stood speechless. A fireplace, constructed from beautiful white marble which covered the whole of one wall, stood regally in front of her. She ran over to one of the five full-length windows overlooking gardens, which were laid out in the style of Capability Brown. "Mr. Campbell, will you please open these windows?" Frances called.

Alex was convinced this woman was completely mad, running around looking for rooms and appearing to find just what she was looking for. He opened one set of the huge doors onto the garden.

Her heart pounding in her chest, Frances stepped out virtually racing into the garden her eyes shining in anticipation for what she would find next. Could this be "The Grange" where her mother was born in 1901?

The story of the bowl and her grandfather's hunting horn had been Frances's favourite bedtime story. The bowl had been given to her mother during the 1926 general strike in the Yorkshire mining village of Halten. Miners and their families suffered great hardship during this time, and Sarah Wiseman, Frances's mother, had shown kindness to a poor woman who, when giving birth, had not had two shillings for the midwife. She asked Sarah for help. After paying the nurse, Sarah cared for the woman and her children and did not ask for a reward. But Sarah had always admired the bowl with the huntsmen painted around it. The picture of the huntsman blowing his hunting horn, followed by a pack of hounds was repeated around the large china bowl. This stood in the window of the small council house in Halten where Frances had spent her very happy childhood.

Frances hurried toward a clump of gorse bushes covered in yellow blossom. She eventually found a path through the gorse, leading out onto a lawn with the most beautiful views of rolling countryside she had ever seen. She stood quietly taking deep breaths. This was just what she had imagined she would find. Although overgrown and in need of attention, everything was as her mother had described it. For some reason the land had not been developed. Her mind was racing along, imagining a man in hunting clothes on a beautiful black stallion riding toward her saying, "This is your home, your rightful place in the world." In her imagination, the huntsman had haunted her for years, beseeching her to search for this place. When life got tough, and Frances had many tough times, she would dream of finding her mother's home and living happily ever after. Of course, it was just a dream. But she now had the finances to look for the imaginary place and at last lay some of ghostly memories to rest.

The fortunes of the Bingham family covered one hundred years of gentry and gypsies, love and hate, wealth and poverty, tragedy and social inequality. If this did prove to be the mythical Grange, she must act before it was too late. Lambecote Grange must not be lost at the eleventh hour to greedy speculators, and she must, if it was at all possible, save it. This was her destiny. All those years of deceit and treachery had come full circle. She could be standing on the very land where her mother was born into a wealthy landowning family in 1901 and lived a privileged life until she was five-years-old when tragedy struck and banished the family into poverty. Had Frances really solved the mystery of her mother's bedtime stories?

She must read all the history of this place before she committed herself but knew in her heart that this was the place. Could it be possible that she wanted so much for this property to be the house in her mother's story that she was making everything fit the picture in her imagination? This thought worried her, but she decided that the deeds would answer all her doubts. If the previous name on the deeds was Bingham then this was indeed her grandfather's land, and she had no time to waste.

Chapter 2

The Grange, December 1889

C harles Bingham reined in his horse, and after catching his breath, turned to look back. George, his son, was galloping his beautiful hunter, Storm, toward him over the frost-covered fields toward him. He felt exhilarated after his early Sunday morning ride around his land. He looked around, taking in the magnificent view. How he loved this place. He loved the smells that reminded him of his childhood when he would ride here with his father. Memories of picnics with his mother, and his two sisters, Grace and Lillian, came flooding back. He counted his blessings every time he rode around Lambecote Grange land.

The cold December wind chilled him, but he hoped it would blow away the heavy head with which he had awakened that morning. He had been presented with an exquisite hunting horn at the Hunt Ball the night before, inscribed in silver with the names of the last three hunt leaders, Charles, his father Henry, and grandfather William. He had lovingly hung the horn from its black velvet ribbon above the portrait of his father on the main staircase at Lambecote Grange. Charles, as the local squire, had been the toast of the ball and had consumed far too much alcohol. Not being a regular drinker he was suffering the consequences today.

"Are you all right, Father?" George called out to him.

"Yes, I am fine son," Charles replied. "Shall we ride back together? I need to talk to you."

Avoiding the main roads, they began to trot back to the farm together, enjoying the fresh air.

Lambecote Grange was on the outskirts of Nottingham, two miles from the beautiful English village of Lambecote. Charles was very well respected in the village. He was the main employer, farming three thousand acres of farmland and owning and supplying eight butcher shops in and around Nottingham. He was the absolute model of what the English call "a gentleman farmer." In the unequal class sectarianism of the Victorian Age, he lived a charmed life, having no concept of the poverty that surrounded him.

"Is there a problem?" George asked his father.

"No, George, I just want to talk to you about the business after I retire," Charles replied.

"Retire! Why? You are not ill, are you?" George looked alarmed.

"No, George, I am not ill, but we should discuss the future plans for the estate. As your mother and I are not getting any younger, it is sensible."

"Father, I don't want to discuss this now. You are too young to think of retiring. We need to work together for many more years!"

"George, I want to start taking your mother abroad in the winter months. It will be a good chance for you to start taking over the reins. This land has been in the family for three generations. Your grandfather and my grandfather have been hunt leaders. I expect you to carry on the tradition. We have to learn to move with the times and keep up with modern farming changes, and it needs a younger man looking at it. You should be thinking about settling down, George. We need an heir to groom for the job." Charles spoke quietly having carefully considered the responsibility he was about to put on his son's shoulders.

George responded angrily. He understood very well where this conversation was heading and had no intention of listening to a word his father had to say. "I don't want to discuss this, Father. I have not met anyone with the right attitudes for me and shall not be rushed into relationships with these spoiled overdressed women that you keep pushing at me. You wonder why I avoid family discussions when this is the only subject you feel you can discuss with me. Mother is obsessed with finding me a wife."

Charles was not going to let this opportunity pass. "Good God man!" he shouted. "Half the women in the county are throwing themselves at you. All you give them is a smile, oh, and an occasional trip to the theatre. The best will be snapped up if you don't pull your finger out."

"I will decide when and whom I shall wed, Father, and that is an end to it." With this, George angrily rode off, leaving his father to follow at his own pace.

Charles watched him go. He had to agree with his son. Most of the women that Charlotte, George's mother, had invited to Lambecote Grange were empty-headed silly girls looking for a lifestyle rather than a life-long commitment to a family.

Charlotte had insisted that Charles ride out this morning with George. She would not listen to his protestations regarding his unhealthy state and had great expectations of George taking a liking to her latest protégée, the daughter of a very well-respected family from Derby. She had been invited to the Hunt Ball by one of Charlotte's friends. George had been perfectly charming to the girl but had refused an invitation to visit her family in Derbyshire.

Charlotte would be impossible all day when he told her that George refused to discuss it. He would have preferred an easy day as he had this strange feeling in his chest—something that had been recurring quite regularly. He decided he would visit old Basil Judge, the family doctor, one day next week.

The horse was not happy about the valley into which they had started to descend. Charles encouraged him with a squeeze of his heels and the horse responded instantly, racing up and over the other side before dropping back into a gentle trot. Charles looked down towards Nottingham Road where a long procession of wagons was winding its way into Nottingham.

"Must be the Goose Fair," he said. "The Romanies, gypsies, would not have this problem with their sons. They arranged their sons' marriages. If they do not do as they are told, they are ostracised as gypsies. They have to leave the family and fend for themselves. Perhaps that was the best way to arrange for their future. Who knows?" George was becoming a problem.

Charlotte was obsessed with organising dinner parties and bridge evenings, hoping to find the girl with the right background for her son.

The horse slowly wound his way down to the road and then trotted alongside the well kept wagons that were painted in bright colours.

When he reached the leaders of the group, a swarthy-looking man called out to him, doffing his cap in the process. On their regular routes up and down their particular section of the English countryside, gypsies knew who owned the land.

"We shall put up in t'same field, sir! Two nights should do us, I reckon," the gypsy suggested.

"Very well but remove your rubbish when you leave," Charles replied.

"Will yer sell us some milk for t'bairns, sir?" a dark-skinned woman called to him.

"Just go to the kitchen door at Lambecote Grange. They will give you what you need."

The woman gave him a toothless grin.

He said, "Good morning to you." Then he rode away.

The Goose Fair in Nottingham would take place the following week. For the past five days, the gypsies and fairground people had been arriving from all around the country for the annual Christmas Goose Fair.

The sight heartened Charles. He would make quite a good profit during the next seven days, mainly in the butcher shops. He had purchased a stall at the fair that would sell hot peas, hot pies, and faggots. This had proved very successful over the years.

The farm workers who had very little work to do in the winter months welcomed the opportunity to earn a little extra money before Christmas, and it was possibly the highlight of the year for the country folk around Nottinghamshire.

The Romany women started early, selling their bits of homemade lace, promising good luck to the buyer, and doing a bit of duckering, fortune telling, from door to door.

Their men folk pitched their benders, tepee-style tents constructed of several poles leaning into the centre and wrapped around with strong waterproof cloth, and found grazing for the horses, which they had gathered from around the country over the last months.

Appleby in North Yorkshire was the main horse fair, but deals were struck at all the fairs. The Romanies selected the best horses from around the country to sell at Appleby. They never mixed with the fair people, and Romany women were not allowed to fraternise with *gorgios*, people not of Romany blood.

Romanies should not be mistaken with the tinkers, people living on the road but not of gypsy blood. They travelled around the country dealing in anything they could lay their hands on and generally giving the gypsies a bad reputation. Romanies were a proud race but true Romany gypsies were all one extended family of sisters and brothers.

Charles arrived at Lambecote Grange just in time to change his clothes before the carriage would be brought round for the journey to church. He, Charlotte, and their son George had their own family pew in the village church. George was approaching his thirty-first birthday and was the most eligible bachelor in the county.

Horses were Charles Bingham's passion. He took pride in having the finest horses in the county. Hounds were kept at the farm, and such a large number of dogs meant extra pay for the farm workers. The wives and daughters of the farm workers served in the house and the dairy.

Charlotte had a lady's maid and a full complement of staff afforded to the wife of a man of such standing. Violet Grimwood was Charlotte's personal maid, and her husband, Arthur, was the blacksmith. They had two children, Nellie and Billy, who attended the local village school.

Elsie Buttle was Violet's mother and had been housekeeper at Lambecote Grange for twenty-five years. This position gave her and her family privileges not afforded the other estate workers. In return, Charlotte and Charles expected complete dedication to their family needs, and indeed, Elsie considered George with as much love and affection as she did her own flesh and blood.

Elsie held the purse strings for the smooth running of the household, and Charles trusted her implicitly. Charlotte professed to run the household, but in reality, Elsie hired and fired maids, and kitchen workers watched over by Charles.

Elsie's husband, Fred, was the stable manager. He also looked after the ploughs and other equipment needed to plant and rotate crops. Working horses had to be in tiptop condition, and Fred's skills were as revered outside in the yard and stables as Elsie's were in the house.

The whole workforce was expected to attend church on Sunday, gathering outside the litch gates to follow their master and his family into church. Only workers needed for duty were excused.

Violet, Nellie, and Billy Grimwood were in the kitchen on this particular Sunday after luncheon had been cleared away, all happily stirring the Christmas pudding and making their wishes. Elsie had wrapped the little silver three penny pieces carefully, and all the kitchen staff had dropped one into the pudding mixture, making a wish.

Little Nellie closed her eyes tight and shouted loudly to ensure the wish came true, "I want to be a lady when I grow up!"

Elsie, her grandmother scoffed, "Well that's one wish that won't come true. Yer fill that girl's head with all sorts of rubbish, Violet. Why don't yer teach her how to scrub a floor? She's too soft."

"Never!" exclaimed Violet. "I am not working here to pay for her education just to waste it on her scrubbing floors and being bullied by housekeepers!"

"Yer watch your mouth, Violet Grimwood." Elsie retorted. "Yer are getting above your station. Just remember were you come from."

"I do remember, and that's not where I want her to go," Violet argued. "Not if I can help it."

"Well, madam, you can leave anytime you like!" Elsie, face beetroot colour now, bellowed at Violet, "Yer got this job 'cos I put in a word with the mistress, telling her how well brought up yer were!"

"Yes, and I've seen the other side of life now, Mam, and that's where I want our Nellie to be," Violet declared.

Still feeling unwell and complaining of pains in his chest, the master had taken to his bed after luncheon. Charlotte admonished him for over indulgence at the Hunt Ball the previous evening.

Agnes Smith donned her cap and apron, and lifted the tea tray. She was the fourteen-year-old daughter of the pig-man and a not-very-bright kitchen maid. Agnes had a tendency to sniff a lot. Elsie only allowed her to go upstairs when Mary, the dining-room maid, took her day off.

Elsie thought it must be the smell that pervaded from her father, Jimmy Smith, who had caused the nasty habit in Agnes. "Come here let me look at yer!" Elsie bellowed at Agnes.

It had been a long day, and Elsie's temper was short. Poor Agnes usually got the brunt end of Elsie's tongue whether she deserved it or not. She had risen at four-thirty that morning to light the fires in the breakfast room and clean the kitchen stove before she stoked up the fire to heat the water for the family. She had prepared the vegetables for lunch before the very grumpy overweight cook rose at six, scratching and picking at sores on her arms and legs and giving Agnes a clip round her ear for not taking her a cup of tea.

Agnes scrubbed, cleaned, and dipped her knee to everyone. Mary, the upstairs maid, had the day off, and Agnes had to do her duties along with her own. Serving afternoon tea was a rare privilege for her. On Mary's day off, Elsie usually served tea but she was too busy with stirring the Christmas pudding this afternoon.

Master was resting, and tea would be just for the mistress.

Master George had gone riding after luncheon. He had heard enough of his mother's whinging about the lass from Derby whom she had presented to him with high hopes of a romance. Elsie thought the woman would drive the lad away if she persisted in harassing him about marriage. George was an independent character and would only marry when he met the right girl. These snooty pieces his mother was parading for him irritated him with their pouting and preening.

Mistress said it put her off her food when Agnes continually sniffed, but the more nervous the poor girl became, the more she sniffed.

Elsie was too tired to take the tray upstairs. She and cook had not only mixed the Christmas puddings since luncheon, but prepared dinner and baked cakes and bread for tea.

"Get thyself upstairs, and for God's sake, don't sniff!" Cook shouted at Agnes. Cook had been at Lambecote Grange for six years, and was frequently at odds with Elsie, the housekeeper. Agnes slowly and carefully carried the tray upstairs.

"Come in!" Charlotte called, answering the timid knock on the door.

"Tea, ma'am," Agnes said nervously.

"Oh, it's you, Agnes. Where's Mary?" Charlotte asked.

"Beg your pardon, ma'am," Agnes replied, dipping her knee in reverence to this lady who terrified her just by looking at her. "It's Mary's day off, ma'am. She has gone to see her mam in Nottingham."

"Does her mother live in Nottingham now? I thought they lived on the estate," Charlotte said.

"Her mam had to leave when her dad died of fever last year, ma'am. Master wanted the cottage for the new ploughman so Mary's mam went to live with her sister in Nottingham. Master looks after her with food and bits. Mary takes it when she has her day off," Agnes babbled.

"The master's too kind, Agnes. Too kind!" Charlotte exclaimed angrily, having no understanding of life outside her class. How poor Mary's mother would live without the help from Lambecote Grange was of no concern of hers. "Agnes, have you taken tea into the master yet?"

Now flustered, Agnes had completely lost her composure saying, "Cook never said owt about giving master owt, ma'am." Agnes's face turned the colour of puce, and the sniff got worse.

"Well, just pop upstairs with a cup of tea for him, my dear. Here you are." Charlotte passed the frightened girl a beautiful china cup and saucer with tea for her husband. "Run along and ask him if he would like anything to eat."

Agnes took the cup with shaking hands and made her way upstairs. Outside the master's door she stared at the tea that had spilt into the saucer, and looking around to be sure no one was watching her, she poured the tea from the saucer into the cup. *That's better*, she thought, boldly knocking on the door.

She was not as frightened of the master as she was of the mistress. He was always kind and asked if she liked her job. There was no answer. She knocked again and again. After some time, she decided to put the tea down on a side table and go and tell the mistress that the master was asleep.

Charlotte said, "Oh. Just put the tea by his bed. He will drink it when he wakes."

Agnes went back upstairs and again knocked on the master's door. She then picked up the cup and saucer and quietly went into the room. "Excuse me sir," she said when she got near to the bed. She intended to put the tea down and leave, but did not want to catch him in some compromising position. Looking down at the bed, she immediately dropped the cup and saucer and screamed.

The master was half in, half out of the bed. His face was contorted in pain. He was a dreadful colour, his eyes bulging from his head. Agnes ran so fast her feet hardly touched the stairs. She was shaking from head to toe when she ran into the mistress's room screaming.

"It's Master, ma'am. Come quick. I fink he is deed."

It was a typical bleak misty-grey December day—perfect for a funeral. The funeral cortege, accompanied by a black carriage bedecked with black ostrich plumes and pulled by four proud black horses, wound its way through landscape that Charles Bingham had loved so much during his fifty-nine years of life at Lambecote Grange.

Charles was born on Lambecote Grange in 1830 and was the eldest son of Henry Bingham and his wife, Eleanor. He had been brought up in a very genteel environment knowing that as eldest son, he was expected to marry well and into his own class.

On his shoulders, he carried the responsibility of everyone who owed their living to Lambecote Grange. It was important for his family to maintain the structures that had governed this particular piece of English countryside for four generations.

After the death of his father in 1861, the farm had been left in trust for him to run and provide for all the dependants including his two sisters, Lillian and Grace. His sisters had married well, and had an annuity from the farm for life.

As the procession reached the field where the gypsies had camped just a few days earlier, a dusky man holding the reins of a piebald pony removed his cap and lowered his head in respect. Romanies in general had very little respect for *gorgios*. Most landowners blamed Romanies for thieving and spoiling crops, but this gentleman on his last journey knew the difference between fair folk, tinkers, and Romanies.

The Romanies had a pride in their ancient race. They were honest hardworking people with their own customs, but the only thing they had in common with tinkers or travellers was that they lived on the road. The whole world was theirs, and if they were left alone, they would never harm anyone or anything that did not belong to them. The tinkers or travellers did not have these strong principles. They lived on the road and took anything that was not fastened down, figuring that if they did not take it, somebody else would. The Romanies would not camp with anyone not of their race, giving them a reputation of being odd. Charles Bingham had respect for the Romanies. In the summer, they worked hard on Lambecote Grange land, helping to gather in the harvest.

Standing at the back and around the sides of the church and spilling outside into the well-kept churchyard, the farm workers and their family's watched the landed gentry arrive in their splendid carriages. Women wailed at the thought of their men losing their work, and prayed that the son would be half the man his father was.

Charles was laid to rest in the churchyard in the family plot. After the service, the carriages made their way up to Lambecote Grange to pay their respects to the new squire and commiserate with the widow.

After the mourners left, the family solicitor arrived to read the last will and testament of Charles Bingham. All the family were congregated in the morning room. Charlotte was devastated. She had not been in her room since that dreadful day last Sunday, when the sniffy girl had burst in babbling the gruesome news of her beloved Charles' heart attack. She vowed she would only leave to travel to the funeral. She rested after the funeral, but George brought her down for the reading of the will.

George was worried that his mother would have a bronchial attack. He would take her away after they had had a respectable period of mourning. Charlotte would not be strong enough to come out of this and continue running the household staff. She had admonished him for not providing an heir for her beloved husband, moaning and groaning about her fate.

Aunt Grace and Uncle Ambrose were there with their son, Harold. Aunt Lillian and Uncle Edwin had been a power of help and kindness during the past week. Unfortunately they had no children, and Lillian had always doted on George. She found Harold, her sister's child, untrustworthy and sometimes downright rude when her husband would not back his schemes. Aunt Lillian suffered with her heart. She was a very frail lady.

The house was in deep mourning. All the mirrors and main entrance doors had been covered in black and the drawing curtains had not been opened since Charles' death. The servants were in shock. Being in no such condition to work, poor Agnes had been sent home to her mother, and Elsie had not spoken a good word to anybody all week. She and cook had organised the food and the cleaning of the house. The house would be on show to the whole county after the funeral, and it was a matter of pride to the housekeeper for everything to be cleaned whether it needed cleaning or not. The staff had no had time to think about their future or to wallow too long on the master's demise.

Morgan Bryce, a senior partner in the law firm of Bryce Coombes and Braithwaite, rose from his chair and began to read the will. The whole estate was left to George, with some small legacies to the church and an old farm worker whom Charles had befriended. Charlotte was left an annuity with a proviso that she lived out her life at Lambecote Grange in the manner to which she was accustomed. The legacy was to continue to Charles' sisters, Grace and Lillian. This they had received since the death of Grandfather Henry.

One thousand pounds was left to Harold Sutton, with a provision that after his mother's demise her annuity would pass to Harold for the rest of his life. Harold Sutton almost burst a blood vessel when he heard this. He believed he should have a half stake in the estate. Grandfather Henry had left it to the male line, missing the female line, including his mother, but surely he was due for more than a measly one thousand pounds, and eventually, his mother's annuity.

Ambrose Sutton, Harold's father, had a very lucrative wholesale grain business. He had tried to encourage his son into the business in many ways, but Harold objected to working, spending most of his time in Nottingham, drinking, gambling, and womanising. He would lose one thousand pounds in a very short time.

George thanked everyone for their kindness and took his mother upstairs, away from Harold and his protestations.

January 1890

George sat in his office looking out over the snow-covered fields. His mind was unsettled. How he wished he had not angered his father when they were riding out on that fateful Sunday. He thought his heart would break when he allowed his mind to recall the conversation his father tried to have with him. He had been so arrogant, riding off and ignoring him. Perhaps Father knew he had a weak heart and was trying to make provision for the future. Father had said that he wanted to take more time away from the farm. If only he had listened. George would never forgive himself.

After speaking with Fred Buttle and having been assured that at least until March the farm could be managed quite easily without him, George decided to take his Mother to Italy where she would recover from the dreadful chest complaint that had bothered her since Charles's death. He had assured her his father had intended to do this, remembering the conversation they nearly had on that fateful day two months ago. She had reluctantly agreed. He rang the bell, and Violet answered.

"Hello Violet," he said, smiling at her. "How are you?"

"Very well sir,"

"Will you ask your mother to come and see me?" George asked. "And please bring a tea tray with two cups."

"Yes, sir." Violet smiled back at George. *Oh. He is such a nice man*, she thought.

"What does he want two cups for? Who has he got in there?" Elsie retorted when Violet gave her the message downstairs in the kitchen where Elsie sat with her feet up in front of the large black cooking range.

"Nobody as I can see, Mam. He looks a bit down though," Violet answered.

"I'll take him some a these biscuits," Elsie said. "Straight from the oven. That'll cheer him up a bit, you see." Elsie knocked at the office door and waited to be asked in before she entered and put the tea tray down.

"Thank you, Elsie. Take a seat. Won't you join me in a cup of tea? And what is this? Biscuits? You spoil me, Elsie. You really do." George laughed.

"Thank you, sir. Are you all right, Master George?" Elsie asked. "I hope there's nothing wrong."

"No. No, Elsie, far from it! You and Fred do such a good job that I have decided to take mother away," he replied.

"Good idea, sir, if you pardon me saying so. Shall I pour, Master George?" Elsie asked.

"No." And passing her a cup, he asked, "Do you take sugar?"

"Yes, sir. Yes, please. Two spoons, if yer please." Elsie was beginning to get a little nervous now. *Why is Master George taking tea with me?* she thought.

"I have been thinking Elsie," George said. "You could change things, rearrange things a little whilst we are away—for Mother's sake.'

"I don't understand yer, Master George. In what way?" she asked.

"Do not let her come across Agnes for a while. Poor girl, not her fault. But just the mention of her sets mother off with a breathing spasm."

"I'll use her in the dairy, sir. That should keep her out of the way," Elsie said, feeling a little easier now. "Mary's getting wed to a bloke in Nottingham, so we'll need a new maid for the dining room," Elsie informed him.

"Very well, Elsie, you see to it. Get somebody who did not know Father. Less chance of slipping up when she is serving Mother," George said.

"Very well sir," Elsie replied. "I'll start getting Mistress's trunk ready today. When do yer plan to leave, Master George?"

"There is a boat on January 31st. I think we could manage that, don't you?" George asked.

"Certainly sir, I think that is a very good idea." Elsie could not wait to get back downstairs and tell the news. She ran into the kitchen saying that she was in charge until March and that there were going to be some changes. "Mark my words!" she bellowed out as she strutted around the kitchen like the captain of a ship.

Cook groaned. "Yer had better not start on me, Elsie Buttle 'cos I'm off first change that yer makes to me job!"

"Agnes is to go in the dairy, and I need to go into Nottingham and get a new dining room maid to replace Mary," Elsie announced.

"Our Beatie's lass is looking for work. I'll ask her on me day off!" Cook declared beaming.

"Yer'll do no such thing! I want somebody who looks like a lady. Not a spotty-faced ragbag," Elsie spat at her.

Cook screamed back, "That's it! Yer've gone fur enough, Elsie Buttle. I'm going!"

"If you want to go cook, yer go!" Elsie said. She had never liked cook, and certainly could manage without her dizzy spells and bad backs. She also coddled her gin too much for Elsie's liking.

Cook stormed out of the kitchen, banging the door.

"Mam, now look what yer've done!" Violet said angrily. "We'll never get another cook at short notice."

18

"We don't need one!" Elsie said "Master and Mistress are going travelling at end of the month, and not coming back 'til March. Why do we need a cook?"

"Have your way!" Violet said. "Think on, I'm not doing her work at all."

"Yer'll do as you're told!" Elsie shouted at her, buoyant now with her new-found power.

George decided to ask Aunt Lillian and Uncle Henry to travel with them. Henry Braithwaite, now being a retired partner in the law firm Bryce, Coombes and Braithwaite, had on his retirement purchased a beautiful villa in Florence where he and his dear wife, Lillian, spent most winters. Lillian found her sister-in-law very tiresome. Charlotte constantly moaned and groaned about her fate now that her husband had died. Poor George had the patience of a saint when listening to his mother about her disapproval of his lifestyle without a wife and heir.

The carriage left Lambecote Grange on the 29th of January with its occupants set to travel by coach, boat, and train, taking in several European cities before settling in Florence.

George hoped the ladies would find other things to occupy their minds in Florence. He had become fearful for his mother's health. Charlotte refused to eat properly and spoke only of the dreadful events she had witnessed when her dear departed Charles had left this world broken-hearted because he died without an heir to carry on the tradition of hunt leader. No amount of loving care could console her.

Elsie thought Charlotte was getting so much attention from the situation that she would carry on until she died herself. She decided to put up notices in all the Bingham butcher shops in Nottingham. She had to find a new maid suitable to serve the mistress her food. Charlotte was very particular who served her at table and had been known to refuse to eat her meal if the maid was not suitable. They must have references and apply in writing to Lambecote Grange.

The cook had left Lambecote Grange after several altercations with Elsie. She realised that life would be impossible with the master away.

Elsie Buttle reigned supreme—at least for a while.

Chapter 3

Nottingham, February 1890

C arrying her shopping basket, Rosina Morton walked along, her head back, letting the cold February wind blow through her long mane of dark brown thick curly hair. She was a striking girl who loved to be outdoors. Rosina was working with her sister, Gladys, at a vicarage in Nottingham. Gladys did the cleaning, and Rosina, general housekeeping. She always volunteered to do the shopping and was a very thrifty shopper.

"I do not know what I would do without Rosina," Ophelia Kendall, the vicar's wife, told people when they came for tea at the vicarage.

Rosina's and Gladys's parents, Kisaiya and Leonard Morton, lived in Nottingham. Len Morton was a good-for-nothing layabout. His wife lived from day to day on what little she could forage from cleaning and scrubbing. Kisaiya was a true Romany gypsy who fell in love with the wrong man and paid the price for her mistake. The gypsies disowned her, and her husband continually abused her. Kisaiya scrubbed for the butcher, Mr. Sykes, who ran the shop for Bingham's farmer butchers. The butcher would give her a few scrag-ends of meat on a Saturday along with a wage of two shillings.

Rosina crossed over the road to the butcher shop. She was looking for a good piece of beef for the Sunday roast. Sunday was the day Rosina and Gladys had dinner at the vicarage. She would try to spend the meat allowance carefully, and perhaps she would have a bit left over to buy her mam a bit of something. She walked into Bingham's and waited in the queue. Mr. Sykes saw her come in. He could not keep his eyes off her. She was the most beautiful creature he had ever seen.

Rosina looked around at the meat hooked on iron bars that were drilled into the ceiling. The shop had a nasty smell, and the floor was covered in sawdust that had patches of dried blood festering. Several large blue bottles were laying eggs in the sawdust, and others were buzzing around in a feeding frenzy. She decided to ask for a piece of tail end of rump having nice bit of fat on it. That usually went down well with the vicar.

"You certainly know your meat, Rosina lass," Josiah Kendall, the vicar, would say when he was carving the Sunday joint.

A notice behind the counter caught Rosina's eye. It read, "Silver service maid wanted." She thought this was a funny place to advertise for a maid. Mr. Sykes was not married so it could not be for him.

After haggling over the price of the beef, the butcher reduced the price by two pence, and she put the piece of tail end of beef into her basket. Then, looking straight into the butcher's eyes, asked, "Are these eggs fresh, Mr. Sykes?"

Sykes said, "Wait there just a minute, madam." He was really turned on by this creature. If she played her cards right, she would eat well for the rest of her life—her snivelling mother along with her. "I have got some fresh duck eggs in t'back. Take some of 'em. Vicar'll love 'em!" He could not contain his excitement. The spittle was stuck in the corners of his mouth. Ignoring everyone else in the shop, he blubbered and spat his way past Rosina to get into the back room, disappearing into the stinking area where a lad was boning disgusting-looking carcasses and making sausages, faggots, and meat balls made from any unusable waste meat mixed with strong seasoning to cover the smell.

Sykes roughly pushed past the lad swearing obscenities at him. He muddled through the mess on the filthy wooden block, trying to find bits of steak to impress Rosina. She loved faggots. Her mam sometimes brought them home if the butcher had any left of an evening. Kisaiya, her mam, said you had to be very careful with faggots it was dangerous selling them the next day, all the rubbish went into them 'cos butcher never wasted an ounce of meat even if it had been on the floor. He would pick it up, scrape it, and put it into the ice cupboard. Ice was bought in every day, so the ice cupboard door always had to be shut. If they did not shut the door, the lads who worked there would have to pay for anything that went off.

Sykes came out from the back room with the eggs and a little parcel, which he put into Rosina's basket. Giving her a wink, he said, "That's for yer, pretty lass—a present like."

Rosina's back stiffened and her blood boiled. How she hated men who thought women could be bought by a bit of meat. "No thank you,

Mr. Sykes," she retorted. "I only want the meat I can afford." She handed him the parcel and thanked him as she left.

Sykes was furious. Who did this little upstart think she was? He had never been so humiliated in his life. He would see her starve before he would give her family another sausage.

Rosina turned, held her head high, and flounced out of the shop, briskly walking down the back streets to where her parents lived in a dingy little two-up-two-down slum. Her father was sprawled out in front of the fireplace. The fire had gone out, and the room was very cold.

"Oh look who it is," Len, her father said. "Lady Muck, been called to see t'peasants, have yer?"

"Where's me mam?" Rosina asked.

Her father sickened her. He had been drinking and had probably spent her mam's wages, earned last night scrubbing out that butcher shop.

"She's gone to see if she can get more scrubbing. We can't manage on t' butcher's throw-outs, I'm a big bloke. I need some real food in me belly," Len scoffed.

Rosina rounded on him. "You are an idle fat good-for-nothing!" she shouted at him. "Why don't you get out and find some work. Me mam will kill herself by not eating and giving you all the money she earns."

Leonard stood up to his full six-foot-four. "Let me get me hands on yer. I'll break your neck, yer jumped-up little bastard! Where did yer get t'money from to buy that fancy coat? Aha. Bet that vicar gets more than his dinner when his wife's out doing her good deeds," he sneered.

"You are disgusting, you foul-mouthed drunken animal!" Rosina was furious. "I am not working to keep you in idleness." She stood her ground with her hands on her hips. "You won't get another penny from me while you drink and gamble it away," she shouted.

"Well, if that's your attitude," Len said. "Get out and don't come back."

Rosina groaned in exasperation, clenching her fists she left the house, slamming the door behind her. Gladys and Rosina had provided the rent money since they were eleven-year-olds. If she took him at his word, he would be homeless.

On her way down the passage between the terraced houses, she met her mother. Kisaiya had a threadbare old shawl pulled tight around her thin wan face.

"Mam," Rosina said angrily. "Where is your coat? It is so cold out today. You will get your cough again."

Kisaiya Morton looked sheepishly at her daughter. "I had to pawn it, lass. Last week we had nowt to eat."

"Mam, why do you give me dad the money? He does not give a damn about you. He is so selfish, he makes my blood boil," Rosina said angrily.

"That's not all, lass. The butcher just gave me marching orders. He says to ask yer why," Kisaiya said tearfully.

"What? The pompous idiot. I would rather starve than work for him!" Rosina exclaimed.

"It's all right, yer saying that. But where do we get money to eat?" her mother cried.

Rosina was so angry. "Mam, there is a notice up in the butcher shop just behind the block. I think it was for a dining room maid. Who is it for, do you know?" she asked Kisaiya.

"It's at Lambecote Grange, Rosina. Mr. Bingham just died, and I heard the butcher saying that his son has taken his mother travelling to recover from the shock."

"Do you know where it is?" Rosina asked.

"I could take yer. We used to camp on that land when I was a bairn. Elsie Buttle is housekeeper there. She's no man's fool, Elsie. I wouldn't want to work with her, but still, beggars can't be choosers. It does say that yer have to write to her first. That'll whittle it down a bit. Not many lasses can write."

"Well, I can write and am no man's fool either." Rosina threw her head back in the way she did when she took on a challenge. "I think I shall buy some paper, pen, and ink and have a go at that, Mam. Me money would be good, and if I earned a bit more, it might mean you did not have to scrub for idiots like that butcher. Now come here, put my coat on and give me your shawl."

"Nay, lass, I can't take yer coat. I shall be all right." Kisaiya shivered.

"Now, Mother, how much did you get for your coat at that pawnshop?" Rosina asked.

"Six pence," Kisaiya said.

"What!" Rosina exclaimed. "I paid four shillings for that coat." She glared at her mother. "Doctor's wife gave it for the church jumble sale. I paid over the odds for it then so you would have a warm coat for winter. I am not buying it back again. Here, put my coat on and let us go and see what we can find." She gave her mother the shilling she had made by shopping carefully for the vicar, and threatened that if Mam gave it to her dad she would not get anymore. Putting her arm around her mother's shoulders, she said, "Come on, Mam, let us get some decent food. Our

Gladys will be home soon, and she will go for me dad if she finds out you have had no food and he has spent the money on booze."

"Rosina, shall we go to the market? It's late and you can buy things a bit cheaper when they are packing up on a Saturday," Kisaiya said, feeling humiliated. She wished she could be as strong as her daughters when it came to dealing with Len.

Rosina held her mother's arm and shivered as the cold wind blew through her thin blouse. Her mother's shawl gave no protection from the cold. "I hate me dad for doing this to us, Mam. Why do you put up with it? Nobody should live like this. I tell you I shall not live like this for any man. Why does he not go and find a job? There is work out there for everyone. You have to go out and find it," Rosina mumbled as they walked along.

The vicar carved the beef at Sunday lunch after morning service and congratulated Rosina on her shopping skills saying, "We would miss you and Gladys sorely if you ever left us, Rosina."

Rosina bit on her lip. She had not said anything about writing for the job at Lambecote Grange. Gladys had sneaked some paper from the vicar's study while she was cleaning, and Rosina had written the letter while the family was at church. She had used the vicar's ink. The vicar did not like waste so he would understand she could not spend money on ink when her mam needed medicine.

Since the day when Rosina had met her freezing cold and hungry, Kisaiya had been very ill. Rosina asked the doctor for something for her mam's chest, and he had very kindly gone to see Kisaiya at no charge. Later, he told Rosina that her mother needed regular food or she would not have the strength to fight these chest infections.

Gladys had given her dad a real good telling-off and threatened to take her mam away and leave him to fend for himself. Things had looked up a bit since then, but Rosina thought that when Len got her mam on her own, he bullied her. She hoped the vicar had not found out about her trying for the job at Lambecote Grange. She liked working here at the vicarage, but the pay was poor and she had to live at home. Lambecote Grange was a live-in position. The food would be good and a uniform provided, Rosina really needed to get away from her dad. She hoped the vicar would not sack Gladys as revenge.

If Gladys could stay on at the vicarage, perhaps they would make her general maid in Rosina's place. And they could take on her mam to do the cleaning. If her dad misbehaved, he would be on his own with no one to bully. The plan began to take shape in her mind. If she handled this carefully, it might just work. She decided to tell the vicar about her plans. She knew she was jumping the gun, not having heard from Lambecote Grange yet, but if the vicar was put in the picture, he might look kindly on Gladys and possibly her mother as replacements. Kisaiya Morton was an excellent cook, and Gladys worked like a horse.

"Well, well, well!" Josiah Kendall exclaimed.

Rosina had finished her story about her wanting to work up at Lambecote Grange and set her mother and sister up for life there at his vicarage.

"What if I don't want your family, Rosina? What if you don't get the job at Lambecote Grange. You will be in a pickle, won't you?" he said furiously.

Rosina's heart banged against her rib cage. "I am being honest and aboveboard with you, Vicar. I expect to be treated fairly. I don't want to leave you in the lurch. I need to help my mam and can't do it without earning more money. I like working here, but it does not pay enough to keep our family. Me mam is a good cook. She taught me to housekeep and be thrifty with money, I am sure she could do that for you just as well, and with our Glad's help, they could run your house together, costing you no more than it does now," she said nervously.

Josiah was shocked,. He was used to people standing in awe of him, not planning out his life. Who did she think she was? He did not know whether to be angry, humiliated, or happy at the proposals that had just been put before him.

"I, err, will talk it over with my wife," he stammered, brushing past Rosina. In his embarrassment, he left the room.

Rosina felt weak. She could not believe what she had just done. Where on earth did she get her ideas from? She just opened her mouth, and there she was telling the vicar how to run his household. She had better find Glad and tell her to start looking for another job 'cos neither Vicar nor his wife was going to like this at all.

Ophelia Kendal listened to her husband. He jabbered on about how humiliated he was when Rosina dared to sort out a replacement for her job, providing she was lucky enough to get the job at Lambecote Grange. Ophelia liked Rosina very much and was not surprised that she wanted to better herself in this way.

"Josiah, sit down, my love," she said calmly. "Think about what she has done. I admit it is not the usual thing for a servant to do, but Rosina is not a usual servant, as you have very astutely pointed out on many occasions. If those at Lambecote Grange are as adept at assessing human nature as you are, my love, they will jump at the opportunity to employ this intelligent woman. She has fulfilled all her duties here with the utmost propriety, and we have come to rely on her so very much. She has tried to be sure that we will be taken care of to the standard that she herself has set here, by asking you to employ the one person whom she knows will able to carry out the work—her mother."

Josiah became calmer. His lovely wife had pointed out he had been astute as to choose this girl in the first place and then commented on her abilities on many occasions.

"We should help her in her decision, Josiah," Ophelia pronounced.

"In what way, my love?" Josiah asked, growing in stature as he rose from his chair, his chest blown out with his ego.

His pretty wife twisted him around her little finger. "Well, perhaps if we could call on Lambecote Grange and give Rosina a character reference, Josiah. We have the knowledge that she will be honest and truthful to the Bingham family as she has been to us, my love." Ophelia smiled lovingly at her husband.

"Excellent idea, Ophelia!" Josiah exclaimed. "Excellent. We will go today."

Ophelia smiled to herself and left the room.

Lambecote Grange. February 1890

Elsie Buttle looked out and thought how lucky she was. The house was quiet. The work was done. The pantry had just been emptied and lime washed. So had every cupboard and drawer in the kitchen.

Tomorrow she would start the job of answering all those letters she had received applying for Mary's job. *By gum, some of these lasses have a lot to learn*, Elsie thought. It was obvious they had gotten somebody to write for them. Even their Violet could not write like that and she was educated. They would not have time to learn. That is if they were half-decent workers. They would have to have been working since they were eight or nine-years-old. She would sort them out—no messing her around.

"One of them letters came on real quality paper," Elsie told Violet whilst they were having lunch. "Now, where do yer think she got that from?" She laughed. "Well, she won't get a reply. Her fancy paper doesn't fool me."

Elsie was in the middle of the dishwashing. She had to do most of this herself these days. Violet refused to do work because that job should have been done by a kitchen maid. Elsie also had to cook since cook had left. "I'm saving money," Elsie said, consoling herself when she began to get tired of doing everything herself. It was now February 15, and Master would be home the first week in March. She had to get herself organised and get some decent staff.

Violet came into the kitchen announcing that they had visitors.

"What!" Elsie retorted. "We do not have visitors. Everybody knows the family's away. Who is it, for God's sake?"

Violet laughed. "It's the vicar from that church in Nottingham where Mary was wed. He's outside with his missus."

Elsie dried her hands, tidied her hair, and proceeded to receive the vicar on behalf of the family. This was an honour. Walking toward the front door, she felt quite regal.

"Good morning, sir, madam," she said in her best voice.

"Good morning, madam," Josiah replied, helping his wife from the carriage.

"I am afraid the family is travelling at the moment, sir," Elsie trilled in an almost unintelligible voice—affected because she believed she had taken on the mantle of gentry to receive the vicar and his wife.

Ophelia assessed the situation in her usual way, realising that poor Rosina would not stand a chance with this silly woman. "How are you managing my dear?" she asked Elsie with a sweet smile. "What a responsibility you have here. If you need any advice or help in any way, my dear husband and I are at your disposal."

Elsie was in her element. She could not believe her power. "Please come into the morning room. I shall have refreshments brought in. Yer must be tired after the journey from—" Elsie realised they had not said who they were, and she felt quite stupid. Should she admit she knew who they were or what?

Ophelia smiled sweetly at Elsie and said, "My dear husband's position, as vicar in a Parish in Nottingham, gives us some free time at the week on occasions."

"Of course," Elsie replied. She was thankful for a chance to redeem herself from an embarrassing situation. "Would yer like to remove your cloak, sir?" she asked.

"No thank you," Josiah answered quietly. "We will not be staying long as your master is unavailable. My wife and I have travelled here to give a verbal reference for one of your applicants for the job of dining room maid. I knew Mr. Bingham, God bless his soul, and would like to think that his poor widow is provided with the finest care in the county, which I am sure you are very well experienced to give her, Mrs. Buttle."

"Thank yer, sir," Elsie replied. "I was going to start that selection this very day and was not looking forward to making the decision myself. The mistress was in a very disturbed state when she left for Italy."

"Well, worry no more, Mrs. Buttle," Ophelia assured her. "If we can be of assistance in any way, we will be only too happy. It came to our notice only this very day that my maid of the last five years has applied for the position. Indeed, we are very distraught at the prospect of losing her, but when she told us that she had applied here, we realised how honest and trustworthy a servant we had. She has found replacements for herself to ensure that we will not suffer in any way when she has gone, as go she will when you meet her, Mrs. Buttle. There will be no changing your mind. My husband and I have travelled this distance today to ensure that you know what a wonderful opportunity you are being offered. Also to put our minds at rest that Rosina would be in good hands, and good hands she will be in with you, Mrs. Buttle. Of that I am sure."

"My dear Ophelia," Josiah said, taking his wife by the hand. He gently stepped between Elsie Buttle and Ophelia saying, "Not so fast, my dear. You are putting this poor woman at a disadvantage. She has to make a decision herself based on her own experience and not ours. Please forgive my dear wife, Mrs. Buttle. In her exuberance to help, I fear she goes a little too far."

"No, not at all, sir," Elsie quickly replied. "I am very grateful for the help of such revered people as your wife and yerself. Where could I find such a reference than in the church? And yer travelling all this way from Nottingham to help the mistress find a girl, to help the mistress recover from her poor husband's death. I am very grateful indeed, sir," Elsie said fluttering around the couple like a moth around a flame. "Very grateful indeed."

A knock on the door redeemed Elsie from making a complete fool of herself, and Violet entered with a tray of tea and light refreshment.

The refreshments were taken with chitchat regarding the weather in their respective parts of the county. Elsie, pulling herself together, asked the name of the maid in whom they held such very high regard.

Josiah replied, "Rosina Morton."

Elsie said she would find the girl's application and left the room. She looked through the disorganised heap of applications she had received, and finding the one on good quality writing paper, she said to herself, *Ah, this is the one. Well, she can certainly write a good letter I'll say that for her.* She proceeded back to the morning room and her guests.

"I have her application here on good quality writing paper. That says a lot about a person, I always think. Some of these girls can't write a word. Vicar, yer would not believe the scrawl on the paper." Elsie showed the letter to Josiah.

Josiah instantly recognised the paper from his desk and looked across at his wife who said, "Rosina has the use of my husband's desk if she wishes to write letters, Mrs. Buttle. The quality paper is, of course, my husband's choice."

Josiah was happy to believe that his choice of writing paper had so impressed he forgot the fact that he would not have allowed Rosina to use it if she had asked or that the paper had been stolen.

"Perhaps yer could ask Miss Morton to call and see me, Vicar, as soon as possible. The girl has to be pleasant to the eye, being a dining room maid. The master would have the final say on the matter. If she is as yer describe, and I have no reason to believe that she is not, then she will be taken on a month's trial."

"We will bring her ourselves," Ophelia said. "I am sure you will not be disappointed."

"Ophelia, my dear," Josiah said. "I have a funeral service tomorrow and cannot possibly leave the parish until next week."

Elsie said, "There is a coach once a day from Nottingham. It arrives in the village at one o'clock and leaves the village at three. She can come on that. I will see her off, and she can return on the same day."

"She will, Mrs. Buttle," Josiah replied. Thank you for your attendance on my good wife and myself. We should make our way back to Nottingham before it gets dark."

"Yes indeed, sir, and thank yer for travelling such a way on our behalf. The master will be told of your kindness when he returns," Elsie trilled in the affected accent she had used when they arrived.

Ophelia sat quietly in the carriage on the way home. "You are very quiet, my dear," Josiah said. "Are you well?"

"Oh yes, Josiah. Everything is very well indeed," Ophelia smiled sweetly back at him.

Rosina stepped from the coach in the village of Lambecote. She wore the new plum-coloured suit she had bought when the vicar had told her he had visited Lambecote Grange and spoken with the housekeeper regarding her eligibility to be dining room maid. Rosina was very dubious. She had always worked hard for the vicar and his wife but thought he was less than pleased when she told him of her plans regarding her family taking over the running of the vicarage in her absence.

Elsie watched her walk along the drive to the back of Lambecote Grange. Rosina, head held high and walking confidently, looked perfect for the job of dining room maid to the mistress.

Elsie had this feeling she had not made the decision herself, but God had somehow intervened in this. She had been so impressed by the vicar and his wife and she felt so important. "Just think, Violet. a vicar treated me like gentry," Elsie boasted to her daughter.

Rosina was very reverent toward Elsie. She was nervous and aware that she was being watched everywhere. She went into the house. Elsie questioned her all the while about her background.

One thing for sure, without the intervention of the vicar, Elsie would not have given her the job. Her background and address were far from ideal. The mistress would never hire someone with her background to take care of gentry. She would be lucky to work in the kitchen. Elsie gritted her teeth and agreed to give her a month's trial. After all, she could not go against a vicar, could she now?

Rosina was told to report for duty on March 1st, ready for the return of the family. No need to have her here any earlier because all the work had been done, and Elsie did not want the master to think she had had help with it. If he were going to bestow glory on anybody, it would be on her.

The carriage travelled along the bumpy road toward Lambecote Grange carrying the intrepid travellers returning from their European tour.

Uncle Edwin and Aunt Lillian were to stay at Lambecote Grange for several days to help Charlotte settle in, and face the memories that she must cope with for the rest of her life. Charlotte had used her grief to the full during their travels, but Lillian noted that when George was not around, she was much happier.

Charlotte insisted that she was not strong enough to deal with a new maid, especially one whom she had not had any influence over hiring. Of course, she usually did not have such influence, except when she was with her bridge-playing friends and proclaiming how she ran the household with a firm hand.

Poor Charlotte had never done a day's work in her life and had no knowledge of how much a person would be paid for pandering to her whims and fancies. Her husband always let her believe that she was in charge of the housekeeping affairs.

George, aware of his mother's character, asked Aunt Lillian and Uncle Edwin to stay for several days on their return to Lambecote Grange. This would help his mother settle down into her usual routine of afternoon teas and bridge parties where she could recount her experiences of Europe. He had no doubt that she would soon forget the trauma of his father's untimely demise.

The trees were just about to burst into the fresh green of spring, and the fields were looking healthy with the spring wheat growth. George opened the carriage window and took a deep breath. Oh how he loved this place.

"Close the window, George. Do you want me to catch my death?" wailed Charlotte.

George put his face as far outside the window as possible, and closing his eyes, he took a long deep breath. When he opened them again, the carriage was overtaking a figure struggling to carry a portmanteau. Walking a few paces, then stopping and changing hands, the figure turned and stepped aside to allow the carriage to pass.

As he looked out of the window, he realised that the figure with the portmanteau was a young woman. He instantly called to the driver to stop. As he was opening the door to alight from the carriage, his mother became almost hysterical.

"What are you doing, George?" she screamed.

Uncle Edwin and Aunt Lillian had been dozing and awoke puzzled at the sudden cessation of movement.

George stepped out of the carriage and said, "I believe this young lady needs a hand with her luggage. I shall ask her where she is headed." He then started back along the road towards Rosina.

Rosina was standing in the road. She was dressed in her best plum-coloured suit and the pert little hat the vicar's wife had bought for her as a leaving present. The hat was askew on her head. Her hair had broken out from its clips, and the wind was very nearly blowing her away. She stood by the side of the road when she heard the carriage coming along the track. Her arms aching with the weight of her bag, she decided to take a rest before carrying on along the road to Lambecote Grange.

31

Elsie Buttle was a real tarter. Rosina had decided she would need all her buttons on to cope with this hard-nosed woman. Even though she would have a heavy case to carry, Elsie had snorted with laughter when Rosina asked her if someone could meet her in the village with a pony and trap.

"Well, that's a good start," Elsie had quipped. "We are not servants for the likes of you, madam," she snarled. "You can carry your own case and don't take too long about it 'cos I shall expect you to be working and looking smart by five o'clock.

Rosina thought she was being hired to wait in the dining room. The master and mistress didn't arrive home until Friday and today was only Monday. Still she would soon find out what this bossy woman was really about. Better get going.

As she started on her journey again, she realised that the carriage had stopped twenty yards along the road. The door opened and a tall gentleman alighted. He seemed to be speaking to someone inside the carriage.

Shrugging his shoulders, he began walking back towards her, smiling. "I think that portmanteau is rather too heavy for you to manage, madam. Can I be of assistance?" George asked.

She was trying to answer intelligibly, not having much breath in her lungs after the long haul and being a little afraid of what was happening to her. She stood and looked at the man and desperately tried to get her breath and to work out what this gentleman wanted with her.

George took the portmanteau from her. "Can we take this for you?" he asked. "Where are you bound?"

"Th-thank you," she stammered. "I am on my way to Lambecote Grange. It seems much farther than when last I came without a heavy bag to carry."

"Lambecote Grange is my destination also," George said. He could not stop the excitement he felt, looking at this beautiful woman, struggling with this infernal bag. "Let me put your bag into the carriage, and you can ride the rest of the way with my family and I.'

"I will manage sir. Thank you," Rosina protested.

George would hear none of it. He put the bag on the back shelf of the carriage and helped her inside next to his mother whose face was a picture. If George had put a bag of horse manure into the carriage his mother could not have pulled a more distasteful face. Turning her head away, she refused to look at this untidy and dishevelled creature.

Aunt Lillian smiled at Rosina, and Uncle Edwin, always delighted to see a pretty face, helped her to find space to sit comfortably.

"Do you have business at Lambecote Grange?" George asked.

"Yes sir!" she replied nervously "I am to take a position there at five o'clock today."

Charlotte nearly exploded. "What!" she exclaimed. "You are only just arriving for work. What time of day is this to arrive for work?"

"I have travelled from Nottingham ma'am," Rosina said. "The coach arrives in the village at one o'clock, and I have been walking along this road for over an hour."

"Piffle!" Charlotte retorted. "You could have organised a pony and trap to bring you the short distance to Lambecote Grange."

"Please forgive my mother," George implored. "We have been travelling many days, and she is not feeling well."

"Oh, I am sorry, ma'am," Rosina answered. "If you will ask the driver to stop I will walk the rest of my journey."

"You will do no such thing," George said angrily. He stared at his mother in disbelief. "What position are you to take up at Lambecote Grange, Miss—? I am sorry but I did not ask your name. I am George Bingham and this is my mother and my aunt and uncle. We have been travelling in Europe and are returning home to Lambecote Grange."

Rosina was struck dumb. Here she was sitting in a grand carriage with this lovely man and his mother who would probably dismiss her before she could take up any duties at Lambecote Grange. Servants should not have the nerve to ride in the same carriage as gentry.

Lillian leaned over and touched her hand. "What did you say your name was my dear?" she asked.

"R-Rosina Morton, ma'am," she stuttered. "I am to be the new silver service maid, ma'am."

Charlotte threw her arms in the air in a dramatic gesture saying, "We are returning to a disruptive household with staff arriving with the family. What will people think?"

"Mother, you forget we are not expected until Friday. It was your idea not stay on in Southampton but to travel straight home. We could not possibly contact Mrs. Buttle to prepare for our arrival. Please calm yourself. Miss Morton has had a long journey as have we, and I am very pleased that you are going to be our silver service helper, Miss Morton. I am sure we will all be very happy together." George tried to console his mother whilst not offending this lovely young woman.

Elsie Buttle, who was a very obese woman, was sitting with her skirts above her knees and her legs akimbo in front of the iron range in the kitchen of Lambecote Grange. She had become quite accustomed to her afternoons, resting in front of the kitchen range. She pondered what would happen when they returned at the end of the week. She had employed a new cook to arrive on Wednesday, and the dining room maid who should be here anytime now if she knew what was good for her. Elsie didn't like this girl at all and felt she had been hasty in listening to the vicar and his smiling wife with their verbal reference, as they called it. She closed her eyes and nodded off, enjoying the peace and quiet of the warm kitchen.

"Mam. Mam!" Violet came running into the kitchen, screaming at her mother. "Quick. Get up. There is a carriage coming up the drive. I think it's Master's."

"Away we yer," Elsie said. jumping up from her ungainly pose in front of the fire. "They are not home 'til Friday."

Violet ran back to the front window to get a better look. "Well, they are here now so hurry up get yer boots on and get out front quick."

Elsie pushed her feet into her boots, pulled her skirts down, and tried to tidy her hair whilst running around like a headless chicken. Just as she reached the front door, she saw Master George alighting from the carriage, pulling down the steps, and holding out his arm towards a lady in a plum-coloured suit with long unkempt hair flying from underneath a stupid hat.

The woman emerged from the carriage, smiling at Master George. She then went to the back of the carriage to help herself to her portmanteau.

Elsie nearly collapsed on the spot. It was that woman from the vicarage. What was she doing in the carriage with the family? Elsie knew Rosina would be trouble. Well, she would not stay one night under this roof.

Oh no! Bloody hell! What am I going to do—no cook, no beds made-up, and hardly any staff? she thought. Elsie ran outside to help the mistress from the carriage. When she saw the mistress's face she did not feel any easier.

Charlotte was beside herself. She had never in her life had to ride in a carriage with mere servants. George had gone too far this time. She would have to make sure that he was not as lenient with staff as his father had been. It was her job to run the household, and she would make sure this chit of a girl was sent packing as soon as possible. She flounced into the house with Elsie bowing and scraping and protesting how she thought they would be home on Friday.

Today was only Monday, and Elsie had nothing prepared for dinner. She dared not let on that the household was without a cook, a kitchen maid, a boot-boy, or Alfred, the butler, who approaching retirement, had walked out soon after the family left for Europe. She had intended the master to thank her for saving money and being thrifty, for not taking on the staff until the last minute, but now she was in a right pickle. That vicarage woman—how had she wheedled herself into their carriage? But she would catch it when she got her on her own.

George took Rosina's bag from the carriage dismissing her attempts to take it from him. He strode into the house, and after making exclamations on how wonderful it was to be home and how lovely it looked, he asked Elsie where he needed to put Rosina's bag.

"W-what?" Elsie spluttered to herself. *Needing her bag indeed! She will not be needing any bag when I am finished with her. Huh!*

"Mrs. Buttle, I asked you where Miss Morton would be sleeping," George repeated.

Elsie turned her very large frame around to face George. Her face turned red as she blustered, "Follow me, Miss Morton!" Striding out, she tripped over the boot-laces that she had not had time to tie in the panic of the last ten minutes, and fell on her face.

George and Rosina rushed forward to help Elsie who was close to tears and completely flustered by now. George helped her to her feet, asking her again to tell him which room Rosina would be using. He had no objection to taking the bag himself and leaving Elsie to prepare refreshments for the travellers.

"We have been on the road since dawn, Elsie," George explained. "We are very tired."

Elsie told Violet to go and show the girl where she should sleep, but George insisted on carrying the bag.

Violet took them to the top of the house, a garret room, which she supposed would be the room for the dining room maid.

George was too tall for the door, and dipping his head, he moved into the room. He was aghast at the condition of the place. He had no idea his home had such places within its walls. Water ran down the outside wall which had a tiny window with a pane of glass missing. The bed was a straw-filled mattress on a rickety wooden frame. Propped up with bricks, a broken chest of draws stood in the corner. It was so cold he could not imagine anyone sleeping in here without suffering pneumonia. He stepped out of the room taking the bag with him.

Rosina did not know what to think. She was not staying in a room like that. She thought it might be better to leave now. Elsie was never going to forgive her for arriving in the carriage with the family. The mistress was a bitch of the first order, and Rosina did not want to stay in this godforsaken place.

George asked Violet, "Who usually sleeps here, Violet?"

"Agnes used it when she was kitchen maid, sir."

"So that is why poor Agnes sniffed," George said. "That room is not fit for a dog. Where is the new kitchen maid sleeping, Violet?" he hardly dared to ask.

"We don't have one, sir. Not till Wednesday," Violet replied sheepishly.

"Oh." George's brain was working fast now. "Where is the cook's room?"

"We don't have a cook either sir—not till Wednesday."

"Do we have a butler?" George asked, noting the look of fear in Violet's eyes. He answered himself sarcastically, "Not till Wednesday. Don't get upset, Violet. I think I understand. I am sorry we caused you so much grief!"

"Come with me, Miss Morton. I shall try to get this sorted. Come into the morning room and take some refreshments. You must be cold and hungry after such a long journey. I know I am," George, said taking Rosina's arm gently.

"If you don't mind, sir, I would rather take my refreshment in the kitchen. Then I shall be on my way. I really do not think the housekeeper is requiring someone like me. Mrs. Buttle has different ideas on how to keep house than I was led to understand from the vicar. I am sorry, Mr. Bingham, but I could never sleep in a room like that," Rosina said, pushing her shoulders back and straightening her hat. George was shocked and angry to find that people were living under his roof in such dreadful conditions.

"Miss Morton, please do not be hasty," George implored. "I shall find you a suitable room, and we can sort this mess out tomorrow after we have rested and eaten. This is a confusion caused by my family returning earlier than Mrs. Buttle expected. That does not excuse the room you were offered. I know things will change. Now that I am home, I intend to take control. I shall need help to get the household running smoothly again and would like to think I could count on your help." George could not believe he was putting his trust in a woman he had met only minutes before. He had a feeling that this woman was a godsend and would do his best to keep her.

Rosina felt sorry for Mr. Bingham. He had shown her such great kindness, and she agreed to stay at least until morning. Elsie sat at the large wooden table in the kitchen. The whole episode was beyond belief. The fall she had taken in the hall had knocked the wind out of her sails, and her face was ashen.

Violet had taken over, and with the help of the master, had found Rosina a room on the first floor next to her mother's room.

Rosina helped Violet prepare a meal—vegetable soup, cold meats with cauliflower au gratin, and potatoes roasted in their jackets, followed by fruit compote, made from the delicious preserves cook had bottled in the autumn a year earlier.

Rosina served the meal in the dining room, and Charlotte continued to ignore her, turning her face away every time any part of the meal was offered to her. Rosina insisted on eating her meal in the kitchen with Elsie and Violet.

After dinner, Violet persuaded Elsie to take an early night. She tucked her mother up with a warm drink. And after explaining to Rosina that she lived in a cottage in the village with her family, Fred Buttle drove her home in the pony and trap that was kept for shopping trips to the village. The estate workers used the carriage to travel to church of a Sunday, and it should have been sent to meet Rosina when she arrived in Lambecote earlier that day.

Rosina checked all the doors and windows and proceeded to her room. She knocked quietly on Elsie's door, and getting no reply, went to her own room.

She was exhausted and did not unpack her bag fully, just taking out her night attire and what she needed for the morning. She lay for a long time thinking on the day's events. She could not believe that she had travelled in the master's carriage. Mr. Bingham was very personable and seemed so genuine. He was not like the vicar, professing God's will all the time yet selfish as the next man underneath. Mr. Bingham seemed different. His Aunt and Uncle seemed like real gentry, not just sitting and being waited on hand and foot. The mistress, on the other hand was not as gracious. Rosina thought Mrs. Bingham was a spoilt selfish woman, ignorant of the ways of the world. She only knew what she picked up from other silly preening woman of high birth. After all, why should they know anything other than trivia? They would never need to know any skills except perhaps a little stitching and musical knowledge.

Rosina felt angry. Her own mother had to scrub her fingers to the bone to eat the meagre rations that she could buy. The little she earned at the vicarage actually changed life for the Morton family. Rosina knew her father was beyond help. She was grateful that she had been able to procure that position for her mother and sister.

Things could be a lot worse, she thought. She would give this job a try if only to show the arrogant mistress that she was not afraid of her. If the master turned out to be after something else, then he would get the shock of his life if he tried it on with her. She smiled to herself and fell into a deep sleep.

For what seemed like hours, George lay awake, tossing and turning. Perhaps he was too tired to sleep. He would have to take charge of this household starting tomorrow. Elsie had had it her own way far too long. He knew his father left a lot to Elsie and Fred Buttle. George thought that was because he spent too much time entertaining mother's silly friends. He was sure they were only fair-weather friends, pandering to his mother's whims and fancies for the privilege of being included in her afternoon teas.

He decided to ask the new girl to stay on, perhaps offer her a little more money, feeling sure she had the makings of an excellent organiser. Look at the way she had organised the dinner tonight. There was not a hair out of place when she served the delicious meal after Elsie had completely lost her composure. The girl had organised Violet, who after all, was only a lady's maid and not accustomed to cooking a meal for the dining room. The meal had been concocted out whatever she could lay her hands on, and it tasted delicious.

George was ashamed of his mother's behaviour and would tell her so when she had rested after her trip. People could not sleep in conditions like that when two-thirds of the rooms in this house were left empty. He would make sure that staff was employed to provide fires in everyone's room be they family or staff.

Mother and Elsie needed a few lessons in management. A happy household was paramount to the success of any estate. People worked much better when they had had a good night's sleep and plenty of good food. And by God, he would see to it that that was what they got.

Chapter 4

June 1890

Rosina looked through her window onto the back of Lambecote Grange. The stable lads and the farm workers were busy grooming the horses and cleaning the farm implements. Every piece of equipment had to be cleaned each night before it was put away.

The master had taken on many more lads from the village to be trained for various trades, and they worked happily with the skilled men. The girls in the dairy were thrilled when they heard the master was taking on extra lads. Lots of preening and parading up and down the yard was taking place. The whistles and whoops from the lads and their elders could be heard clearly in Rosina's room. Elsie had also heard the goings on, as she put it, and had a word with the mistress about it.

After dinner, Charlotte spoke to George and told him he was ruining his father's farm. "Harold Sutton could do a better job, George." she moaned. "Your father will turn in his grave. You employ the riffraff and have become the laughingstock of the county."

George was sick and tired of his mothers continual whining. "Mother!" he proclaimed one day, after she had spent a journey to Nottingham decrying the Morton girl who, in her opinion, was from a bad lot.

No doubt Elsie, who did not take kindly to Rosina's smooth organisation, fuelled this opinion. "I have doubled the production on the farm in the last three months and it is only June. When we have harvested this year's crops and collected the profits from the butcher shops that I have modernised, we shall have made a profit which promises to double that of last year. When I begin to lose money, and I see reason for your stupid complaints, you may get me to listen. Until then I fear you are wasting your breath. Rosina Morton is a very astute businesswoman. She manages the accounts perfectly and saves money when she buys sensibly. Very few provisions need to be brought in. Rosina bakes the bread and has taught Violet how to manage accounts. She can read and write and is also a good conversationalist. That is more than you can say for most of the silly woman with whom you are acquainted."

Charlotte was overcome and had decided to tackle George on the journey knowing that she would have his undivided attention. Her dear departed Charles always listened to her opinion on staff, and if Elsie disliked anyone Charlotte recommended, she would be fired and rightly so.

"George! I plead with you," Charlotte cried, turning on the tears. This tactic had usually worked with Charles. "This Morton woman is an impostor. Elsie says she only employed her because the girl beguiled a vicar to give her a verbal reference. Verbal reference indeed! She is a charlatan. Mark my words! Her background is a home in the slum area of Nottingham, and you have her waiting on gentry in your father's house. It beggars belief."

Rosina had been at Lambecote Grange three months now. She had worked very hard and had full co-operation from George regarding the changes she had made in her roll as buyer and account keeper. This allowed Elsie to carry on as housekeeper but with less authority on staff matters. Rosina understood the master's thinking.

Elsie carried on with running the house. She needed some help now, and he had taken on more staff. George had more business meetings at Lambecote Grange and this entailed dinner parties for the elite of the county. George had succeeded his father as hunt leader and keeper of the hounds. His position was greatly revered by the county people and they expected to be wined and dined in style. He understood now why his father always dined at the Crown on these occasions. He wanted to avoid the trauma that a formal dinner party would cause his mother, Charlotte. Elsie was not capable of organising such an event without bringing in outside caterers.

Today was Rosina's day off. She would have liked to go home to see her mam but could not get there and back in the day. She usually took her day off, taking a small picnic basket and walking out onto the farmland to explore small thickets and watch the fish in the beck that ran through the land. She walked out to the west of Lambecote Grange today. She had not been this way before, and carrying her picnic and a book, she had borrowed from the library at Lambecote Grange, she enjoyed the sun on her face as she strode out along the hedgerows.

George rode back toward Lambecote Grange. He had been exercising Storm, his beautiful hunter. He thought Storm was the closest living creature to him since his father's death. They had an affinity, an understanding of each other. They had covered a fair amount of the farm today. Most days, he would ride Storm after breakfast, checking the crops and generally enjoying the open air. He preferred solitude and was always glad to be away from the stupid tittle-tattle of his mother and Elsie. He would check fences and thickets, measuring the growth of the crops. He loved every blade of grass that grew here. It was part of his own flesh and blood. He counted his blessings many times when riding around the farm. He was in sight of Beckett's Thicket now—so called after a woman called Beckett had been executed there when she was accused of being a witch several centuries ago.

As he trotted up towards the thicket, Storm suddenly pulled up short and reared as if afraid to pass any closer. George knew of the superstitions about Beckett's Thicket but had been here many times as a boy and a man. He had never experienced fear.

"Whoa Storm!" George struggled to hold the horse who was really spooked. He dismounted, and leading the horse, proceeded to walk past the thicket when he heard what he thought was a girl's voice coming from inside.

He tied Storm to a tree, and walked farther in toward the beck that ran through the centre of the wood. The land dipped here which caused a little pond in the middle of the trees. He walked closer to the singing voice. His heart leapt in his chest as he silently moved the branches of a gorse bush to get a better view of the figure sitting barefoot with her feet dangling in the water. Rosina Morton was singing a most beautiful song about the lass with the delicate air.

George stood quietly for several minutes. This was a beautiful sight and he wanted to savour the moment. He decided to make himself heard so as not to alarm the girl.

"Hello there," he called out. "What brings you up here?"

Rosina jumped up and spun around, her heart beating fast with fear. "Master George." She smiled. "You startled me. I was taking my day off in the country. This is my first visit here I came across this thicket and decided to have my lunch here among the birds and these beautiful trees." Rosina glowed.

George thought he never had seen such a glorious sight. Rosina had a look of the ethereal, her smiling happy face, her hair long and flowing

41

with the soft warm breeze taking little strands across her face. She was the most beautiful creature he had ever seen in his whole life.

"May I join you?" he asked.

"You certainly can, sir. I only have a little food. If you are hungry, I think you should make your way home."

"I won't take your food, Rosina," George said as he sat beside Rosina and removed his shoes and socks. "My horse heard you singing and was startled. I tied him to a tree and came to investigate."

"Oh, that bad was it?" Rosina laughed.

"No, no!" George reassured her. "It was beautiful. I thought I was dreaming. This thicket has a legend, I fear, and when Storm would not ride past. I began to wonder if the legend was true. Then I found you."

"What kind of legend?" Rosina asked curiously.

"A woman accused of being a witch was burned here sometime ago."

"Poor woman!" Rosina said, having heard of women being burned alive for no worse crime than curing a child with herbs.

"Well, this is a lovely place to die if that's your fate," she said.

"Thank God we don't burn people now."

"People are still punished for being different," Rosina said sadly.

"In what way, Rosina?" George asked, puzzled. "How do we punish people today?"

"Oh, let us not speak about it now," Rosina said thinking of her mother, a gypsy who married a *gorgio*.

Poor Kisaiya Morton believed it was her fate to suffer poverty after her shamed family had cast a curse upon her and her offspring.

"This is my day off, and I want to spend it with the trees and the witch, if she doesn't mind." She smiled.

George dangled his feet in the freezing water, yelping at the cold. They laughed and shared the picnic, and George told Rosina how he loved the Grange and every thing that grew and lived on it. Time flew by, and when the sun began to fade, Rosina gave a little shiver and said. "I think we should start back, sir. I have a long walk and do not care to be out here in the dark."

George led Storm and walked alongside Rosina. They chatted easily. "Why don't you go home on your day off, Rosina?" he asked.

"It's too far, sir. My home is in Nottingham and there is only one coach a day in the week. But none runs on Sunday."

"Well, on your next day off, Rosina, I shall organise my business to coincide, and you can travel in with me. I shall drop you wherever you want and meet you later, if you would allow me," George said eagerly.

The excitement he got from just being with this girl gave him an urge to spend more time with her—alone if possible.

"No, sir, I don't think that would be appropriate for you. You must think of your reputation," Rosina replied feeling her face flush with embarrassment.

"If you don't want to travel with me, Rosina, I understand, but from where I am standing, I would be proud to accompany you to Nottingham," George said. "I can think of nothing that could be construed from it that could harm my, or indeed your, reputation. It is quite acceptable for me to help one of my household visit her home."

"Well, if put it like that, sir, I don't suppose it could, but Mrs. Buttle would not agree. I am sure of that," Rosina said. Her heart was pounding. She was so happy with this man. *I must watch my step here*, she thought. She would protect this man with her life if need be. She did not want to end up like many girls she knew in Nottingham. They had fallen for their employer and come home with a bairn in tow, their futures ruined by some fine-talking gentleman turning their heads.

"Mrs. Buttle does not run my life, Rosina, or yours for that matter. I give her respect for the years of work she and her family have given to Lambecote Grange. But there it ends. I shall consult my diary this very day and organise for your day off to be taken when I can accompany you."

Elsie checked to see if the fires had been lit in the dining room. It was that Morton woman's day off, and she was in charge of her duties today. If she could find something amiss with Rosina, she would have a better chance of making Master George see that the girl was a bad lot and should go.

Elsie didn't enjoy working at Lambecote Grange any more since Rosina had been given so many of her jobs. Violet said she liked her— that she had a lot of good ideas and worked hard. But Elsie wished she had never set eyes on her. As she walked past the back windows overlooking the stables, she saw something that made her blood rush around her body like a storm. The Morton woman was walking beside Master George. He was leading his horse and laughing and joking with her in an intimate way. If that was what she did on her day off, she was as good as gone. After the mistress found out, her feet would not touch the ground. Oh this was good news. Elsie nearly broke her neck to get to Charlotte's room and report what she had just seen.

George left Storm with Tommy, one of the new stable lads. The lad had a real way with horses. They liked him and would go anywhere with him. Horses told you a lot about a stable lad. If they liked him he was encouraged.

Running upstairs to his quarters, he had almost been knocked over by Elsie, flying like a mad woman toward his mother's room. He asked her if everything was all right, and she had dipped her knee, given him a weak smile but not seeming to have enough breath to speak. She was acting strangely these days. *Must be her age,* he thought wryly. He took his bath and was dressing for dinner when there was a knock on his door. "Come in!" he called.

Violet entered and looked very upset. "Your mother wishes to see you, sir." she said, not looking at him.

"Is there something wrong, Violet?" George asked.

"No. No, sir, I don't think so," Violet answered sheepishly.

"Very well, Violet," George said. "I shall go along shortly." He finished dressing and proceeded to his mother's room a little puzzled. Entering, he found Charlotte having one of her vapours, as she called them. Elsie was administering smelling salts, and Charlotte was milking the situation, whatever it was, for all it was worth.

After dismissing Elsie, Charlotte lifted a tearful face up toward George and wailed, "George, George! What are you doing? Your father was a paragon of virtue and had a blameless reputation. How could you tarnish our name in such a way?"

"For God's sake, Mother, what on earth has happened?" George was shouting now, his mother's attitude angering him greatly.

"Don't try to deny it, George. I have it on firsthand authority that you are carrying on with that dreadful woman. That is why she virtually runs this house and does as she pleases," Charlotte sniffed.

George began to understand the situation. Obviously someone had seen Rosina and him walking back to the farm together, and he wouldn't have to look far to identify the taleteller. He went over to the bell pull, and tugged it so hard, he pulled it from its anchor. He stood motionless holding the dysfunctional bell rope waiting for someone to answer.

Violet arrived. "Yes sir, did you need something?" she asked. Her mother had sent her to say that she was not very well and had to go to bed. Violet had told her mother that she had gone too far this time, and Master George would not stand for this.

George said, "Will you please ask your mother to come up here immediately, Violet?"

"Mother has taken to her bed, Master George," Violet replied. "She has taken a funny turn."

George bellowed at her, "Violet, bring your mother up here now or I shall bring my mother to her myself. While you are at it, ask Miss Morton to come up here also. Thank you, Violet."

Violet dipped her knee and left the room. She ran into the kitchen and told Elsie the master had summonsed her and to be quick because he was in no mood to wait. She then ran upstairs to Rosina's room.

Rosina was sat at the small writing desk. She was writing a letter to her mam and was bemused by what had happened that afternoon. *I count my blessings every day, Mam. I love this job. It's hard work, but I enjoy it so much. Mr. Bingham has offered to give me a lift into Nottingham next time he goes on business. I don't know what to think about that. My gut reaction is that he is a perfect gentleman. He gets a little lonely with no friends of his own age. I shall watch my step but it would be nice to come home and see you all. I miss you very much. I am glad that you are feeling better now that you are getting regular food. Don't let the vicar put too much on you, Mam. He is not as kind as his wife you know,* she wrote.

Violet knocked on Rosina's door but didn't wait for an answer. She ran in babbling out what her mam had told the master. "Excuse me, the master has asked me to get Mam back again too," Violet said, leaving the room once more.

Rosina was furious. She stood up, pushed her shoulders back, and made her way to the mistress's room, leaving Violet speechless. She hoped the master would not sack her and all the family because Elsie interfered and told tales. Master would not do such a thing. For that matter, he would not do it to Rosina either. Master George was known for his courteous way toward women. Rosina was great and would soon be putting tradesmen in their places when they said anything out of line.

Rosina knocked on Charlotte's door and walked straight in to see the master with his mother and Mrs. Buttle. She was not going to be servile to this woman anymore. *Bitter twisted bitch!* she thought.

George turned as Rosina came through the door. Seeing the straight posture and the shoulders pushed back in defiance, he knew she had been told what had taken place after they returned to Lambecote Grange. He spoke immediately, not allowing his mother to open her mouth. He was afraid of the accusations his mother would throw at her. He certainly did not want to lose Rosina from his life, but he also had to be careful not to show his very fond regard for her or she would run a mile.

"Rosina, I am so sorry to bother you on your day off," George started. "My mother and Mrs. Buttle saw you and I walking back home this afternoon, and although I do not need to answer to either, I do not want any accusations levelled at you. If you would tell my mother what you do on your day off, Rosina, I would be very much obliged. Of course, if you decide that it is not any of her business, then I respect your decision."

Rosina took a deep breath and tried to calm her temper. George was giving her prominence over his mother, and she had intended to tell her what she thought of her before packing her bag and leaving first thing in the morning. George was giving her the opportunity to do it with dignity. She must not betray his trust. She coughed a little and said. "I take a picnic as Mrs. Buttle knows, ma'am, and walk around the farm somewhere different each fortnight." Rosina only had a day off once a fortnight.

"Where did you go today Rosina?" George asked smiling.

"I went out toward the west field sir," Rosina said.

"I, mother, was riding out by Beckett's Wood when my horse was spooked at the sound of someone close by. After dismounting, I walked into the wood and found Miss Morton taking her picnic, which she very kindly shared with me, I might add. As it was getting dark, we walked back to the farm together, and I was reluctant to let a lady walk all that way on her own whether she wished to or not.

"Now, Mrs. Buttle, I think you owe Miss Morton and me an apology, don't you?" he said, looking at Elsie. "You, Mother—I expect better of my own mother—when you and Mrs. Buttle have apologised, you, Mrs. Buttle, can carry on, looking after Miss Morton's duties."

Charlotte was dumb-struck. She had no intention of apologising to this trollop and was hardly able to breathe. With anger, she feigned a breathless palpitation. Elsie took her cue running to her mistress with the smelling salts at the ready.

George took Rosina's arm and ushered her from the room. "I am afraid you will have to wait for your apology, Rosina," he said. "But believe me, you will get an apology if these two gossips wish to live in this house."

Rosina said, "Please do not upset your mother over this. I think it would be much better if I left in the morning as I had decided to do before you kindly absolved me from any wrongdoing."

"No. No, Rosina!" pleaded George. "This is just silly posturing by two ladies who for many years have had their own way in their different positions in the household. They must realise that I am the master at

Lambecote Grange now, and I want to successfully go into the future without the dreadful class barriers of the past century. You must believe me, Rosina. I would deal with anyone who was so badly misjudged as you are in the same way. I do not listen to gossip whether it is from my mother or a member of staff.'

"Your mother seems ill, sir," Rosina said quietly.

"She is not ill, Rosina. She manoeuvred her own way with my father many times, using this silly fainting act. I do not subscribe to it," George replied.

Rosina went back to her room and reread the letter she had been writing when Violet had interrupted her. *How life can change from one minute to the next,* she thought.

Served by Violet, George dined alone that evening. His mother had taken dinner in her room as she was not well, and Violet had been told to tell the master.

Rosina went into the kitchen for her meal at eight to find only Violet there waiting for her. "Me mam says she's not going to apologise, Rosina," she cried tearfully. "And me dad says she's not to come home to him if she's lost a good position like this. He won't stand up for her. He likes you and says me mam's just jealous."

"Don't worry, Violet. Your mam is wrong. You know I was taking my picnic in Beckett's Thicket when my singing spooked the master's horse. I thought I was alone. He told me the story of a witch who was burned there years ago. I did nothing wrong, and Master was telling me about the hunt and how he loves his horses."

"I know Rosina," Violet said. "Me dad's right. Me mam is jealous. She has had her own way here for too long and should be grateful for some help instead of trying to get rid of yer. Don't cry, Rosina. Come and get yer dinner."

Rosina tried to eat but was pushing the food around her plate rather than enjoying it. She decided to go and find Elsie and break the deadlock. After knocking on Elsie's door with no answer, Rosina decided to go inside. She found Elsie folding her clothes, ready to pack them into an old bag that had seen better days. Her hair, very grey now, was hanging loose around her shoulders, and Rosina was shocked at how aged she looked.

Elsie looked up and saw Rosina. "I don't want any more of this," she said. "I can't stand all this friction. You will be glad to know that I shall leave tomorrow morning. You have taken everything I worked for. You made it worthless." Elsie began to sob.

Rosina could see in the dim light of the oil lamp that Elsie had swollen eyes. The poor woman had a bowed look about her.

"I don't want to take your job, Elsie," Rosina said.

Elsie scoffed. "You could have fooled me. You have wormed your way in here and changed everything. Master George is besotted with you. It seems like you have him under a spell or summat."

"No. No, Elsie," Rosina said. "You have the wrong impression of me. I only want to do my own job. I never had any intention of being anything more than a dining room maid when I came here. It takes more than one person to run this household. Neither you nor I can do the job alone. We need each other. I don't have your skills in the kitchen. I would not know where to start on preserves, for example. I come from the city. We don't have abundant fruit in the autumn in Nottingham. We do not know how to live in the country like you. You have all the experience that I don't. I only have youth on my side, Elsie. I have the will to learn everything, and like the silly girl I am, I want to learn it all in one day. You are the one to teach me to measure myself out, Elsie. I don't want to change things just for the sake of it. I need you here and so does Master. You are the only woman of the mistress's own age in this house with whom she can confide. She is like a child who also needs teaching how the world outside lives. I feel so sorry for people who have had husbands who cherished and protected them so much that they have a poisoned view on reality. The master has never so much as noticed me. As a woman, I can assure you, I need to work here to help my family back in Nottingham. I send all my spare money to my mam. I don't have any ideas above my station. I have no intention of getting me self mixed up with the gentry. Believe me."

This was too much for Elsie. She sobbed uncontrollably.

Rosina put her arm around her shoulder and said. "I shall go and get you some supper and a warm drink. Then we can talk about tomorrow."

Elsie dried her eyes, and nodding her head, agreed to have some supper.

Whilst Rosina was in the kitchen putting a cold plate together for Elsie, the door opened and George came in.

"What on earth are you doing, Rosina?" he said. "It is very late."

Startled, Rosina spun round to face him and found herself looking into his beautiful grey-blue eyes. "I was just getting Mrs. Buttle some supper. She feels a little better now but has not eaten since luncheon," Rosina stuttered, the blood rushing to her face making her cheeks glow.

George was smitten. He was looking at Rosina with such tenderness, she felt her legs go weak. Here was this beautiful gentle woman, caring for that bitch of a woman who had not two hours ago accused her of unimaginable acts of indecency. He thought she was so strong yet so kind. George figured she must be an angel sent to help this household recover from the great loss of his father. His mother had no idea how to run this house, yet she would send away the one woman who could make life go on for all of them. He felt so protective towards her he wanted to touch her, hold her in his arms and say, *I will take care of you Rosina for always.* George knew he must not let these feelings be known to Rosina. She would leave immediately and would misconstrue his intentions. He must stay calm and strong and encourage her to be herself. "Can I carry this upstairs to Mrs. Buttle's room for you, Rosina?" George asked, his heart pounding in his chest.

"Oh no, sir!" Rosina exclaimed. "I can manage." Rosina thought Elsie would have a fit if she walked in with George whilst she was in such a state.

George was glad no one would see his dithering hands, especially not Elsie. She might have got the wrong impression.

Elsie had pulled herself together when Rosina returned with the supper tray and was sitting at her writing table ready to eat her food. She was hungry.

After placing the tray in front of Elsie, Rosina asked, "Do you need anything else before I retire, madam?" she smiled at Elsie mischievously.

"I am sorry lass," Elsie said. "I have had it all me own way for so long now and thought I was going to go on forever. Fact is, I enjoyed having a bit of spare time when the family was away. I think I might speak with Mistress about living in the village in my own cottage now that you're here to take a bit of the strain like."

"Well, don't make up your mind tonight," Rosina said. "We shall talk tomorrow when we have both had a good sleep."

Chapter 5

Rosina would remember that summer for the rest of her life. The sun shone, and she was happier than she could ever imagine. George was true to his promise and once a month he took her to Nottingham when he went to see his bankers.

Kisaiya enjoyed her work at the vicarage, and Gladys found herself a man friend. Len Morton was not so happy. Gladys made sure her mam did not give him all her wages. He had managed to get himself a job in the market, humping boxes for a green grocer and earning just enough to pay for his drink. He didn't go home every night. Gladys thought he might have some gambling debts after some bloke came around looking for him late one night. She told the bloke her mam never heard from him, and he left grumbling saying he would find him if it was the last thing he did.

The carriage was parked in a Nottingham market place. George sat waiting for Rosina. He had been very busy, having had a very profitable day. The butchers were not happy with the regular visits they were getting from the new master. His father never came into town. He always sent an accountant to collect the takings. There was less opportunity to fiddle the books when George collected. He seemed to ask so many questions.

George had organised for the booths to be set up at the Goose Fair the following week and quietly reflected on the changes in his life over the last year. He really looked forward to these outings with Rosina. She had blossomed in the last six months and was such a strong-willed woman. Yet she always knew her place and had opinions on most subjects. She was very well read, which was a minor miracle considering her background.

Rosina hurried along Market Street where she had arranged to meet George. Having spent more time than she had intended at the vicarage visiting her mam and sister, she hoped she was not late. The vicar and his wife wanted to know everything about her job and her life at Lambecote Grange.

Josiah frowned when he learned that the Master was bringing her into Nottingham every month. "Mark my words, Ophelia," he said to his wife. "There will be trouble afoot. Gentry does not have truck with the likes of the Mortons without payment."

"Josiah! How can a man of your breeding have such thoughts?" Ophelia said angrily "This man is a good man who out of the goodness in his heart gives a poor girl a lift home to see her family. We know how Rosina works hard and earns a day off with her family once in a while. How can you accuse her of misbehaviour? You have no evidence or knowledge of the man you are accusing."

"Mark my words, Ophelia. That is all I am saying. Just mark my words," Josiah postulated.

Rosina saw the carriage waiting for her. She quickened her step, eager to get back to her life at Lambecote Grange and George. She lay awake at night telling herself that she had no business thinking about this lovely man. It was only a dream. Her heart would break if he took to one of those silly women that his mother paraded for his attention. She could dream a little, couldn't she? There was no harm in that.

"Oiy!" a voice bellowed at her just as she was about to be seen by George

Rosina turned startled.

"Where are you rushing off too?" Len Morton called to her. He walked over to her unsteadily, looking tp the entire world like a tramp.

"Dad," Rosina said, startled. "What are you doing here?"

"Just in time to see me daughter turn a trick by the look of it." Len leered at her. Seeing his daughter well-dressed and about to be helped into a fancy carriage by a gentleman, only meant one thing. He knew what the gentleman was after. And if the wanted his daughter, he would have to pay him something for the privilege. "Just a minute," Len bellowed at George. "Where do you think you're gonna take my little girl, eh?"

Startled, George held Len back with his left arm whilst he helped Rosina into the carriage with his right. Len stumbled backwards and fell onto the cobbled road. George closed the carriage door and stepped over toward Len offering his hand to help him to his feet. Len was winded and took a little time to get himself together. By this time Fred, who usually drove the coach when George went into Nottingham, had jumped down from the front of the carriage, and although he was getting on in years soon took over the situation, telling Len to push off or he would call the constable.'

"Constable. I'll call the constable. By God I will!" Len shouted at George "That is my girl in there, and you have just assaulted me in my defence of my little girl. I think the constable would like to hear that."

Rosina sat in the carriage, paralysed with shame. The look on George's face was one of complete astonishment.

Fred looked from Len to Rosina, waiting for Rosina to disagree with this statement. But she just sat there staring into space, not moving a muscle.

George was the first to take hold of the situation, and speaking to Fred, he said. "Make sure the horses are not spooked, Fred. I shall deal with this." Rosina had told George her father was a no-good drunk who beat her mother and kept them poor with his drinking. Here was proof. Poor Rosina must be dying a thousand deaths sitting in that carriage.

George held out his hand to Len saying, "I am pleased to make your acquaintance, Mr. Morton. The circumstances are disagreeable, but I can assure you Rosina is returning to Lambecote Grange with Mr. Buttle and I after taking her day-off in Nottingham."

"Oh uh," Len scoffed. "And yer are looking after her out of the kindness of your heart. Is that it?"

Rosina had become angry now. Opening the carriage door, she jumped down onto the cobbled stone road. Attacking her father with her fists, she screamed at him, "Yes, Mr. Bingham is taking me back to Lambecote Grange. You care so much for your family you have not been home for a week. Get yourself away from Mr. Bingham, you stupid little man. I am so ashamed of you. You are probably drunk on the money I earn and send home to feed you. Send for the constable, Mr. Bingham. Get this man locked up before I do him some harm myself!"

George took Rosina's arm and said, "Rosina please get into the carriage. I can deal with this. Do not fret yourself on my behalf."

Rosina was in tears now, and shaking with rage, she let George push her into the carriage and close the door. George took hold of Len and roughly pushed him a few yards away from the carriage. Holding him against a wall, he told him he should be proud of such a well-educated daughter and not shame her in such a way.

Len blubbered. Now he was scared. He had gone too far with this gent who was looking after their Rosie. "Sorry, sir," Len said. "I have not eaten today and am hungry. She don't send money to me. She sends it to her bitch of a mother who spends it on god knows what but not on me.'

George felt sick at this snivelling man. He put his hand in his coat and brought out his wallet. Opening it, he took out a five-pound note saying. "Take this and buy some food. Smarten yourself up, and your family might be proud of their father. Spend it on drink and you will never get another penny."

Len grabbed the white fiver. He could not believe his luck. He began to dip his head and touch his cap in reverence to George.

Rosina sat in the carriage waiting for George. She could not see what he was doing with her father. She hoped he did not give him any money. Len would take that as proof of her guilt. God knows what he would tell the world she was doing in the market. She would not be able to hold her head up in Nottingham again.

George returned to the carriage, his face red with anger. Seeing Rosina cowering in the corner of the carriage, his face softened, and taking her hands in his, he crouched down in front of her saying, "Rosina, do not cry. I can't bear you to be hurt like this. You mean so much to me, Rosina. I know this will come as a shock to you, but I have loved you for such a long time now. I must tell you or I will burst."

Rosina stared in disbelief at George. She must be dreaming. He had said he loved her. How could he? She was a maid in his employ, and he was gentry. He had seen her father and knew now what her background was.

"I know this is not the time or the place to say all this, Rosina, but will you marry me? I love you so much. I can look after you and your family. You do not need to worry about any of them ever again." George had opened the floodgates now and there was no stopping him.

"What!" Rosina exclaimed, her eyes wide in disbelief. "You marry me? But I am only a servant. How could you have these feelings for me?"

"I have feelings for *you*, Rosina, not your position in life. You run my home for me. Lambecote Grange as never been such a happy place. Everyone, indeed even my mother, is happier for your presence. Please say yes, Rosina. If you could put up with me, I would be honoured to have you as my wife," he pleaded.

Fred was struck dumb. He had been driving gentry for thirty years or more and had never heard the likes of what he heard in this carriage the night. Master George, who was the most eligible bachelor in Nottinghamshire, was proposing marriage to a maid in his coach. This would never have happened in the old days. Oh, no never.

Rosina's mind raced.

George said, "Do not give me your answer now, Rosina. Take some time and think about it, but I assure you I shall ask again and again. I have loved you from the first day I set eyes upon you struggling with that silly portmanteau on the road to Lambecote Grange." He gave Rosina his handkerchief to dry her eyes and wrapped a travel rug around her feet before settling into his seat for the long journey back to the Grange.

Rosina sat in silence during the drive back. She could not make sense of the day's happenings. It was dark when the carriage arrived at the Grange. George helped her down into the courtyard.

After Rosina had moved toward the house, he went to Fred and said, "I don't want any of today's events repeated to a soul, Fred! Do you understand? Not a soul."

"Yes, sir!" Fred replied.

"I mean it Fred! If I hear one word of this, I shall know who to blame." George said threateningly.

"It won't come from me, Master George! I have been driving your family for over thirty years now and you can't accuse me of any tittle-tat-tle." He was very hurt by the implication that George was making.

"Yes, I know that, Fred, and I don't want to offend you but I can't stress enough how important it is to keep quiet," George said.

"You can depend on me, Master George."

Rosina entered through the back door and went directly to her room.

Elsie brought her a pot of tea and asked if she had had a good day. Elsie and Rosina were good friends now. "I shall be going home with Fred tonight," Elsie said. "Do yer want any supper, lass. Yer look tired."

"No thanks Elsie. You go home. I shall have a bath if the water is hot and then have an early night."

"There is plenty of hot water, lass. I'll put some towels in before I go," Elsie said, puzzled at Rosina's lack of conversation. She was usually full of beans when she had been home for a visit—but not this night.

"Thanks Elsie," Rosina said wearily.

"Well, I'll say goodnight then Rosina," Elsie said, leaving the room.

"Good night Elsie," Rosina replied. She slept fitfully that night. She was dreading meeting George in the morning. She thought the day before must have been a dream.

Rosina and George avoided each other during the next week. After lunch on Sunday, George decided to confront Rosina. She sat at her writing table writing a letter home but had not mentioned George's proposal, having decided that he had made it on the spur of the moment after the dreadful scene her father had caused in the market place. She was so embarrassed about it, she tried to remove it from her memory by keeping busy sewing, writing letters, and taking on extra duties in the house to allow Elsie to spend more time at home with her family.

Rosina and Elsie were becoming very close friends, and Violet was like a sister. Rosina shuddered to think what Fred had told them when he got home that night. They had not mentioned it or even hinted at knowing of the proposal. George must be too embarrassed to speak to her. He had carefully taken his meals in his room all last week, and Rosina dared not ask Elsie why. Perhaps he was ill.

A knock came on the door. Rosina called, "Come in." Turning towards the door she was shocked to see George. He was smiling and asking if he could speak with her. "Yes, yes," Rosina stammered.

"Rosina, I have purposely kept out of your way for over a week now. I think I have given you enough time to make a decision regarding my proposal. I can't sleep or eat until you give me my answer," George said, not giving her the opportunity to speak first.

Rosina's jaw dropped. She was gaping at George, her brain forming words but her mouth refusing to move. Eventually she said, "I thought you were just being kind to me after my father embarrassed me so," she managed to stutter.

George moved toward her, and taking her hands in his he said, "Rosina, Rosina, I love you. I have loved you since the first day I saw you. I am in torment waiting for your answer. Please, please say yes."

"Master George, do you realise what you are saying?" Rosina asked.

"Yes, Rosina. I am asking you to be my wife—to be my partner in life, and to have my children. I could not be happier to be in a position to offer you a home at Lambecote Grange. You have made it such a happy place for everyone."

"I don't think your mother will agree to that," Rosina said.

"It has nothing to do with Mother," George said, putting his arm around Rosina's shoulder. "This is our decision, yours and mine. It does not affect anyone else."

"But George, I am not of your class," Rosina protested.

"Rubbish, Rosina. You are the sun, the moon, and the stars. There is no class high enough to hold you. You are kind, intelligent, beautiful, and accomplished at many things. The staff loves you. You have encouraged them to take pride in their own accomplishments. In the past, Rosina, workers were not allowed to learn to read or write and have their own dreams of prosperity, but you have changed all that."

"Oh, I am sure workers had their dreams, Master George. Everyone has their dreams. You do not need money for dreaming," Rosina said, her mind in turmoil. How could she make sense of this?

"Rosina! Rosina! Rosina!" George exclaimed. "I love you. Shall I run around this house proclaiming it to everyone before you will give me your answer?"

Rosina laughed at his exuberance saying. "You would be the laughing stock of the county if you wed a mere maid from Nottingham. And when they discovered my father's background and my mother being a gypsy, you would not be welcome at the hunt either. No this is ludicrous." Rosina first raised her voice and then began to cry. She was so confused. Every part of her body wanted to be with this man. She had never had feeling like this before. This could not happen. She would be done for if he was trifling with her, but this was George Bingham. He did not possess a bad bone in his body. She had to believe him. George held her in his arms, and she was melting into him. The only answer she could give was. "Yes! Yes! I love you but do not think it will work. We are not compatible," Rosina said, sinking deep into this feeling of completeness.

Charlotte took to her bed when George announced his intention to marry Rosina saying, "This is the end of respectability for this family. I am glad your dear father is not here to suffer such immoral behaviour."

George was ready for his mother's reaction and had asked Elsie to wait outside the door just in case she was ill. Immoral was not the word to use. It inflamed George. He could have screamed at his mother. She had no idea the meaning of immoral. To her your birthplace and bank balance stated whether you were moral or not. "Rosina is the most moral person I have ever met in my life mother," he said. "You had better get used to the idea for we shall be wed at Christmas."

"So soon? She has beguiled you. I knew she would," Charlotte wailed.

"Christmas Eve. We shall be wed on that day. I shall leave you now. Elsie will spend the night with you. Good night, Mother." Placing a light kiss on her cheek, George left the room.

Chapter 6

George took Rosina into Nottingham on the day of the Goose Fair. They arrived at the back street where Rosina's Mam and their Glad lived. Len was never at home these days. Children came out to hang onto the back of the carriage, and Fred cracked his whip to scare them off. Carriages did not come down here. There was not enough room to swing a cat round, but Mr. George insisted on driving to the door of Rosina's home.

After asking George to wait in the carriage, Rosina left. To her dismay, Len was at home.

"Ho ho. Here she comes. The loose woman," he yelled as he noticed the good coat and bonnet she was wearing.

"Rosina love, I didn't know you were coming today," her mother said, hugging her close.

"Rosina held her mother at arms length. How did you get that black eye?" Rosina asked.

"I walked into a door, love, at the vicarage," Kisaiya lied.

"Has the vicar seen it?" Rosina asked.

"No, No. He wasn't in," Kisaiya said hanging her head in shame.

"Where's our Glad?" Rosina asked.

"She's gone out with the boyfriend a nice feller, Dawson they call him Sam Dawson," Kisaiya replied, eagerly changing the subject of her black eye.

There was a knock on the door. Kisaiya flashed her frightened rabbit look at Len. A knock on the door usually meant trouble.

"Open t' door, woman," Len said.

Kisaiya opened the door to find George standing there. Looking past him, she saw the carriage and all the neighbours crowding around it—women and kids, dogs, and cats. Rosina thought she would die of shame. She knew she should not have brought George here. Well this would put an end to it if nothing else would.

"Mrs. Morton!" George said, holding out his hand to Kisaiya.

"Y-yes," Kisaiya managed to mumble.

Rosina said, "Mam, this is George Bingham. George, this is my mother."

"I am very pleased to meet you, Mrs. Morton," George answered, taking Kisaiya's hand. Turning to Len, he nodded his and said, "Mr. Morton."

"I have some news for you," George said, smiling at them. "I want to ask you for the hand in marriage of your daughter, Rosina."

Kisaiya grasped the top of an old chair and the colour drained from her face. George put his arm around her shoulder and steadied her, leading her to a seat.

Len, who still had not risen from his chair said, "What? Yer and our Rosie? I don't believe it. You're havin' us on, man."

"Does that mean you give your approval, Mr. Morton?" George asked politely.

Rosina looked at her dad with eyes of steel. She hated him, but George had insisted on doing it correctly and asking for permission to marry her.

"Yes. Yes, sir," Len spluttered, shaking George by the hand and bowing and scraping.

"Well, Mam, put your coat on, you are coming with us to Nottingham. We intend to get married on Christmas Eve, and as I am only twenty, you have to sign the papers," Rosina said nervously whilst she looked around for Kisaiya's coat.

"You're not up the stick, are yer?" Len laughed.

Kisaiya cowered at this thought.

"No, I am not," Rosina said indignantly.

"Well what's he marrying yer for then?" Len asked.

"I am marrying your daughter because she is the most wonderful woman I have ever met, Mr. Morton. I love her with all my heart and soul," George said.

"Am I to come with yer all?" Len asked, shocked and stupefied.

"Yes, if you behave yourself and keep off the booze," Rosina answered

Later that day, they all arrived at the vicarage. Ophelia was delighted at the news. Her husband was nearly as bad as Len for bowing and scraping to George, telling him what a fortunate day it was when he took it upon himself to go to Lambecote Grange with a reference for Rosina.

"Mark my words, Mr. Bingham, the housekeeper would not have seen her but for my good wife and I taking the time to travel to Lambecote Grange in the middle of a very busy week. But my dear wife said that poor Mrs. Bingham has lost her husband, and we should be of all the help we can to the family. How is your dear mother?" he asked George. "Happy I am sure with such a prize as our Rosina."

"My mother is very well indeed, sir," George answered. "The reason we came to see you today, Vicar, is to ask you to officiate at the ceremony. We shall of course wish to be married at Lambecote, but do you think you could fix it with the bishop to officiate at that parish?"

"Of course, yes. Yes, of course," babbled Josiah Kendall who was overcome with joy. He was to officiate at the marriage of gentry. What a credit to his name.

"I cannot thank you enough," George said. "Mr. and Mrs. Morton have come here today to sign the documents required for Rosina to marry."

"Of course, Mr. Bingham," Josiah said, looking at Len suspiciously and then noticing Kisaiya's black eye. "Kisaiya, what have you bumped into this time? You have only just recovered from the last fall. You must be more careful."

Rosina spun round on her father saying, "My mother has bumped into a door, Vicar, but I do not think it will be happening again, will it, Father? You are going to take good care of her now, is that right?"

Looking down at the floor, Len shuffled his feet uncomfortably.

The papers were signed. and the little party moved on to Nottingham for the Goose Fair.

George knew Rosina enjoyed the fair, and he had quite an interest in surprising the butcher who was running the stalls for him. They took lunch at an inn. Len refrained from drinking when Rosina took him to one side with a warning of any allowance he might receive from her would be stopped if he touched one drop of ale whilst in George's company.

George and Rosina walked hand in hand around the fair. When they reached one of the faggot stalls, Rosina stood aside with her parents until George had done his business. When George appeared, the butcher, whose face was puce in colour, followed him.

Kisaiya's hand went to her mouth when she saw the butcher. It was Sykes. *He had better not say owt about our Rosina now 'cos he will be in big trouble*, she thought.

Sykes saw the little group. After he had taken Mr. Bingham round the stalls he had been running, he thought he would sort that bitch out. What was she standing around here for? Did she think she would get a hand out or something?

Rosina noticed George was not himself. She wondered what the butcher had been saying but did not move towards him while he was doing business. George looked over to her and smiled.

Sykes saw this and said to George. "You don't want any truck with that trollop. She's no good. Neither is any of her family."

George carried on walking toward the next stall and disappeared into the back. Some minutes later Sykes was thrown out of the canvas door at the rear of the stall. There was blood on his mouth. Someone had hit him hard.

Kisaiya said, "Yer don't think it were Mr. George do yer, lass?'

"I have no doubt it was, Mother, but for what reason I have no idea." Rosina said, dreading what lies Sykes was telling, George.

George eventually joined them and said he had to stay in Nottingham longer than he had expected. He asked if Rosina could stay at home with her parents that evening. He would find an inn for himself and Fred.

"Of course, George!" Rosina said. "Is everything all right? You look quiet flustered."

"I will discuss it later, Rosina. But do be careful. I want Fred to drive you back to your parents' home, and I wish you to stay there until I come for you tomorrow. Mr. Sykes can be a very violent man, and I need to collect some facts from all the stalls he has running here before he removes the evidence. Do you understand, Rosina?"

"Yes, George, but you be careful too. Sykes is nasty. He employed my mother and paid her in scraps. I have had course to put him in his place," Rosina warned.

"I realise now that Sykes is a scoundrel, Rosina, but I need more evidence. I have upset him today, and he may try to take revenge on you and your family. Fred will see you home, and you must stay there." George gently put his arm around Rosina's shoulders, and after lightly kissing her cheek, he left.

Rosina and her family had a wonderful evening. George had sent a hamper of every kind of delicacy you could think of, and Gladys could not believe this fairy story their Rosina was telling them. Their Rosie was marrying gentry. It beggared belief. She secretly thought Rosina must be up the stick but kept her thoughts to herself.

They decided not to tell all their relatives, as they were all Len's family who were layabouts and would turn up at the wedding and ruin the whole day. The gypsies of course had cut Kisaiya out when she married Len.

Rosina told them George had asked her if she wanted a fairytale wedding, but she had laughed and said, "No George, I am not interested in dressing up to look like a fairy. Something simple will be what I choose, but thank you for offering."

George said that he did not think she would, but if she wanted a fairytale day, then she could have everything. That is when they decided to wed quietly on Christmas Eve and just have Kisaiya and Len and Gladys.

"Rosina, do you think I could bring my fella?" Gladys asked.

"Of course you can." Rosina laughed.

Sykes was arrested for fraud. He had been fiddling with the books for years and had become so complacent. He did not think he would ever be caught, but fate sometimes decides things, and a chance visit on a fair day was something the gentry had never done. "Fairs are for t'working classes, not namby-pamby gentlemen. I'll sort out that Morton bitch one day if it is last thing I do," Sykes said.

December 1890

Rosina and George had the most beautiful wedding. Charlotte refused to get out of her sick bed. Aunt Lillian and Uncle Edwin came as well as Aunt Grace and Uncle Ambrose.

Harold Sutton was George's best man and could not believe that George was marrying this maid when she was not even up the stick. He always thought George was weak. He had been to see his Aunt Charlotte and commiserated with her, agreeing that George was ruining the good name of the family. "Uncle should have left the farm to be shared," he said to Charlotte.

Kisaiya and Len had new clothes and so did Gladys. They really did Rosina proud. They had never slept in a room with such fine furniture and bed linen so soft. Kisaiya hardly dared move in her sheets. Len had been promised enough money to pay the rent and look after Kisaiya in the way she deserved. Rosina asked her mam if she wanted to come and live at the grange with her and leave her dad, but Kisaiya declined, saying that she loved Len with all his bad ways, and that perhaps if they had a bit more money, he would not be as bad. Rosina doubted that but agreed to give him a pound a week. But if she heard of him drunk once or hitting her mam, it would stop.

George had wanted to move them all to a cottage on the estate, but they had their own lives to live. Rosina knew they would be happy for a little while, and then trouble would start. George agreed to let Rosina handle the whole thing.

When Rosina arrived at the church, she expected no more than a dozen people, but the building was full of villagers. The women had gathered berries and holly and decorated the aisle.

"It was perfect," Rosina told George after they had retired.

George delayed going into the bedroom until he thought Rosina would be in bed. She looked like an angel, lying there with the sheets pulled up to her chin, nervously trying not to look when he got into bed.

"What a magnificent day, Rosina," George said. "Earlier, I was thinking about the amazing events of the past twelve months. First Father's death and the catastrophic effect it had on the household, and then the miracle of you coming like a gift from God to sort out the chaos. Life is so strange and so precise. If we had stayed in Southampton overnight instead of travelling home straight off-the- ferry to please mother, I would not have seen you on the lane, and perhaps you would have left the next day. When I think of the room you were expected to sleep in, I can't see how you stayed. But here we are, the happiest day of my life with a beautiful wife and her family on my wedding day."

Rosina said, "I do love you, George."

He tenderly took her in his arms, and their lovemaking completed their happiness. They were so perfect. Rosina felt a little afraid. She wanted this night to go on forever. She worried that if she let morning come she would lose him and this gossamer delirious happiness would be gone.

Rosina and George had decided to have Christmas at Lambecote Grange, inviting both of their families to a grand Christmas Day party. Elsie and Fred and Violet and her family had moved to the farm for the week. Kisaiya, Len , Gladys and her friend Sam were staying for three days. Lillian, Edwin, Grace, Charles, and not to mention the parasite, Harold, were the Binghams' guests for the festive season.

Lillian coaxed Charlotte out of her room on Christmas Day, and although Charlotte ignored Rosina and her family, she did seem to be enjoying the company.

Kisaiya and Len spent most of their time in the kitchen with Elsie and Fred saying, "This is where we feel more at home."

Fred had no time for Len. He could not forget the episode in the market place. Elsie thought Fred was emphasising the class difference, but Fred knew better. He thought Len Morton did not deserve a lass like Rosina, and he thought that Master George would have trouble from him before too long. But he could not tell Elsie any of this in case she let it slip.

Uncle Ambrose had given the couple the use of his villa in Florence for as long as they wanted to use it. He liked Rosina. She was good for George, and by God, she had got this house running like he had never seen it run before.

George had booked a passage on the ferry on New Years Day, and they would travel until they decided to come home.

Chapter 7

November 1894

Beaming, Elsie came out of Rosina's room. George stood, looking out through the front windows over the land—his land, as far as the eye could see.

That is what his father told him as a child. "Look out there, George. That's yours, all of it. You must have a son to pass it on to!" That had been the last conversation his father had had with him on that fateful day five years ago.

George and Rosina had thought that they would not be blessed with children. It had been four years since they were wed, and no sign of a child until now.

George turned, and seeing Elsie walking towards him, he said, "How much longer, Elsie? It has been twelve hours now. Rosina will be exhausted."

"Master George, the child is born, you can go in now," Elsie said, beaming. She ushered George into Rosina's room.

George ran into the room. Seeing Rosina resting now, not in the unbearable agony she had been in earlier, he exclaimed. "Rosina my darling, how are you?"

Rosina smiled weakly at him and said, "George meet your son."

A crib stood by the bed. He had not noticed it earlier because he was so upset about Rosina. But now he looked into the crib, and his child lay there, peacefully sleeping.

"A son, Rosina! Oh how wonderful, a son!" George was in tears. Throwing his arms out in jubilation, he cried "Rosina thank you for making my life so perfect."

Charlotte came into the room, and after a cursory glance at Rosina, went over to the crib and said, "A boy, Rosina, how clever of you. What will you name him?"

George looked at Rosina, and they both said, "William George!"

Charlotte bent over and kissed Rosina gently on her forehead, saying, "Thank you for my grandson, Rosina."

Rosina and George lived in a world of wonder they cooed and talked to the child not having time for any one else. It was many years before Rosina found she was pregnant again. George was ecstatic.

The baby girl was born seven years later in 1901. They named her Sarah.

"Little Sarah," George called her. "Where's my little Sarah?" he would say when he came into the nursery.

Sarah loved her. She was a really beautiful child with soft brown hair and George's eyes of a pale grey-blue, which seemed to draw everyone in. She was a child you could not take your eyes off.

George would take William around the farm, sitting him on the front of his saddle. He would constantly talk to the child about the farm and the hunt. William's big eyes took in the views in absolute wonder when his father told him. "This is your home, William. This is where your children will be. All of this is for you my little huntsman."

Just before the Goose Fair when William was eight-years-old, George took him down to the Romany encampment. The Romanies had just arrived for the fair.

A toothless old hag came over to George and said, "Come inside, sir, and take tea."

George had many times taken tea with the Romanies. They were very interesting people. He lifted William down to the woman, and she led him into the wagon. William sat close to his father. He was not sure of these people. The woman grinned at the boy and gave him something to drink. He had not tasted anything like it before, but it was sweet so he liked it.

While George was taking his tea, her man came into the wagon, and nodding to George, asked if he needed a horse.

"What have you got?" George replied.

The man motioned for him to go outside. George told William to stay and finish his drink. The woman sat quietly watching William. He was afraid of her. She had great big eyes that never blinked and was not smiling now. A younger woman came into the wagon with a girl about four or five-years-old. The girl sat beside William and gave him her doll to play with.

"Thank you!" William said politely.

They played for sometime, and the older woman left, muttering something to the younger woman who laughed.

George returned and William said, "This is my friend, Fluere, Daddy. We have been playing."

"Hello, Fluere," George said smiling broadly at the dark-haired dark-eyed child playing with his son.

Fluere grinned at him.

"We have to go now, Fluere," George said. "But we shall come again tomorrow."

George mounted his horse, and the old woman lifted William up to him, saying in a gravely voice, "There's trouble ahead sir. A woman, an older woman—be ready!"

George smiled saying, "I will, I will." He was accustomed to the gypsies' prophesying and did not pay much attention to them, but he knew Rosina did.

After dinner that evening, Rosina and George were sitting by the drawing room fireplace, which was constructed of magnificent white Italian marble covering the whole of one wall. Rosina loved this room in the winter when the children were asleep and life was so perfect.

Rosina said, "William tells me he has a friend, George. Where did you go today?"

"To the gypsy camp—I may buy a couple of horses from them. William quite took to them, and a little girl, her name was Flower or something."

"Fluere," Rosina said. "He has not stopped talking about her all day. He says you are to take him again tomorrow."

"Yes, I did say that we would go back tomorrow, but I was not aware that he was so taken with the girl," George said.

"Do you think it wise to take him there? He is so young."

"Of course, Rosina. They are capital people. I have known them all my life. They always camp on the flat field just before the Goose Fair," George said smiling at her.

"George, the Romanies ostracised my mother when she married my father. They never forget, never! We are cursed by them. My mam believes everything they prophesy. Please do not take William there again George. I am afraid for him. They know who his mother is and will try to make trouble for us. George, promise me you will not take him again." Rosina was so worried about the gypsies harming her children she began to cry.

George put his arm around his wife's shoulders saying, "Don't listen to these old tales, Rosina. Nothing will harm William. I intend to purchase a pony for him for a Christmas present. The gypsies know horses better than anyone I know. I have to return tomorrow. I have promised."

Elsie knocked quietly on the drawing room door, and when Rosina called for her to come in, she opened it and softly went in. "Mistress is not well, Rosina. She looks queer to me. Could you take a look at her?" Elsie asked.

Rosina and George jumped up and ran upstairs to Charlotte's room. She was an ashen colour and breathing badly. George fell to his knees by his mother's bedside. taking her hands in his, "Mother. Mother," he cried. "What is it? Are you in pain?"

Charlotte smiled weakly at her beloved son and tried to turn her head toward Rosina.

Rosina knelt beside her husband, gently, lovingly, stroking Charlotte's forehead. She had sent Elsie to the stables to get a boy to ride into the village for the doctor.

Charlotte slowly moved her hand from George's grip and held Rosina's hand. "Rosina." She spoke faintly now. "I am so sorry for the way I treated you in this house. I have been a fool."

Rosina put her fingers on Charlotte's lips saying, "Shush. Save your strength, Mother. Tell me later when you feel better."

"No." Charlotte's smile weakened. "I have only a little time and need to say I love you both so much—and William and little Sarah. You have made this house so happy. It was a fortunate day when you arrived here, Rosina."

George was in tears. He held his mother close to him rocking her gently saying, "I love you, Mother. I need you here with me, guiding me through to bring up my children in the ways of Lambecote Grange. I need you to tell them that they belong here on this land for generations in the future, Mother. Do not die. Please do not die."

Charlotte was limp in his arms. She had died happy in the arms of her son, having made her peace with her daughter-in-law. Now Rosina was the true mistress of Lambecote Grange.

Chapter 8

Christmas 1902

W illiam whooped for joy when he saw the pony standing outside the front door of Lambecote Grange. Little Sarah clung
to her fathers neck as he raced down the stairs with Rosina,
laughing and running behind them. This had been a surprise Christmas
present for William.

Santa Claus had left lots of presents underneath the Christmas tree,
and they had been so happy opening them. Sarah loved her doll with real
hair and a beautiful dress.

Rosina had been embarrassed when she opened her present from
George. It was a magnificent eternity ring set with diamonds, rubies, and
emeralds. She had not known what to give George, and had ordered a
photographer to take a picture of all of them. Rosina sitting next to
George, with Sarah sitting on her fathers lap. William was standing at the
right of Rosina with his arm on his mother's shoulder. Rosina had had
the picture framed in a beautiful solid silver frame and this she had
wrapped and presented to George. He wiped the tears away from his eyes
and taking Rosina in his arms held her so close with affection she was so
happy she could burst.

George had been teaching William how to sit a horse for some time
now. He had been looking out for a suitable pony for him. Whilst he was
visiting the Gypsy camp in November when the gypsies were camped for
the Goose Fair, he saw this prize. Fluere had been riding the pony bareback, and he responded to her every move. George thought he was gentle yet strong. He was perfect for William.

Fluere had named him Skye because she loved the sky and the stars
and the moon. She would fantasise with William about people who visited the camp from the stars. William loved Fluere. He was very sad when
the gypsies moved on and was always first to know when they had
returned.

George had a little pony and trap to take little Sarah out. With William trotting Skye alongside, they would travel around the land. He showed them every little corner of Lambecote Grange, always telling them how it was their birthright to live here and how William would be expected to be hunt leader and keep the traditions of the countryside. He taught him to treat all people fairly and not judge anyone until they knew them. "Never judge anyone based on where he was born. All people have a soul," he would tell them. "And that soul will know where it has to be and what it has to do in the span of life. That it is given here on earth. We are here to look after this land and provide food, good healthy food, for everyone. In doing that, we give them work and a home to live in. Never believe that you will always have what you have now. You will keep this land only if you use it well. If the land is lost, and you ensure that it is used for the purpose that God has entrusted this family with for over four generations then so be it. But if the land is being used for greed then it will be your duty to regain it and put it to the best use possible."

These were days of sheer bliss. Rosina still ran the household and baked the bread. She could no more sit entertaining idle women than they could bear to take tea with a mere maid.

The Bingham family certainly gave the county something to gossip about during the time after Charles' death. But Rosina and George were so happy bringing up their children in this idyllic world of gentry interspersed with common folk.

George nearly lost the role as hunt leader when the gossips discovered that Rosina's mother was a gypsy. Needless to say the hunt dinners were still held at Lambecote Grange, and the gentry always turned out in full for the occasions.

Elsie told Violet that they were just waiting to see Rosina fall on her face. How could a common woman like that know how to entertain gentry? Wives whispered under their fans whilst eating the splendid food and drinking the finest wines they had tasted anywhere in the county.

What they could not seem to understand was the fact that unlike these woman who could not manage to wash themselves without help from another human being, Rosina could cook the whole thing herself.

The farm continued to thrive. George bought more land from an adjacent farmer who suffered from gout and could not manage to plough the fields or bring in the harvest without great help from Lambecote Grange workers. This farmer had never married and not produced an heir. George paid above the going rate per acre for the land and allowed the farmer to stay on in his home for as long as he lived.

1905 was a year of great joy and happiness.

William and little Sarah helped in the fields. Sarah was taught how to make bread and pies. Elsie adored her. In the Autumn, Elsie would take Sarah into the kitchen garden and pick fruits. First gooseberries, then raspberries, blackcurrants, blackberries and plums were bottled, and apples were carefully wrapped in paper and stored to eat through the winter months.

During spring, Fred would show the children how the winter spring wheat had grown and the blossoms on the fruit trees would turn into fruit in the autumn.

Sarah loved the summer when the drawing room windows were left open and she could run all the way down to the beck without her shoes and paddle her pretty little feet in the water. Daddy would tell them the story of how he fell in love with mummy when she was paddling her feet in the beck whilst singing a song about a girl's hair.

Sometimes Grandma Morton came to stay. She always asked if she could hold Sarah's hand before she touched her. Then she would cry when she looked into William's eyes, telling him he reminded her of her father.

"Where is your father, Grandma?" William asked.

"Oh far away, son, far away," Kisaiya answered.

Sarah lived a charmed life with the best of both worlds. She had a maid to brush her hair and had lots of pretty clothes to wear. Her grandmother taught her how to make flowers from tree bark and told her stories about the gypsies living outside, even in the winter. William wanted to know all about the gypsies and asked Kisaiya so many questions Kisaiya began to worry about him.

"Rosina!" Kisaiya exclaimed when she was alone with Rosina one summer afternoon. "I think William is a Romany."

Rosina shrugged her shoulders as a cold shiver went down her spine

Grandpa Morton was different. Sarah thought he smelt of something nasty. She didn't like him to visit. He always made Grandma cry and Mummy angry.

Auntie Glad was funny. She spoke funny. She had a husband who smelt funny like Grandpa. Mummy used to tell him to look after Glad and not gamble her money away.

Wesley and Wilfred were Auntie Glad's children. Wilfred was a little younger than William, and Wesley a bit older than Sarah. Rosina liked Wesley, but he was a little slow. Wilfred was horrid. He nipped Sarah when no one was looking and blamed things on Wesley that Wesley had not done. Uncle Sam always hit Wesley on the head and believed Wilfred even when he told lies. Sarah didn't like Uncle Sam.

Sarah asked her mummy what *gamble* meant.

"Nothing to bother your pretty head about," she replied, shrugging her shoulders.

In the summer of 1905 George took them all to Blackpool for some fun. Apparently Blackpool was where everyone went when they were unhappy. They always seemed came back happy. Sarah asked George if he was unhappy.

He swooped her up in his arms, and laughing loudly, bellowing, "I am the happiest man alive, Sarah—the happiest man alive!"

"Is Auntie Glad going to Blackpool? She was unhappy yesterday when she came to see Mummy," Sarah asked innocently.

"No, poppet, Auntie Glad has to go into hospital," Rosina said. "That is why she was unhappy."

What she did not say was that Auntie Glad had come with a sad tale of woe. She had been infected with pox, and Rosina had nearly died of shame when she turned up. She asked George for the money to get treatment. She swore blind she had caught it from Sam, but Rosina was not so sure. Gladys drank far too much for Rosina's liking. She blotted out the realities of life with a bottle, which was the way most women who were living in poverty went. Gladys said it was the only way to survive and that Rosina had no idea what she had to endure.

George knew Rosina was very upset at Gladys for turning up with such a tale and decided to take them all to Blackpool for a week. They would take Elsie, Violet, Nellie and Fred. Violet's husband couldn't leave the farm, but George said for him to come for a couple of days in the middle of the week.

Sarah was afraid to go up to the top of the tower that was five hundred and nineteen feet high, but George took William right to the top. Blackpool Tower was a very famous venue for holidaymakers since it was opened in 1894.

Rosina and the rest of the little group of holidaymakers excitedly bought tickets for the Tower Circus that would perform in the afternoon. Sarah's eyes were like saucers when they arrived at the circus, which was built in the base of the tower. The wooden bench seats were almost full and the lights and music thrilled children and adults alike.

William sat on the edge of his seat absolutely enthralled with the performers. Fluere had told him of her escapades with the circus people—how the freaks were not really freaks and the the strong man who was scared of mice, but most of all, the bareback riders whose daring stunts left William wanting to join the circus. He chatted on and on about Fluere and what she could do on a bareback stunt horse. Rosina watched her beloved son with dismay when she realised he could not help but love this kind of life.

Violet and her children took William on the big wheel, which had been built in 1896. Rosina was terrified when she could see them at the top of the wheel waving. George purchased two more three-penny tickets and took little Sarah on the wheel but she was not happy about the height and looked very pale when she returned to her mother.

The pleasure beach had been the last attraction to open at the turn of the century and there was so much fun there. Sarah loved every minute of it.

Chapter 9

November 1905

George and William were out riding one Sunday morning in late November when William's face suddenly lit up and he called to his father, "Look, Father, the Romanies are here for the Goose Fair." William was off down the hill onto the road. riding his little pony at a breakneck speed, weaving in and out of the caravans looking for Fluere.

"Hey you, *gorgio!*" the voice screamed at him from inside one of the caravans at the front of the line. "What are you trying to do, kill yourself?"

William spun Skye around and galloped over to the wagon waving and calling out. "Fluere, Fluere. I have been waiting for you. Have you got a pony to ride?"

The girl disappeared inside the wagon. William dropped back and watched as she jumped from the wagon onto the bare back of a piebald pony running alongside. Fluere galloped off up the hill toward Lambecote Grange with William, laughing and trying to keep up with her.

Rosina heard William's happy laughter coming from the kitchen. She walked in to find Fluere and William sitting around the fire with Elsie, eating bread straight from the oven and covered in butter that Elsie had just collected from the dairy.

William was retelling the story of Fluere jumping onto the back of the piebald and racing him up to Lambecote Grange.

Rosina felt a cold chill travel down her spine. Nothing good would come out of this friendship that William enjoyed so much with Fluere. Rosina cast her mind back to a time when a gypsy had struck her mother down at the Goose Fair.

Rosina had not understood then the implications of the act but later was to learn that her mother was indeed a Romany, ostracised for marrying a Gorgio. Gypsy curses went through generations and William was the grandson of a *pauno-mui*, a woman who prefers the company of a gentile, and Fluere was Romany. Rosina was frightened at the thought of what that could entail.

William was innocent but the Romanies left nothing to chance. If they could stop this friendship now, they would by doing whatever was necessary to remove William from Fluere's life.

William called out to his mother. "Mummy, can Fluere stay for lunch? Oh please say yes, Mummy. Please."

"William, Fluere must go home. Her family will be worried for her," Rosina said unconvincingly.

Elsie, not knowing the fears that Rosina harboured said, "They can eat in the kitchen with me Rosina. I would like that."

"As you will," Rosina retorted.

Elsie noted the edge in Rosina's voice but picked up her mug of tea and carried on listening to the stories that Fluere was entertaining them with—stories of fat ladies at fairs and bareback riding. Elsie laughed 'til her sides ached. She laughed at the tale of the bearded lady and the strong man getting wed at Appleby.

George arrived home just as lunch was being served. Rosina was quiet and brooding. George asked if she was unwell. She told him she had a headache and would take a walk after lunch. He offered to accompany her but she refused, telling him she liked to walk quietly sometimes. Rosina strode out towards the gypsy camp. She had not realised how far it was but had made her decision. She had seen the look on William's face whilst he was listening to Fluere give her account of life in the camp.

As Rosina came upon the first wagon, a toothless woman poked her head out and said, "Cross me palm with silver lady, and I'll tell your future."

"Not today. Thanks," Rosina replied nervously. "Can you show me the wagon that Fluere lives in?"

"Never heard of her," the toothless woman spat out.

Rosina was annoyed with herself. She knew no gypsy would let on knowing another. As she proceeded to walk along the line of wagons it went deadly quiet. She could only hear the crackle of the fires outside the deserted wagons.

"Hello," Rosina called out at one wagon door. "Is anyone about?"

A voice came from behind her. "What do yer want, lady?" a deep throaty voice called out.

Rosina was startled and began to shiver.

"Come here near the fire, lady. Yer shaking like yer seen a ghost."

Rosina turned to run, but when she looked around her, gypsy men all grinning with an array of gold teeth, bad teeth, and no teeth surrounded her.

One man took hold of her arm saying, "Steady now steady. Sit down." Pushing Rosina toward a wooden bench outside a wagon, he stood in front of her menacingly.

Rosina's heart beat so fast she could not get her breath. Her legs would not move. She opened her mouth to speak and no sound came out.

A woman's shrill voice called at the man. "Let her be, Sake. Get on your way." The woman climbed down from the wagon and the men vanished into several benders encircling the camp.

"Here, drink this," the woman said to Rosina, pushing a cup of something sweet and hot into her shaking hands.

Rosina began to feel a little better and stopped shaking.

After a few minutes the woman said, "You're the *chavi* of Narrilla Lee?" Then, leaning back into a chair, which was made up of straw and blankets, she puffed on a white clay pipe, looking suspiciously at Rosina through hooded eyes.

"My mother's name was Lee, yes." Rosina stammered. "But her name is Kisaiya."

"Ha!" The woman spat on the ground just in front of Rosina. "That's what she called herself after she went off with that drunken carter—after he'd deflowered her at Goose Fair," the woman growled. "She was a good girl before he got his hands on her. She worked hard, and many a good *chavo* she would have spawned if she hadn't got taken down with him."

Rosina thought she should try to leave while the men were away, but each time she tried, the woman put her foot out to stop her escaping from the corner the woman had hemmed her into.

"What yer here for?" the woman asked.

"I was just out walking," Rosina lied.

"Walking and looking for Fluere, yer mean." The woman laughed. She could see the fear in Rosina's eyes and was enjoying the power she had over her.

Rosina was getting angry. This woman was trying to scare her off. She knew that. Rosina was the wife of the landowner. Gypsies knew everything about the areas they travelled.

She stood up saying, "I shall be off now." She began to fasten her bonnet and push her shoulders back.

"Not so fast," the woman said. "I asked yer what yer came for. Don't tell me yer was just passing 'cos yer travelled five miles to get here and it's not walking weather."

"I came to ask you to stop Fluere from spending so much time with my son," Rosina said, holding her head high.

"Romanies not good enough for him, eh," the woman said, grinning all over her wizened face. "Or yer don't want his father to know that he's married a gypsy," she said, getting to her feet and pushing her face right in front of Rosina's.

"That is not the case at all," Rosina said. "My husband knows full well where my mother was born, and I am certainly not ashamed of my roots. My mother is a wonderful woman who brought me and my sister up with strong values of fair play and family worth. This she learned from the gypsies."

"So what's wrong with us for your son, then?" The woman spat at her.

"You know what will happen if this friendship goes on into his manhood. My son does not have any idea of the difference between Romanies and *gorgios*. I am looking after his welfare as a mother," Rosina said with a little more confidence.

"You're a brave woman to come here when yer know what could happen to yer," a voice called from inside one of the benders.

"Shut your mouth, Sake," the woman said.

There was laughter from the men at this.

Rosina started to walk around the woman's foot. "Hold," the woman said. "So what yer gonna do now?"

"I shall forbid my son from seeing Fluere again," Rosina said.

"It's his destiny. Women have known since littlens were babbies that they are for each other. They won't have a chance of putting a stop to it. It's what's for 'em," the gypsy woman said, pushing her face close to Rosina's.

Rosina stood for a second, taking in what the woman said before walking away.

"Watch out for yerself," the woman called after her. "Yer've had yer happiness. It's near over. Time's passing. Yer'll not have him, that man o' yours, long. Yer'll be on yer own with youngens."

Rosina walked back to Lambecote Grange, tears rolling down her face.

She felt that she had met with someone who knew her inside out, and yet she knew the gypsies always used fear to get their own way. Her mam had told her many stories that had come true after old gypsy women had seen the future. Rosina wished with all her heart that she had not gone to the camp. She should have known better. She had just made things worse. Anyhow, the Goose Fair would be over soon, and the gypsies would move on. They would not be back again until late spring. What could they do to her? She would put it out of her mind for good. George would be angry if he found out where she had been.

She decided to keep quiet about the whole affair.

Christmas 1906

The week before Christmas, a ball was held at Lambecote Grange for the members of the local hunt. The household worked furiously to get everything ready for the big occasion. Rosina told Elsie to allow William and little Sarah to watch for a short time from the safety of the back stairs.

Rosina broke the news to George that she thought she was with child again. He picked her up and danced around the bedroom, telling her again and again how much he loved her.

Rosina looked gorgeous at the ball. Elsie and Violet peeped out with Sarah and William to see George and Rosina greet the guests at the front entrance of Lambecote Grange. Rosina wore a beautiful French blue silk velvet dress. Her hair was taken up and away from her face. She had fastened it with a diamond clip.

Harold Sutton arrived with a terrible woman in a red dress.

"She's showing all she's got!" Elsie exclaimed.

Harold introduced George and Rosina to the woman as my dear cousins who robbed me of my inheritance. George ignored him and Harold winked slyly at Rosina when George announced, bursting with pride, that they would have another child in the summer. Rosina hated Harold. She tried to like him, but he was so crude. She found herself avoiding him whenever possible.

The ball was a great success, and even Edgar Fitzwilliam from the bank and his spiteful little wife congratulated George on his news about the baby.

Rosina looked at George. He looked so happy dancing with all the young girls, whirling and waltzing, always returning to her side to introduce his partners to his darling wife. Suddenly out of nowhere Rosina heard the gypsies words ringing in her head. *It's near over. Time's passing.*

Yer'll not have him, that man o' yours, long. Yer'll be on yer own with youngens. Rosina shivered at the thought.

"Come along Rosina." George laughed, taking her arm. "One dance will not hurt. You look as if you have all the worries in the world."

The music struck a waltz, and George and Rosina Bingham swirled around the floor, bound together in happiness.

"Oh look at Mummy," Sarah screamed. "She is like my dolly. Look William. Look at Mummy and Daddy."

William clapped his hands to the music after he stuffed another of Elsie's cakes into his mouth.

"No more cakes, Master William. You've had enough for one night. Come along, both of yer. Time for bed," Elsie called to them.

They fell asleep tired and happy.

Christmas was a joyous occasion at Lambecote Grange. Kisaiya came, but Len had gone on a bender. Glad and her man, Sam Dawson, came with their children, and Rosina was happy to have them all around her. Boxing Day was a special day at Lambecote Grange. This was the day when the hunt met. The hounds were out barking at the heels of the local gentry, mounted and dressed in their red hunting jackets and taking a cup before the chase began.

Rosina was so proud of George. She watched with Sarah and William. "This is what you will be doing next year, William," Rosina said, putting her arm around his shoulders.

"I don't like chasing the fox, Mummy," he said. "Fluere says it hurts the fox when the hounds catch it."

"But, William, the foxes are always stealing our chickens. I suppose that hurts the chickens."

"Yes it does hurt the chickens, Mummy, but that does not mean that we can hurt the fox does it?" William replied.

"No, William, I suppose you are right," Rosina said quietly.

George was at the head of the line looking magnificent in his hunt leader roll, the beautiful silver hunting horn fastened to his jacket. He lifted the horn to his lips and blew. All the dogs were barking madly, and the excitement was mounting. Everyone followed George. Then the hounds got the scent of a fox and the cry went out. "Tallyho!"

Rosina watched until they were out of sight and then took the children inside. Elsie had made tea and put it in the morning room in front of a huge fire. Kisaiya and Glad and her brood had been watching from upstairs. They had no love for the gentry as Glad told William when he asked if she had enjoyed watching the meet.

"What are gentry?" William asked her.

"You're gentry—yer, and yer mam. That's who gentry are." Wilfred shouted at him accusingly.

William sat quietly by his mother who just put her hand on his and smiled. Rosina and the children, with Glad and her family, and Kisaiya all had Boxing Day luncheon together. Sam was worse for drink and objecting to every thing the maid put in front of him. Rosina felt tired. She wished she had not invited them for Christmas. It was like a battleground. Wesley always snivelled because Wilfred had done some dastardly thing and blamed it on poor Wesley. And Glad and Sam were forever arguing. Kisaiya always apologised for them. Just as they were finishing their coffee there was a commotion at the front of the house. Rosina went out to see what was happening.

Several hunt members were gathered around a makeshift stretcher.

She ran toward them saying "Is someone hurt? Bring him inside. Have you called the doctor?"

One of the huntsmen took hold of her arms and looking at her, grimly said. "It's Master George, ma'am. He's had a bad fall."

"George! George!" Rosina cried. "Are you badly hurt? Do something, can't you?" she shouted at the man who was holding her arms. "Let me go, will you? Elsie get Fred. Get the doctor. Take him upstairs." In her despair, she frantically shouted orders to anyone and everyone.

George was taken to his bedroom, and Basil Judge visited him within the hour. He came out of the bedroom after what seemed like an eternity and took Rosina's hand. "George has had a very narrow escape, my dear," he said.

"How is he, doctor? Is he conscious now? Can he be moved?' Rosina asked, half-crying and trying to keep some kind of composure.

"Rosina, he is going to be fine," Basil Judge comforted her. "He has concussion and some bruising but he is a strong fellow. With your care, he will soon be on his feet."

"Can I go in to him, doctor?" Rosina asked.

"Of course you can, Rosina, but do not tire him. He needs rest." Basil Judge said, most likely wanting to get back to his family for their Christmas celebrations.

Rosina ran to the bedroom, and kneeling beside the bed, she held George's hand and kissed him, tears rolling down her face. They laughed and cried together. She was so relieved that he was not seriously hurt.

George smiled weakly and said, "Rosina, darling, do not get upset. I have had many a fall. I do not know what happened. Storm was spooked by something in Beckett's Wood and refused to take the fence, throwing me over the hedge and into the beck. I am just winded my dear. I shall be up and about tomorrow you see. Do not fret. You must think of the child. Now go and rest while I sleep."

Rosina kissed his forehead and reluctantly left him with the nurse that Basil Judge had brought with him from the village. He had anticipated the need of medical skills if George was badly injured. Thankfully he was not and should recover in no time at all.

She entered the drawing room where Kisaiya and the rest of the family were entertaining Sarah and William, trying to keep up their spirits.

"Mummy, what has happened to Daddy?" William cried, running to his mother.

"Daddy has had a fall," Rosina said. "But he is not badly injured and just needs to rest for a while. He is very lucky."

"That's what ye' gets when yer chases after bloody foxes," Sam slobbered. Drink had taken its toll by now, and he could only just speak.

"Glad, perhaps you should get Sam to bed to sleep it off," Rosina suggested to her sister.

"Don't worry about me, Rosina; I can take, me drink. I'm not like them bloody idiots out there on t'hosses," Dawson spluttered.

Glad stood up and whispered something in Sam's ear. He staggered to his feet and followed her out grabbing at her backside as he went.

Rosina put the children to bed and told them not to worry. Daddy would be up and about in no time at all. She went to see George to find he was still asleep. The nurse said he had taken a sleeping draught that the doctor had prescribed and she suggested Rosina slept elsewhere so as not to disturb him. Rosina was not so sure that she wanted to leave him but did as the nurse said. Not wanting to cause George any more stress, she kissed him lightly on his head and left the room to spend the night on the bed in the children's room that was used when they were ill.

She woke, suddenly aware that someone was shaking her. "What is it?" she asked, startled when she realised that it was the nurse who was shaking her.

"Please come, Mrs. Bingham," the nurse said. "It is Mr. Bingham. He is not well. He is asking for you. I have sent for the doctor."

Rosina jumped out of bed, not stopping to put on her robe. Running into George's room she was terrified when she saw that his face was grey. He was staring out as if into some other place.

"George! George!" Rosina cried. "What is it?"

George lifted his head toward Rosina and smiled at her weakly, the love in his eyes showing through the grey pallor of his face.

"Rosina," he whispered. "My love, Lambecote Grange must go to my heirs. Do not let it go to Harold. This is your home, darling, and you must stay here as long as you can. I am sorry, Rosina—"

Rosina was held him in her arms, rocking him to and fro, begging God not to take him from her. "No, no," she wailed. "You can't go now! No! No! No!"

George died in his darling wife's arms early on the morning of December 27, 1906. Basil Judge thought he had suffered a blood clot to his brain, caused when he struck his head earlier in the day.

The gypsy woman had seen it, and Rosina believed the curse put on her mother when she married a *gorgio* had struck again, not allowing any issue of her parents' doomed marriage to settle in one place or find peace.

Chapter 10

Lambecote Grange, 1907

Rosina did not speak a word to anyone until after the funeral. The children were taken care of by Kisaiya and Elsie. She was in such deep shock that the doctor kept her under sedation for fear of her losing her child.

Sam had taken over as man of the house and general pandemonium reigned. Elsie tried in vain to bring Rosina out of the shock. Basil Judge said she was going to need a lot of care to get through this pregnancy.

What was going to become of the business? George had done most of the management himself with Rosina taking care of the house. What indeed was going to happen to Lambecote Grange? Young William was only eleven-years-old. It would be years before he could take over.

Rosina was grief-stricken. Although usually a strong woman, she was unable to cope with even the smallest task for several weeks. The doctor had told Glad, who had stayed to help Rosina, that she would lose the child if she did not have absolute rest.

Rosina wanted this child so much. George had been so happy when she had told him she was to have their third child. She must rest for the unborn child's sake. She was given sleeping droughts to help her sleep away the pain of losing her beloved George.

Sam, Rosina's brother-in-law, played the roll of squire, whilst there was no man of the house. The work force despised the man. He groped the young dairymaids and drank anything and everything he could get his dirty hands on. Throughout the next six months the butcher shops began to lose money. The managers were refusing to hand over a penny to Sam Dawson, who boasted that he was taking over at Lambecote Grange. Many of the farm workers left, complaining that they were not being paid. The treatment they were getting from Sam Dawson was more than any man could take.

Fred was very concerned. "If Rosina doesn't get herself together soon, Lambecote Grange will be finished," he told Elsie.

The Doctor kept Rosina under sedation. Some mornings, she felt so weak she could not even make it to the kitchen let alone take over the household chores. After just a few minutes, she would become breathless and have to take a seat, Sometimes, she would just sit on the stairs. She was so huge with this child, she asked the doctor if he thought she should take more exercise.

"You are carrying a lot of water, Rosina," Basil Judge answered. "Don't worry. Everything will be all right."

Rosina dreamed of George and how happy he had been about this child. It was to make their lives complete. Now she would be so glad to get this over with. She went into labour at the end of July on a hot sticky day with very little air. The twin boys were delivered stillborn after a torturous twenty-five hours, leaving Rosina barely alive. It took Rosina six months to recover physically from the birth of her dead babies. Mentally, she would never be the same again.

William and little Sarah were completely traumatised throughout this time. William rode around the countryside looking for the gypsies with whom he felt a peculiar belonging. They tried to lose him, but he always found them. They would take him back to Lambecote Grange, but he always managed to escape. Of course, who would care where he was? His father was dead, and his mother was always asleep.

Poor little Sarah cried herself to sleep every night. She wanted her daddy. She walked around this great house, pretending her daddy was there. She found his hunting horn thrown onto a table in the kitchen. It was dirty, and Elsie said she had rescued it from Uncle Sam who wanted to sell it. But she would not tell him were it was.

Sarah put it under her skirt and took it to her room. She looked down the silver horn believing that she could speak to her father through it. Asking him what she could do. He would answer her, but only in her imagination.

"Be strong, Sarah," he would tell her. "You have to be strong. Do not let anyone stop you from being who you are."

Glad drank heavily. She had no idea how to run a household like this and most of the staff had gone. Fortunately, Elsie and Fred stayed on at Lambecote Grange with their daughter Violet. Fred argued with Dawson constantly. Dawson refused to pay anyone, workers and merchants alike. Fred discovered Dawson had large gambling debts, when an unsavoury character visited Lambecote Grange early one morning looking for the squire, Fred told him the squire was dead. But there was an impostor here, taking advantage of the mistress who was ill.

The debt collector thanked him for the information and left, assuring Fred that he would soon put a stop to Sam Dawson's games.

Glad told Rosina to try a drink at night instead of the sleeping drought to which she had become addicted. Rosina began to find solace in a bottle. She became untidy and always had a headache. She could not cope with life anymore.

Glad suggested they all go to the Goose Fair on Saturday. She told Rosina this within earshot of William who ran to his mother begging and pleading for her to be allowed to go.

Rosina said, "No. I am not well enough."

The look of disappointment on William's face forced her to change her mind, and the trip to Nottingham was organised. Rosina, accompanied by the children who were very excited, took the coach to Nottingham. Fred could not drive them because Sam had sold the carthorses that were always used to pull the carriage on long journeys. The Binghams, Glad and Sam, with their two boys, Wilfred and Wesley, and Kisaiya walked arm in arm along the road toward the fairground. The boys carried the picnic basket put together by Elsie in the kitchen at Lambecote Grange.

They laughed at the sideshows with the strong man and the bearded lady, and the bareback riders daring stunts. William looked out for Fluere. He was sure to see her here at the fair. The stories she had often told him of her exploits, earning a shilling riding a pony bareback or pretending to fall off to get the sympathy of the crowd, made him smile to himself.

The day was filled with happiness for Sarah and William. They had been so unhappy for so long it was great to let themselves go a little, running around eating sweets and other goodies freely available at a Christmas fair. The baked potato man was doing a great business with potatoes baked in a large drum set on a huge bonfire. He also had chestnuts cooking on the lid. There were toffee apples and fudge and marshmallows roasted on a fire. Sarah began to feel quite sick.

Rosina was so much happier. She told Glad this was a great idea to come to the fair. Rosina's mother said she would take all the children home and Rosina and Glad should stay with Sam and have a drink. The pub bar that Sam took them to was on the edge of the fairground. The room was packed with all kinds of people, merchants and fair folk alike.

Rosina scuffed her feet in the sawdust that covered the floor and remembered what life was like away from Lambecote Grange. The day had been charmed whilst the children were around her, but now she felt afraid and lonely.

Sam gave her a glass with something akin to whisky in it. "Drink that down, Rosie." He laughed, his smelly breath making Rosina recoil.

Glad drank down her drink in one swallow. "Here. Get a bottle next time yer goes to the bar," Glad said to Sam, giving him two sovereigns.

"Where on earth did you get money like that to spend on drink, Glad?" Rosina asked.

"Oh, where there's a means there's always a way," Glad shouted over the noise of the crowded room.

Rosina thought that the money must have come from Lambecote Grange. How disappointed she was in her sister's attitude. The farm was almost lost because of the dreadful way she and her husband had acted during the last twelve months.

Sam brought in a man with flaming red hair to join them. "This is Len Marshall," Sam said to Glad. "This is the fella who says I can have a job sinking a new pit in South Yorkshire."

Glad poured whisky into Len Marshall's half-empty glass, saying, "He'll do for me then if he's getting you a job."

The man seems pleasant enough, Rosina thought.

He was very polite to Rosina. She was trying not to drink too much but felt like a fish out of water, standing in a pub and not drinking. She carefully sipped on the drink that Sam had given her but was not comfortable.

The noise got louder and Glad and Sam were singing raucously. Len Marshall stayed by Rosina, telling her about his job in mines. Rosina was appalled that men had to work in such dreadful conditions.

Len told her things were much better than they used to be when his father started down the mine fifty years before. In those days, children were used to pull the coal tubs along the pit bottom. Children were cheap labour and small enough to crawl through tight tunnels. Many children were killed, but there were always others ready to take their place. "They would rather risk death in the pit than starve to death," Len Marshall said. Rosina thought of William and Sarah, and shuddered at the thought of them having to earn their own living. She was beginning to feel tired. She looked around for a seat but could see none. Len asked someone to give up a chair, and when they refused, he gave them a shilling to help change their mind. Rosina sat down thankfully and Sam returned with another bottle of whiskey. Her head was hurting. She told Glad that she wanted to go home. Glad was too far gone to care about Rosina. She was just trying to get her hands on the bottle her husband was dangling in front of her eyes.

Len Marshall gave Rosina a glass, saying, "Drink this, lass. This'll make you feel better."

Rosina drank the sweet smelling liquid and wished with all her heart that she had gone home with her mam and the children. The room began to sway and she felt sick. She looked around for Glad or Sam but could not see anything clearly. Eventually everything went dark. When she opened her eyes the pain in her head was unbearable. She was outside with Len Marshall leaning over her wiping her face with a dark coloured handkerchief.

"What happened to me?" Rosina cried, feeling so ill she thought she would die.

"You passed out Rosina," Len Marshall said.

"Where have Glad and Sam gone?" Rosina asked, beginning to feel afraid now for the position she was in.

"I have asked around but no one knows where they went. They are not in the pub, and I don't want to leave you here alone while I look for them."

Rosina and Len decided to walk around and look for Glad, but Rosina could hardly put a foot in front of her. "What am I going to do?" Rosina cried.

Len Marshall put his arm around her shoulder and told her not to worry. He would get her home safely.

"What's the time, Mr. Marshall?" Rosina asked.

"Half past midnight."

"Oh my God, the children will be fraught. They have never been away from home for so long without their father or me," Rosina cried. She was almost hysterical by now.

Len Marshall put his hand in his pocket and brought out a hip flask. "Here!" he said. "Take a drink of this. It will make you feel warmer while we walk."

Rosina eagerly drank from the flask. She was so cold her hands could barely hold it still. Len Marshall steadied her hand as she gulped down the brandy. The drink was so strong on her throat she began to cough. Tears rolled down her face as she looked around for Glad and Sam. Where could they have gone? Just as she was giving up hope of finding them, she heard a voice bellowing,

"Lost something, have yer Mrs. Bingham?"

Rosina turned to confront by Sykes, the butcher who had been summoned some years ago for fraud regarding one of George's shops. She began to run down the road. She was still near to the fairground but Sykes was not going to give in. He stumbled after her, laughing and calling abuse at her.

Len Marshall caught her arm and pulled her down a side street into an alley that was very dark. Rosina opened her mouth to scream but Len put his hand over her mouth to smother the sound.

"Rosina. Rosina," he whispered in her ear. "I won't hurt you for God's sake. I am just trying to lose that drunk who seems set on getting his hands on you."

She leaned on his arm and rested her head on his shoulder, sobbing and sniffling.

Len Marshall again produced a clean handkerchief from his pocket and dried Rosina's eyes, saying to her. "Look, don't take this the wrong way, but I lodge down here. It's not very smart, but I don't need luxury when I travel to recruit men for the pit."

"No, Mr. Marshall, I must get home," Rosina said, pulling her hat straight and trying to walk away but failing to be able to move.

"Rosina you can't possibly walk home alone at this time of night. It's dangerous!"

Rosina knew he was right. Her mother's house was at least five miles away from the fairground. She had paid for a carriage to take the children home. No carriage driver would be sober at this time of night—not on a fair night.

They arrived at a mid terrace house, and Len Marshall said, "I can't take you in the front, Rosina. The landlady only takes men lodgers, and women visitors are not allowed. I'll have to go in and come through the back to let you in. Just hide yourself behind this bin. No one will see you. It should only take me a couple of minutes."

Rosina shivered and pushed herself behind the dreadful smelling bin. She was terrified of Sykes, terrified of going into this house with this stranger, terrified of being alone in the world and not taking enough care of herself, and annoyed with herself for trusting Glad yet again. At least the children would be in bed asleep.

The door opened and Len whispered, "Rosina come with me quick. Don't speak a word."

Rosina slunk through the door into a filthy kitchen. It was dark, and the smells were putrid. They tiptoed upstairs and into a filthy room with two beds. She stood staring at the bed in horror. Len lit a candle on a saucer on the floor that gave a little light saying, "You'll be safe here until morning, Rosina. I'll sleep on the floor in the next room. The chap in there is so far gone he won't know I am there."

"Thank you Mr. Marshall. I do not know what I would have done without you." She was so scared now she could hardly speak at all.

Len left the room, and Rosina sat on the edge of the bed. She must not sleep in this place. After struggling to keep awake for an hour or more, she allowed herself to lean back on the pillow. She closed her eyes. She woke struggling for air. Something was pressing down on her face. She tried to scream but was unable to make a sound. She lost consciousness.

Rosina's eyes flickered. She began to focus on a weight on her body. She was being raped roughly and repeatedly. A hand came down on her face again before she could make a sound. Her blouse was ripped open and her skirts were round her waist. She struggled to free herself, thinking she was going to die. She could not breathe. The smell coming from the man was sickening. He was grunting like a pig. He could not believe what he had found in his bed, all laid out waiting for it.

Len lay awake in the next room. He must not go to sleep. He had not dared tell Rosina that he was sharing the room with an Irishman who may or may not come in. depending on where he had fallen down when he could drink no more. Len heard the noise of a stair creaking and waited for the sound of the outside door to open. Perhaps someone was going to the midden. He heard nothing. A noise came from somewhere, he thought he heard a muffled cry, but his mind was dulled with drink. He listened but heard nothing but snoring coming from around the house.

Len lay for a while still trying not to sleep and still he could hear muffled snoring coming from somewhere. He thought about going to check on Rosina, but she would think he was after something else, and he did not want to scare her anymore than she was already.

Len opened his tired eyes and slowly realised that what he could hear were the sounds of grunting and groaning with rhythmic banging on the wall. He ran into the next room. There, to his horror, was Rosina spread-eagle on the bed with the Irishman fondling her breasts having obviously just satisfied himself on her limp body.

Having disposed of the Irishman who lay unconscious on the floor, he lifted Rosina up in his arms and crept out of the stinking house as furtively as he had crept in. He had to get her out of there before the landlady brought the constable.

He left through the back door and ran down the same alley he had brought Rosina along for safety just a couple of hours earlier. What had he done to this poor woman? She was still in a state of shock. Her eyes staring out, not blinking. Even her breathing was so quiet. He thought she might be having a heart attack. He must find somewhere to make her comfortable.

Len ran toward the fairground. He would surely find someone to help there. He heard voices coming from inside a bender placed outside a wagon. He called out. "Is there anyone who can help me please?"

A dusky man opened the flap on the bender and screwed up his eyes to see what the commotion was.

"Please help me?" Len pleaded.

The man opened the flap further and ushered Len inside. He lay Rosina on a *pallias* on the floor. He could not believe what he saw. She was covered in scratches and bruises on her face.

My God, she must have put up a fight, Len thought.

A woman's voice shouted through the half-light. "Get out of here all of yer. Let her be."

Rosina opened her eyes to find the peering eyes of the old hag whom she had met at Lambecote Grange. The woman was gently cleaning her face with a cloth that smelled very nice. She began to remember the attack and started to shake uncontrollably.

"Nay. Yer rest a while. Don't fret. I've cleaned thee up and yer can be on your way as soon as day breaks. That man's waiting outside for thee."

"I do not have a man," Rosina sobbed.

"Well, a decent bloke brought thee here to get help when he could a left thee to the mercy of the night," the gypsy woman said quietly.

Rosina gradually calmed down and began to understand what had happened to her. She asked the gypsy to let Len in so that she could thank him for his help.

He looked at the distraught Rosina sitting on the *pallias*. "God, lass, you shouldn't be here. You're a lady. I can't tell you how sorry I am for what's happened. I tried to stay awake to make sure you were safe. Oh, God, this is just terrible." He almost sobbed.

Rosina stood up. She was very unsteady on her legs but she had to get home to the children. She would never leave Lambecote Grange again as long as she lived. She thanked the gypsy woman and said she would see that she was paid for her kindness and left. She walked along the road with Len beside her, ready to catch her if, in her weakness, she stumbled.

"Rosina," he said. "Let me take you into that cafe over there. They are just starting to cook breakfasts for the fair folk. You can't go home looking like that."

She agreed. In the cafe she had a cup of sweet tea and asked the proprietor if she could use the midden outside at the back. He looked at her dishevelled state for a long time and then agreed. He did not want any trollop using his midden. She might have the clap. But this woman looked different somehow.

Len waited outside the midden. When she eventually came out, she had straightened her hair and looked a little more presentable. She looked for her bag and realised that she must have left it in the place the night before.

"Thank you so much for helping me, Mr. Marshall," she said. "I must get back to my parents' house. I have to catch the morning coach with my children. I seem to have lost my bag. I have no way of repaying you, but if you could help me get back to Lambecote Grange, I will see that you are well paid for your trouble."

Len found a carriage and helped Rosina in. He told the driver to take them to wherever the lady wanted to go. They arrived at her mother's house and collected the children. After running the gauntlet of her father's jibes about her being a loose woman, they travelled to the coach station just in time to catch the carriage to Lambecote Grange.

Len Marshall paid the carriage driver for Rosina, and Rosina pleaded with him to give her a forward address to send money onto him. He refused.

Chapter 11

January 1908

To all who had not been involved with the trip to Nottingham, Rosina seemed to be back to her old self. She was vigorously trying to get things organised at Lambecote Grange. The fact that she had not had a proper night's sleep since she arrived home had escaped everyone's attention. Glad and Sam Dawson had not been seen at Lambecote Grange since that terrible night at the fair.

One day, Rosina had a visit from Harold Sutton, George's cousin. Elsie informed Rosina of Harold Sutton's arrival and said she had put him in the morning room.

Rosina walked into the morning room where Sutton was looking through the books on George's desk. "Mr. Sutton, what are you doing at my husband's desk?" she asked angrily.

"I am trying to find out just how much money you have lost in the last year, woman," he said. "While you have been lazing in your bed, your brother-in-law squandered all your wealth, the family wealth, my wealth."

"My sister and her husband have been kindly helping me since my husband died. I have also lost my babies, Mr. Sutton." Tears fell down Rosina's face as she sat on the edge of a chair. Rosina was furious. "You have no right to be here, Mr. Sutton," she said angrily. "This is my house, and I shall take care of my own affairs. Kindly leave or I shall call the stable lads to throw you out."

"Ha! Ha!" Sutton laughed. "You don't have any stable lads," he snorted. "You don't have anybody left here. That bloody convict has sent them all packing. You are the laughingstock of the county. That's why I am here to rescue my Lambecote Grange."

"This is not your Lambecote Grange!" Rosina exclaimed. "This is to be kept in trust for William and Sarah to run when they are of age." She went to the bell rope and pulled so hard it came off in her hand. Standing there with the bell rope in her hand, she felt so vulnerable she almost gave in.

Elsie came to her rescue with Fred standing at the door.

Rosina shouted. "Get out of my house, Mr. Sutton, or we shall call the constable."

Sutton, his face red with anger, left but not before a warning that he would be back to remove her and her brood.

Following his departure, Rosina began to put a plan to rescue Lambecote Grange into action. She would have to be desperate to let Harold Sutton get his hands on William's heritage.

She and Elsie cleaned the house, and Violet took Sarah and William in hand. At least life began to get back too normal for the children.

Sam Dawson had robbed every account that had been paid into Lambecote Grange from the butcher shops. Last year's harvest had rotted in the fields when workers refused to collect it in until Dawson paid them their dues.

Not one invoice had been paid to the merchants who supplied the Binghams with the provisions they needed to run the farm and feed the small amount of livestock that remained.

Rosina put together a plan to be presented to the bank. She thought that if she could lease the shops to the managers on a contract. Insisting that they could buy only Lambecote Grange produce, she could recoup much of the income that had been lost from the shops. This income would enable her to plant the wheat for next spring after she had reinstated the workers that Fred assured her would work for her anytime. All she needed was a loan, short term, to put things back together.

Fred told Elsie, "There is as much chance of the bank loaning Rosina money as pigs flying over the moon, but yer have to give her credit for trying. She's got guts all right."

Surely the bank would see that this was the way to keep Lambecote Grange going so William could take over when he was of age. Why had she listened to Sam Dawson? She supposed it was the easy way out when she felt so ill and unhappy. She had let her family take over. She knew deep down that he would rob her but at the time did not care what was happening to Lambecote Grange. Now Lambecote Grange was the most important thing in her life—to keep it going for George and his children.

Rosina wrote to the bank, asking Edgar Fitzwilliam to call and see her. This is what George would do when he needed to—he would speak to the local manager of Henderson's Bank.

Fitzwilliam explained the position to his clerk in the carriage on the journey to Lambecote Grange. Rosina Bingham was not gentry by blood. A banker of Fitzwilliam's standing did not feel it was his place to visit a woman to discuss business—even a woman with education, and this woman was scum of the first order.

George Bingham married her for her beauty. Poor sod. He could have had any woman he wanted. He had been chased for many years by every eligible young lady in the hunt but had shown no interest in the fair sex until he met this maid. Poor Charlotte Bingham, his mother, was distraught when he announced his marriage to Rosina Morton, his mother's maid. Many thought it was that which caused her untimely death.

Now she had inherited the farm and the shops, and what a mess she had allowed it to fall into. The rumour was that her brother-in-law had run the place into the ground before he left.

"We no doubt find her pitiful," he said. "The bank will have to sell up and give her what we can salvage. Oh, how I hate pathetic women, especially uneducated women who have stepped above their station in life," he postulated.

With Violet's help, Rosina had cleaned the house. Bread was baking in the kitchen. Fresh flowers had been arranged in the hall where the floors were polished so well you could see your face in them. The house was alive again and smelt wonderful.

Sarah practised her piano. William played with the dogs. The sounds stopped Rosina in her tracks as she checked. Everything was in its place to receive the bank manager. She smiled happily to herself. *Please God let him loan me the money to carry on. I am sure I can make a go of it and have prepared the proposals very carefully. If I rent the shops to the present managers and take on a good farm manager, the arable side of the farm would soon pay its way. We could gradually buy animals and build up the stock side. If the shops are kept open, I would have a guaranteed market for my produce. I calculate it to take her twelve months to rebuild, and thirty-six months to repay the bank the loan.*

Fitzwilliam had never heard such a thing in his whole experience as a banker. A woman was asking for a loan to run a farm alone. She even had the nerve to expect him to say *yes*. He told the clerk after their visit to Lambecote Grange, "I shall offer her a tidy sum to move out into one of the cottages on the estate, and the bank will take over the farm until we can find a buyer." Fitzwilliam thought he might have a go at this one himself. What an opportunity!

Rosina refused to move out, and with the help of many workers, who had returned, stubbornly prepared for the next season. "Please, God, let us survive until then," Rosina said to Elsie and Fred. "I shall show that bank manager how wrong he is."

Harold Sutton called at Christmas with gifts for the children and a different attitude toward Rosina. Rosina was polite but noncommittal. Christmas came and went with many sad memories for all of them. Sutton returned in the New Year with an offer to buy Lambecote Grange, leaving William as the heir to the land when he was of age. He would, in the meantime, spend money on the farm and pay for the schooling of Sarah and William, but only if he could stay there until his death.

Rosina refused politely, saying she had no intention of sending her children away. They had lost their father. That was enough for one lifetime. Sutton told her to think on the offer.

Mid-January brought a bout of sickness that would not stop, and Rosina could no longer keep food down. At the end of January, she began to realise that she had not escaped the ordeal on the dreaded night at the Goose Fair. She was pregnant and terrified of the consequences of having the baby.

She plodded on, keeping the truth to herself and hoping that she was wrong, but as February blew in, she was certain. What was she to do now? She cried herself to sleep every night.

Rosina wrote a letter to Harold Sutton asking him to visit regarding the future of Lambecote Grange. She had to act fast. If Sutton guessed, or anyone else for that matter, that she was pregnant, she would be on the road to the workhouse. She had no bargaining power and time was not on her side. She would soon be showing signs of her plight. Sutton would not care for the children if he knew of her condition. He would think they were family flyblows and be overjoyed with the situation.

When he received her letter he thought she was just not able to manage financially. He travelled to Lambecote Grange, ready to take over as soon as possible. He made an offer which Rosina could not turn down— one thousand pounds in cash and two hundred and fifty pounds a year to be paid to her for life. The children would not have any rights to their father's property, and George's will would be classed as null and void.

Rosina was frantic. She had no option but to take the offer and move away as soon as she could. A carriage was provided. All their belongings that could be carried were taken to Nottingham where they rented a small cottage in a respectable area. Only Violet was given the address. She was the only person in the world who Rosina could trust—but not with the truth. Instead, she told her about needing to get away from the memories.

Rosina agreed that she and the children would not set foot on Lambecote Grange again. Poor Rosina was frantic. All she could think of was getting away before anyone realised her condition. She had not had enough time to ask Uncle Edwin for legal advice or contact Aunt Lillian for fear of the dire consequences if she was found out. William and Sarah were told that their life at Lambecote Grange was finished. They would have to make their own way in the world.

"No good looking back. We have a new home to look forward to and must forget Lambecote Grange," Rosina said, pushing her shoulders back and holding her head high. She tried to look confident saying, "Take one last look before we drive away. We will not be returning to Lambecote Grange."

Sarah was distraught, but William was very angry. He needed an explanation, but Rosina said nothing.

Chapter 12

Summer 1908

After some months in which Rosina stayed indoors for fear of anyone guessing the awful truth about her swollen stomach, a midwife was booked.

The neighbours were informed that her husband had suddenly died. William and Sarah had been told never to tell anyone that they were Binghams, or Harold Sutton would take them away and she would never see them again. They were very confused and afraid at the changes going on around them. William asked his mother repeatedly why they had not stayed at Lambecote Grange until he was old enough to take over. Rosina was tired and broken. She yelled at William, telling him not to expect to have a comfortable life without earning it. William wanted an explanation but Rosina was not forthcoming. When she told the children that she was going to have a child, they believed it was their sibling.

The girl child was born in September 1908, and Rosina was up and about immediately after the birth. The child was very content and no one ever heard a cry or whimper from the bundle in a drawer in the corner of the bedroom.

Life was miserable for Sarah and William. William only wanted to find the gypsies and was forever talking about Fluere and what she could do. Sarah had secretly hidden her fathers hunting horn in her nightdress case when they left Lambecote Grange. Speaking to her father through it was her only salvation. She also rescued the photograph of Rosina and George with William and Sarah which Rosina had given to George one Christmas. Sarah had not been allowed to carry many possessions when they left Lambecote Grange and had cut out the picture, leaving the frame behind. Fearing Rosina and William would take them from her, she hid them, only taking them out when she was unhappy.

Both children were enrolled at the local school. William settled down, but Sarah was not accustomed to mixing with children in large numbers and became withdrawn and nervous.

Rosina spent most of her time feeding the baby. Sarah was not allowed to take part in the care of little Alice, her name having come into Rosina's head on her way to register the baby's birth. She could not say who the father was because she really did not know who he was. Not wanting the child to be a bastard, she gave the name "Len Marshall," as the father. Little Alice had a father on paper, and Rosina would think of some explanation later. She became bitter, believing that the Romany curse was on the whole family. She would never avoid poverty however hard she tried. Her mind began to torment her with thoughts that Len Marshall was the child's father. After all, he was the only person she saw in that dreadful house. He could have raped her after she fell asleep. He could then have covered his tracks by helping her. She began to hate him and wanted revenge.

One day after the children had left for school there was a knock on the door. Rosina dried her hands and opened the door.

There stood Len Marshall, smiling. "Hello, Mrs. Bingham," he said. "It was difficult to find you. I searched everywhere. Your mother and sister told me they have not seen you since the night of the Goose Fair. They are very worried about you. I eventually persuaded a woman at Lambecote Grange to tell me where you were living. She was really scared about losing her job and said she had been told to say that they had never heard of you."

Rosina was struck dumb. She stood for what seemed like hours, mouth gaping and eyes not blinking—just staring at this man on her doorstep. Eventually, she pulled herself together, and pushing her shoulders back, smiled and said, "Oh, Mr. Marshall, I am so sorry. I did not know where to send your money. Please forgive me. I was very grateful for your help. I can never thank you enough." She tried to keep her head up and push her shoulders back in her usual manner, but her face was distorted, holding back the fear and shock of seeing this man again. Where could she go to escape this nightmare?

"I have not come for the money, Mrs. Bingham. I have been in Yorkshire since we last met and hoped you had made a good recovery," he replied.

Rosina started to shake uncontrollably. She had not spoken about the dreadful night since it happened. This visitor brought back the horror of what had really happened.

THE CALL OF THE HUNTSMAN

"I am so sorry, Mrs. Bingham," Len Marshall said. "I would not have come if I thought I should cause you any pain."

Rosina ran and picked up Alice. She pushed the pretty little baby toward Len saying, "This is what happened. This poor child does not know who her father is. I don't even know who her father is. You could be the father for all I know. The children believe she is their sister, but they will work it out soon enough. How I wish I had not gone to that fair. I ruined my children's lives, forever. They lost their home and their heritage. We had to flee before anyone realised that I was pregnant or we would have been for the workhouse. How could I fight to keep the farm, knowing that I was with the child of God knows who? I have seriously considered taking my life and the children's too." All these words came spilling out one after another until she had emptied herself of all the grief and anguish she had bottled in over the past year.

Len Marshall stood in awe of her. This was a nightmare for which he felt responsible. If only he had slept on the floor in her room, she would not be in this predicament now.

"I would love to be the father of this beautiful child, Mrs Bingham, but I am not. She is better off not knowing the name of the bastard who raped you. Please let me help you. I know I am not fit to clean your shoes, but just for the children's sake, let me take care of you."

"No, no!" Rosina exclaimed. "I would not even think of it. I can look after my own children. I don't need help from any man."

Len stood, holding this baby gently. Tears were running down his face. He looked so helpless. Rosina knew she had no love for the child. She had seriously thought of placing the baby in an orphanage because she was not capable of feeling anything for it. She fed and bathed her but it was all done in silence. The poor baby girl was looking into Lens face and seemed to know that this man cared for her. *Why?* Rosina thought. *He is not the father. How could anyone care for a child who was conceived in such horror?*

Len Marshall visited Rosina daily, bringing food and gifts for the children. William and Sarah began to run home from school, hoping he might want to take them out into the town or to ride in a pony and trap into the countryside. They liked him. He was kind, and they had not had much kindness shown to them for such a long time.

Len begged Rosina to marry him. It would be in name only, but it would allow him to give her a life of respectability. He accepted that she would never be his proper wife.

Len constantly pleaded with Rosina, and she was aware that if the truth ever came out, her annuity from Lambecote Grange would stop, and she and the children would go to the workhouse. She could not deny little Alice's existence forever. Len Marshall had found them. It would not be long before someone from Lambecote Grange followed him.

Rosina Bingham married Len Marshall, a marriage of convenience. She showed poor Len nothing but bitterness. She blamed him for the whole sorry mess but still had the good sense to realise that two hundred and fifty pounds a year would not keep her and three children from the Grange.

Chapter 13

Halten, 1909

In January 1909, Len took his new family to the village of Halten in South Yorkshire where he was in charge of employing men to sink a mineshaft.

They lived in a newly built house in a pit village created to accommodate miners and their families and situated on the main north/south route to London. Until the mining company arrived, it was a very desirable place to live. A new school had been built, and the little village had a beautiful church. The arrival of such a mixture of men and their offspring was sure to change the village—and it certainly did.

Sarah and William were installed in the local school, but William was very unhappy. He spent more time running away, looking for the gypsies than going to school.

Rosina became hard and bitter and drank heavily as did most of the people living in such hard conditions. Their men folk were often badly injured in the pit, or even worse, killed—everyday events in a mining community. Children were thought of as a commodity—if you had lots of lads they would earn money within a few years. The more children you had, the more chance of the mother having a few bob for the drink—seemingly the only light in a very dark life.

Most families in Halten lived in fear of their fathers. After their shifts in the pit, the men usually drank in the alehouse, using money their bedraggled wives needed for food and medicine. Illness was rife in such conditions.

The village doctor in Halten was a kind Jewish man who worked day and night, trying to help these hardworking uneducated people. His pay, if he was lucky, was a treasured piece of furniture or jewellery, probably the woman's wedding ring. Money was very rarely used to pay such bills. The main currency was coal and included in the miner's wages and became as valuable as money to the miner's wives. They would sell what they could spare to the farm workers in exchange for vegetables or even a chicken at Christmas time, depending on how much they could save out of their fuel allowance through the summer months when they needed less fuel for heat. If the mine owner heard of anyone selling coal, their men would be sacked on the spot. A very clandestine transaction, moving black market coal usually took place at the dead of night.

The houses in the pit village had all been fitted with a fireplace in each room, although only the cooking range and the copper were ever used. The kitchen had a copper for boiling clothes. A black iron range had an oven on one side of the fire, and a water tank with a tap on the opposite side for heating all the water the family would need for washing.

When the men came home from their shift in the pit, they would be unrecognisable, black coal dust stuck to their skin, thick and sticky, smelling of the stale water in which the men had been working underground for the last twelve hours.

The houses did not have bathrooms or inside toilets. The local publican would not allow men into his alehouse if they had not bathed after leaving the pit. Consequently bathing for the men was a necessity, not the luxury it was for their wives and children. The children would all bathe in the same bathwater on Saturday night. This saved both coal and soap. The eldest would go in the bath first, followed by the siblings in order of age. The women usually had an up-and-downer, their quick wash which they took if they needed to see the doctor or a midwife. More often than not, they did not wash, and the smell was not pleasant.

The tin bath was taken down from the hook outside in the yard and placed in front of the fire in the living room. Water from the tank beside the oven would be drawn into a tin ladle and poured into the bath, which was just big enough for a man to sit in while his wife scrubbed his back.

The pitmen would then eat their dinner before they left for the alehouse. This is what they had worked for all day in the God forsaken bowels of the earth. There was little else to dream about in a village like Halten. Not all the pitmen drank. Some of them were regular churchgoers who lived in fear of God. These men ruled their families with terror, believing that God had given them the right to beat their wives and children.

Rosina did not appreciate Len Marshall, a good kind man who loved all the children as his own. He gave her and the children everything they needed. Sarah loved Len. She was a delicate child and found life in Halten difficult. She often lived in her own world of dreams, where her father, George, told her what to do. She had smuggled her fathers hunting horn with her when they came to Halten, not letting anyone know that she kept it upstairs under a loose floorboard in Osborne Street.

Alice grew very sturdy, with long flaming red hair that Rosina hated. She often accused Len of being Alice's father, saying, "Look at her bloody hair, Len. It's red, just like yours."

"Rosina, I am not the man who raped you but I can tell you that he did have red hair," Len argued.

"Oh, and I am supposed to believe that, am I?" She was never sure and gave Len no thanks for the home he provided for them.

The children loved him. He was as near to a father as anyone could be to all of them. Rosina would scrape the red hair back from little Alice's face, fastening it back out of sight and making the child wince in pain. She hated to be reminded of the past.

Sarah, very delicate and withdrawn, longed for her real home and dearly wished she had a piano to practice her music on. Rosina was cruel in her treatment of the children and indeed of Len. She despised the man and ridiculed him when he came home from his shift at the mine. Len always brought his wages home to Rosina and pretended not to see that she was worse for drink most evenings. He read to the children and played with them, taking them out into the surrounding countryside when Rosina was on the rampage.Sarah had to scrub the scullery floor everyday, and when with bleeding sore hands and in tears, pleaded with her mother to stop being so angry. Rosina would tell her she was not at Lambecote Grange now and had better toughen up because life was hard, and if you want to survive you have to work hard.

Sarah would be sent to the Beer Off, a shop licensed to sell alcohol, with a jug and three pence to collect beer for her mother and the smelly old women who frequented the house when Len was at work.

Rosina would laugh and say "Do as you're done by."

Sarah did not understand the implication of this but went and waited outside the Beer Off until an adult would go in and buy the ale for her mother. Sarah would bring the jug of beer in through the scullery and pour half down the sink before filling up the jug with water in the vain hope that this would stop her from mother getting drunk. But Rosina or one of the gnarled old cronies would notice the watered-down beer, and Rosina would storm upstairs and beat Sarah. Sometimes she would beat little Alice by mistake when, in the darkness, little Alice would be on the side of the bed that Sarah usually slept on. Rosina would beat the first child she came to when she was in her drunken rage.

The house had gas lamps downstairs, but upstairs was unlit. It was not thought that miners needed the luxury of lighting upstairs. When someone was sick, a bed would be brought down into the front room, and a fire would be lit in there. This was the only time a fire would be lit in this room as it was thought to be an extravagance.

Rosina hit bottom more and more during the next few years. When Sarah was nine and William was sixteen, she got so drunk one day that she fell in the midden at the back of the house and broke her arm. Len Marshall came home from the pit and took Rosina to a doctor. The doctor warned Rosina that she would have the children taken from her if the drinking did not stop.

Len pleaded with Rosina to try to forget the past and make a good life for them all here in Halten where he was very well thought of at the pit and earned a decent wage. But Rosina was miserable. She hated herself and knew that she had given up, unable to look at Sarah or William without shouting at them.

Sarah took hold of Len's hand one day after Rosina had finished berating him, saying, "When my daddy was unhappy, he took us to Blackpool. We all came back happy."

Len looked down at Sarah's tearful little face and thought his heart would break. He knew Rosina had no love for him but how could she treat these children so badly? Sarah must be suffering so much, living in this place after her life at the Grange. He took the family to Blackpool for a week's holiday. They had such a lovely time. Alice had never seen the sea before, and she and Sarah ran in and out of the water, laughing happily.

Rosina and Len sat in deckchairs, watching the children having so much fun when suddenly Len took Rosina's hand in his. "Rosina, I feel that I have failed you so badly when all I ever wanted to do was care for you. I have grown to love you so much."

"I do not believe a word of it!" Rosina retorted. "I have made your life hell. You know I have, Len Marshall. I do not deserve to live. I should have been the one to die, not my poor George. I see him in Sarah's eyes and hate her for looking like him. It is not her fault. I need help, Len. I do not know what to do."

Len put his arms gently round her and said softly, "Please let me be a proper husband to you, Rosina. I will make you happy. I know I will."

After she had returned from the holiday Rosina settled down for a while, Len brought the local vicar to speak to her.

"We all have to suffer, Rosina, in whatever way God has planned for us. The secret is to do it with strength and courage, trying to be a beacon of light to other poor souls who suffer much more than we do," he said patronisingly, not having the slightest idea what pain and poverty meant to this little family.

Rosina remembered the vicar in Nottingham whom she had no respect for. It was unfortunate that she had had that experience regarding religion because it could have made a difference to the fortunes of the family if Rosina had believed in God and tried to care for Len. He was a good man, but she saw him as a wage packet, someone who paid the rent and bought the food and clothes for the children. After all, the two pound ten shillings a week she got from Harold Sutton, barely paid for the drink that she consumed when she was at the bottom. She never told Len about the deal with Harold Sutton. He believed she had left the Grange penniless.

Sarah took Alice out onto the common and told her stories about the huntsman and his beautiful horse, Storm. He had told her that she was special. Sarah told Alice to look for the Grange when she was grown. Sarah tried to persuade William to take her back. She was sure Elsie or Violet would take care of them, but William had no ambition to go back. He wanted to live on the road with Fluere and the gypsies.

Alice asked Sarah, "How does the huntsman talk to you if he is dead?"

Sarah smiled at her and said, "Through the silver hunting horn, Alice—my daddy's silver hunting horn."

"What's that, Sarah?' Alice asked in wonder.

"It belonged to my daddy. You must not let mam know that I have it or she will pawn it for more drink like she did with daddy's gold watch that William was keeping. Alice, you must promise me that you will not speak about it ever!" Sarah pleaded. They linked their little fingers in a gypsy's promise. Nobody dared break a gypsy's promise.

Alice did not want to upset Sarah. She was the only person who was kind to her, except her dad, of course. But he was only her dad and not Sarah's dad so she felt special with Len.

Sarah was ten-years-old when Rosina said, "You had better be getting prepared to share your bed with another one 'cos we are going to have a baby soon."

"Will it be a girl?" Alice asked excitedly.

"By God, I hope not!" Rosina retorted, pushing her to one side. "I need a lad to earn some money when I'm old and Marshall has pegged it."

Rosina's speech had become like her neighbours who ridiculed her if she spoke posh. Sarah was very often ridiculed at school for talking posh, but she did not understand most of the slang words that the local children used.

Len was over the moon at the news. He told Rosina she had made him the happiest man alive and bought her a new coat and hat. The hat was black felt with red poppies on it. Alice thought the hat was beautiful and would sit looking at it for hours on end saying, "I shall have a hat like that one day."

The little girl, Kisaiya, named after Rosina's mother, was born the following summer. She was so beautiful even Rosina smiled at the miracle she held in her arms. Sarah and Alice loved little Kisaiya so much they took turns feeding and dressing her. Rosina soon took to going out in the evening when Len was on the late-shift at the pit. She was always home in time for his return, and he never knew that she had left baby Kisaiya with Sarah and Alice.

Kisaiya had much better care than Alice ever had. She was in the care of Sarah who had been cared for at the Grange and knew what love was and how good people felt when they knew that someone cared for them.

Life at the pit carried on for almost twelve months. Len was oblivious to what Rosina was up to when his back was turned. She drank at the King's Head with all kinds of characters that made her laugh and joke. Len was very well respected by the pit men, and one of them told him that Rosina was making a fool of him when he was at work, telling him that Rosina would do anything for a drink when her money had run out.

This was not true. Rosina hated men and only spent her own money on drink. Of course, she was the only one who knew of her pay off from Sutton, but the pitmen thought that she was spending Len's hard earned wages or earning it on her back somewhere else like most of the drinking women in the pit village.

Len knocked the man to the floor and left the pit to make his way home. He stormed into the house, and going over to Rosina, smelt her breath. "And who paid for you to drink today, Rosina?" He bellowed.

Rosina laughed at him. "Not you, Len Marshall," she shouted.

Sarah took Alice and little Kisaiya upstairs and out of the way. She had never seen Len angry like this before. She felt so sorry for him. He was crying, sitting with his head in his hands and his elbows on the wooden table that she had scrubbed clean earlier in the afternoon.

The noises downstairs got louder and louder as Rosina taunted Len about what she thought about him.

She is bad, Sarah thought. *When she drinks, she is so bad.*

Len went out and banged the door shut.

It went quiet, and Sarah heard her mother come upstairs and go to bed.

The next morning Sarah got up early before anyone was awake, and taking the hunting horn from its hiding place, went downstairs. She usually walked to the front room when she needed to console herself with her memories of home, and the hunting horn was the only link that remained. She opened the door quietly to the front room and walked in.

The sight that met her was unbelievable.

Len lay on the floor, covered in blood. She stood, stricken with fear. She could not move a muscle.

Alice called her, and after some time, Sarah stumbled out of the room and back up the stairs. After putting the hunting horn back in its secret place, she went to see Kisaiya and Alice.

Alice was pulling at her skirt. "Sarah what's up?" she asked. "Kisaiya wants her nappy done and needs a drink."

"Sarah, come here," Rosina called out from the bedroom at the front of the house. "Don't stand gaping, girl, get that child a drink and bring me a cup a tea."

"Mam." Sarah tried to speak. "Mam," she cried pitifully.

"What is up with you?" Rosina asked.

"Mam, c-come down and look in the front room," Sarah stuttered.

"What!" Rosina shouted "What are you talking about?"

"Mam, it is Len. I think he is hurt," Sarah cried.

Rosina got out of bed and went down stairs, grumbling all the way.

"Oh my God," Rosina screamed. "Go get Lily from next door. Quick!"

Sarah ran and told Lily that Len was hurt and that her mam said to come quick.

Lily had just got up and said, "I'll come in a bit Sarah, when I've had a drink."

"No, no!" Sarah yelled. "Now. You have got to come now!"

The woman followed Sarah to the front door.

Rosina wailed. "Oh my God, Lily, Len's dead. I think he has cut his throat. Oh my God!"

Lily took one look at poor Len and ran out screaming.

Chapter 14

Halten, 1912

T he following days and weeks passed slowly for Sarah. The one person in her life on whom she could rely was gone forever—just like her daddy.

Rosina had been in shock since the terrible discovery of Len's body. She had not had a drink since that night when Len had accused her of ridiculing him in front of all his workmates at the King's Head.

Most of the neighbours knew how Rosina despised Len. It was nothing out of the ordinary for a woman to despise her husband. Eighty percent of the women that lived in such deprived existences commiserated with her. Rosina would have to leave the house now that her man had gone. The owner of the mine would want their family house for his replacement within six months. Where would she go now?

Rosina knew all this, of course, and this, not grief for her dead husband, kept her awake at night worrying. Leaving out the bit about Alice's conception, Rosina told the vicar the sad story of losing her first husband. The vicar decided that this is why she had taken to drink. He could save this woman and her family from the gutter. After all, they came from gentry—at least the children did. He could not let the children of gentry live like mere workers.

Rosina went to church every Sunday, taking the children. This pleased Sarah. It reminded her of her life at Lambecote Grange. She loved to listen to the organist and always sat in a position where she could see his hands on the keyboard. The vicar asked Rosina if she had thought about Sarah's future.

"I think she will have to go into service, Vicar."

"But she is not like the other girls in the school Rosina. She is so refined. I believe that working in such circumstances will be detrimental to her," the vicar said, shocked.

"Well, that is where she will have to go," Rosina retorted. "I have two other daughters to think about. William is as good as useless. All he ever does is follow the damn gypsies. I have not seen him for a month."

"Perhaps if I speak with William he will listen to me," the vicar answered.

"I would appreciate that Vicar," Rosina said.

Rosina stayed on in the house for more than twelve months. The neighbours tittle-tattled about her and the vicar. Any other woman in those circumstances would have been out on the street begging, but not Rosina Marshall. She was in thick with vicar. In fact, the vicar had asked the mining manager for time to sort out Rosina's problems, telling him that she had come from gentry and would be an asset to the village.

"That is not what the pitmen say about her," Jimmy Wiseman, Sr., the pit manager, replied.

"Well, we don't always listen to gossip, Mr. Wiseman, do we?" the vicar replied.

The manager said he would give her a little more time but he would need the house, which was one of the better houses in the pit village. Houses were allocated according to the employee's skills. The villas were built around a village green, which had been planted with trees and shrubs. These were occupied by the manager in the detached house, and the overmen and deputies in the semi-detached houses. These were educated men, and houses were "The Villas." Behind "The Villas," looking on to their backs, terraced houses with small front gardens housed the skilled men. Behind these were rows of terraced houses without gardens or any refinements for the labourers and their families.

Rosina and her family lived in a skilled man's house with a well kept front garden in which Len had always taken pride. Sarah decided to keep the garden up with the help of Alice and baby Kisaiya. They enjoyed life now that they had the church and the vicar to relate to. The vicar seemed interested in Sarah and spent quite a lot of time talking to her about the Grange, her daddy, and the Bingham family.

One day, the vicar called to see Rosina. "I would like to find a place for Sarah if I may, Rosina."

Rosina said, "I have already got somewhere, Vicar. She is going to Ingells' farm to work in the dairy."

"Rosina, you can't send the child there. It's a terrible job. She would suffer agonies. They do not treat their workers very well. I know that Mr. Ingell bothers the young girls. I have just placed a girl in a workhouse after she became with child, and she swears the father is Mr. Ingell. Oh no, Rosina, she can't go there." The vicar was appalled.

"Vicar, she is almost thirteen. I do not have enough money to live on. William will not give me any of the money he earns as a blacksmith's lad at the pit. He will only bring food into the house and pay the rent,"

"William is a good lad, Rosina," the vicar said. He knows what he wants. He wants to work with horses. I have asked him if he would like to go back to Nottinghamshire and find his Uncle and perhaps claim his inheritance, but he wants none of it, and mind you, he is the reason that you are staying in this house. He would be allowed a house at sixteen but not on this level. Len Marshall was a skilled worker, Rosina, and he earned this house, but William is only an apprentice and would be given a house in "The Backs."

"You should mind your own business," Rosina said. The mention of Lambecote Grange struck fear in her. If any one found out that she was receiving payment for giving it up, she would be thrown out of this house. Not to mention what William would do with such a piece of news. "None of us has any rights to Lambecote Grange. I had to leave it to the relative of my dead husband and sign away all rights. William has no inheritance nor does Sarah."

"Rosina, how much will Sarah earn at the Ingell's dairy?" the vicar asked.

"Three shillings a month," Rosina said, angry with the vicar's inter-ference.

"And where will she live?"

"At home. Where do you think?" Rosina spat at him.

"Well, I think I can do better than that for you and her," the vicar said, rising to his feet and walking over to the window.

"She can go wherever it is if you can get me more than three shillings a month," Rosina said. She wished the little man would go away and leave her alone. She did not need to be reminded of Lambecote Grange every five minutes.

"I have written to a family in Bingley regarding Sarah. I am still awaiting a reply. I am sure she will earn more than three shillings a month, and what's more, she will be a live-in, giving you more money to spend on the other children," the vicar said, watching Rosina's face for a favourable response.

"I can't wait long," Rosina said. "I need Sarah to be working—and quick."

Sarah listened to this conversation. She was in the kitchen doing the wash, helped by Alice who seemed to enjoy rubbing the clothes on the scrub board.

Sarah felt sick with fear. She had no idea that her mam was sending her out to work. The girls at school talked about Ingell's farm and how Mr. Ingell was a bad man. She hoped the vicar had found her somewhere else, but she would probably not be able to come home from Bingley, wherever it was.

She started to cry, and Alice put her arms around her saying, "I love you, Sarah. I love you so much!"

This made Sarah cry more than ever.

After the church service on Sunday, which Rosina missed, the vicar took Sarah to one side. "Is your mother at home, Sarah?"

"Yes, Vicar," Sarah said. "She has a headache this morning."

"I will walk home with you. Just wait a little while until I have finished here," he said.

Sarah waited outside. Perhaps he wanted her to clean the church. He always said she was a good cleaner when he watched her scrubbing in the kitchen or polishing the floor at home. They walked back to the village in silence. The vicar smiled as he nodded to people along the way. Rosina was drinking with one of the old biddies when they arrived. She was not pleased at seeing the vicar.

"Can I have a word with you in private?" the vicar asked.

"Yes, Vicar, Mrs. Marsh is just leaving," Rosina answered, glaring at the drunken Gertie Marsh.

Old Lass Marsh, as she was known in the backs, smiled a toothless smile at the vicar and left.

"Well, Rosina, I have heard from my friends in Bingley, and they will be happy to take Sarah. She will be paid five shillings a month and her keep. They will also take William on one pound a week to work with the horses, if that is acceptable to you. You don't have to leave this house. The church will pay your rent for twelve months provided you don't drink away the money that William and Sarah earn in Bingley."

Rosina was stunned. She felt humble and began to cry uncontrollably."

"Don't cry, Rosina. We know you have done your best, but circumstances got the better of you. You are a good woman at heart who only drank when her dear husband died, leaving her pregnant and vulnerable."

"How do you know this, Vicar?" Rosina sobbed.

"I made inquiries through the church in Nottingham. After the children told me of your previous life, I thought we could help you, but you must also help yourself, Rosina," he answered.

"Where is Bingley?" Sarah asked fearfully.

"In North Yorkshire, Sarah," the vicar answered. "Don't be afraid. William will join you as soon as I have made the arrangements with Mr. Wiseman at the mine."

"Have you told William?" Rosina asked.

"No, not yet," the vicar replied. "I thought I had better speak with you first."

"He won't go, you know," Rosina said sadly. "It is too late for him. He has got his heart set on a gypsy lass, and there is no changing his mind."

"We'll see," the vicar said.

William was shocked when the vicar told him the news. "Four pounds a month, Vicar. Me mam will drink herself to death on that."

"Well, she has got the chance to put her life back together, William, and bring up her children in a God-fearing way. It is up to her now, but you need to get away from here and build your life as your father would have wanted," the vicar replied, knowing that William should be squire of Lambecote if that were true.

"I will think about it, Vicar," William said.

"Don't take too long," the vicar said. "Sarah is going next week. It would be good if you could travel together. She is very nervous."

"What are these people like?" William asked.

"Gentry, William. That is why I know you can fit in. You know the ways of gentry," he answered.

"But that was another life, Vicar. I do not think I ever would have fit in with gentry. I always wanted to be free, free to roam and stay wherever I felt happy," William said.

"We would all like that, William, but sometimes it's not practical." The vicar was disappointed in William's attitude. "Let me know by tomorrow, and I will purchase your ticket when I purchase Sarah's."

After the vicar had given Rosina time to consider the offer, he returned to ask if she had come to a decision. "She will go as soon as possible. These people need her now." Rosina looked at Sarah.

"No, Mam, no. I do not want to go away. I need to stay here with our Alice and Kisaiya. Who will look after them?" Sarah pleaded.

"Your mother will take care of your sisters, Sarah. You don't have to worry about them," the vicar said, putting a gentle hand on Sarah's arm.

Rosina was not going to turn an offer like this away. She said, "Thank you, Vicar. I shall accept. Sarah will be ready when you want her."

Sarah fled, running outside, down the road, and out onto the common. She wished she had her hunting horn. It had become a sort of comforter. She felt close to her father when she polished it and imagined she could hear him calling to her.

"Be strong Sarah. You have to be strong!"

Chapter 15

Bingley

Monday morning, Sarah sat on the waggonette going to the railway station. Her mother sat beside her. Alice had gone to school, and Kisaiya had been left with Lily next door. Sarah was so miserable she thought she would die. How could her mam let her go away to someone that she did not even know? It was such a long way to Bingley. It would take two hours on the train. She was to be met by a pony and trap at the station and driven to the farm.

The waggonette stopped and her mother took her hand, pulling her across the road to the railway station. Rosina wanted to get this over with as soon as possible. It broke her heart to see Sarah's sad face that sported George Bingham's eyes, pleading to let her stay at home.

"Sarah, hurry up!" Rosina said "The train is in." She pushed Sarah into a carriage. "You behave yourself and do not forget to send me the five shillings every month." Rosina then vanished into the steam from a train just pulling out of station.

The train started to move. Sarah was scared. The *clackety-clack* of the wheels went on and on. Eventually, she fell asleep. She had not slept properly for several nights since the vicar came with the news of her job. The train screeched to a stop. She jumped up, startled and disorientated, looking around her. People were pushing to get off, and others were pushing to get on to the train.

She panicked. "Please, are we in Bingley?" she asked a lady who got into her carriage.

"No, me dear. This is Leeds. Bingley's a good while yet," the woman answered.

Sarah sat down again, and checking for her bag, she began to settle down. After what seemed like an eternity ,the train arrived at Bingley. She held her bag nervously and waited for the train to stop. She could not believe her mother had sent her to strangers that may be worse than Mr. Ingell. If he were, she would run away and find the gypsies. William had told her to do that if she was in any trouble. He said to tell them who she was, and they would get word to him.

A man helped her down from the carriage. As she straightened her coat and hat, a well-dressed lady approached her smiling.

"Are you Sarah Bingham?" she asked.

Surprised, Sarah said. "Yes I am!"

"Yes, I can see you are," the lady said. "You have your father's eyes."

"Excuse me, but did you know my daddy?" Sarah asked.

"Yes, Sarah, I did. And I knew your grandfather and your mummy too," the lady replied.

Sarah's face lit up, and she excitedly said, "I am here to meet someone who will take me in a pony and trap to Longcliffe House. Do you know of it?"

"Yes, Sarah. I am Mrs. Arkwright from Longcliffe House and I have come to meet you myself." Edith Arkwright had been so excited to learn that Sarah was coming at last.

Aunt Lillian and Uncle Edwin had searched Nottingham, looking for Rosina and the children. When Violet Grimshaw had eventually broken her silence telling Uncle Edwin where Rosina had gone, he arrived there to find she had moved on with no forwarding address. The neighbours told him she never spoke to them, but she had a man friend and married before moving out.

Sarah was shocked to find someone who knew of her other life. "Thank you, Mrs. Arkwright. That is very kind of you," she said.

"Give me your bag, my dear, and we shall find Robinson with the carriage and get you home. We should just be in time for tea," Edith said kindly. She had decided not to tell Sarah who she was until she had time to settle in.

Sarah was pushed along in front of Edith to a carriage with a driver waiting to settle them in with a warm rug and a cheery smile. Sarah began to feel at ease a little. The carriage bumped along for several miles before it turned into a long drive at the end of which was a beautiful house in such lovely gardens. Sarah was enthralled.

Edith had made light conversation with Sarah not asking anything about her mother or brother. Sarah needed to know how this lady knew her parents, but when she asked Mrs. Arkwright, the woman just said, "All in good time, Sarah. All in good time."

Waiting at the door of Longcliffe House was a lovely young girl of about Sarah's age.

"Sarah, this is Amelia. You and she will be companions. I hope you will become good friends," Edith said, smiling with pride.

The little girl who took Sarah's hand and said, "Hello, Sarah I have been waiting all day for you to arrive. Follow me and I shall show you your room."

Sarah followed the girl up a curved staircase, Amelia running ahead excitedly. Sarah looked around her room in absolute wonder. It was so pretty. She could just remember her room at the Grange with its lace and frills, but this was satin and silk in pink and white. She just stood in silence.

"I hope you like it, Sarah," Amelia said. "Mummy let me choose. I do hope you like it."

"Oh, I do, I do." Sarah was in tears now.

"Do not cry please," said Amelia. "I suppose you are tired. I always get teary when I am tired. When we have had some tea you can have a rest, and then I shall show you around. This is your home now, Sarah, just as it is mine."

Sarah sipped her tea in silence and nervously looked around the morning room in which the tea had been served. The maids in their white lace pinafores and hats fussed around them. *Perhaps this is what I shall be taught to do?* Sarah thought. She hoped she did not mess it up. They looked very smart and knew just what to say to everyone.

Edith took her back to her room, telling her to get some sleep before dinner. Then she would tell her exactly what was happening. Giving her a hug and saying, "Little Sarah, I never thought we would find you again."

Sarah removed her boots and lay on the bed. It was so comfortable she sank into the feather mattress and stroked the soft silky cover until she fell asleep. She awoke to the sounds of a maid unpacking her clothes into a beautiful white armoire.

"What would you like to wear for dinner, Miss?" the maid asked.

"I, err, do not know," Sarah said nervously. "What should I wear?"

"Well you only seem to have brought outdoor clothes. Perhaps your other bags are coming along later. Maybe you should wear this dress," she said, holding up Sarah's best church dress. "If you would like to bathe, I will help you with your hair. We have to hurry as dinner will be served in half an hour," the maid said.

Sarah remembered dressing for dinner at the Grange. She went in to the vestibule and found a jug and bowl with fresh warm water fragranced with Rose petals. This brought back memories of home. Sarah was nearly in tears. She thought she must have been dreaming all this. The maid brushed her long soft chestnut brown hair and tied a fresh white silk ribbon in to hold it from her face, several wisps fell down around her lovely light-blue eyes that shone in wonder at the happenings of this day.

Amelia rushed into the room with her mother, saying, "Are you ready, Sarah? Daddy is home and wants to meet you. I hope you had a good sleep and are rested enough for me to show you around after dinner."

"Amelia, do not fuss the girl," Edith protested. "She needs to meet Daddy and listen to what he has to say before you rush her off to play. There is plenty of time for that later."

Sarah looked puzzled. She certainly did not expect service to be like this. She wondered when she would have to start work.

Thomas Arkwright looked over his spectacles at Sarah, smiling and taking her hand. He knelt down to her height and said, "I am pleased to meet you, my dear. I have heard so much about you."

Sarah smiled nervously and said, "Pleased to meet you, sir."

"Sit down, my dear," Thomas said. "I need to speak with you."

Amelia and her mother were beaming with happiness, knowing what Thomas was about to tell Sarah. "Sarah I have some news that you may find interesting," he began.

Sarah felt her stomach tighten. She had suffered so much over the last eight years. She had learned to steel herself for the worst.

"Yes, sir," she replied.

"I have been notified by our local vicar that you are the daughter of George and Rosina Bingham of Lambecote Grange in Nottinghamshire," he said.

"Yes, sir, that is correct," Sarah said.

"Well, your father's Aunt Lillian is married to my dear wife's Uncle Edwin," Thomas beamed.

Sarah thought about it for a while. "Who is that, sir?" she asked.

"He, my dear girl, is Edwin Braithewaite of the law firm Bryce, Coombes and Braithewaite. These were solicitors to your father and his father for many years. We had no idea where your mother had taken you and your brother. Mr. Sutton, who owns the Grange now, said he that had not been told where your mother moved too after she left the Grange.

"We moved to Yorkshire, Mr. Arkwright, and my mother married a very kind man who had an accident and died last year," Sarah said in a high-pitched nervous voice. Rosina had told her never to tell anyone who she was or she would be taken away.

"Was he kind to you, Sarah?" Edith asked.

"Oh yes, he was to me and to Alice, my sister."

"How many sisters do you have?" Edith asked.

"Two—Kisaiya and Alice. Kisaiya is little, and she will be crying for me. I know she will 'cos Alice can't look after her like I do when Mam is not in," Sarah said as she remembered home.

"Where does your mother go, Sarah?" Thomas asked.

"I don't know, but William follows her sometimes, and they argue when she comes home," Sarah said.

"Never mind that now," Edith said. "Let us eat. This looks delicious, what do you say, Daddy?'

"Capital my dear. I am hungry as an ox," Thomas Arkwright said, laughing.

Sarah smiled and looked at the array of cutlery. Now this she remembered from the Grange. They always had a knife and fork for every course starting from the outside. Edith watched her choose her cutlery and smiled to herself. After dinner Amelia took Sarah off on a grand tour of the house.

"I do not think she has come to much harm, Thomas, but I do think there is a story behind Rosina's sudden departure from Lambecote Grange," Edith said when the girls were out of earshot.

"Yes, Edith, I agree, but we must let the girl settle in before we throw anymore questions at her."

Later, Amelia ran into the lounge where Edith and Thomas were taking their coffee and brandy. Sarah followed with eyes has big as saucers. She stopped when she saw the grand piano with the silver candelabra standing on top.

"Do you play, Sarah?" Edith asked remembering how well George Bingham played the piano.

"I had lessons when I was at home, at the Grange that is, but I have not seen a piano for such a long time," Sarah replied.

Amelia has a teacher twice a week. "Would you like to join her next time she comes?" Edith asked.

"Oh please. Could I?" Sarah said excitedly.

"Certainly. It will be a pleasure to listen to you two girls practice the piano," Thomas said with a wry smile.

"Mrs. Arkwright," Sarah said. "When do I start work and what shall I be doing? I am supposed to be in service. That is what Mam said, and she said to be prepared to work my fingers to the bone. But eating in your dining room and sleeping in a lovely bedroom and piano lessons—that is not working, is it."

Thomas looked up from his newspaper saying. "Sarah, my dear, we want you to be a companion to Amelia. She does not have any brothers or sisters like you, and we would love you to share her lessons and live here like our daughter, if you would do us that honour."

Sarah could not believe her ears when she heard this. Would this wonderful day that had started so unhappily ever end? Eventually Amelia took Sarah upstairs and they both went to bed. Sarah's nightdress had been laid out on the silk bedcover ready for her to put on. She was so happy she lay in bed thanking God and the vicar—but adding, could you find room for our Alice and our Kisaiya as well, God?

William did not turn up at Longcliffe Farm, but he did write a thank you letter, explaining that he intended to marry soon and was not in a position to take up work so far away from Nottingham. The Arkwrights were very disappointed. They were looking forward to having a son about the place, but William seemed to have little interest in farming or settling down in a regular place.

Sarah's life became one long string of happiness. She took to the piano so well the music teacher told Edith that she thought she could be a teacher of music. She was such a natural.

The girls were taught all the accomplishments that girls of that time were thought to need—sewing, cooking, Mathematics and English—so they would be able to keep good accounts for their husbands when they eventually married. In fact, they were educated to become wives—wives of educated men. They would have to have a degree of conversation, but never stray across the boundaries of men's subjects like Political Science, Religion or Business. These were for male conversation after the ladies had left the table.

Rosina received a money order from the post office in Bingley on the first of the month, usually accompanied by a letter telling her that Sarah was doing well and was a bright girl. Nothing about her education or that she was with George's relatives.

Thomas had told Sarah that it would not be wise to tell her mother who they were because they did not know why Rosina had run away in the first place. "I do not want to teach you to tell lies to your mother, Sarah, but I do not think it would be wise, my dear," he said.

Sarah looked sad but she understood what he was saying, and although she would like to tell her mam and their Alice about her life, she knew her mam would bring her back, and she might have to work in Ingells' dairy if she had to go back. She was due a visit home once a month, but Rosina said not to come home until she told her to. Sarah worried about Kisaiya. She knew the vicar and God were looking after Kisaiya and their Alice, but could God look after such a little girl as Kisaiya?

Christmas came and went, and Sarah began to get very homesick. She wanted to see their Alice and Kisaiya. "Mr. Arkwright!" she asked at dinner one evening.

"Sarah, please call me Uncle Thomas, will you? Mr. Arkwright sounds so formal."

Sarah smiled, and embarrassed, whispered, "Uncle Thomas."

"Yes, Sarah." Thomas beamed at her. "What can I do for you?"

"I would like to go home to see my mam," Sarah said nervously.

Edith looked across at Thomas. "Very well, Sarah. When would you like to go? We will take you, won't we, Edith?"

Edith relaxed. "Yes Sarah. We could make it a holiday. We shall stay in Derbyshire with some friends, and you can spend a little time with your dear mother and sisters. When shall we go Thomas?" she asked.

Thomas left the table and went to his desk to look through his diary. "We could go on the twenty-ninth, and I could take a whole week. How would that suit you Sarah?"

"I shall write to my mother tonight and tell her I am coming home for a week. She will be very happy, and Alice will and so will Kisaiya," Sarah said happily.

The carriage stopped at the end of the road where Rosina lived. Edith and Thomas had insisted that they see Sarah into her mother's house—much to the consternation of Sarah who said she would rather they did not see were she lived.

She jumped down, and after arranging when they would collect her, she ran down the road toward home.

Rosina was waiting with Alice and Kisaiya. The house was gleaming. Sarah was so happy to be home with them. Rosina had spent a week getting ready for Sarah's return. She hoped she was well and not too bitter at the fact that she had sent her away. *Here she is looking like a lady,* Rosina thought. *It must be in her blood. She was gentry through and through.*

Alice stood with her mouth open looking at Sarah. Sarah looked like a doll. Her hair was shining. Her velvet coat and hat were just the same blue as her eyes.

Sarah hugged them and picked up Kisaiya and swung her round and round. "Oh, I am so glad to see you!" she said. "I have missed you all so much."

"Come and sit down and tell us all about it," Rosina said. "And before you start, I know who you are living with. The vicar told me after you had gone to make me feel better about it."

"Oh, Mam I wanted to tell you, but I was scared you would make me come home. I am learning to play the piano and can sew my own clothes now. I am going to measure our Kisaiya and Alice and make them some clothes. I can make clothes for them out of the bits left over from Amelia and my clothes." Sarah excitedly babbled her story to her family.

"So you like it then?" Rosina said, standing with her hands on her hips and smiling at her beautiful daughter. *George would be so proud of his Little Sarah*, Rosina thought.

How she wished that William had gone to Bingley with Sarah, instead of running around the country looking for the gypsies. It would have changed his life.

"Where is our William? He did not come to Bingley, and Uncle Thomas was really looking forward to having a man around. Why didn't he come, Mam?" Sarah asked.

"He has got some fool idea that he wants to be a gypsy," Rosina replied. "He knows the gypsies do not want him around but he will not listen to me."

"He loves to be with Fluere, Mam. That is why."

Rosina sighed and shook her head sadly. "I know, Sarah love, but it will come to nothing. Mark my words," she said. "Now come with me round to next door and let them see how well you look. Lily will be chuffed to see you."

Lily was very surprised when she saw Sarah dressed up like a lady. She thought Rosina had been lying when she had told her the story of Lambecote Grange and their previous life. Well some of it anyhow. Rosina told people what she wanted them to know regarding Lambecote Grange. The only person other than herself to know about Alice's father was Len, and he was dead, so she would never let on that Len was not Alice's father. Alice would be devastated and Rosina would have an even worse reputation than she already had.

They had a lovely week together. Alice and Kisaiya did not leave Sarah's side for a minute.

They questioned her about every aspect of her life. What kind of food did she eat? What was her room like? When Sarah told them that she had her own maid to wash and clean her clothes and brush her hair, their eyes were like saucers.

"Tell us more, our Sarah. Tell us some more." Little Kisaiya laughed.

The time came to go back to Bingley, and Alice and Kisaiya walked to the end of the road with Sarah. Rosina refused to meet the Arkwrights, much to Sarah's disappointment. Edith gave presents to Kisaiya and Alice, which she had purchased when they had travelled to Derby for a day's shopping.

Amelia was full of excitement, telling Sarah how much she had missed her. They had purchased silk cloth of several different colours to make dresses for all of them, including Edith.

Life soon got back into its routine, and Sarah was happier, knowing that everything at home was well and that her mam did not seem to be drinking. No one had told her that her mam had stopped drinking. That would have been too much to ask of God all in one year.

Chapter 16

1917

Several years passed and Sarah visited her family regularly. Rosina was looking drawn the last time Sarah went home. Alice said her mam only drank a bit when Sarah asked her if her mam was going out at nights.

"How much is a bit, Alice?" Sarah asked.

"Well, Saturdays are the worst" Alice said.

Kisaiya said, "Me mam fell downstairs, Sarah, and we had to get doctor out."

Sarah went cold. Oh please, God, do not let her start again. She returned to Longcliffe Farm and asked if she could travel home again in one month, not letting her mam know that she was going.

Sarah was almost sixteen now. And her beauty was not only of her face but in her gentle ways and kindness to everyone she met. Edith told Aunt Lillian and Uncle Edwin that she thought Sarah had a refinement and that it had to be in the genes. It could never be manufactured. Amelia was a beauty but with strong features. Sarah was like a porcelain doll, so delicate that it would break easily if you did not handle it carefully.

One of the help took Sarah into Bingley to catch the early train to Doncaster where she could get a waggonette to Halten. She dreaded what she would find at home as she walked along Blythe Road after she left the waggonette. Walking only a few yards, she heard a young man approach from behind. He asked if he could carry her bag.

"No thank you," Sarah replied. "I can manage it myself." She was struggling a little trying to carry the bag that was full of clothes and other bits and bobs she had brought for Alice and Kisaiya.

The young man said, "Don't be silly, I can see you are having trouble carrying the bag. Here, let me help you." He took the bag with some force from Sarah's grip.

"Where are you heading?" he said. "By the way, I am James Wiseman. I haven't seen you before. Do you live in Halten?"

"No, I live in Bingley, but my mother lives here. I am just visiting," Sarah said giving in to the pressure this very pleasant young man had put her under.

"Well, which way are we headed, miss? I, err, what is your name?" Jimmy Wiseman asked.

"My name is Sarah Bingham, and my mother lives on Osborne Street."

"Oh! I live over that way. I can see you right to the door," he said, smiling a smile that made Sarah's heart race. He handed her the bag when they got to the back gate of Rosina's house and said, "Perhaps I can see you again, Miss Bingham, before you go back to Bingley?"

"On no, Mr. Wiseman," she answered. "I have only come for four days. But thank you for your kindness."

"Not at all," James said. "But I shall be waiting for you whenever you leave this house. I insist that you let me take you to the pictures." We have a picture house in Halten I would love to show you," he said, insisting that she answer.

"I am tired, Mr. Wiseman. I have travelled a long way today. Please let me go." Sarah was embarrassed. She wanted to surprise her mam. If this man did not leave soon, the surprise would fail, and her long journey home would be to no avail.

"Very well," James said, seeing her embarrassment. "But I will be back."

Sarah tentatively turned the door handle and quietly walked in. When she walked through the door from the scullery into the back parlour she could smell the beer and tobacco smoke.

She was confronted by old lass Marsh and another woman that she had not seen before. Rosina was well past caring about Sarah seeing her in a drunken state and with a sarcastic sneer on her face said, "Oh look here, lady muck has come to visit us."

The other women laughed, and one of them pretended to courtesy to Sarah.

"Mam, where are our Alice and Kisaiya?" Sarah asked.

"They have gone out for a walk somewhere. I do not know when they will come back—never, if I had my way," Rosina slurred.

They all laughed at this remark. Rosina said, "What are you doing here? Spying on me, are you?"

Sarah put her bag down in the front room, and removing her purse before she left the house, went looking for her sisters. She found them on the common sitting huddled together to keep warm. They did not have coats or cardigans on, and the wind was chill. Kisaiya saw her first. She got to her feet and ran with her arms outstretched toward Sarah.

"We have just been praying that you would come home, Sarah. Mam has been so bad since you went back last time." Alice was crying.

"What happened, Alice?" Sarah asked. "What set it off?"

"It's our William. He's got married to Fluere, and me mam's gone mad."

"When did he get married?" Sarah asked, not so surprised as she always knew he would marry her sometime.

"He says they have been married for ages, but me mam says he must have got married when he was twenty-one 'cos she would have had to sign the consent papers if he had got married before he was twenty-one," Alice gabbled.

"How long has she been drunk, Alice," Sarah asked.

"About three weeks now. I don't know where she gets the money from. Sometimes she sends out for fish and chips and a jug a beer and I know she hasn't had any money from our Bill for ages. He brings us some food when he comes but travels around a lot," Alice said, shivering.

"When did you last have food?" Sarah asked.

"We bought a loaf yesterday and have been putting dripping on it when we got really hungry, but I don't think we have any dripping left now," Alice said.

With her face set hard, Sarah said, "Come on. We can just catch the shop on Low Road if we hurry."

The shopkeeper was just about to close the doors when they arrived there out of breath. Sarah bought fruit and vegetables and some tinned meat because the butcher was already closed. She would have to buy fresh meat tomorrow.

Rosina was asleep when they arrived home. They cooked a meal and left a plate on the hob top for Rosina when she awoke. She was always starving hungry after she had been on a binge.

Sarah gave the girls the dresses she had made for them, telling them that they must keep them out of sight until she had spoken with her mam about her drinking. "She will pawn them when she runs out of money," Sarah warned.

The next morning Rosina was in a quiet mood. She felt dreadful after the booze she had consumed the previous few days. She had spent all

Sarah's wages and the money from Harold Sutton in a three-week booze-up with her drinking pals and now hated herself and everyone around her.

"When are you going back?" Rosina asked Sarah.

"I am not going back until I get some answers from you about this mess you are getting into again," Sarah replied.

"You had better go and earn some bloody money 'cos our William has gone and got married, and we do not get any money from him now," Rosina spat at her.

"Well where did you get the money from for the booze, Mam?" Sarah asked.

"Mind your bloody business," Rosina answered.

"It is my business, Mam. I am sixteen and I want to know how you can feed three people, pay the rent, and supply drink for all your pals on my five shillings a month," Sarah said angrily.

"Where do you think I get it from Sarah?" Rosina said. "Do you think I've been hawking me duck downtown. Is that what you think?"

"I want you to tell me, Mam," Sarah said, staring into her mother's eyes. "Come on. Where did you get it from?"

"I sold Len's gold watch if you must know," Rosina lied.

"Len never had a gold watch," Sarah said. "So whose gold watch did you sell?"

"Bugger off," Rosina said, turning her back on Sarah's piercing glare.

"You pawned my father's watch, didn't you, Mam. Or better still, William's gold watch," Sarah accused her. "Uncle Edwin says William is the rightful heir to Lambecote Grange, and you must have made a deal with Harold Sutton. Is that where the money comes from, Mam? Are you drinking away William's and my inheritance? Alcohol costs money, and if our William is not giving you money, you must have a supply from some other place." Sarah was angry. These thoughts had been worrying her for some time now.

"William never had a gold watch," Rosina retorted. She was flustered now. She wished she had not let Sarah go to Bingley. If she had known the connection to the Bingham family, she would have not allowed it.

"Yes, Mam," Sarah shouted at her now. "He had my father's gold watch that was for William. Len told us that."

"You had better watch your p's and q's, me girl," Rosina shouted at Sarah, "'Cos I can still bring you back home as fast as I let you go. You are still underage," Rosina bellowed.

There was a knock on the back door.

Alice went to see who it was. "It's for our Sarah," she said, smiling when she came back into the room. Sarah went to the door and was shocked to find James Wiseman standing there with a jaunty grin on his face.

"I told you I would be back," he said.

Sarah was so embarrassed. He could not have chosen a worse time if he had planned to.

"Oh, Mr. Wiseman," she stammered. "I am afraid it is not very convenient at the moment."

"Just say you will meet me tonight at the picture house, and I will go away," he said laughing.

Sarah looked over her shoulder and nervously said, "Yes. Oh please just go away and leave me alone."

"Six o'clock then tonight," he said. "I shall come back if you don't turn up."

"How do you know him, our Sarah?" Alice asked.

"He helped me to carry my bags when I got off the waggonette." She wanted to know were her mam had got the money from for the booze, and Rosina was just about to tell her when he knocked the door.

"Do you know who he is?" Alice asked.

"No! And what is more, I am not interested in who he is," Sarah said, embarrassed.

"What's that?" Rosina said. "Who is she talking about?"

Kisaiya said, "Our Sarah's going to the pictures with Jimmy Wiseman."

"What, that old man? She is not!" Rosina said.

"No, Mam, the young one. His son is really nice-looking and he's after our Sarah," Kisaiya giggled.

"Is he now?" Rosina said. "Well our Sarah had better play her cards right if she knows what is good for her, and get friendly with Jimmy Wiseman."

Sarah was very angry now. "I shall catch the afternoon waggonette to go back to Bingley. I have suffered enough insults on behalf of your drinking." Sarah ran upstairs and began to pack her bag, which was not so heavy now that the presents had been taken out.

"Don't go, Sarah," Alice said. "We need you here."

"I must go, Alice," Sarah said. "It's up to you to get out and away from here. You should look for a position somewhere. I shall start looking for you."

"I'm not old enough Sarah," Alice cried. "Don't leave us, Sarah We don't have anybody now our Billy's gone and we don't know what to do."

"I shall call at the grocer and give him five pounds. That should feed you if Mam carries on drinking, but do not let her know that the money is there. Just feed you and our Kisaiya. I will see that you do not starve, Alice. Don't worry, but I am going back before I say something I will regret forever."

Rosina kept out of the way until Sarah left. Rosina had very nearly blurted out the truth about Lambecote Grange when confronted by Sarah, glaring at her with eyes just like her father's. She felt it was George, accusing her not Sarah, and she was afraid.

The waggonette was full and smelled of sweat. Alice and Kisaiya had been in tears as they waved goodbye. Sarah told Alice to just get enough food for a day and not to tell their Mam how much she had left at the grocer.

Chapter 17

1914-1918 War

Soldiers crowded the railway station. The newspapers were full of stories of the war with Germany. There was a picture of Lord Kitchener pointing a finger ominously with a caption reading, "Your Country Needs You." It offered a shilling to anyone who signed up there and then.

Even at the railway station there were booths manned by smart-looking army officers, smiling a welcome to the hordes of young men, looking for adventure, and if their parents had their way, a life taking them away from the dreadful pits. Some had left the farm work, objecting to being used as slave labour for the rich landowners.

Sarah was sad, watching the antics of the young soldiers. Some of them that were not of age to sign up pretending to be older. Surely the officers could see that these were just boys, strutting about with cigarettes in the corners of their mouths and nonchalantly whistling at the girls as they passed by.

The train was full. Sarah sat in the corner of a carriage, and closing her eyes, began to let her mind run over what had happened. When she arrived at Bingley, it was raining. She looked around for the stationmaster who ordered a carriage to take her to Longcliffe Farm.

Edith was surprised to see Sarah back so early. After hearing her story, she put her arm around her shoulders and said, "You can't do any more Sarah. Your mother has a problem. It is very sad. When she was married to your father, she was a paragon of virtue. We all loved her, but something has happened to her to make her hard like this. We must not judge her in the absence of facts."

Sarah was tired and went to her room. Amelia came in, looking radiant. "Sarah, I am so pleased you are back," she said, kissing her on the cheek. "I have some news for you."

Sarah poured the tea, which had just been brought in for her and sank her teeth into the ham sandwich made from home-cured ham and bread baked that very day. Oh this tasted good, and life at Longcliffe was so wonderful.

"Sarah, I have met a wonderful young officer," Amelia said, bubbling with enthusiasm.

"Amelia," Sarah replied. "When and who is it? Do I know him?"

"No, Sarah, you do not. I met him at a church bazaar that I helped at. He was putting up the stalls for Mrs. Pringle, the vicar's wife."

"Yes," Sarah said eagerly.

"He asked if he could walk home with me, and I said *yes*," Amelia said excitedly.

"Oh, you brazen hussy," Sarah joked.

"He is coming for dinner tonight. It is just perfect that you are here to meet him before he goes off to France with his regiment."

"Amelia, he is not going away so soon, is he?" Sarah asked sadly.

"Yes, he has to go to help sort out the Germans. They are being very bossy, Sarah, and someone has to stop them before they hurt anyone," Amelia replied naively.

"Yes, Amelia. I saw young men being signed up at the railway station at Doncaster. They did not look old enough to go to war. It is very sad," Sarah replied.

"I think they are very brave," Amelia enthused.

"We should all be able to live together without this arguing."

"Sarah, you are so good," Amelia said. She actually thought that Sarah was too serious for her own good but perhaps would change if Sarah met a handsome young officer too.

The dinner party was very pleasant, and the officer was indeed very handsome. He was the second son of a wealthy landowner. Although the boy loved the land, he was expected to have a career either in the clergy or the military. The elder son would take the land, and the younger son would fight for his king and country—all very right and proper. Amelia was head over heels in love with Robert Grimshaw.

Sarah was surplus to requirements now and felt very lonely. She worried about her family at home and needed a friend, but Amelia was all wrapped up in her officer and had little time for Sarah's silly family problems. Sarah was often left alone when Amelia travelled to meet Robert. She journeyed miles just for a glimpse of him at railway stations here, there, and everywhere.

Edith liked the boy very much, and his background was perfect for Amelia. But she wished her daughter would have a little more decorum. Sarah was the level-headed one, but Amelia had not experienced the world outside in the way that Sarah had.

Robert came home only once during the next two years after he had been injured with gas in the trenches. He convalesced at Longcliffe Farm and dreaded the day when he would be recalled to his regiment in France.

The stories he had told them of young men being used as targets to draw the fire away from the real battlefront were constantly on Sarah's mind. She was so thankful that William had not taken the king's shilling and gone along with the thousands of young men looking for adventure but only finding death and destruction in a foreign land.

Alice had been working in the fields instead of going to school, and Kisaiya took the brunt of Rosina's wrath at home. On the occasions that Sarah visited home, she thanked her lucky stars that she did not have to live there.

Alice and Kisaiya seemed happy. Sarah would sometimes envy them. It was so much easier to accept that this was what your life was meant to be, rather than constantly fight to make a better life. She wished she could have that attitude but was different. She loved them both and their William so much, but Sarah knew that she could not make them think like her.

William and Fluere had three children, two girls and a boy. Fluere had been ostracised by the gypsies because she married a *gorgio*, and she and William had bought their own wagon and travelled around from town to town. William got casual work when he could, and Fluere made clothes pegs and flowers and sold them wherever she could.

Sarah always wondered if they had actually been married because gypsies had different ideas regarding marriage, at least different from Christians. *They are very happy, and that is what is most important*, Sarah thought. William would let her know when he was in North Yorkshire, and they would meet and have a wonderful day together.

Sarah loved her days with William and his family. She met many young officers during this time who were passing through, usually Robert's friends. But Sarah would not lose her heart as easily as Amelia, and breeding and fortune would have no part in her choice of husband. There were many more factors to endear her to a man than money.

This was a very sad time for most of the county's men folk as they fought in France and Belgium. When they came home, it was usually because they had been injured or very badly shell-shocked. Some of the young men would never be the same again.

Robert Grimshaw wrote to Amelia daily. It was his salvation, knowing that he had her waiting at home for him. He had made many friends in France where he had earned himself a medal for valour for saving a French family from certain death in Normandy.

Robert loved Normandy. It was such a beautiful place. The land was fertile, and the crops would be rich if they could ever stop this war. He was certain of one thing. He would not be a soldier after this was over. He knew in his heart that this was a war of idiots looking for power and position. Nothing had been achieved from any of the battles that had taken the lives of so many young men—men who had so much to give to this earth and were just cannon fodder for the stupidity of generals playing soldiers. This must be the war to end all wars.

Jimmy Wiseman was the best-looking young man in Halten, and his dad was manager of the pit. But he never dated a lass more than once. Along with his brothers, he had taken a job at the pit so he would not be called up. If you were in a type of employment that was needed for the war effort, you were exempt from National Service. He had wanted to be an engineer but that meant going to college. He had always intended to go to college, but the war stopped that for the time being. He often took the road past Rosina's house on Osborne Street, hoping to see Sarah again. He asked Alice and Kisaiya whenever he saw them. "When is your sister coming home?" he would ask.

But they never knew because Sarah had taken to dropping in when she felt like it these days. Rosina was going out more now that she had a wage from Alice. This money was in addition to the five shillings she received from Sarah, and of course, nobody knew about the money from Lambecote Grange. She never told anyone, and Harold Sutton was not likely to reveal how he had swindled her out of their inheritance. Life on Osborne Street had settled into an existence that had to be endured for Alice and Kisaiya.

After the war was over and all the jubilation died down, Robert and Amelia made plans to marry. Edwin and Edith were getting old now, and Thomas thought that Robert would want to take over the farm. But Robert had different ideas. He wanted to go to France and farm. He had seen the land that he wanted to buy in Normandy, close to Dieppe where he could have a market for his produce. Being near a busy, port he could perhaps export to England. He just had to find the finances for this, and he was going back to make a life for Amelia and himself. It had been his dream throughout the terrible times during the war.

Thomas was dumbstruck. He was willing to turn over to his farm and property to this man, and he was turning it down. Robert had problems borrowing money in England to take to France, and after many weeks trying every financier who would listen, he eventually told Amelia that he was going to France whether he got the money or not. Thomas was mortified. He did not want to lose his beloved daughter, but she was adamant that she would follow Robert wherever he went. Thomas spent many nights worrying about this. The farm was suffering, and life at Longcliffe was very tense. Edith cried often, and Sarah tried to talk to Amelia, pleading with her to take her time and listen to common sense. But she was headstrong and incapable of seeing the dangers that could befall a young woman in the aftermath of a war torn France.

Amelia and Robert eloped to Gretna Green. Thomas and Edith were devastated. Sarah tried to make up for the fact that their daughter had made them so unhappy, but Edith was inconsolable. This was such a terrible social stigma. How could they hold their heads up again? Poor Edith had a heart attack and died, leaving Sarah with Thomas to console.

Amelia came back for the funeral and persuaded her father to sell the farm and go to France to start a new life with her and Robert. Thomas was reluctant but had nothing left to keep him at Longcliffe.

They told Sarah she would love France. "You could teach music, Sarah," Amelia said. "The farm is so beautiful. It is near the sea."

"I do not speak French," Sarah said.

"You will soon learn, Sarah. Please say you will come with us. I do not want to leave you here," Amelia pleaded.

Amelia wrote to Rosina telling her of the opportunity for Sarah to go to France and teach music. Rosina wrote back and said she had no objection if she still got the five shillings a month. Amelia explained that this was impossible because they were starting a new farm, and the currency difference meant that they could not continue to send a money order each month from a foreign land. Rosina wrote back angrily, saying that Sarah should get herself home as soon as possible and find a decent job.

Thomas went to see Rosina, but she would not relent. She told him that she would not sign a passport application for Sarah, and if they carried on she would get the constable to sort them out. Thomas could not believe that this was the same Rosina who married George Bingham. She was so embittered toward the world.

Sarah did not know what she wanted to do. Amelia made it all sound so romantic, but Sarah thought that she might be stranded in a foreign land if Thomas died. Amelia was so besotted with Robert that she was not thinking clearly at all, and Sarah was not about to make a mistake that she might regret for the rest of her life. She decided to go home and try to find work in Halten. She did not want to return to the squalor of the pit village but could make a start there and try to find somewhere to use her skills.

Chapter 18

The return to Halten

U pon returning home, Sarah found that her mother had secured her a job at a local farm as a kitchen maid. She was not happy with this arrangement but took it. These people were farmers who had made money as publicans over the past twenty years and liked to think that they were the new gentry. Sarah hated every minute at the farm. She worked in the kitchen with a woman called Sadie Ainsworth.

Sadie was subservient to everyone. She had no confidence whatsoever. The first Sunday that Sarah was at the farm, the Greenwoods went to church. Sadie panicked. She had to have dinner ready for exactly thirty minutes after they arrived home, and Sarah had to meet them in the hall with a glass of sherry.

Sarah did not like the farmer's wife, Mrs. Greenwood. She was pretentious and liked to belittle the staff. The work was long and hard, and the staff never stayed longer than a month. Obviously, this is why Rosina had secured the job so quickly for Sarah. Sadie did not have the courage to leave or the gumption to find a better job. This was where she came when she was thirteen, and she would stay here forever.

The pony and trap arrived at the alighting stone, and Mr. Greenwood helped his wife down. Sarah handed the sherry out and went into the kitchen to help cook serve the dinner.

The first bell rang. This meant they were ready for their first course, soup. Sarah served it and returned to the kitchen. Poor Sadie was so nervous she burnt her fingers every day.

Sarah served the second course, roast beef and Yorkshire pudding, but just as she returned from the dining room after serving the beef, Sadie dropped the plum pudding as she was taking it from the oven. The pudding basin broke and plum juice spilt on the kitchen floor. The poor woman was mortified. Her first thought was to clean the kitchen floor. Unlike Sarah, She was a born cleaner. Sarah was a born thinker.

"Leave it, Sadie!" Sarah shouted at her.

"I can't! What if Mrs. Greenwood comes in. She will know what I have done?" the distraught cook cried.

"She is eating her dinner," Sarah said. "She will not come in here until all the work is done." Taking a clean basin and spoon, she proceeded to scoop the pudding from the floor into the basin.

"There," she said when she had finished. "Good as new."

"But what if there are bits of pot in it, Sarah. She'll go mad."

"I checked for all the pieces of pot, and if I serve it on the side server and cover it with custard, she will not be any wiser," Sarah replied.

Sadie shook with fear saying, "I don't think it's right, Sarah. They might choke."

Sarah said, "Well you go in and tell her there is no pudding because you have clumsily dropped it on the floor and see what she says to that."

"Oh God," cook moaned.

"She will not know, Sadie. Mark my words!"

The bell rang for the next course, and Sarah set off with the pudding, winking at Sadie as she opened the door for her. Sarah dipped her knee and served the pudding, an extra large portion for Mr. Greenwood. She returned to the kitchen to find cook in tears of fright.

"Oh shut up. They have no idea," Sarah said.

They sat and waited for the bell to ring. When it did, cook nearly jumped out of her skin. Sarah entered the dining room, crossing her fingers behind her back.

"Thank you, Sarah," Mrs. Greenwood said. "The plums were very good. Were they our own?"

"Yes ma'am," Sarah said, smiling sweetly.

"Capital!" Mr. Greenwood said. "I would like some coffee, me dear. Why don't you serve it in the lounge?"

Sarah went back into the kitchen where Sadie was shaking as she washed the dishes.

"Capital pudding, my dear. All our own plums. Capital!" Sarah mimicked.

"Oh, Sarah, you will get into trouble one of these days," Sadie said, relieved that they had got away with it.

"I will not," Sarah said, "because I am leaving here on Friday. I shall tell them tonight."

Rosina was furious that Sarah had left a good job.

"I want to work in a shop, Mam," she said.

"You have never worked in a shop," Rosina said.

"I have never worked in a kitchen but managed that all right," Sarah replied.

Sarah tried to get work at the new local shop, the Co-operative, which sold almost everything. The customers were supposed to be shareholders. This meant that you had a customer number, and twice a year if the shop had made a profit, you collected a dividend.

There were three sisters working in the Co-operative, all sisters of Jimmy Wiseman. They were not very nice to Sarah when she asked for details on how she should apply for a job. Sarah decided she would not like to work with them. She walked around and called in at the butcher shop for something for dinner.

"Hello Sarah," Mr. Grundy said. "Are you visiting your mam?"

"No, Mr. Grundy. I have had to come home as my Uncle and his family have gone to live in France."

"Oh dear, lass. Why didn't you go?" he asked.

"Something about my passport and not being old enough to sign," she said, not wanting to elaborate.

Mr. Grundy nodded knowingly. He knew what a tarter Rosina was and that she relied on Sarah's money to live. "What are you going to do now?" he asked.

"Well I thought I might get a job in the Co-op," Sarah said. "But the Wisemans seem to have it all tied up."

Mr. Grundy laughed "Aye. They have that, lass. I do not suppose you would like to do a bit of baby-minding, would you?" he asked.

"Who for?" Sarah asked.

"Why my wife, of course," he replied.

"Yes, I would until I find something more permanent," she said.

Because Uncle Thomas gave her an allowance, Sarah had saved quite a bit of money whilst she was in Bingley, and what she did not spend on Alice and Kisaiya, she put away in a savings account with the Trustees Bank. She planned to buy a piano and put it in the front room at home. She missed the piano at Longcliffe Farm so much. It had been her life, playing a bit every day. One of her favourite pieces was "Robins Return," and she had to practice this very difficult piece of music regularly to get it right. She needed a job or would have to dip into her savings because Rosina would not feed her if she did not earn anything.

"My father owned butcher shops, Mr Grundy. Eight of them. It must be in my blood. What do you think?" Sarah laughed.

Sarah began to baby-sit at the butcher shop just a few evenings a week to begin with. Mrs. Grundy was a very nice woman who found it difficult to cope with four young children. Her husband was forever shouting her into the shop to serve when he got busy.

Before very long, Sarah was living in at the butcher shop, and she began to learn the butchering trade. She served in the shop, made savoury ducks, which were meat off-cuts that would have gone to waste if they had not been utilised. She mixed them with onion and herbs. These were very profitable for the butcher, and the miners bought them instead of the more expensive cuts of meat. She also became very proficient at baking pork pies. Jack Grundy became more and more reliant on Sarah to organise the shop and deal with the customers.

Sarah still looked after the children but insisted she have Sundays off. She liked to go to church on Sunday.

One of the customers at the butcher's was the minister of the Wesleyan Chapel who had called in the shop one day and was telling them that he needed someone to play the organ at the chapel.

Jack told him that Sarah was a pianist. "I haven't heard her myself, Minister, but if her work here is anything to go by, I think she would be good."

"Would you consider it, Sarah?" The minister asked.

"I have never played for anyone but myself, Minister," Sarah answered. "I shall need to come in and practice as it has been some time since I played piano. I have never played an organ in my life."

"That would be wonderful! When can you get away to come and practice? I shall be only too happy to open the chapel for you at any time."

Jack looked at Sarah and asked, "How much time do you need, Sarah?"

"Oh! I will have to take a look at the organ before I can tell. Is it a pump organ minister or a pedal?" she asked.

"It is a pump organ, Sarah. I will have to be there with you to pump the air into the pipes," he said.

"Why don't you go now?" Jack asked. "I can manage for the rest of the day."

Sarah sat at the organ she had not played for such a long time. "Do you have any music, Minister?" she asked.

"Of course, Sarah. Here is the book of hymns that came with the organ when we purchased it," he replied.

Sarah studied the book for a little while, and taking a deep breath said, "Right, Minister, start pumping, and let us see what happens."

Sarah played "The Lord is My Shepherd" to the tune of Crimond. The minister sang at the top of his voice whilst he pumped the organ. They proceeded to play several more hymns from the book and the minister asked, "Where did you learn to play so well Sarah?"

"I had a music teacher when I lived in Bingley," she replied.

"Excellent!" He beamed at her. "You are the answer to my prayers. Will you play on Sunday at our service?"

"What time will that be?" Sarah asked.

"Morning service at nine-thirty, and evensong at six-thirty"

"Sunday is my only day off," Sarah said. "But I will play for the first four weeks. After that, I think I shall have to play just for one service if you agree."

"I would like music at both services but shall settle for one. I suppose you need a day off the same as anyone else." The minister was delighted.

A new picture house, The Grand Cinema, was being built opposite the butcher. Everyone was very excited about it. Rumour had it that Hollywood films would be shown there when it was opened. The cinema opened just before Christmas. Sarah took Alice and Kisaiya to the first showing. When they came out, someone ran over to Sarah shouting, "Well, well. You are back then." It was Jimmy Wiseman.

"Yes," Sarah said, embarrassed.

"You stood me up last time, Sarah. I have watched out for you every time I came passed your house. Are you back for long?" he asked.

"She's back for good," Kisaiya said, smiling happily. "She lives in the butcher shop though so it's no good looking at our house for her."

"I shall see you again then, Sarah," Jimmy Wiseman said, beaming that disarming smile at Sarah that made her heart miss a beat.

"Your face has gone red," Alice said to Sarah, nudging Kisaiya as they giggled.

"Yes it was very hot in the cinema," Sarah lied.

"You like Jimmy Wiseman, don't you?" Alice asked, pointing a finger toward Sarah.

"Grow up, Alice!" Sarah said. "I do not know Jimmy Wiseman."

"I still think you like him though. He likes our Sarah, doesn't he, Alice?" Kisaiya, and Alice laughed happily.

Sarah continued to work hard in the butcher shop. She enjoyed the work and liked the people she met. Some of the women who shopped at

Grundy's were thin and worn out because they had so many children but not enough money to feed them. Jack Grundy was a good man. He often let women take some scraps and pay when their men got paid. In quite a few cases the men's wages would be spent before they got home from the pit.

A Miner's Institute had been opened to cater for the needs of the many workers who came into the area from other parts of the country. Beer was subsidised by the mining company that often tried to profit from the heavy drinking habits of men who faced danger every minute they were down the pit. A large proportion of the working miners drank heavily, and some treated their wives and children very badly, not leaving enough money for food or clothing.

The Wesleyan Chapel organised regular jumble sales to help clothe the poor people who lacked such basic requirements as soap, shoes, blankets, and even beds to sleep on. Many children slept four and five in a bed, which invariably stayed wet from at least one bed-wetting child. Many children were physically abused by their fathers and some by their worn-out mothers. They grew up in a world where the strongest got most and the weak did not survive. Some families had as many as twelve and thirteen children in one household. All the churches were kept very busy trying to keep these men in their place.

One family in Halten had eighteen children. The father only worked on Thursday and Friday. He was always sick on Mondays Tuesdays and Wednesdays. Of course he had to go to the pit some time or he would lose his house. If he went on Thursday and Friday, he could pick up his pay and vanish into the pub for the weekend.

The Catholic Church was strong. Quite a few Irish workers had emigrated to work in the pits. The Catholic priest was very strict. He rode a motorcycle that sounded like a wasp caught in a bottle as he steered it down street after street with his black robes flying behind him. He kept a notebook with the names of everyone who did not take communion and would ride around the village on Sunday afternoons, banging on the doors and walking into the houses of people, preaching fire and damnation on them.

The men were always contrite and asked for the forgiveness of the Blessed Mary, and the priest would take a donation and forgive them. The children would be hiding anywhere they could whilst the priest raved at their dads, but when he had left, they would get out of there so Dad would not take it out on them. Often the women got the "punch-up" from the humiliated men. But if a child was handy, he would catch it too. Of course when the Catholic Club opened in the evening, the men would be down there drinking and playing dominoes, sometimes with the same priest but never with the women.

The Catholic Club had a little room called "The Snug" for the women who could only go in there on special occasions. Only the men were allowed to go to the bar to buy the drinks. Women mostly drank at home when the men had gone to work or to the club.

The local shop licensed to sell alcohol was called the "Beer Off." This shop was open until ten o'clock in the evening. Children stood in line with jugs and bottles, even jars—anything that the licensee could pump beer into for their mothers and sometimes for their fathers. Usually the men drank away from the home where they could also gamble. It was illegal to serve children drink, but there was always someone passing by who would buy the drink for them. If a child went home with an empty jug, he would be in trouble.

Sarah knew how they lived. She had seen it first hand when she was at home with Rosina before she went to Bingley. She worked hard collecting old clothes and bric-a-brac for the chapel to distribute to the needy. At least the poor people had work and a roof over their heads.

In other parts of the country, there was unrest when men objected to low wages for working long hours in dangerous conditions.

Jimmy Wiseman pestered Sarah. He would call at the butcher shop to ask how much beef was or if there were any duck eggs. He only really wanted to speak to Sarah. Jack Grundy laughed at him. He was such a likeable fellow. Eventually Sarah said she would go to the pictures with him.

Jimmy was delighted. "I shall pick you up at half past six," he said.

"I can walk across to the cinema on my own Jimmy," Sarah said. "I do not need to be picked up."

"I want everyone to see me take you into the cinema," he said. "I'll pick you up and you can walk across the road with me."

Sarah laughed. He always made her laugh. "Oh all right, pick me up if you must."

Jimmy and Sarah went out often during the next year. Jimmy wanted Sarah to marry him. He said, "I can get a house straight off, Sarah."

Sarah laughed at him saying, "I do not want to get married until I have enough money to have the home that I want, Jimmy."

"Well, will you promise me and not anyone else?" he asked.

"I will, I will," Sarah said, saying anything to get rid of him.

Sarah had been thinking about starting her own business for some time now. The council was building some new shops just on the fringe of the village. She had been to look at them and thought she could make an excellent butcher shop out of one of them. There was enough trade in the village now that all these extra workers had been brought in for at least two butcher shops. Jack would not like it, but if she did not do it someone else would. She wanted a better standard of life than living in a pit house for the rest of her days. She had saved up almost five hundred pounds now.

She still yearned for her piano, but she at least got pleasure from playing at the chapel. She played for weddings and funerals, and when she had time, the minister allowed her to play for her own pleasure. Jimmy would pump the organ when she played popular music or Beethoven whilst the minister sat in the pews listening. Sarah loved Chopin but it depended on her mood. If she could buy her own shop, the piano would have to wait a while. She could wait for a piano if she could sometimes play at the chapel.

Chapter 19

Spring 1922

O ne spring day 1922, Sarah was working in the shop when she saw her mam walking across the road toward her. *She looks lovely*, Sarah thought. *She is a really good-looking woman.*

Rosina had her shoulders back and had a purposeful look on her face. She was wearing the black felt hat trimmed with poppies that Len had bought for her all those years ago.

Sarah thought she must have been going somewhere special and ran outside. "Hello, mam," she said. "Where are you off to all dressed up?"

"Oh just into town. I can't stop to talk, Sarah. I have to catch the waggonette," Rosina said, rushing past Sarah.

Sarah liked seeing her mam going off to town. She looked happy.

Jimmy called for Sarah in the afternoon. Jack had given her a half-day off after she told him she had some business to see too. Jimmy and Sarah went to speak to the council officer who was in charge of building the new shops. After Sarah told him what she wanted, he laughed at her.

"Eh, lass, I can't let shops to the likes of you," the council officer said, patronisingly.

"And why not?" Sarah asked.

"Because a slip of a lass like you couldn't run a butcher shop on her own," he replied.

"She won't be on her own," Jimmy said. "I shall be with her."

"And what do you know about butchering, lad?" he asked.

"I know that I can do the job as well as Jack Grundy, if not better, and Sarah can do the make-up stuff. I can do the heavy work. We can start a delivery service to our customers, especially the ones who live outside the village."

"And what are you going to use for money, lad?" The official asked.

143

"We have money," Sarah said. "I have been saving for years. I have enough money to start this business and pay the rent for one year before we even take one penny from customers."

"And where did you get money from to save?"

"What do you mean?" Jimmy asked, angry now.

"I mean she must have been on the fiddle if she has that kind of money, 'cos you only work in blacksmith's shop at pit," he scoffed.

Jimmy grabbed the officer by the collar saying, "You take that back, or I will knock your head of your bloody shoulders."

Sarah pulled Jimmy away saying, "Come on, Jimmy. We will have to find some other way of getting the shop."

"Over my dead body!" the officer shouted after them, straightening his tie.

Sarah and Jimmy walked hand in hand back toward Osborne Street. Sarah wanted to find out what her mam had been up to earlier in the morning. As they turned the corner near to the butcher shop Sarah saw Alice and Kisaiya waiting for her outside the shop.

They ran to Sarah, both crying their eyes out. "What's up?" Jimmy asked Kisaiya.

"Me mam went out in her best hat with the poppies on and came back married," she wailed.

"What?' Sarah said.

"She did, Sarah!" Alice said. "She's at home with him now."

"Come on, I shall sort her out," Sarah said, and they marched along home, or what was supposed to be home.

They walked in to find a house full of people who Sarah had never seen in her life before. Rosina was worst for drink, sitting by the fire with an old man with a long moustache that curled up at the ends. He had hairs growing out of his nose, which made him look like a horse.

"Who is this?" Sarah asked.

"This is your new dad," Rosina said, laughing.

"He is not my dad," Kisaiya said, and Alice put her arm around her shoulders to comfort her.

"You had better be nice to him," Rosina said, "'cos we were married this morning, and he lives here now."

Sarah was stunned. "Well, Mam, this is the last straw! Why didn't you tell me this morning?"

"It was not your business!" Rosina shouted at her.

"You get married to a complete stranger, and it is not our business? This is our home. I pay the rent," Sarah said to Rosina. "Well, I can tell you this. I am never coming back to this house again as long as I live. He can pay for the rent and the beer."

Her new husband, Albert Edwards, laughed. "I don't want yer rent money, lass. You can find a fresh place to live 'cos I don't want trouble from thee or anybody else."

Sarah was disgusted. Jimmy stood motionless, watching this scene. He could not believe what he had just seen.

Sarah did not know what to do. She could not walk out on Kisaiya and Alice and leave them to this houseful of flotsam and jetsam.

Jimmy said, "Sarah, get your things. You are not stopping here."

"Jimmy, I am not leaving our Kisaiya. Alice can go and stay at the farm where she works, but our Kisaiya needs caring for," Sarah cried.

"Come on, let us go and find somewhere for you all to stay," Jimmy said.

When they got outside, the stunned children walked away, not knowing which way to go.

"I know," Sarah said, "Let us go and ask the minister if he knows of someone who will take us in."

"You can go back to the butcher shop, our Sarah!" Alice said. "You don't have to come we us."

"I am not leaving you anywhere until I make sure you are safe," Sarah said, putting her arm round Kisaiya who was so scared she could hardly breathe.

The minister was horrified to hear their story and took them into his very comfortable home where his wife gave them tea.

"I don't know what we can do about it," the minister kept repeating to himself, whilst walking up and down the kitchen where they were all sitting.

After some time Sarah realised he had no more idea of how to deal with the problem than she did. She said, "Well thanks for the tea, Minister. I think we had better be going now. It is getting dark, and we have to find somewhere to sleep tonight."

The minister, looking very embarrassed, said, "I am sure you will find a good-hearted family, Sarah. God, in his mercy, will guide."

Jimmy coughed and stood up grabbing Kisaiya by the arm. He walked out of the door failing to look back or thank the minister. He could not wait to get away from him. They walked the two miles to the farm where Alice had been working. Sarah said that she would only have one to worry about if Alice was safe.

Mrs. Mullet, the farmer's wife, came out red-faced, wanting to know where Alice had been all day. She should have been at the farm, helping with the milking. Sarah and Jimmy explained the situation to her, and when she realised that Jimmy was the pit manager's son, she took a different attitude toward Alice.

"Well your sister is safe here, Sarah," she assured her. "But what about the young one?"

"I am looking for somewhere for our Kisaiya, Mrs. Mullet. But she is only ten and not old enough to work," Sarah replied.

Mary Mullet looked at Kisaiya "Can you iron, lass?" she asked.

"Yes, Mrs. Mullet," Kisaiya said. "I am a good ironer. Me mam said so."

"What about school?" Mary Mullet asked.

"I go to school but I can still do your ironing for you," Kisaiya said.

Kisaiya did not like school. She had learned early in her life that she had to be tough to survive and had a reputation for sorting people out who crossed her. Rosina had beaten her so many times when she drank that she had become crafty, quick to dodge blows, and blame others when she was in trouble. Kisaiya would love to work at the farm and not have to go to school again.

"Ummm," Mary Mullet thought. "I think I'll give you a try. You will have to sleep with your sister 'cos I don't have a spare bed. You can stay here but the first sign of trouble and you're out," she said firmly.

"Oh thank you, Mrs. Mullet," Sarah said. "Are you sure you want to stay here, our Kisaiya? Will you be all right?" Sarah asked the girl.

"I will Sarah, I will," Kisaiya beamed.

As Jimmy and Sarah walked back to the village and the butcher shop, Jimmy asked, "Sarah, why don't we get married. We can have our own home, and Kisaiya and Alice can come whenever they want."

"I shall not get married just for a home, Jimmy," Sarah said.

"But I love you, Sarah. I want to see you every day of my life," Jimmy said fondly.

"I think I love you too, Jimmy. You are the best man I have ever known apart from my father, and I can only just remember him. But I know he wanted me to have a better life than living in a pit house. I know it, Jimmy." Sarah remembered the silver hunting horn and her father's promise that the land was theirs. She should never forget it.

The week after Rosina's marriage to old man Edwards, as the girls referred to him, Jack Grundy took Sarah to one side and said, "What's this I've been hearing about you wanting to start your own shop, Sarah?"

"Yes, Jack. That is what I intend to do," Sarah replied.

"I trusted you, Sarah. I never thought that would do the dirty on me like this," Jack said.

"I am not doing the dirty on you Jack. There is enough trade in this village for both of us to make a decent living," Sarah answered.

"You can't run a shop on your own, lass," Jack scoffed.

"I can do anything you can do, Jack. You forget I have been running this shop for the past two years. You have had very little to do with the running of the shop! I do all the made-up stuff with Tommy Bates. All you do is go to market and buy the meat. Tommy butchers it, and I deal with the customers. I also run your household or had you forgotten that? You have more days off than the king," Sarah said.

"Sarah, that's what I pay you for," Jack said angrily.

"You pay what I could get as a kitchen maid, Jack Grundy. So don't run away with the idea that you are overpaying me. Your life would change considerably if I walked out of that door, and you know it."

"Sarah, who do you think you are?" Jack bellowed at her.

"I am Sarah Bingham, the daughter of George Bingham, gentleman farmer and butcher. Who do you think you are, Jack Grundy, exploiting an educated woman so that you can have an easy life?" she said, pushing her shoulders back and holding her head high in indignation.

"By God, Sarah Bingham, that had better be it, 'cos I won't take this kind a talk from anybody, let alone a woman!" Jack was absolutely furious. He had never been spoken to in this way by anyone.

"Very well, Mr. Grundy, I will sort myself out. I shall leave right now. I mean to get that shop on the new High Street if it is the last thing I do!" She flounced out of the shop into the living room. Sarah went straight upstairs and began to pack her belongings.

When she came down with her bags, Jack and his wife were sitting in the living room waiting for her. Lily Grundy did not want to lose Sarah. She had been such a blessing to her. The children loved her. She was so gentle and had an attitude that Lily wished she could acquire, but Sarah, the daughter of gentry, evidently had it built-in. Everyone loved her. She helped people no matter what they were or how they spoke. She had taught their children to play music, sew, and paint pictures. No, she was not letting her go.

"But she wants her own shop, Lily," Jack Grundy said.

"Well you had better talk to her, Jack, 'cos I need her around."

"Sarah, sit down a minute, lass," Jack said.

"I shall not change my mind, Jack," Sarah said. "I shall not spend my life working for someone else."

"Well, how can you buy a shop, Sarah?" Jack asked.

"I have been saving since I started in Bingley when I was thirteen. My uncle gave me an allowance, and after I made clothes for Kisaiya and Alice, I saved the rest in the Trustees Savings Bank," Sarah said proudly.

Jack looked at Lily.

"I don't want to lose you, Sarah," Lily said.

"I don't want to lose you, Lily," Sarah replied. "But I have to move on some time."

"Yes, lass, that you do." Jack was panicking now. When old Robbo from the council had told him about Sarah trying to get lease on a new shop, Jack had laughed with him. But now that Jack could see she was capable of doing it, he began to worry.

"Jack, you'd better do something 'cos I don't want her to go," Lily cried.

"Sarah," Jack said quietly and uncomfortably. "What if I buy the shop, and you manage it?"

"You must think I am stupid, Jack. That is another way of you exploiting me," Sarah said.

"My God, Sarah, you're a damn stubborn woman," Jack said. "Well, what if I buy the shop and you pay me the rent. You buy the meat from me and keep the profits," Jack offered.

"What!" Sarah said. "Why would you do that?"

"Because if you decide you want to wed, I have got the shop. I will buy more cattle from the farmers, and will have more bargaining power. You will profit from my buying skills, and I can slaughter at the back of the shop, saving money again." Jack was excited now that he could see this working.

Sarah thought about this. "Jack, I shall think about it. I need to work it out," she said.

"Well, Sarah," Lily said. "Take your clothes back upstairs while I make a drink. We had better get that shop open again before we lose all the customers we have."

Sarah met Jimmy that night, and they talked about Jack's offer. Jimmy had the idea that he would be able to be a butcher if Sarah got the shop. Sarah knew this could not happen as he had no idea how to kill a pig or butcher a side of beef. In fact, Jimmy did not realise the amount of work involved in butchering the meat that he ate. Actually, Sarah had had moments of apprehension when Jimmy took time off work for silly reasons. She put it down to the fact that he had lived a charmed life with his father being the pit manager. They had always had plenty.

Jimmy Wiseman, Sr. was a womaniser. He had women throwing themselves at his feet. Women seemed to believe him when he told them they were the most beautiful creatures he had ever seen. He had a motorcar, which was one of only three in the whole of the village. The manager of the pit, owning a motorcar, and handsome and free with his money—the world was his oyster. His wife, Elisa, was a beauty, but she had born him nine children, the eldest being young Jimmy. Poor Elisa stayed home, caring for her children. Jimmy had his father's grin. But she hoped he would not have his father's ways because the poor lass that got him would rue the day.

Sarah built up the new shop and with the help of Tommy, who Jack Grundy had sent to help with the boning out and the heavy stuff, the shop turned out to be very promising indeed.

Chapter 20

Sarah and Jimmy marry, 1923

Jimmy pestered Sarah to make marriage plans, but Sarah was not so sure she was ready.

On most Sunday mornings, Sarah and Jimmy went out walking. Sarah wore a pale blue Georgette dress and a white stiff-organza wide-brimmed hat trimmed with forget-me-knots. Jimmy was proud when people saw him out walking with Sarah. She was by far the best-looking woman in Halten, and her reputation was spotless, which was quite something coming from a background like the pit village. They decided to wed on Christmas Eve 1923.

"Christmas Eve is when my father married my mother," Sarah said dreamily. Sarah told her mam.

Rosina scoffed and said, "I hope he is not like his father or you will be in for a boatload of trouble."

Alice and Kisaiya were going to be bridesmaids. Sarah asked Jimmy's mother if Jimmy's sisters would like to be bride's maids too. Elisa asked them excitedly when they came home from work.

"What!" Jane, the eldest girl, replied. "Make a spectacle of myself with that riffraff? Never!"

But Ellen and Annie said they would love to be bridesmaids. Sarah bought the material and sewed their dresses. Kisaiya and Alice were in very pale blue, and Ellen and Annie in a very pale yellow with Sarah in a sax blue calf-length. They all wore cloche hats, which Sarah made from the same material. She sewed swatches of the sax blue silk for her own dress. It fell from her waist to her calf with embroidered seed pearls in a very delicate design. Her fashionable cloche hat was made from the same coloured silk, stiffened to hold its shape and trimmed with hand-made flowers. Unfortunately, fresh flowers were out of season. She would have loved to use them.

Jimmy was measured for a suit and bowler hat.

"Boy does he look smart!" His brother, Horace, was to be best man and his brothers, Jack, William, and Harry were ushers. He had the keys to a new house on Devonshire Street in the Woodlands, a new area being built for the miners away from the pit village.

Sarah had not needed to use any of her savings now that Jack had financed the shop, and spent some of her money on new furniture of the finest quality. The front room had a rust coloured three-piece suite, a carpet covered in autumn leaves, and a walnut veneered cabinet with a glass front, complete with a full china dinner and tea service. In the front room stood her finest possession, an ebony piano with candlesticks in solid silver. The bedroom had a full suite of furniture comprised of a bed, armoire, dressing table with three mirrors, and a tall boy, all in Rose walnut veneer. The floor was covered in a sumptuous carpet in crushed strawberry colour. The kitchen had a gas cooker, gas washing machine, and the house had an inside toilet with bathroom. The coal range in the kitchen also heated a tank at the back of the fire, which kept the house serviced with hot water on tap, unlike from a tank beside the fire which needed a ladle to carry hot water to the kitchen.

The only lighting available was gas lighting, but the housing agent told them that there was a new thing called electricity which was going to be put into the houses as soon as they could manage it. Then you could have light by flicking a switch. Alice and Kisaiya thought this was absolute luxury.

The wedding was a big event in the 16th century church. Sarah had not been back to the chapel after the minister refused to help her when her mam remarried. To make the day complete for Sarah, William had agreed to be there to give her away. She had been sending messages with gypsies and travelling people for almost a year, but when he turned up the day before Christmas Eve, she was delighted.

It was a magical time for Sarah and Jimmy. They had a beautiful home, good jobs, and Sarah still had a little money left in the bank.

Jimmy was learning to play the piano.

"He is very good," Sarah said. "Although he vamps his left hand rather than learn the correct notes." This irritated Sarah, who was a perfectionist when it came to music.

Jimmy soon learned how to read music, but he did not have a lot of patience when it came to practising. He bought a radiogram, which cost a fortune, and Sarah was shocked at such extravagance until she heard the music. Each week they bought a new record. Jimmy copied the records, especially Charlie Kunes piano music after seeing a film with Charlie Kunes playing piano in a restaurant. Jimmy had remembered all the hand movements, and played tunes over and over, crossing his hands over from left to right just as Charlie Kunes had. Sarah hated this type of music. She had been taught classical music and thought that this was a lazy way to play the piano.

Jimmy also joined the male voice choir, which the miners had started at the Institute. His dad had asked all his sons to join and support the efforts of the new music committee. Jimmy, Sr. had sung a solo at their first concert, and everyone said how much they had enjoyed it, so Jimmy, Jr. had become a singer to please his dad.

1924 was a year they would remember for the rest of their lives.

In early March, Sarah discovered she was pregnant. Jimmy was over the moon. Sarah was a little worried about not being able to work. She wondered how they would manage on Jimmy's pay.

Jimmy said, "I can keep my own family, Sarah. I do not need a woman to work for me. Now do not mention it again and make sure you tell Jack straightaway."

Sarah thought this is what Jack figured would happen. She wished she had had a little more time to settle down to her new life with Jimmy. But she also dreamed about her new baby and how happy they would be when it arrived.

Jack Grundy was sorry to lose Sarah, and he and Lily became regular visitors to Devonshire Street after she left the shop. Lily Grundy gave Sarah a pram, which must have cost a fortune, and Jack had gone mad when she bought it, but Lily had said. "I can't push that old pram around any longer Jack." Jack was quite happy for the new pram to go to Sarah.

Sarah bought the cot, and the layette was stitched and prepared lovingly. Jimmy was as good as his word. He worked every shift, and some overtime, after she left the shop.

Kenneth James was born in October 1924. Jimmy was thrilled to have a son.

Jimmy, Sr. took his son out and bought him a pint and sent Sarah a crisp white five pound note to buy the little chap something. Kisaiya came to look after Sarah while she was lying in. She loved it at Sarah's house. She had her own room, and Jimmy was so funny, making her laugh all the time.

Rosina came to visit. Sarah did not have a lot of time for her mother since her marriage to Edwards. Jimmy said he thought she had married him so she would not have to give up the house. That was what his dad had said, but Sarah did not know.

Rosina looked at the child without saying anything for a long time. Then, looking at Sarah with tears in her eyes, she said "Your father would be so proud of him, Sarah."

This made Sarah cry for hours. Her mam never talked about her dad, and when she asked questions about him she shouted at her to shut up. Then Mam turned up at a time like this and cried for her dad. Sarah was upset for days. She could never work her mother out. Never!

William and Fluere were in Doncaster when they got Sarah's letter about her baby being due in October. Sarah regularly sent letters to an address that they called at when they were in Doncaster. On their way to Nottingham for the Goose Fair, they called at Sarah's house to see the baby. Kisaiya asked Fluere to read her hand, but Sarah would not listen to any of Fluere's predictions.

She said, "It is not right, I do not believe in it."

Fluere told Kisaiya that she would live in a house like Sarah's one day in a few years time. In fact, this is your house, Kisaiya.

Kisaiya was delighted. "But where will our Sarah be going?" she asked, a bit worried.

"Sarah will have somewhere else to live," Fluere prophesied. "A new house. But it will be her last home, and she will live there for many years."

Christmas 1924 was wonderful. Kisaiya and Alice stayed over, and they all looked after the baby like little girls do when they have their first dolls.

Chapter 21

1925

In early 1925, the men at the pit started to strike. They had a union now that was trying to get them more pay and better conditions.

Jimmy, Sr. left the Halten mine and got a job at a new mine close by. He told his son to watch out or he would lose his job. Jimmy only worked three days during most weeks and was always at meetings. He worked less and less as the year went on.

The workers hoped to bring down the current government and vote in a Labour government that would look after the workers. Sarah just hoped they would sort it out. Her savings were almost gone. In 1926 there was a general strike.

"This is the last push," Jimmy said.

All Sarah could see was that she had no savings left and now Jimmy had no wages either. "How do we eat, Jimmy?" she pleaded with him.

"Like everybody else, Sarah. We are all in the same boat," Jimmy replied.

"You mean we should beg food from the soup kitchen," Sarah said angrily. "I would rather starve."

"Well, that is up to you, Sarah, but we have stick to together or we are finished," Jimmy said angrily.

"That does not help, Jimmy. I need some money for food for the baby."

"Sell something. There is enough to sell," he said, walking out and banging the door behind him.

Sarah looked around the room. *What can I sell and who could afford to buy it,* she thought?

Lily came to visit, bringing scraps for her. "What are you going to do, Sarah?" Lily asked.

"I don't know, Lily. I could sell something but who has the money to buy it?" Sarah asked sadly.

"Um," Lily said. "What about the piano? You know how I always wanted a piano?" Sarah's heart sank. "Not the piano Lily. I could not."

"I will have a talk to Jack and see what else I can buy."

"Thanks, Lily. You are a good friend," Sarah said.

The next day Jack turned up in his horse and cart.

"Hello, Jack, what are you doing round here?" Sarah asked. "Have you come for the piano?"

"No lass, I know you don't want to part with the piano but I thought of something if you're willing."

"What is that, Jack? What do you want?" Sarah asked.

"Come back to work for a while. Lily will take care of the baby, and it will save you selling something," Jack said.

"I will have to ask Jimmy," Sarah said. "But I can't see why not. Thank you so much, Jack."

Sarah went back to work, and Jimmy went on the picket lines. His father had warned him about getting involved.

Jimmy, Sr. had said. "I can't help you if you make a fool of yourself. Mark my words. Hell will freeze over before they give them what they want!"

The strike did not affect Sarah and Jimmy badly because Sarah was capable of working and supplementing the family income.

In early 1927, Sarah was pregnant again but tried hard to continue working. Jimmy was back at work at the pit. He had developed a skill for cutting men's hair. During the strike, he had cut the strikers hair for nothing, but now he was charging sixpence and all his weekends were taken up barbering.

Sarah worked until she was seven months gone. She wanted to replace the savings that she had spent during the strike, but with Jimmy taking time off for every reason he could think of, she found it difficult to pay the bills with what she earned. Jimmy hated the pit, and Sarah understood his reluctance to get up and go. But unless he could think of some other way of providing a living for them, he would have to do just that.

The baby was born in September, a beautiful baby girl. Kenneth loved his baby sister, and Jimmy was over the moon. They named her Jean. Jean was as fair as Kenneth was dark. They were a handsome family. Jimmy began to work regularly, and life returned to the happy state they had enjoyed before the strike.

When Jean was eighteen-months-old, Sarah had another child. Lorna, born on St. Valentines Day, was a perfect child who never cried, slept through the night, and cooed and gurgled all day long. She was a delight.

Jimmy began to slip back to his old ways of working only three days a week. He did not drink or gamble, as did most of the other pitmen, but he hated the pit.

Sarah had used all her savings now. Three children needed so much care and attention. She intended to teach them all to play the piano and started to teach them music at an early age. Kenneth and Jean loved to sing in the evenings just before bedtime. Jean would stand on a chair and look out of the window she loved the moon. I Love the Moon. I Love Stars" was a popular song she had heard on the wireless, which stood in the corner of the living room. The house was always full of music, and the children responded to music whenever they heard it.

"They are such happy children," Lily said to Sarah after one of her many visits to Devonshire Street.

Jean knew all the words to the song, and to Sarah's delight, she would twirl and swish out her skirt, dancing and singing. Lorna giggled and tried to sing like her sister, and Kenneth marched up and down waiving a stick in time to the music.

One day, Jimmy brought home a puppy, and the children loved him. They named him Jackpot. Jackpot became a part of the family. He guarded the children faithfully, following them every time they ventured outside.

In late October 1930, Lorna went to bed as usual but was very fretful all night. Sarah was concerned. She asked Jimmy to ring the doctor's surgery and ask the doctor to come and take a look at her. She was so hot and feverish. It was later the next day when the doctor arrived. He told Sarah to give her some Fennings fever cure, and she would be fine by morning.

As the night got darker, Lorna became very ill indeed. Sarah was distraught. She had never seen a child sick like this before. Jimmy ran to the doctor's surgery banging on the door, shouting to wake up the doctor who was known to like his drink of an evening and would probably be sleeping it off.

When the doctor saw Lorna, he said, "This child is very ill, Mrs. Wiseman. She needs oxygen." He wrote a note for Jimmy to take to the pit top and ask for a cylinder of oxygen and to be quick about it.

Jimmy ran all the way to the pit, which was probably two miles. He could not speak when he arrived at the pit top. He passed the note to the man on duty and bent over trying to get his breath before he starting back with the heavy bottle.

The doctor was looking grave when Jimmy arrived with the oxygen. They ran upstairs to the room where Lorna was fighting for breath with Sarah desperately trying to comfort the child.

Alice and Kisaiya were in tears downstairs in the kitchen. Kisaiya said. "Look at that dog, Alice, it seems to know that something's wrong. He won't move from the bottom of the garden. He won't eat or drink. He just sits there howling."

Alice shuddered, saying, "It makes me go cold, Kisaiya, just looking at him."

Jimmy came down stairs in a terrible state and ran for the door.

The doctor ran after him, shouting, "It's no use Jimmy. It's too late."

Jimmy fell in a heap on the floor saying, "Oh God, it's empty. Why didn't I check it? I was just trying to get back as fast as I could."

"I know, Jimmy, but it would not have helped. She was too far gone, lad. I think it is meningitis, and there's no cure for that, Jimmy. None at all," the doctor said.

Kisaiya began to cry. Alice was trying to be strong, but her lips shivered as if she were out in the snow without a coat.

Sarah refused to leave Lorna all night long. She had been in a coma for six hours now and still Sarah talked to her and cuddled her, singing nursery songs. She did not seem to understand what the doctor had said.

"Lorna is dying, Sarah. There's nothing I can do. She has meningitis," the doctor told her.

The poor child died suffering great pain in the early hours of the next morning. The neighbours, who would not go near the house for fear of their child being next, could hear Sarah's cries. Jimmy's dad offered them the grave, which he had bought for his daughter, Margery, who had died after being scalded two years previous. In payment, he took the piano. Sarah never forgave him for profiteering on the death of his own granddaughter.

The dog sat in the garden for days after Lorna's death. Nobody noticed if he ate anything or not, except Kenneth, who was six-years-old now. Kenneth took to caring for the dog. He sat with him and told him his secrets. But he never mentioned Lorna or why his mam and dad were crying all the time.

Everyone missed Lorna. She had been such a happy child. Sarah's heart was broken, but she had to make a face and get on with things. She thought she was expecting again. The doctor thought perhaps she was suffering the shock of losing Lorna, but Sarah knew better. Six weeks after Lorna's death was Jean's birthday. Sarah had made a beautiful white dress and bought her a straw bonnet with daisies around the rim. Jean loved the Marguerites that grew in the front garden. After they picked a bunch they took them to the cemetery for Lorna.

Later when they arrived home, Jean stood at the kitchen table with Sarah holding her hands and they sang out, "I Love the Moon. I love the stars," with Jean twirling to cause her skirt to swish out. *She looks like an angel.* Sarah thought, thinking of her other dear beautiful little girl, buried in the ground.

Jean would not eat her dinner. Sarah thought she was just excited on her birthday. She did not eat her cake, and after the party, lay down on the settee. She was vomiting. Oh my god Sarah's heart dropped to her feet. Jean had meningitis. She knew it!

Mrs Worthington, the lady next door, ran for the doctor who came to the house quickly this time. Sarah would not speak to him because she knew what it was. The doctor left and sent an ambulance to collect Jean. They would not let Sarah into the ambulance. She protested, but the driver said he was not allowed to let anyone in a fever ambulance. Sarah had to catch the trackless bus, which had replaced the waggonette. It took forever. She arrived at the hospital and was ushered away from the patients who were infectious and into a corridor where she could hear Jean screaming for her mam.

"Please! Please! For God's sake, let me go to her," Sarah pleaded.

"Rules have to be kept, Mrs. Wiseman." The big strong nurse told her not to make a fuss. "We have more to do than comfort you, Mrs Wiseman. Go home and look after your other child. We will look after this one."

Sarah tried everything she could think of to get inside the room where she could hear her suffering child, but the strong woman was not going to give in.

Jimmy arrived, and on the insistence of the big woman, he took Sarah home on the trackless bus. Sarah sat rigidly, staring into space all the way home. The bus had wooden seats and rattled along slowly and very uncomfortably.

When they arrived at Devonshire Street, Kisaiya was there with Alice. Both looked after Kenneth.

"Kisaiya, take that child out of here," Sarah said. "This is a house of death. Take Kenneth with you and scrub him in carbolic. Do not bring him back until we know that it is gone."

After Kisaiya had gone, a knock came on the door.

"Mrs. Wiseman?" The policeman asked.

"No! No! No!" Sarah screamed.

Jimmy asked the policeman in, and he told Jimmy that Jean had died just after he and Sarah had left the hospital.

Sarah blamed herself for Jean's death. "The cemetery, that is where she got it," she shouted at Jimmy. "I took her to the cemetery for her birthday. It should have been me not her. I hope I am next. Do not bring Kenneth back here, Jimmy, ever! You hear? Never!"

The doctor came and asked if they would allow a post-mortem on Jean. Sarah screamed.

"Have you no feelings, man?" Jimmy shouted at him. "We have just lost two children. How can you ask such a thing?"

"I am so sorry, Jimmy," the doctor said, sitting down dejectedly. "I can only imagine your sorrow. But we need to find a cure for this terrible disease. We know very little about it, and until we find how it attacks the brain so quickly, we will lose more children. Please let us try to stop any more children from dying in this way."

Sarah thought about Kenneth. "If I agree, what will you do to her?" she asked.

"We are interested in how it has damaged her brain, Mrs. Wiseman," the doctor said. "We need to take a look and test her blood."

Sarah was in torment. She thought she had caused Jean's death and did not want to cause Kenneth's death by not allowing this terrible thing to be stopped. "How will I know it is Jean in the coffin?" she asked, looking at the doctor with the saddest eyes he had ever seen.

"I will pay for a glass top to little Jean's coffin, Mrs. Wiseman," he answered. "You can then see her for the last time. You would not be allowed to have her coffin at home because of the fear of infection, and without a glass top, you would never know whether she was in it or not."

Jimmy put his arm around Sarah's shoulders, saying, "I think we should let them do it, Sarah love. We do not want to lose Ken and all."

After a long bout of sobbing Sarah agreed.

Chapter 22

1931

S arah went into a deep depression lasting for some years after the deaths of her girls. She refused to leave her room. She thought that if she died now this terrible pain would go away. She would never have to wake to another day to realise the horror of reality. Both her beautiful little girls were in the cemetery and they should be here with her. Why oh why didn't God take her? Sarah eventually came to the conclusion that God did not exist. He was just a figment of her imagination and the concept of a greater being had been used over the years to control and manipulate people. She would not allow the local vicar or anyone spouting religion into the house.

Sarah's pregnancy progressed with Sarah denying the presence of this new child soon to born. When Amelia was born in May of 1931, she was a beautiful child. Poor Sarah wanted to die so much she would not nurture another child just to lose her. She ignored the baby. Kisaiya gave Amelia all the attention that her mother should have been giving during the first two years of her life.

Jimmy loved little Amelia so much. She looked so much like him. He loved to take her out and became very angry with Sarah. He bought a second-hand piano, trying to make life more bearable for her, but she had nothing left to give. She did not want to live. What was the use of trying when death took her children, creating such agony? She would not speak about it to anyone. The wireless must not be played, and the house was like a morgue, so different to the home they had before the deaths of her girls.

Jimmy thought, *Poor Amelia has been born into a house of misery*. She would sit at the piano trying to make a tune with her little fingers, moving them along the keys in the way she had watched her dad's fingers play the notes. Sarah would get very angry and close the piano lid down roughly, dragging Amelia from the stool and telling her to go and find her brother.

Kenneth had begun to take an interest in sport and objected to taking his baby sister tagging along everywhere he went. Jackpot followed Kenneth around even to school. The dog would sit outside the school gate, waiting faithfully for the children to come running out.

Auntie Kisaiya moved into the house on Devonshire Street with her new husband, Eddie Fitzgerald, an Irish migrant worker whose family had bought a small plot of land in Halten to rear pigs.

Kisaiya looked after Amelia and ran the household. She had taken to religion in a big way after having instruction at the Catholic Church before she could wed Eddie. Sarah would not listen to Kisaiya and Eddie when they tried to convince her that there was life after death.

"Why bring the children into the world just too cruelly put them through such agony," Sarah screamed at them.

Eddie was losing his temper with Kisaiya who would not leave her sister and her family to go and live with Eddie's family. Jimmy could not bear to see his wife in such distress and spent much of his time out of the house. He was not a drinker, but Sarah had taught him to play the piano, and he loved every minute he spent practising music. He played in the brass band and sang in the local male voice choir. Anything, rather than stay home in the misery of that house.

Alice had married Arthur Brody in 1926 when the pit was out on strike. Rosina grumbled but did offer them lodgings in Osborne Street. Alice and her husband lived with Rosina for a short while. Rosina and Edward's soon moved to Doncaster where he took a job on the railways. This left Alice and Arthur in the house, Arthur being a regular hardworking miner had earned the right to a good house, and Alice was overjoyed in her own home. She had a child every year and she was the happiest woman you could ever meet. Her husband worked hard, and he and Alice always went out together dancing and drinking.

In 1936, Kisaiya and her husband were given a newly built council house in a lovely woodland area of Halten. They decided to ask Sarah if she would like to take the house, and Kisaiya would stay in Devonshire Street. This meant that Sarah would be away from the nightmares of memories, but could come back and walk through the garden when she felt the need to remember her beautiful girls.

After some strong words from Jimmy who had had enough of this misery day after day, Sarah agreed to the move. Little Amelia was over joyed and carefully packed her few meagre belongings in an old wooden box, which she had been using as a dressing table. Kenneth liked the idea of moving to the woodlands because the house backed onto open fields with a large wooded area that was going to be great for Jackpot and him to explore.

Moving day arrived, and Sarah tried hard to cover her feelings of despair. Her troubled mind told her that Jean and Lorna would be left behind if she moved away, and she could not bare the thought of them roaming around, looking for their mam. Kisaiya and Jimmy persuaded her that because Auntie Kisaiya was staying there, they would just follow Kisaiya when she came to the Woodlands.

Eventually they moved the furniture with poor Sarah sobbing and crying at the sight of every item connected to the lost girls—the wireless set and the gramophone, Jean's little bed, which was Amelia's little bed but Sarah saw only Jean sleeping in there. Each item brought floods of tears and the whole experience was a nightmare.

Jimmy, with the help of Eddie and Kisaiya, patiently little by little cajoled Sarah out of the Devonshire Street house and into the Woodlands.

The new house had electricity upstairs and down but Sarah would not use it upstairs. She thought the children might be harmed by this new-fangled idea. When she went to bed she would light a small gas burner, which was minus its mantle and had only been fitted as a secondary lighting system. Electric lighting was the latest technology in Halten, and the miners and their wives were not too happy about this unknown phenomenon.

One night Sarah was lying awake in the darkness with just a flicker from the gas pipe, which was protruding from the wall. She had not wanted to sleep in the dark since the death of the girls. She imagined that she saw Jean and Lorna in a scene on the wall next to the gas light. Perhaps it was in her imagination, but Jean and Lorna were laughing and playing together with her father, George Bingham. He had baby Lorna in his arms, and they were playing in Beckett's Wood. Jean was dangling her feet in the beck, and they all looked so happy. Sarah jumped up from the bed and ran over to the picture it seemed so real she thought she could touch the girls. She called out, "Daddy, Daddy, it is me, Sarah. I am here, look."

Jimmy woke startled at the noise Sarah was making. He sat up and his heart sank when he saw Sarah clutching at the curtains and smiling happily at something above the window. He jumped out of bed and put his arms around Sarah's shoulders. He tried to get her to get back into bed. Sarah protested and struggled. She wanted to get back to the window. Jimmy could take no more of this. He crumpled into a heap on the bedroom floor and sobbed uncontrollably. She was talking to someone and laughing. Jimmy thought she had lost her mind. What was he to do? Kenneth came into the room, and seeing his dad on the floor and his mam talking to the wall, he was scared stiff. He ran into Amelia's room and snuggled down beside the sleeping child and covering his head with the blankets to block it all out.

The next day Jimmy went to see the doctor and told him the sad tale of Sarah's decline.

"Jimmy me, lad." The doctor laughed. "Sarah is suffering grief of the first order. She will only improve in her own time. Everyone takes his own time and comes to terms in his own way. I know it's hard for you, lad, but she needs you more now than she ever did. Stick with her, Jimmy. She will come round. For what it's worth, I think she has hit bottom. We might see some improvement from now on. Go home and just love her, Jimmy. That's all she needs."

Sarah began to improve dramatically after she moved to Woodland Park, and the picture of her father playing at Lambecote Grange with the girls stayed with her forever. She began to play the piano again, teaching little Amelia. For the first time since the death of her beautiful little girls, she began to feel happy sometimes. She never told anyone about believing that she had seen her father playing happily with her children in Beckett's Wood. That was her salvation, and she would not share it with anyone. People may have thought she was losing her mind, but that was not true. She was just regaining her life.

Amelia's life improved when Sarah began her recovery. Her mam danced with her and taught how to play "The Rose of Tralee" on the piano. Little Amelia practiced for hours, her little face was a joy to watch when she had successfully struggled through the piece with no mistakes. Sarah would praise her and told everyone who visited how well she could play the piano.

Sarah would not allow Amelia or Kenneth to go with her when she visited the cemetery. She had this terrible notion that she had caused the death of Jean when she took her to put flowers on her sister's grave.

Jimmy thought life had been split into two—before the girls' deaths and after the girls' deaths. He had been working at the coal face for some time now. This was the hardest job in the pit, and he was always looking for ways of earning money without having go down the dreaded pit. He began to cut hair again and would spend most weekends in a shed in the garden at Woodland Park cutting hair. He charged a shilling now. After all, men were working and earning. He could still beat the local barber on price, and would cut hair at any time day or night. When the miners spent long shifts in the pit, they needed to get a hair cut between shifts. Jimmy was sought after for his skills in barbering, and on weekends, he could also earn ten bob playing piano at the local pub. Sarah would not hear of him leaving the pit but she wished he would get a job on the pit top where he would be safer.

One afternoon shift, Jimmy was cutting hair in the pit bottom whilst waiting for the paddy train to take them men back to the shaft. There was a shout from the lookouts, and Jimmy promptly put his shears and scissors into his snap tin and stood in line with the other men.

The over man obviously knew what had been going on and would not let the men leave the pit until the culprit had owned up to cutting hair in the mine owner's time. After all, the floor was covered in freshly cut hair. "How did that get here?" he shouted. "Did the rats start up their own barbershop?"

Jimmy owned up. It was what he had been wanting to do for a long time. He hated the pit. He could spend more time cutting hair at home and get more piano playing jobs. This was favourable to going down the hole day after day. The shed in the garden at Woodland Park was busy all day and every day. Sarah began to bake pork pies and sell them to the waiting line of miners.

One day they were visited buy the housing officer who told Jimmy that he was contravening the terms of his lease by running a business from the garden, and if he was found cutting hair on the premises again, he would have no alternative but to evict the family from the council house. Jimmy agreed that he would never cut hair there again. Later, he was to learn that the local barber had tipped off the coalmine owner and the council about Jimmy cutting hair, taking his trade.

Sarah was positive she could go to the council and get a shop with living accommodation. That would solve their problem.

The council agreed to put Jimmy on their waiting list for a shop with living accommodation, if possible, but only after Jimmy, Sr. pulled a few strings with his buddies.

Kenneth was an excellent cricketer, and Jimmy, Jr. with Jimmy, Sr. took great pride in following his progress. Kenneth adored his mother.

He took on a paper round when his dad lost his job at the mine. But even after doubling his round he could not provide enough money to pay the outgoings at Woodlands Park. Sarah began to get depressed again.

Jimmy Wiseman, Sr. was killed in the mine in 1937, crushed by a rock fall. He had been called out one Saturday morning to check out a broken pit prop when the whole area caved in.

The miners dug for a week to recover his body which Jimmy, Jr. identified from his fathers gold watch and chain. The watch was badly squashed but Jimmy Wiseman's name was still clear on the inscription added when he was presented with it after record tonnage of coal had been brought out of the new mine in Halten.

War was threatening again, and Jimmy's youngest brother, Harry, joined the Army in 1938. Harry was a boxer in his leisure time and often represented England. Elisa, his mother, had his cups and trophies displayed in a glass cabinet in the lounge. Every week, she polished them with pride. After her husband's death, she doted on her youngest child, Harry. When he joined the army, she was devastated, but thought it would be preferable to going down the pit. Her thoughts were the opposite of most of the other parents in Halten who preferred their sons to be in the pit rather than fighting a future war. But poor Eliza Wiseman had just waited for a week for her husband's squashed body to be dug out of the black hole, and she certainly did not want to lose her youngest son in the same way.

Jimmy pestered the council for a shop but the threat of war was halting all investment in the future.

"We have had to stop all our plans for building, Jimmy lad," the council officer told him when Jimmy begged him for a chance to start a shop. "You're lucky you're too old to get called up 'cos that what's coming next. You mark my words."

Jimmy was despondent, he had taken to travelling with the brass band since he had lost his job, and these weekends away were getting more and more frequent. Sarah was having a hard time making ends meet.

Kisaiya and Eddie had taken stewardship of the local Catholic Club with Eddie still working on the pit bottom. Kisaiya learned the art of changing barrels and general care of beer. The pitmen worked hard and drank hard and knew a good pint of beer when they drank it. Kisaiya worked all hours at the club. She had given birth to two daughters in the first two years of her marriage to Eddie and they still lived in the house at Devonshire Street. Molly and Peggy, Kisaiya's daughters, looked after the house while their mam worked at the club, and Sarah kept an eye on them each day. Kisaiya paid Sarah a few shillings a week, which helped her make ends meet. But life was not easy.

One night, Amelia woke up to hear her mam sobbing downstairs. She crept downstairs and found her mam and Kenneth sitting in front of an empty grate, Kenneth was telling her mam he would kill his dad if he had his way, but Sarah was sobbing and pleading with him not say a word to Dad when he came home. She would deal with it in her own way.

Life was very quiet and miserable in the Woodlands. Sarah had her suspicions regarding Jimmy's weekends away with the band, but she was so tired and worried about the war, which every one said would start soon with Hitler causing trouble in Germany again, she just struggled through each day hoping that Kenneth would not be called up. She decided to go to the pit and try to get him a job as an apprentice fitter. She dressed in her best clothes and walked to the pit office where Jimmy's brother, Horace, was chief engineer. Sarah pleaded with Horace, and Kenneth was taken on as an apprentice fitter. This meant he would not be called up if there was a war. Sarah could breathe again.

Late 1938, Sarah was pregnant again and was not happy about it. She thought she would spend the rest of her life-producing babies to worry about. She discovered by accident that the band had never left Halten when Jimmy had supposedly been with the band on a weekend trip. One of the band members told Sarah that Jimmy was meeting a woman who lived in Manchester, which was at least fifty miles from Halten.

Sarah went home and made her decision. She would go and find this woman and confront her with this information. If Jimmy was innocent, then she would apologize to him. But if he was guilty, he would have to leave. She had had enough.

Travelling by tram and train, she found the address given to her by the band member and knocked on the door. It was opened by an elderly woman. When asked if she knew Jimmy Wiseman, she replied, "Yes, me duck, he is engaged to me daughter."

Sarah was eight and a half months pregnant, and the journey and the stress were too much for her. She passed out on the doorstep of this strange woman. An ambulance was called, and Sarah was promptly taken into the local hospital were her condition was assessed. After a night under observation, she was discharged to have her baby at home as planned. Jimmy had to pay for transport to bring Sarah back to Halten and life took on a very unhappy turn. Poor Sarah was heart-broken. She almost lost the will to live during this dark time.

Rosina came to visit the Woodlands when she heard of Jimmy's misdemeanour, and poor Jimmy was subject to Rosina's wrath. She cooked a meal for him after telling Sarah to go to bed for the afternoon and rest. Sarah was only too pleased for someone to take over the family for a short time. Jimmy sat down to his dinner, and Rosina sat opposite him, her elbows firmly on the table. Her hard eyes, which had at one time been so beautiful and soft, never blinked. He was sure she had poisoned the food, but dared not suggest that he did not want to eat it. The way Rosina was staring at him, he thought he might get a knife in his back if he objected to anything. He thought about trying to apologise but was to scared to do anything but eat the dinner in front of her.

The food was foul. Rosina had poured a whole box of pepper in it and sat, never flinching, to watch Jimmy eat the dreadfully disgusting food on his plate. Amelia watched her grandmother and wished her mam would get up because she was scared of this nasty woman who was making her dad eat his dinner.

When he had finished the food, Rosina laughed and pushed her face straight up to Jimmy's nose and said, "Let that be a lesson to you, Jimmy Wiseman. Any more of your shenanigans and you are in for the high jump. Like father like son—that is what I think."

Jimmy thought it best not to tell Sarah about her mother's dinner and hoped the episode was over and done with.

Chapter 23

1939 World War 2

Amelia stayed at Auntie Kisaiya's because her mother had been really bad the night before, and her dad had fetched the doctor out.

She was skipping down Woodland Park on her way back home when Mrs. Allan, a neighbour, shouted to her. "Hey, Amelia, you've got a baby sister."

Amelia could not believe it. How could she have a sister? Her sisters were dead. Her mam had told her that. She ran to her house to see a strange woman, washing in the kitchen."

"Where's me mam?" Amelia shouted to the woman.

"Come with me I have a surprise for you," the nice woman said, taking her hand and pulling her up the staircase and into Sarah's bedroom. Kenneth sat holding what looked like a doll wrapped up in a blanket.

Sarah held out her arms to Amelia saying, "Come here and look at your sister, Amelia."

Amelia backed away. She did not want to look at her sister. Her sister was dead.

"Do not be scared," Sarah said. "She was born in the night.'

"Mam, I thought you said my sister was dead. How did she get alive?"

Sarah, with tears in her eyes, said, "This is another sister, Amelia. God sent my two little girls back—first you and now Frances. Come and say hello to Frances."

Amelia slowly walked over to the baby who had lots of black hair and rosy red cheeks. "Hello, baby sister," she said. "I am glad you have come."

Frances was born into a household of misery and arguing. If she did not have Amelia to spend time with her, she would have been very miserable. But her character was showing from that first day.

Sarah said she came out saying, "Hey, here I am. Look at me. I can do it. Just watch me."

On September 3, 1939, war was declared with Germany, but war had already been declared in the Wiseman house for some time. Harry Wiseman died in November 1939. He was one of the first casualties of the war. Jimmy's mother became senile after the deaths of her husband and her son in such a short time. Sarah took his mother to live with her in Woodland Park after she had been passed around the whole Wiseman family until she had no money left. She was very seriously disturbed.

Jimmy came home one day and announced that he had joined the RAF. He professed to be so enraged with the Germans for killing his brother that he wanted to do his bit for the war effort. When Jimmy joined up, he was really too old and could have spent the war years at home caring for his family. But he volunteered to become a rear gunner in a Wellington Bomber. A rear gunner's average lifespan was seven minutes. He was lucky and made twenty five missions over occupied territory. He was finally shot down in 1941 and broke his back, spending the rest of the war in hospital in a plaster cast.

Jimmy's mother, Elisa, died in 1942 after a fall, and the usual family arguments over who had her few belongings went on for twenty years.

Sarah took a job in the local munitions factory working three shifts. Amelia, on her way to school each day, would leave three-year-old Frances at the local Catholic club with Auntie Kisaiya. Frances hated the Catholic club.

It was a smelly hut with a black stove in the centre of the floor where Irish migrant miners cooked kippers and eggs. The floor was covered in sawdust and there was a spittoon in the corner. Most times the men missed the spittoon and spat on the floor. Frances watched as a man dressed in dirty black clothes poked the eyes out of a kipper, and after removing his bootlaces, proceeded to thread the boot lace through the eye sockets. He would then hold the string as close to the coals in the black stove without burning the boot lace. While this took place, the man's little black and white dog sat with his nose as close to the kipper as he could get without burning his whiskers, knowing that when the man ate the flesh off the kipper he would get the head and tail. Frances watched hoping the kipper would not fall into the fire because then the man would not have any dinner.

"Miners always have to spit," Auntie Kisaiya said. "Because the coal dust gets in their lungs and they have to get it up."

The toilet was a midden at the bottom of the yard where a bull terrier named Bruce was tied up. His job was to protect Auntie Kisaiya from anyone who might have had too much to drink.

On cleaning days, Auntie Kisaiya would put Frances in the snug. The snug was a room in which the wives of the Catholic men could sit on weekends. They were not allowed to drink with the men. Frances screamed and kicked when Kisaiya locked her in the snug. It was the most hated place of all. It smelled of something that Frances could never understand until many years later. The experience of the snug would affect Frances for the rest of her life.

In the yard behind the Catholic club, a joiner worked in a shed. Outside the shed, the yard was very untidy with off cuts of wood strewn around. Frances would peep over the fence when she visited the midden and waited for Auntie Kisaiya to come for her, and Auntie would have to walk her past the dog because it had bitten Frances several times when she had been playing in the yard. Perhaps he could smell the fear she had whenever she used the midden.

In the joiner's yard, Frances had noticed that sometimes people would congregate, and the joiner on these occasions was usually dressed in black. She thought he must be a very nasty man because the people in the yard were usually crying. Sometimes they would look up and see the little face looking over the fence.

The women would go over to Frances and pat her on the head saying things like, "Life goes on, doesn't it, lass? Life goes on."

If Auntie Kisaiya caught her looking over the fence, she would get very angry, shouting at Frances. "Never look over that fence, Frances. Do you hear me? I have enough to do without having to watch you all day."

Most days a man dressed in black visited the club. The Irish men always stood up when he came in and doffed their caps saying, "Mornin', Father" or "Arternoon, Father." This puzzled Frances. *He can't be all their fathers*, she thought. *Where were their mothers?* She never saw them.

One day she heard the father-man shouting at Uncle Eddie saying, "You are not pulling your weight here, Eddie. I know you work in the pit, but Kisaiya is not a carthorse. She runs this club alone without bar staff and gives all the profit to the church. She's only taking a meagre sum for her labours. I have seen you gambling away your wages and asking Kisaiya to cover your card playing. If this doesn't stop, Eddie, I shall have to think about giving the stewardship to someone else. You are the steward, and she is doing all the work. You understand, Eddie? I am warning you. I have watched you for sometime now."

Uncle Eddie was very upset, bowing his head nearly too the floor. "Yes, Father," he said quietly. "Sorry, Father. I will work in the bar more often at weekends."

"Good man," the father-man said as he lifted his glass to his mouth. He drained the beer before he left with a final warning. "I am watching you, Eddie. Mark my words!"

Frances thought he must be Uncle Eddie's father. At least she knew he was not her dad 'cos he was in the hospital with a big plaster on his back. Her mam had told her that.

Eddie waited until the priest had left and then complained to Kisaiya. He was so humiliated having been told off by the priest. He blamed Kisaiya who cried. Frances needed to go to the midden but dared not ask. She waited and waited for Uncle Eddie to stop shouting at her Auntie Kisaiya, but it was too late and she wet her pants. She hid all afternoon cold and uncomfortable in her wet clothes.

Auntie Kisaiya was still crying and had started to drink the beer to make her feel better but it just made her nasty. When Kisaiya found Frances hiding behind the beer crates in the yard, she lost her temper and slapped her legs, which were sore with the urine that had dried on her. Frances cried to her mother that she wanted to stay at home and not go to Auntie Kisaiya's, but Sarah had no option but send her to Kisaiya. She hated the work at the munitions factory, but it was compulsory to the war effort and the money was necessary.

One afternoon Frances was at the club with Auntie Kisaiya when the sirens went. The men in the club said, "The sirens are early today. Must be a false alarm."

The sirens mostly went off at seven in the evening when Sarah would take the children into the air raid shelter at the bottom of the garden in Woodland Park. The shelter was smelly and wet. Sarah would cuddle under a blanket with Amelia and Frances close and tell them the stories of Lambecote Grange and her father, the huntsman. Most of the neighbours who shared the shelter thought Sarah was a bit odd, always trying to be posh. She always wore a stylish hat and cleaned her shoes before she went out. She never wore a headscarf like most of the other women in Halten and always had gloved hands. Who the hell did she think she was? They used to whisper amongst themselves. Sometimes in the winter, Sarah would make a bed in the pantry underneath the stairs for Amelia, Frances, and herself. Frances loved her mam's stories about Lambecote Grange and vowed that she would find it one day. They could all go to live there and have their own air raid shelter.

Kenneth would not go into the air raid shelters. He and his friend Billy would bring home a jug of beer and sit in the dark, laughing and-joking when the ornaments rattled off the walls. But this afternoon the noise from the sky was frightening.

The father-man came into the Catholic Club and said, "They are bombing Sheffield. Get into the cellar as fast as you can."

Kisaiya wrapped Frances up in a blanket and asked the father-man what was happening at the school.

"Don't worry about the school, Kisaiya. They are safe underground in the shelters. All the children of school age are underground," the priest assured her.

Unlike most other Yorkshire pit villages, the worry in Halten was that there was work being done at the munitions factory as well as Halten having a coal mine. When the Germans came at night, they could not see the coal mine because it was black, and the munitions factory was also painted black to camouflage it. In broad daylight they were vulnerable.

After some thirty minutes or more, Sarah was banging on the door of the club, screaming for Kisaiya. She ran in and scooped Frances up and ran back outside with Kisaiya pleading with her to wait until it died down. Sarah was not sure it would die down and wanted her children near her. She had run from the munitions factory when they had ordered everyone into the shelters, but she just ran first to pick up Frances, then to pick up Amelia. Kenneth worked at the pit and would look after him-self, she hoped.

After leaving the club, Sarah raced on, frantically trying to keep Frances covered with the blanket, but Frances could see out of the fold.

The sky was black with aeroplanes and bits of rubbish were flying around all over the place. They arrived at Amelia's school to be told by the caretaker that they were all in the shelters. He persuaded Sarah to take Frances into the shelter, which had been constructed a ways from the school buildings in area known as "The Craggs." The shelter was buried deep in the earth and well constructed.

This was frightening. Sarah was passing her daughter down a hole in the ground. Someone told her to hold on to the metal ladder running down the side of the hole, but Frances was too scared to move. It was so deep a teacher had climbed halfway up the hole to help to pass her down to someone else. Sarah followed her down the hole, and they went along a long tunnel looking for Amelia's class. When they found her, Sarah hugged her children thankfully.

Each class was singing with the teachers following a well-rehearsed routine. Frances began to enjoy herself. She was the centre of attention, and she loved to perform and show off. When they eventually climbed out of the hole, there was such a mess, and people were running around frantically looking for their families.

Sarah left the munitions factory when Jimmy came home. He needed to be cared for. He was in a plaster cast for three years and wore a steel back support for the rest of his life. He had many friends from the RAF Benevolent Fund who looked after the family well until he could work again. Sarah began taking students for the piano and soon had quite a busy time teaching. She taught singing and piano accordion, which were very popular at that time. In 1944, Jimmy was still in a plaster cast but one that was adapted to keep his back straight.

Soon, Sarah was pregnant again. She was very ill throughout this pregnancy and was confined to bed with high blood pressure for most of the nine months. Alice sent one of her boys down to Sarah to tell her that her mother had had a stroke, and Edwards brought her over to Alice's to look after her. The old bugger had washed his hands of her. Sarah got up and began to get dressed. Jimmy came in just in time to stop her rushing off to see her mam. He was still in a plaster cast and had limited movement, but he offered to visit Rosina and assess her condition.

"Sarah, you are not walking anywhere," Jimmy said. "You will kill yourself and the baby. Your mother has not been to see you for over a year, and I won't let you risk everything to visit her now." Jimmy went to the house and knocked on the door on Osborne Street.

Alice was cooking in the kitchen. "Hello, Jimmy lad," she said smiling. She was always smiling. "How's our Sarah. She's not bad, is she?"

"Well she's not good," Jimmy answered. "Her blood pressure is so high the doctor says she has to stay in bed until the baby's born. She was up and getting dressed when she got your note, but I've put my foot down and make her stay in bed. That's why I'm here. How's Rosina?"

"Oh she's bad. Jimmy," Alice cried, wiping her hands on her pinny. "I think she's dying. Come and take a look at her."

Jimmy went into the front room where Rosina lay on the bed. She looked very old. Her hair was white and wispy, and her mouth was slack and dribbling.

She recognised Jimmy and asked, "Where is our Sarah?"

"She's in bed with the baby, Rosina," Jimmy said, kneeling beside her and taking hold of her hand. "I had to make her stay there or she would have been down here."

"Jimmy, I am dying. I need to see Sarah and William," Rosina pleaded.

"Rosina, I shall try to find William, and we shall have to see how Sarah is tomorrow," Jimmy said kindly.

Jimmy knew that some gypsies were camped down on Gypsy Lane and managed to struggle from Alice's house to the piece of land usually used by them. When he arrived he was exhausted.

An old woman gave him a chair and said. "Sit yer down, lad. What yer doing walking about in that state?"

"I am looking for Billy and Fluere Bingham. Billy's mam is dying and needs to see him," Jimmy told her.

The old women lit her clay pipe and puffed while she thought.

"They'll be up north, lad. It'll take three weeks for us to find 'em, but we'll try. I likes young Billy even if he is a *gorgio*."

Jimmy thanked her and struggled home. On his way, he called the butchers.

"Hello, Jimmy lad," Jack greeted him. "What do you want?"

"Jack! Rosina is dying and wants to see Sarah before she goes. But Sarah is too badly to walk all that way. Can you take her on your horse and cart?" Jimmy asked.

"I can, lad. Shall we go now?"

"If you have time," Jimmy replied gratefully.

Jack and Jimmy rumbled up to the woodlands on the old cart that Jack used to go to market. Sarah was wrapped in blankets and made as comfortable as possible on the cart whilst they rumbled back to the pit village. Rosina was worse when they arrived and could barely speak to Sarah.

"Lambecote Grange should be yours and William's," she whispered through laboured breathing. "You must get it back."

Rosina began to shake uncontrollably, and Sarah became very upset. Jimmy forced her out of the room, and Jack took them home to get Sarah back into bed.

Sarah cried bitterly all the way home on horse and cart. "What does she mean, Jimmy?" she asked when they got home. "What am I supposed to do about Lambecote?"

"You will do nothing Sarah. Lambecote has gone. It's in the past. Rosina was just trying get rid of some of her guilt before she passes over. Don't you even think about Lambecote. We have a good life here. That rubbish is all in the past. Forget it."

Later, Jimmy told Kenneth and Amelia that their grandmother was dying, and he had taken their mam to see her for the last time. "If you want to go and see her then you must do it today."

Amelia put Frances's coat on and all three of them went to the pit village to see Grandma Edwards for the last time. Frances was only four and had no memories of Grandma Edwards alive let alone dead, but Amelia and Kenneth said they had to go. They all stood in line tside the back door of the Osborne Street house. Kenneth, Amelia, Auntie Kisaiya's two children, and all ten of Auntie Alice's children filed through the kitchen and back parlour into the front room.

Grandma was laid on the bed with her mouth open, and her eyes never blinked once. Tears were rolling down her face as all her grandchildren filed past her, looking terrified. The children filed out of the front door and out into the garden after seeing their dying grandmother. They would remember the scene for the rest of their lives.

Rosina died in January 1944. Sarah was not allowed to go to the funeral, but William made it just in time. He unfortunately arrived after his mother died but he led the mourners, and Rosina was buried in a pauper's grave. Sarah told William what Rosina's dying words were, but William had no interest in finding Lambecote Grange now or in the future.

Old Edwards refused to attend the funeral and swore that Rosina was destitute.

Chapter 24

1944

Tommy's birth was a difficult one for Sarah. She was forty-three years old and was never quite the same person after it. Jimmy worked hard to make a good life after the war, but food rationing lasted many years after it finished, and most working families had only a very meagre diet with very little, if any, fruit. Orange juice could be bought at the co-op, but only if a family had a child under the age of five. Apples were plentiful in season because they were grown in England, but fruit that had to be imported was scarce.

When she was nine, one of Frances' friends was given a banana that caused much excitement in the woodlands. None of the children born during or after the war had seen or heard of a banana. They were all sitting in an overgrown garden, their den of sorts, looking at this odd thing, when a pitman passed by.

"Hey Mister," one of the children shouted to the pitman. "Do yer know what this is?"

"Aye, lad, it's a banana. Haven't seen one of them fer years," he said, laughing.

"What do yer do with it?" the boy asked.

"Eat it, son. Thy eats it," the pitman said.

All the kids looked at this thing. "It don't look like nothing yer would want to eat," one of them said.

"Yer peel it first," the pitman said.

"What? How do yer peel it?"

The pitman took the banana and showed the kids how to remove the peel from this odd-looking item, and then, breaking off a small piece he ate it saying, "Bloody lovely that. Bloody lovely."

They all ate a very small piece of this "banana-thing." Some liked it and some spat it out, but they all had a tale to tell Mam when they went home.

Tuberculosis was rife in Halten just after the war as were rickets, probably due to the poor diet. One family in the woodlands had lost two children to TB, and the father had just lost his fight for life.

Sarah warned Frances and Tommy they should never go near this family's house or they might die. Sarah was always in fear of some disease taking her children. Tommy was terrified when the daughter of the dead man gathered all the children together in the overgrown den, telling them they had to give her two pence so she could show them her dad who was dead in the front room. This girl was a bully. She usually bullied Frances either on her way to school or on her way home from school. Frances spent a lot of time trying to find new ways to get home without meeting the bully.

Frances took Tommy home, he was only a baby, and she did not think that he would be hit if he could not find two pence to look at the bully's dad. Frances knew her life would be hell if she did not do what she was told and searched everywhere looking for a pop bottle to take back for the bottle refund. Eventually she found one at the back of the pantry. Her mam would go mad if she found out what she was doing, but she was more scared of this girl than of her mam. All the children, twenty or more, were lined up in the ginnel, an alleyway beside the house. One by one she took their money and pushed them up to the front room window where the curtains had been left open just enough to see the bed with her dad laid out dead with pennies on his eyes.

Frances had been standing in the line for ages not daring to breathe in. All the other kids were happily talking about the dead body they had seen or were about to see, but Frances was trying not to breathe any air from the ginnel. She would run down the ginnel into the street and have a good breath. After filling her lungs with air she would then run back into the queue for the body-watching. The problem was, every time she moved, she lost her place. Eventually, it was her turn to look through the curtains at the dead body. She looked at the poor man. It certainly looked like him, but somebody had put pennies on his eyes, and he was a very funny yellow colour.

Just as she moved away there was a bellowing from across the road, and running across towards them came Granddad Hayfield waving his stick. He caught Frances around her shins with his stick. She screamed in pain. He was running around waving his stick like a banshee, striking out indiscriminately at anyone close enough.

All the kids vanished like magic. The street was empty. Frances went home. She wanted to get a wash, but her mam was cooking dinner in the kitchen, and she dared not tell her what she had just done. Frances could not get near the sink. She would not allow Tommy to go near her and decided to go down the garden out of the way until she could get to the sink and wash all this TB off her.

Frances was a child who demanded attention from the day she was born. Sarah had told the story of the hunting horn to all her children, but Frances was the one who asked for the story over and over again. "I will find that house, Mam! When I grow up, you see if I don't. We should be living there, not here in this little house. I want my own bedroom with a wardrobe of my own and lace curtains like you had in Bingley," she said, dreaming.

Sarah smiled at Frances sadly. How she wished she could give her children a better life. She would make sure they knew of their roots. Then it was up to them to dig themselves out of the trap of not quite having enough money to eat and dress well. Education would be the key, but she cosseted the children so much, keeping them from school when the wind blew on them. She was torn between pushing them into school and cherishing every minute she had with them. Sarah taught the children to be different from the children with whom they mixed, both at school and at home. Her children would have discipline in their lives. They had to use their manners at all times. Food could be only eaten at the table, and watch out anyone drinking tea from a cup without a saucer.

Chapter 25

Winter 1947

The winter of 1947 was bitterly cold, Sarah could not afford to buy coal after Kenneth had finished his apprenticeship. He had procured a job many miles away, taking his coal allowance with him.

Jimmy worked in a steel mill in Sheffield, but the travelling costs took most of his pay. When the pain in his back was bad, he very often took time off work and could not travel on the trackless bus into Sheffield because it aggravated his back.

In order to keep the family warm in this unusually cold winter, people who did not work at the pit had to burn whatever they could lay their hands on. The coal slag heaps were patrolled by a man who lived just a few houses away from the Wiseman family. Sarah decided to try to steal coal from the slagheap. Many other neighbours did the same after dark. Jimmy was at work, and Sarah and Amelia placed a sack and some rope onto the sledge the children played with during the day. They were very nervous, waiting for the pit bobby to pass their house on his way home at about five in the evening.

"He is here, Mam," Amelia shouted. "Come on. Let us go. He only takes half an hour. We do not have much time."

Frances was told to stand on a stool by the window with three-year-old Tommy. If she saw the pit bobby go back into the woods after he had taken his break, Frances had to leave Tommy next door and run as fast as she could through their back garden and into the woods to tell her mam that he was coming. Frances watched every movement in the street carefully. The lamplighter came, and she was distracted, watching the snowflakes fluttering in the light of the gas street lamp outside their house. Then she saw him muffled up with scarves. The bobby was going toward the wood where the slagheap was. She grabbed Tommy and pushed him into house next door, and sped through the garden and over the fields with the snow freezing and blowing in her face. She knew just where her mam would be near the old burnt-out tree, a landmark that the kids called the bowler tree. She wore her coat, hat, and black Wellington boots, but she was still freezing and very frightened. She had to get to her mam, or Sarah and Amelia would be put in prison.

Sarah and Amelia had only filled the coal bag half full. It all had to be sifted from the slag, and everything was frozen solid. When Frances came running to them, she was so out of breath and could not speak. Sarah looked around and decided to hide the sledge under some bushes, hoping that the pit bobby would not see the tracks in snow. If they did not have any coal with them, he could not summons them. But she was ashamed of herself sinking to this. All three hid a good distance from the bush where the coal was hidden. Then they slowly found their way home, cold and frightened, without any coal or the sledge.

Very early the next morning, before the children were out of their beds, Sarah watched the pit bobby go home. Then she ran terrified through the fields at the back of the house and into the woods where the sledge was still untouched under the bushes. She had to have a fire, and if she got caught, she would have to take the consequences. The water had frozen, and she had burnt every thing she could burn. When the children awoke they found her cooking breakfast on a lovely warm fire and their school clothes hanging on the rail above the black-leaded fireplace. The trauma of the night before was forgotten.

Halten was fast becoming an area for entrepreneurs starting small sweat shops and making anything and everything. Here was a generation ready to be exploited after the war years when goods had been so scarce. Everyone wanted everything they could get their hands on and wanted it now.

Women worked on piecework, but after the austerity of the war years, they were prepared to do any sort of work if they were strong enough. Being considered decent was one of the best compliments a woman could get in 1954.

It seemed to Frances that to qualify to be "decent" was when you kept a clean house and washed the dishes straight after a meal. A woman would be very well thought of if she did the laundry early on Monday morning, hanging the clothes out to dry in a particular order like whites at the bottom of the garden. The whites went out first because they went into clean hot water which had been boiled in a copper set into a specially built chimney where a coal fire would be burning underneath. The white clothes would be rubbed on a scrubbing board, rinsed in a dolly tub twice, before being boiled in the copper. When they were pegged on the line, they were the women's pride and joy, the wind blowing through her man's shirt sleeves early on Monday morning. It was something to be proud of. The remaining clothes were pegged out next to the whites depending on their value finishing with the work clothes and old clothes being pegged out as close to the house as possible so as not to be seen by all and sundry. Frances would daydream, watching the wash blow in the wind and feeling sad for her mam who was never the first to get her whites pegged out. Sarah worried about washdays. She was always so tired after scrubbing and rubbing the clothes and would never receive the accolade given to the good washers. The neighbours would stand at the garden fence after they had completed their washing, eager to pick up the latest piece of gossip. The women usually had their hair fastened up in scarves tied into turbans.

Frances would listen to the chatter of the women. It followed a pattern. Each one would fold her arms over her ample bosom and nod her head as the others told their tales. They all had the same mannerisms. Frances thought perhaps you learned a special way of talking when you got married. They also passed secrets, lowering their voices and clasping hands, their faces distorted in horror, surprise, or delight. Frances thought that all the women were cut from the same pattern, some a little bigger than others, some a lot bigger than others, but all with the same intelligence and all jostling for position in the group. Everyone liked to be the first to know of bad news or the other exciting stuff, like someone expecting. Frances had no idea why expecting brought so much interest. What were they expecting, she wondered—a letter, perhaps, or a visit from someone? Maybe it had something to do with the men coming home from the war. This usually caused a big fuss.

Most of the men had come back now. She heard Mrs. Asprey from next door say that anybody who had not come back was not likely to come back, and had probably found another woman.

Frances attended a dancing school from the age of seven. The school expected her to provide her own costume when they performed a pantomime. These costumes did not cost much, but it was a struggle for Sarah to pay for them.

Jimmy was not always able to work at this time. Sometimes he suffered badly with the pain in his spine, and he had been fitted with a steel jacket, which must have been very uncomfortable to wear. He worked in

Sheffield, and the travelling each day amounted to thirty miles by bus. The steel jacket made him sweat and chaffed him where the straps fitted under his arms and around his waist. This caused financial difficulties when he could not work for long spells. He had been awarded a War Pension for his injury, but still Sarah and the family found it difficult to manage on the eight pounds a week.

Sarah had made Frances a ball gown out of the bedroom curtains for a pantomime in which she appeared. On the last performance, all the actors and dancers were called on stage to be given little presents of flowers or sweets. They always pretended that it was a surprise, but in truth, they had made sure someone had left a gift for them at the stage door. Frances had never had a gift. On the last night of the year she would be fourteen and would not be appearing in anymore pantomimes. How she would love to walk down to the front and hear everyone clapping for her and then be given a box of chocolates. Sweets had been rationed for so long that people had become accustomed to not having them. Frances and Tommy had never had sweets. They had not been part of their life throughout the war years. Other more important food was bought with the very little money available during and after the war.

There was one family in Halten, the Oakleys, who had sweets regularly. Frances had been told that Mrs. Oakley was a naughty. She had no idea how that got Billy Oakley sweets but he did and sometimes his family had sweets to sell.

Word would go around the woodlands that Oakleys had lollipops for two pence, and every child in the woodlands would be looking for bottles to take back to try to be the first in the queue at Mrs. Oakley's house. Each hoped to buy a lollipop made of toffee that had been poured into small tart tins with a piece of firewood stuck in for the stick.

Frances and Tommy never managed to find a bottle in time to buy a lollipop. Mrs. Oakley could only afford to use enough of her extra sugar coupons to make eighteen lollipops, and even if they were in time to get into the queue, they never managed to be lucky enough to be in the first eighteen. Frances was not really a lover of chocolate. It made her feel sick, but she just wanted to walk down on the last night and be given a box of chocolates, just once.

"Mam, have you got any spare money?" she asked

"What do you need it for?" Sarah asked.

"I thought I might have a present tonight on stage," Frances said sheepishly.

182

"I am sorry, love" Sarah said, not realising how important it was to Frances. "I spent all my money going to watch you last night. I only have your dad's bus fare for work next week."

"Do not worry about it, Mam. It is only daft anyhow. And I do not really like chocolate," Frances said, seeing the pain in Sarah's eyes.

She waited until her mam was out of the room before starting to search for pop bottles to take back. After calling next door, they gave her two bottles and sixpence to go to the post office to post a letter. After knocking on several other people's doors asking if they needed any shopping or if they had any bottles to take back, she collected one shilling and sixpence.

She only had fifteen minutes to get to the church hall after she had done all the errands for the neighbours, and on the way, she bought a box of Payne's Poppets, the cheapest thing you could buy in a box. She could not wrap them nicely so she asked the shop assistant to put them in a brown paper bag and wrote on the bag, "Frances Wiseman. Well done. From Mam and Dad."

She went through the stage door and luckily there was no one about. She placed the package on a window ledge and went into do her last pantomime. After the finale, all the prizes were being given out, and she was the only person left without a present. She thought someone must have stolen her Payne's Poppets. She was so disappointed tears welled up in her eyes.

The stars received their flowers with sweeping bows. The audience stood to sing the National Anthem, and Frances held back the tears, still wanting to walk down and receive a present.

"Ladies and Gentlemen," the dancing teacher shouted. "Please take your seats a little while longer. We have missed one of our dancers. I am afraid her present had dropped down behind the stage manager's desk. Frances Wiseman, will you come down and collect your present from your mother and father? Well done, Frances." Frances was so happy she walked to the front and curtsied holding her box of Payne's Poppets in sheer delight.

During the war years, clothes had to be sewn with a minimum of cloth and only a certain number of pleats and buttons or pockets were allowed in the design, but Sarah loved to dress Frances in clothes she could make out of bits she found on market stalls.

She would watch her daughter, remembering Jean and how she loved to dance and sing. Frances had ribbons in her long dark brown hair and rags had to be put into her hair every night before she went to bed. The next day, Sarah would curl the ringlets around her finger and fasten Frances's hair into bunches of curls.

Amelia decided to cut Frances's hair one day when Sarah was out shopping. All the ringlets were chopped off one by one and put into a muslin cloth. Amelia had heard you could sell long hair if it was not tangled.

Sarah arrived home and took one look at Frances, very short straight hair with a straight fringe across her forehead, and yelled. "Amelia, what the hell have you done?"

Amelia produced the hair wrapped in the muslin cloth, telling her mother they could probably get some money for it and anyhow, Frances was too old for long hair. She was not a baby. She was fourteen and looked silly with curls and ribbons in her hair. Sarah kept the hair for years.

Sarah and Jimmy wanted Frances to go to the Gregg School of Commerce, but she had to be sixteen to enrol. They decided she should get a job with her sister at the local factory until she was old enough to go to college. Frances left school at the age of fifteen on the last Friday of the summer term and started her first job the following Monday as a sock linker, sewing up the toes in socks which were knitted in long circular rolls of twelve dozen socks per roll. She had to link twenty-four dozen pairs of socks per day, and for the first three months, would only be paid thirty shillings a week.

After her National Insurance stamp had been paid along with her other dues and demands, including sixpence a week to the Union woman who scared the life out of Frances, she only took home to Sarah twenty-five shillings a week. This work was very hard, and the hours were long.

Frances always lay in her bed listening to the noises coming from the pit. She could hear the tubs banging against the overhead rails as they carried the pit waste up to the top of the slag heap. Then they would tip the slag out before travelling down again to be refilled at the bottom. The tubs made much more noise on the way down when they were empty than they did on the way up. It only bothered Frances when they stopped. The silence was unnatural. The pit buzzer would blow at four in the morning, ready for the night shift to finish and the day shift to start. Then, after a few minutes, she could hear the men's pit boots shuffling down the road and their snap tins banging against the miners belts.

This was all very comforting to Frances she was tucked up in her bed, while outside, the day was just starting. She had to get up at five-thirty to start work at six fifty-five in the morning and work until four forty-five in the afternoon with thirty minutes for lunch and two ten minute breaks. If she needed the toilet in between these break times, she would be timed by the supervisor who was a woman who had been jilted at the altar and seemed to take her revenge out on all the poor young girls in her charge.

Sarah gave Frances five shillings back from her wages, which paid for her travelling to work and her dinner, not leaving much to spend on herself. But she was happy to be taking some money home to her mam. Most of the girls who worked in the factory kept all their pay, not giving their mothers anything toward their keep. These girls spent money on makeup and clothes. Lots of them smoked cigarettes in the toilets or in the canteen.

Frances was still very much a child. Sarah had smothered her and her little brother because she was afraid she might lose them both. Frances and Tommy were very ignorant of the world, believing everything they were told and not knowing that some people used anything or anyone they could to get what they wanted.

After three months working in the factory, the girls had to go on piecework, which paid approximately ten pence a dozen. With twelve pence making a shilling and twenty shillings in a pound, Frances was struggling to earn five pounds a week, which was the target the supervisor had demanded. Frances became a constant worrier, always scared she would get the sack. Her sister, Amelia, an invisible mender, had worked in the factory for several years, always earning good wages. She was married when she was twenty-one, and Frances was only thirteen. When Frances was sixteen, she struggled to keep up with the piecework target.

One day, the supervisor poked her in her back and said, "You, in the office. Now."

This was the call everyone dreaded. Frances put down her work straightened her hair and started the long walk past all the other girls, including Amelia. She walked past the partition that had been built six weeks before. It was causing great speculation amongst the girls in the factory. What went on behind the partition was the topic of conversation at the moment.

Albert Frost, the floor manager, had watched her walk. She did not look at anyone, but held her head high and did not listen to the jibes from the older women. He had watched Frances Wiseman before. She was not like the other girls in the factory. She was so innocent, not having a clue that she was a very desirable young woman.

Frances knocked on the door. The dreaded supervisor pushed her inside and followed her in, closing the door behind them.

"Don't look so nervous, Frances," Albert said. "I won't bite."

Frances's eyes were like saucers. She wished the floor would open up and swallow her.

"You are sixteen now, Frances, is that right?" Albert Frost asked.

"Yes, Mr. Frost," she answered.

"Do you agree that you are finding it hard to keep up with the targets on the line?" he asked.

"Yes, she is," the spiteful supervisor put in.

Frances looked Albert straight in the eye, saying, "My work is perfect, Mr. Frost. You do not lose any time having to redo any of my linking."

Albert smiled at her. "I know, Frances. That is why I want to move you if you'll agree. Next week we're starting a new venture, and I'm hand picking the people who I think will help us to get it off the ground."

The supervisor sniffed. She must have thought this little snob was going to get the sack. Frances would have if the supervisor had her way. She had been waiting for her to drop below the twenty-four dozen set as a target, but these pretty girls always seemed to get away with everything.

"What is it?" Frances asked.

"Fully fashioned knitwear."

Frances had no idea what it was and must have looked stupid with her blank expression.

"You'll be taught the work, Frances, and you'll be paid a good basic wage until we've worked out how to price the jobs," he said. "Would you like to come along and see for yourself?"

"Yes please," she said.

"I won't be needing you, thank you," he said to the snotty supervisor who left the office banging the door behind her.

Albert Frost and Christine left the office and walked together through the rows of girls toward the partition. Once behind the partition, Frances was deafened by the noise. Obviously the partition was a soundproofing system, blocking out the terrible noise emanating from two strange machines that appeared to be knitting something at a very fast speed. The machines were knitting fully-fashioned sweaters in batches of eight. Eight backs, eight fronts, and sixteen sleeves. Frances was mesmerised. Mr Frost introduced her to the foreman who told her she would have to learn to lip read, but that she would soon get used to the noise.

Frances was to be paid seven pounds a week for the foreseeable future, but she would have to work shifts—six in the morning until two in the afternoon or two until ten at night. This was not a problem for Frances. She had very little social life other than work. She had not been encouraged to mix with her school friends, and usually she and Tommy shared their free time together.

One day, a girl who worked on Frances's shift in the factory asked her if she would like to go to the cinema with her. They would have to go to Doncaster because this was such a popular film, and Halten cinema would not show it for years.

Frances asked her mam if she could go.

Sarah said, "Why do you have to go all the way to Doncaster, Frances, when we have a picture house in Halten?"

"This is a special film, Mam." Frances answered. "Everyone is talking about it at work. I would like to see it."

"What's it called?" Jimmy asked. He considered himself to be very worldly wise.

Rock Around the Clock, Frances said laughing. "It is a funny name for a film, but the girls at work are going to see it. They all practice the dance that they do in the film. Every time I go to the toilet at work girls are dancing around singing "Rock Around The Clock.""

"You are not going," Jimmy said. "I've heard about it. Gangs of thugs calling themselves "Teddy Boys" queue for hours outside picture houses in London, and when they get inside, they dance in the aisle and wreck the place. It's just an excuse for thugs to hang out together Sarah. She's not going."

Frances was surprised at her dad. He usually left things for her mam to decide. She argued a little but gave in when her mam got upset.

When Frances told the girls at work that she was not allowed to go to the pictures, they all laughed at her saying, "You have to live, Frances, there's more to life than working in this place."

Eventually, Frances decided to go and not tell her parents. Mary, the girl who had asked her to go in the first place, asked Frances if she had any clothes that were more *with it*.

Frances said she had her pencil slim black skirt from Marks and Spencer and a pink blouse with a black velvet bow under the collar.

All the girls laughed at her saying, "Never mind. You need some trousers. Everybody wears trouser now." One girl produced a catalogue and showed Frances what she should be wearing, telling her how to pay weekly. She forgot to mention that she made enough commission from selling to all the girls in the factory to buy her own clothes. Frances explained that she would not be allowed to wear such clothes.

"Well," Mary said. "I'll have them delivered to my house and you can get changed from your skirt and blouse into your *with it* gear, go to the pictures, and then go back to my house and change back into your skirt and blouse before you go home."

Frances was not sure but felt like such a fool that she agreed. Grey knee-length jeans with a turn up of black and white checks were ordered from the catalogue and to go with them a shocking pink off the shoulder sweater with black ballerina pumps to finish off the outfit.

The day came to carry out the deceit. If only her mam and dad had let her go, she would have been much happier about it. But she had to face these girls every day at work, and if she backed out now, she would be a laughing stock. Frances made her way to Mary's house.

Mary rubbed pan stick make-up over Frances's face which removed all her fine features. She then drew thick black eyebrows over Frances's natural shaped ones and placed a black spot on her cheek.

Frances had a black spot on her cheek naturally, but Mary said it was not *with it*. You had to draw one on.

To finish this very peculiar picture, bright red lipstick was applied to her lips and long dangly bright pink earrings were clipped on to her almost non-existent ear lobes. Frances was very thin and the off the shoulder sweater had nothing to hold it up. She felt very uncomfortable walking through Halten to the bus stop. She hoped and prayed nobody would recognise her.

The cinema was a sight to see. Hundreds of young people queued outside dressed in various combinations of what Frances was wearing. When they eventually got inside there was pandemonium with police-men and usherettes trying to stop young men and young girls from throwing pepper around. Everyone was sneezing and coughing, and boys were being handcuffed and taken out. It was two hours before the film was eventually shown and then the whole place erupted again when peo-ple started dancing in the aisle. Frances was scared. She wished she had not come. Her dad was right. These were thugs.

Lads dressed in long jackets with velvet trims and trousers that they must have sewn onto their legs they were so tight. She had no idea what the film was about. All she could hear was singing and shouting.

After the film had finished, all the girls said they were going to the pub and catching the last bus home. Frances left them and travelled home alone, after asking Mary if her mam would let her get her skirt and blouse. Mary said her mam would not care what she did. She left the bus on Halten Main Street and ran all the way to Mary's house in the pit village, trying to hold her sweater up. Mary's little brother opened the door to her, and Frances asked if she could wash her face in the kitchen. They did not have a bathroom. She scrubbed her face and quickly changed her clothes.

It was very late, and she had to get home before the gas streetlamps were turned off by the lamplighter. He usually went round on his bike at dusk to turn the lights on. He would return at eleven o'clock to turn them off. All people should be safely in their beds by this time. Times were changing after the war. People had been restricted for far too long, and they were throwing decorum to the wind. The older generation were shocked at some of the goings on.

Frances left Mary's house just as the streetlights were being put out. She was scared it was so dark. She stood on the doorstep, thinking that if she ran like the wind no one would see her. Mary's older brother came home just as she was about to set off and run.

"Hello," he said. "Who are you?"

Frances naively explained who she was and what she was doing.

"I'll see you home, Frances," Gerry Sutton, Mary's brother's friend said. "I live near you."

Frances looked up to see a really nice-looking lad smiling at her. She accepted, and they set off walking at a brisk pace. Frances told him how she had been stupid to get mixed up in this mess. When they got close to Frances's home, she could see someone moving towards them walking as if the devil himself was in him. The figure met them and immediately attacked the nice looking lad. It was Sarah.

Jimmy had been out for a walk earlier in the evening. He found walking helped to alleviate the constant pain he suffered in his back. When he walked past the bus stop there was a long queue waiting for the bus to Doncaster. He was glad their Frances did not dress up like this. He had never seen anything like it in his life.

When the bus arrived he crossed to the other side of the street to avoid the hustle and bustle of the crowd. Girls were pushing and shoving and swearing. Just before the bus pulled away two girls came running from the direction of the pit village. He was mortified. It was their Frances dressed like a tart. She jumped on the bus with no idea Jimmy was watching.

When he arrived home, he told Sarah what he had seen, she was beside herself. Jimmy thought he would have to get the doctor to her. She had difficulty breathing and would not stop sobbing. He asked Mrs. Wood to come and take a look at her.

Mrs. Wood said, "It's just a panic attack, Jimmy. I never thought your Frances had it in her, the little madam. You'll want to sort her out when she gets back."

Gerry Sutton was shocked. This woman was crazy, hitting him and shouting at Frances.

Frances screamed, "Mam. Mam, he is only seeing me home safe. What is wrong with you?"

Sarah calmed down by the time they had reached the gate of their house. Frances apologised to Gerry Sutton and went inside. She then had to face Jimmy who was so angry he hit her, knocking her across the room. Frances was shocked. She had only been to the pictures. You would think she had committed a murder the way they were carrying on. She could not get a word in so she went upstairs and lay on her bed, crying. She was so humiliated. What would Gerry Sutton tell Mary's brother? Everyone at work would find out.

Sarah came in and said "Why did you do it, Frances? Your dad told you not to."

"Mam, I have only been to the pictures," she answered. "I came home before everyone else because I did not like it. That lad was only seeing me home because I got scared when the lamps went out. I can't stay here, Mam, if this is what it is going to be like. Our Amelia has been asking me to go and live with her. She says you should not take all my money off me and not let me go out. I think I am going tomorrow." Frances was so upset she did not know what to think or do.

Sarah put her arms around her, saying, "There is no need for that, lass. I know I went over the top, but I want so much for you. Who is that lad?"

Frances told her who he was.

"I know his family, Frances. They are nice folk. I would not have hit him if I had known who he was. Ask him to come to tea tomorrow."

"I do not even know him, Mam," Frances said. "How can I ask him to tea?"

The next day, Gerry Sutton called at the Wiseman house to apologise for any misunderstanding there had been regarding him seeing Frances home. Sarah asked him in, and they sat drinking tea, waiting for Frances to come home.

Frances was embarrassed to find Gerry Sutton at their house when she got home from work. But her mam had said she was sorry, and he asked Frances if he could take her to the pictures sometime.

Frances said, "Do not talk to me about pictures. I shall not forget last night in a hurry."

"Well just wear ordinary clothes, and we shall go to Halten picture house," he said, laughing.

"He is nice, Mam," Frances said after he left.

"Yes he is, Frances. He is a well brought up lad. Pity he works in the pit, though. Not much future in a pit lad," Sarah said sadly.

Frances went out with Gerry on and off for six months or more. He was a perfect gentleman, and Frances only met two in her whole life.

Unfortunately, Frances messed him about. She was seventeen and wanted to do other things. Unlike most girls in the factory, Frances did not have an ambition to marry and have kids by the time she was twenty. Gerry got fed up of waiting for her and married someone else. Frances was very upset on the morning of Gerry's wedding.

Sarah said, "Well, you have left it too late now, Frances. You should not have messed him about so much."

Frances was confused. She did not know what was best. She seemed to be damned if she did and damned if she did not.

Chapter 26

1955

J immy had some friends from his RAF days who asked him and Sarah if they could take Frances in hand and enrol her in the Gregg school of commerce. She could live with them in Sheffield and would be guaranteed a job in their Engineering works after she had qualified.

Sarah was happy. This is what she wanted for Frances. But Frances decided to go her own way and would not listen to her pleadings. She was earning more money than her dad now and did not want to go back to thirty shillings a week.

Sarah gave up disappointed. With all her heart, she wished that Frances had not gone to work in the factory. It had changed her. Always tired not wanting to go out at all after her shift work, she was becoming cold.

When the knitwear project got off the ground, the work had become very difficult. Frances had to keep up with a machine, which never stopped. Men worked the machines, and the girls had to work at such a pace, they became zombies.

Chapter 27

1958

When she was eighteen, Frances was asked out by the local butcher's boy, Joseph O'Brian. His brother worked with Frances and would tease her about him. He had a car and was older than Frances, which seemed exciting. He took her in his Wolsey 680 to Doncaster to watch a boxing match, which she hated. She had no intention of seeing him again but he was motivated, unlike most of the lads in Halten.

Sarah thought he was charming when he brought her flowers and talked about butchering, which of course, Sarah knew so much about. Joseph told Sarah how he intended to set up his own shops, He would not stay in Halten all his life. Always arriving laden with presents, his latest was a tiny black poodle puppy that was so small it could sit in the palm of Frances's hand. Frances could not keep it at home because they already had a dog, and the puppy might be in danger.

Joseph took the puppy to his mother who looked after it until Frances could decide what she would do with it. This all made it very difficult for a girl like Frances. She had to tell him she had no intention of this friendship going anywhere. But, of course, that was the plan. She decided to tell him so many times, but he always thwarted her efforts. Very often he would be sitting at her home, chatting with Sarah when Frances came home from work. If she was on the day shift, she was always tired and did not want to go out in the evening, but Joseph never took no for an answer. When she was on the afternoon shift, he would be outside the factory waiting for her. She was trapped.

Frances had not encountered this kind of persistence before. She was always taught to be polite to people and not to argue, but this man would not go away. The girls in the factory would soon sort someone out if they felt uncomfortable, but Frances was not very worldly wise.

Joseph would tell her stories of his childhood. Frances had had a happy childhood. Her home was a good home, and she could not imagine what life would be like living in someone's front room with four other members of the family with very little food to eat. Joseph always played this card to get his own way with Frances. It was many years before she saw through him. He asked her to go to Blackpool for the spring break. He said he was going with a group of friends and was sure there would be room for her to share with his mate's girlfriend.

Frances said, "Me mam won't let me go, Joseph. I am only eighteen, and she will not allow me to do things like that."

He accepted this, and Frances thought she had escaped from a difficult situation. Three days later, Frances arrived home from work after the day shift. Joseph was there, chatting with Sarah.

Frances was not very pleased, but Joseph turned the whole thing round to his advantage saying.

"Frances, you are going to Blackpool on Friday. Sarah said it would do you good."

Frances's heart sank. The last thing she wanted to do was go to Blackpool and share a room with some girl who she knew nothing about. After Joseph had left Frances said to Sarah. "Mam, I do not want to go to Blackpool. I am so fed up with being pushed into doing things just to make Joseph happy. I told him that you would never let me go. Why did you agree?"

Sarah looked shocked. "I thought you wanted to go, Frances. He seems like such a nice lad, and I thought it would do you good to get out."

Frances went to Blackpool and drank Babycham for the first time in her life. It made her sick, and she could not wait to get home.

Most of Joseph's friends were married, and Joseph started to pester Frances to get engaged.

"I have only known you for three weeks, Joseph. Don't be stupid," she replied.

He showed a side to his character which should have told Frances to run for her life, but she was so soft-hearted that she turned a blind eye to the temper that Joseph flew into when she refused to get engaged.

She was very confused and more than a little frightened. "Mam and Dad will not let me get engaged, Joseph," she said. "They have only just started to let me go out in the evening."

Joseph left her. He drove off, screeching the tyres of his car as he careened down the road at a stupid speed.

After the afternoon shift had finished, Frances and two friends decided to walk home. They needed some fresh air after being in the noisy factory all day. She had not heard from Joseph for two days. She hoped he would stay away. When she arrived home, Sarah was waiting for her. Her dad was working nights, and only Tommy and Sarah had been at home all evening. Tommy was in bed, but Sarah had stayed up to talk to Frances.

"Joseph called," Sarah said "He wants you to get engaged. I hope you are not in any trouble Frances. I have trusted you, and you have let me down."

"What are you talking about?" Frances asked. She had no idea what Sarah meant.

"Frances, you are nineteen next week and are old enough to know what it is all about. Joseph thinks you are afraid to tell me so he came and told me," she said.

"Tell you what?" Frances asked again. She was tired. She had just done a hard shift at the factory, and her mam was talking rubbish. "I wish I had never set eyes on the man," Frances said, still not understanding what her mother was implying.

"I was not born yesterday, Frances. People do not rush into these things without good reason." Sarah was angry with whatever story Joseph had led her to believe, but Frances had no idea what he had said to her mother.

"Mother, I have no intention of marrying Joseph O'Brian or any-body else for that matter. Will you leave me alone? Go to bed," she said dejectedly.

"He comes from a bad lot, you know, Frances, but he is a likeable lad and has got prospects. You can't live at home forever. Joseph says you need taking out of yourself. He really cares for you, Frances." Sarah was babbling now.

"Mam, go to bed. I am very tired," Frances said. She lay in bed think-ing, *all of a sudden I am supposed to get out and marry someone because they have prospects.* Her mam was making her feel scared. *Why does she listen to Joseph all the time and not to me? He has told Mam something but I have no idea what.*

Joseph called every day, trying to catch Frances before she went to work or when she came home from work. He was puzzled because she had not arrived home by ten-thirty. She had of course walked home, but he was not to know that.

Frances could sleep in late on Saturday morning. "Mam, do not let anybody get me up in the morning," she said before she went to bed Friday night.

"Joseph came again tonight," Sarah shouted from her bedroom. "He says he will come again tomorrow."

"Oh no," Frances moaned as she fell into bed. "How do I get rid of him?"

Joseph bought her flowers and jewellery and constantly pestered her for three weeks. He had told all his friends that they were about to get engaged. Some of his friends bought presents and organised a joint party for Joseph and Frances and Mary and Jimmy, Joseph's friends who had decided to get engaged on the same day.

Sarah had accepted that this was what she wanted, saying, "You know what happened with Gerry Sutton when you messed him about Do not let it happen again, Frances."

She was trapped and so confused. She went ahead and got engaged, telling Joseph she had no intention of getting married until she was well into her twenties. After all, it only meant him giving her a ring, and she thought she could always give it back.

Three months after they got engaged, Joseph took Frances to look at a fish and chip shop that was for sale. The owner showed them round, asking Frances if she had ever fried fish and chips before.

Joseph answered for her, saying, "We have both worked in shops all our lives, and I was a cook for two years in the army."

"Well this is a bit different, lad," the vendor replied. "You have to stand here night after night frying, and when you have closed the door, you have to clean everything down before you can go to your bed."

"I'm a butcher," Joseph laughed. "Don't tell me about cleaning down. I clean down in my sleep."

"Well if you can raise the money for the fittings and goodwill, the shop is yours. You will have to see the owner about taking over the lease. That is not for me to say."

Frances said to Joseph when they left the shop. "I hope you do not think that I am going to do that, Joseph."

"No I don't, Frances. You can work at the factory, and I will work in the fish shop," Joseph replied.

He tried everywhere to borrow the money to buy the fixture and fittings and good will. If he could not buy them he had no chance of getting the lease to the premises. He found a loan company who would only loan him the money if he was married and settled with a family.

He pestered Frances so much, saying this was the only chance he had ever had in his life and she was stopping him from making a good life. Do you want to work in the factory all your life? He went on and on.

Eventually Frances married Joseph. She was nineteen-years-old and on her way to church to marry a man who had railroaded her from the first day they had met.

Sarah saw the look in Frances's eyes. Just before she left the house she stopped her and said. "You do not have to do this if it is not what you want, love!" She had been very worried at the speed of this marriage and hoped Frances was not pregnant.

When Sarah had asked her, she had been indignant and hurt that her mother should even think she was. Frances had become edgy, not her happy self. What was wrong with her? Sarah worried.

Frances swallowed back a lump in her throat and replied to her mother's statement, saying sadly, "It is too late now, Mam. Come on. Get your shoes on or we will be late."

This marriage from hell was a disaster from the first day. The fish and chip venture fell through, mainly because they were so young and inexperienced not knowing one end of a fish from another, and Joseph became undisciplined and violent when he could not have his own way. He spent most of his time with his mates when Frances was at work. She would come home to trouble each day after Joseph had upset the landlady who managed the place where they lodged. This life was not the life Frances had dreamed of at all. After three months, she left Joseph and went home, locking herself in her bedroom. She would not go to work or speak to anyone.

Sarah was distraught. Frances agreed to visit the doctor and tell him her problem. She told him that she had been rushed into a marriage, which she had not wanted. The doctor laughed at her and told her she was wasting his time. He did not want to listen to the fact that she had married to a violent man who treated her like a possession and not a human being.

Divorce was the biggest scandal a girl could bring upon her family, and Frances was not strong enough to deal with life alone.

Eventually she went back to Joseph when the butcher he worked for bought Jack Grundy's old shop. This was the shop where Sarah had worked. The butcher told Joseph that if he brought his wife back, he could rent the house. Sarah cleaned this house. She made curtains and papered the walls, happily reliving her youth.

Frances went back to work and lived like a zombie, trying to look happy for everyone else's sake. But deep down she knew she had taken the wrong turn in her life and could not go back. Joseph's violence got much worse. She lost weight and became withdrawn, not wanting her mam to know how unhappy she was. Joseph took her out one evening to celebrate her twenty-first birthday in the local working men's club and got very drunk. She was very miserable and wanted to go home. After he had started a fight with a doorman, she eventually left him in the club and walked home herself.

Joseph came home very late and in a black mood, saying she had made a show of him. He hit her several times. Usually when he hit her it would be in her back or a twisted arm, but this time he punched her in her eye. Frances left and went home to Woodland Park the next morning with a nasty bruised face. Sarah was upset, and Jimmy was angry. She shut herself in her room again, only speaking when she came down to eat. Her brother, Tommy, tried to make her laugh but to no avail.

Several weeks went by, and Joseph did not show his face at Woodland Park. He knew he could not explain Frances' badly bruised face and carried on as if she did not exist, smiling at his customers who thought he was a lovely fellow.

Frances started to make plans for her life. She began to play the piano with her mam's help, and Jimmy and Sarah took her out for a drink to a lovely little village pub within walking distance of Woodland Park. Frances began to get stronger, and life looked brighter. She was at Woodland Park nearly six weeks before she began to realise she was pregnant. Sarah told Joseph, and after giving her the spiel about his terrible childhood that caused him to do all the violent stuff, Frances was persuaded to return to the house behind the butcher's shop.

Frances started to buy baby clothes, and she and her mam would go to Sheffield window-shopping. Frances would encourage Sarah to try clothes on, and if she found something she liked, Frances would buy it for her. She thought that if she were going to get hit, she might as well get some pleasure for spending his money. Sarah always protested and insisted she would repay Frances at one shilling and sixpence a week. Frances took the money to keep her mam happy but gave it back in many ways.

Sarah always took Shep, the old border collie dog, with her when she visited Frances at the butcher shop. Shep took to visiting Frances on his own, which made Frances so happy. He would scratch the door at the back of the shop sometimes. In the absence of telephones for communication, Sarah would fasten a note to Shep's collar and send him off to

Frances's asking her to come at a certain time for her dinner. People would comment on how intelligent the dog was. He would stand at the curb on the zebra crossing, waiting for the traffic to pass before he continued on his mission.

Joseph was violent throughout Frances's pregnancy. He had no control over his temper. When he tried not to hit Frances, he had to smash something in the home. She would try to keep out of his way when she realised he had been upset by something. Anything could bring on the anger—customers or the butcher with whom he worked, or if she gave him steak for tea instead of lamb chops. She would see it coming and try to escape. She left him several times during her pregnancy.

A son, Richard, was born after an easy birth. Frances had to stay in the nursing home for ten days. In the sixties, mothers were allowed to rest up after giving birth, especially the first baby. Joseph was delighted he had a son, and he wet the baby's head every night after he had visited the hospital. Sarah collected Frances from the nursing home in a taxi. The new pram had arrived at the butchers shop and life looked good.

During the first night at home for Frances and the baby, Joseph had been drinking and objected violently to the baby crying. Frances had to sleep downstairs on the settee and try to keep baby Richard quiet.

On the second day, a midwife visited Frances and the baby, and finding Frances in a state of hypertension, the nurse asked if Francis could go to Woodland Park for a few days. If not, she would have to send Frances into hospital. The nurse could not leave her here in her own house. A taxi was called, and Frances and the baby were deposited at Woodland Park.

Joseph visited once in the first week, showing no interest in Richard. This upset Sarah. He was asked to bring the pram as Sarah wanted to take the baby out into fresh air. Following an old wives tale, Frances was not allowed to go out or visit any household until she had been to church. Frances had to make an appointment with the local vicar to be blessed, or her mam would worry her self to death. The pram was delivered at midnight. Joseph spat out obscenities, telling Sarah that Frances would never get him to look after any kids.

Sarah was appalled. Her heart ached for Frances. What would she do now? Things had gone from bad to worse, and she told Jimmy so when they sat quietly discussing the mess that Frances had got herself into.

Frances eventually went back to Joseph after another of his pathetic stories about his childhood and tried to make a go of things. She had to think of the child now. During the next four months Frances and Richard left Joseph on numerous occasions, due to his violent temper.

On one occasion, he threw the television across the room because Frances was late with his dinner. Frances wanted to get a divorce, but divorce in 1961 was very difficult, and she did not want to be left with the stigma for the rest of her life. The family would be ashamed of a daughter who was divorced, especially if she had a child to bring up.

Sarah loved the boy so much she would stand looking at him saying, "Just look how healthy he is." She would proudly push the magnificent pram around the village.

Frances was pretty useless. She was not a baby person and her mother came every morning to bathe the baby and wash and hang out the nappies. Sarah suggested that Frances leave with the baby with her and Jimmy whilst she and Joseph took a holiday in Blackpool.

Richard was four-months-old, and Frances told her mam and dad, "This is the last try. I shall leave him directly after we return if Joseph gets up to his tricks in Blackpool. I have had enough, Mam," she cried. "I hate him." The week before the holiday in Blackpool, Frances felt quite ill. Her head ached, and her throat was so sore she could hardly speak. "I do not think I will be able to go to Blackpool, Mam," she whispered to Sarah. "My throat hurts, and I really do not want to go,"

"Pack your clothes, Frances, and go away with him. It could be the best thing for you both," Sarah said.

Poor Frances was disconsolate. She did not want to go on this holiday, but how could she get out of it? Saturday morning eventually came. Joseph put the cot and all the baby clothes in the van, and Frances pushed baby Richard to the woodlands in the pram. She was so miserable. On the way, she met a widow woman who lived across the road from her mam. Her name was Mrs. Bollinger, a woman who could not have children and spent her time looking after other people's children.

"Hello Frances," she said. "Let me see your beautiful baby boy. Every time I see him, he's laughing and is so pleasant. If you ever need a baby sitter you know who to ask."

Frances smiled wanly, thinking she would rather be Mrs. Bollinger than Frances O'Brian any day of the week. She felt trapped in a violent marriage. She was only twenty-two. Was this all she had to look forward to all her life?

Sarah waved and waved until the car had turned the corner at the end of the street, holding Richard in one arm and waving to Frances's sad face looking back at her through the window of the hire car that Joseph had turned up in to take them to Blackpool. Tears rolled down Sarah's face as she slowly walked back into the house.

Jimmy said, "Don't cry, Sarah love. She'll be all right and can come home to stay when she gets back 'cos he's never going to be any good."

After they had left, Sarah put baby Richard into the pram, and she and Jimmy walked with the pram to a nearby beauty spot. They chatted and the baby was happily cooed and gurgled in his posh pram.

Neighbours stopped to take a look at him saying, "Is this your Frances's baby? He is so happy and smiley just like his mum used to be?"

Sarah's heart sank when she thought about how unhappy Frances was these days. The day after Frances had gone to Blackpool, Sarah got up, and Jimmy cooked the breakfast. The baby had slept all night, and Sarah decided to take Richard back to the butcher shop to collect a fly net to put over the pram. The baby was in the pram, and Sarah turned to put on her hat. She never left the house without a hat and gloves. Suddenly Jimmy heard a cry. Sarah was on the floor, holding her head in pain."

"What is it, Sarah love?" Jimmy cried.

"My head—the pain is terrible," Sarah whispered. It hurt too much to speak. "Go get Mrs. Wood."

Mrs. Wood was the neighbour who everyone called first before they called the doctor. This custom was left over from the time before the Welfare State when you had to pay a doctor before he would treat you. In most communities there would be a Mrs. Wood who knew everything, and she made the decision whether or not get the doctor.

Mrs. Wood sent for the doctor who visited on his way to the pub. After all, it was Sunday lunchtime. He grumbled to Jimmy. After giving Sarah two pills to put under her tongue he left in a hurry. Mrs. Wood ordered that Frances be sent for and the baby taken to Joseph's mother. Jimmy did as he was told. Joseph's mother was only too pleased to look after baby Richard.

Frances and Joseph came home at four-thirty in the afternoon. Frances thought that she had caused her mam to be ill. Amelia and Tommy were there, but Kenneth was too late.

Sunday August 13, 1961 at six-thirty in the evening, Sarah died of a stroke, leaving the whole family devastated. Frances blamed herself for the rest of her life. Sarah was fifty-nine-years-old and should not have had to look after a baby and worry about her daughter's future. Frances should have left Joseph long ago. He was no good and never would be good.

Sarah's funeral showed that the people of Halten respected her. It was a very sad day that would haunt Frances forever.

Mrs. Green, one of Sarah's neighbours, watched the funeral cars leaving the Wiseman's house and commented to one of her friends. "You would think it was a queen. Look at all those posh cars. I have never in my life seen so many flowers at a funeral."

The front garden and the path into the front door of Sarah's home were covered in flowers. The street outside was lined with wreaths and the mourners could not help but step on flowers on the way to the funeral cars.

Frances and Amelia did not know most of the people who shook their hand paying respect to Sarah. Some people had come from Nottingham, but Jimmy and the children were so upset, they walked like zombies through the crowds into the church where people were standing in the aisle. Sarah had certainly left her mark on so many people.

Chapter 28

Autumn 1961

After the funeral, Frances and Joseph stayed at Woodland Park for several weeks, hoping to come to terms with Sarah's death.

Joseph was charming. After all, he was under the gaze of the whole village. If Frances were seen with a black eye, he would have trouble facing the world.

Monday morning was clinic day in Halten when all the mothers took their babies to be weighed and checked out. Sarah had always gone with Frances after she bathed and dressed little Richard. Now Frances had to go alone.

She had risen at seven when her dad had gone to work and started the washing, but her mam did not have an electric washing machine, and Frances had never used the copper before. The copper would not light and Frances decided to put a bucket on the single gas burner to boil the nappies with Joseph's butcher's overalls. The bucket boiled over and put out the gas. Frances tried to light it again several times before she realised that the gas meter needed to be fed with shillings. Her mam had told her that you must boil nappies or the baby would get some disease. Richard needed bathing and dressing and it was nearly eleven o'clock. She would never get the washing on the line and get to the clinic before the one o'clock closing time. Someone knocked on the back door. Frances opened it, her hair dishevelled and Richard struggling under her arm.

"Are you ready for the clinic?" the women asked her. This woman was an older mother who had had several children and was a competent housekeeper and mother. Not like Frances.

Frances broke down in tears. "I can't go to the clinic, I'm not ready," she blubbered.

"What are you doing with that bucket?" the women asked.

"I can't light the boiler. I have to boil the nappies on Mondays or the baby will get a disease," Frances wailed.

"No he won't," the woman said, laughing. "Come on, just put them in the sink, and I'll show you what to do when we get back from the clinic."

On the way to the clinic the kind women asked Frances what disease she thought Richard would get if she did not boil the nappies on Mondays.

"I do not know," Frances answered. "Unboiled nappy disease, I suppose."

They both laughed so much Frances began to feel better. She thought she would speak with Joseph regarding a divorce. He could have all they had except her savings, which she had earned from the day she left school. She would stay with her dad and Tommy and try to make up to them for the loss of Sarah. It was her fault that Sarah was dead, and poor Tommy had lost his mam. She would just wait until she felt a bit better before she mentioned it.

One evening after Jimmy had gone out with some friends from his RAF days, Frances went upstairs to check on Richard. She pulled back the curtain to let the moonlight into the room and was frozen to the spot. There was her dad coming out of the local widow's house a smile all over his silly face.

Jimmy came in and Frances asked. "Did you have a good time, Dad?"

"I had that!" he replied.

"How did you get home?" Frances asked, her heart banging in her chest.

"Old Wilson dropped me at the gate," Jimmy lied.

"Does old Wilson live with Mrs. Bollinger then?" Frances asked.

Jimmy's face crumpled up. He stuttered and stammered and then got angry saying, "I am a single man and can do what I bloody well like! You had better get back to your own house 'cos I don't want you here, do you understand? You have been nothing but trouble, and I won't have it."

After much heart-searching, Frances left the next morning. She looked around the house for the last time, tears running down her face. She touched her mam's clothes in the wardrobe and buried her face in them trying to smell her mam for the last time. She looked around her mam's room, and seeing the picture hanging on the wall of George, Rosina, William, and Sarah with the silver hunting horn hanging above it, she took the hunting horn and pushed it into the bottom of the pram before she set off for the butcher shop and whatever life had in store.

She would have to stay with Joseph now. She was so unhappy her mind was constantly racing with ideas on what she could or could not do. In reality, she had no choice. She had to put up with this butcher and try to make life liveable.

One afternoon four months after Sarah's death, Frances was preparing the evening meal in the kitchen at the back of the butcher shop when there was a knock on the door.

Two women stood there. One of them had the strangest dark penetrating eyes Frances had ever seen. She was also holding the most beautiful white chrysanthemums she had ever seen.

"Are you Frances?" the dark-eyed woman asked.

Frances smiled and said she was. Those eyes. Frances was spellbound by the woman's eyes. Afterwards she could not remember what the other woman looked like. She just remembered the mysterious eyes.

"We are your mother's relatives," the woman said.

Frances asked them in, and they explained that the dark-eyed one was William's daughter, Gladys. William was Sarah's brother who had married the gypsy, Fluere. The other visitor was a cousin of Sarah and William. They had not heard about Sarah's death until recently and wanted to visit her grave. Frances put Richard in the pram and took the two women to the cemetery where Sarah was with her darling little girls.

The strange dark-eyed one looked around the cemetery, and after finally standing under the tree that was over Sarah's grave, she placed the flowers directly on the grave—not in the vase, just on the soil. She said. "This is a good place. You have done well, Frances."

They left the cemetery, Frances not knowing if she should speak or not to the strange lady. She walked to the bus stop with the two women. They said they lived in Doncaster.

As the bus came into sight and the dark-eyed lady put her hand in her bag and brought out a slip of paper. She handed the paper to Frances just as she was about get on the bus saying, "Ring that number. This man is going to have a heart attack. He is a butcher. You can buy his shop."

The bus drove off, leaving Frances holding the piece of paper and no chance of answering the women or asking any details. She told Joseph about all this when he came home, and they laughed about it. Two weeks later after Joseph had had an argument with the butcher, he decided to ring the number on the paper. He thought he might get a job out of it. An interview was arranged, and Mr. Hather, the owner of the shop, told Joseph that he had decided to sell the shop and retire to the coast.

Joseph asked him, "Why?"

He explained that his daughter lived on the coast, and he and his wife wanted to travel a little before they hit old age. He was tired of butchering. It was a young man's profession. Joseph had no money and no means of borrowing any money. This man wanted four and a half thousand pounds for the house and shop.

"Impossible," Joseph told Frances. "That gypsy woman must be a friend of his or something."

Christmas was dreadful. Tommy had come to live with Frances. He did not like the idea of his dad having a woman so soon after his mam's death. Joseph was drunk most of the time. On Christmas Eve, he smashed up the Christmas tree. The babies eyes were like saucers, watching this maniac break every bauble on the tree. Tommy and Frances were so unhappy they just sat and cried. How could life change so much in such a short space of time? Frances strongly believed it was all her fault.

In the New Year, Frances decided to make plans to move out again. She could not spend her life with this man. On evening of January 6, 1962, the phone rang in at the butchers shop. Joseph had to go round to the front and open up the shop door to answer it. He just made it in time. The distressed lady who spoke to him said she was just about to ring off. Mr. Hather had had a heart attack and could Joseph go to Doncaster right away and discuss the butchers business?

Joseph said. "I still don't have four and half thousand pounds, Mrs. Hather."

"Don't worry about that, lad. Just come and talk to my son," she replied.

Frances and Joseph moved into the Doncaster shop with a personal loan from Mr. Hather. The dark-eyed woman was never seen or heard of again but was obviously a Romany cousin of Frances. How did she know about the heart attack?

During the next seven years, Frances became a baker, a butcher, a mother, a punch bag, and a nervous wreck. After working for a local baker without pay for three months, she opened her own bakery in the garage at the rear of the shop. The work was long and hard but she made quite a good profit.

Joseph worked hard but made some bad economic decisions taking on contracts that he could not fulfil. Life became unbearable for Frances. She worked so hard, but the money just paid off the debts.

Joseph had a pattern to his life. He rose early in the morning. He always believed that the fact that he got up early gave him the edge in life. Frances was so scared of upsetting him, she thought she was living on the edge of a precipice. Any little thing could spark a violent attack.

She visited Auntie Kisaiya who offered to come to Doncaster and help Frances. Auntie Kisaiya was a godsend to Frances. She would arrive at nine-thirty in the morning after travelling from Halten on two buses. She cleaned the house and cooked meals four times a week whilst looking after young Richard. Her help allowed Frances to work in the bake house.

Frances was thin and very tired, and almost always felt unwell. She visited the doctor to find that she was seven months pregnant. She argued with the doctor, but he explained that her life must have been so chaotic that she had not noticed the changes in her body. Auntie Kisaiya looked after Frances, taking over where her mother would have taken over.

A midwife had been booked for the home birth. Only first and fifth pregnancies were considered worthy of hospital delivery. A girl had been employed to work in the bake house and a home help was booked, provided at a cost of seven pounds ten shillings a week from the local council.

After a visit from the midwife, Joseph was informed that Frances could have the baby at any time. She was already three weeks overdue and very uncomfortable. He made a fire upstairs in the bedroom, which had been prepared for the delivery. Richard, who was almost two years old, had his cot in this room. Frances found it easier to care for him in the warm room upstairs rather than in the cold room at the back of the shop. Joseph decided to go to Halten for a drink, which he did every night.

Frances begged him, "Please do not leave me alone. I do not feel well."

He said, "You'll be all right. The phone is there, and I can't stay inside forever. You were supposed to have had the kid last week. Stop moping about. I deserve to go out. I've been working all day and need to get away."

Richard was put in his cot, and Frances stayed downstairs by the phone. She began to worry when she realised the phone was not working. It was February 1963, and the snow had been falling since Boxing Day. The roads were thick with snow, and the phone lines were down. She opened the door into the shop and walked in, hoping she would see someone who might come in for a chat. She was feeling apprehensive about being on her own. When she looked out of the shop window her heart sank, the road was deep in snow, and Joseph had gone all the way to Halten just for a drink when she could have this baby anytime now. She went upstairs to check on Richard who was fast asleep. She sat down wrapping herself in a blanket to keep warm. The fire had gone out downstairs, and she could not get out to the coal place because the snow was too deep and she was too big and clumsy.

The pains started slowly at first but became more and more urgent. Frances cried for her mam. Knowing that the baby would be born if she so much as tried to stand up, she dared not move. She sat terrified, watching the clock and praying that Joseph get back in time to get the midwife. She was scared he would be stranded in Halten overnight. She decided that if he did not come home by midnight, she would have to try to go outside and get help. Just before midnight he arrived worse for drink.

Frances said, "Go and get the midwife, Joseph, and be quick." She managed to get upstairs and lay on the bed. The pains hit her, and she screamed and yelled for someone to help her. Richard stood in his cot with eyes like saucers, his bottle dangling from his mouth. He was terrified. Frances tried not to make a noise but she was in the last stages of labour, alone with a two-year-old child watching her.

The shop next door, which was joined to the butcher shop, was a post office, and the lounge of the apartment above the post office was directly next to the bedroom in which Frances was making all the noise. Luckily the lady who rented the flat heard Frances. Putting her coat over her nightdress, she came to see what the noise was all about.

Frances said, "Please take Richard out of here."

The nurse arrived with Joseph, and seeing Frances just about to give birth, took over the situation. Frances became a mother again. Catherine Sarah, the most beautiful little girl, was born at two in the morning. The baby had been washed and weighed and put into the carrycot prepared for her. Joseph got into bed at three in the morning, after he took the nurse home. Richard was asleep, but Frances had to keep looking into the cot to see this baby girl. She was so tired but just wanted to hold her.

Joseph moved the cot away from Frances saying, "Get to bloody sleep. It's three o'clock, and I have to be up at six to start work."

She did not sleep at all. She was listening to the breathing of the baby. Joseph got up at six and went down into the shop. She could hear him chopping meat long before the shop opened.

John, the lad who worked in the shop and who was from a big family, came up to ask Frances if she wanted a drink. He said he had looked after his mam when his sister was born and knew just what to do. He changed Richard's nappy and gave him his breakfast.

The day went on, and the home help who had been booked had not arrived. Frances looked after two children alone when a woman came in saying she was a customer. Joseph had told her she could come and see the baby. Frances always believed that Mrs. Myers was an angel. She took over, allowing Frances to have a very much needed sleep. She knew she could rest with this woman around. Mrs. Myers stayed around for many years, and Frances would never forget her. Joseph went to Halten again the same night he was to wet the baby's head. Mrs. Myers could not believe that this man put the company of his friends before the lovely little family he had at home. The children called her Myra. She kept the family together for many years. Frances would have been long gone if Myra had not calmed situations down.

Frances was soon back in the bake house with her warm pork pies. She had the feeling that all this was meant to be. For after all, her mother had done exactly this for most of her adult life, and here was Frances, baking pies and bread and cakes and anything else Joseph could think of selling. Perhaps this was her destiny—making pork pies and covering up the odd black eye. One day she would get this sorted! If only her mam was alive. She could have gone home and started again, but she would have to wait until the children had grown up before she made a move.

Auntie Kisaiya was making her way home after helping Frances one bleak winter's evening. Joseph would take her home when he could, and Frances was always paid her with some cash but the rest in meat and groceries. The fog was thick and Frances finished her work in the bake house early. Frances told Auntie Kisaiya to start for home as the weather was getting worse. Thankfully, Kisaiya got on the bus. She had been so cold waiting for the bus to arrive in Doncaster. After the bus had travelled several miles on its journey to Halten, the driver stopped, saying he could not see enough to carry on with the journey. Several people got off and started to walk. The driver asked if someone would walk in front with the conductor and guide the bus along the narrow lanes.

Kisaiya volunteered. The wind bit into her face as she walked on the side of the road holding a white scarf for the driver to follow. It took the travellers some hours to reach Halten, and Kisaiya was frozen to the bone. When she arrived home, Eddie was angry with her for being late for his tea, but Kisaiya was so cold she could not move her hands. That night she took a fever from which she did not recover for many months.

Jimmy had given up the house in the woodlands. He and the widow did not get on after he had moved in with her and upset his children so much. Sadly, he was living alone in a flat.

After Kisaiya stopped coming to help, Frances put Richard into Miss Poskit's School for boys and girls. He wore a blue blazer and grey shirt and trousers. He was only three-years-old but she thought the money that she earned was better spent on education than lost on Joseph's failed business ideas. He lost more money in one day than Frances could make in the bake house in a week.

The butcher shop was very popular, and Joseph was very well-liked by all the customers, but he had a passion for cars on which he would regularly spend all the shop takings. On an impulse, he would spend the week's takings at a car auction on Friday, hoping to sell the cars at a profit before he had to pay the mortgage or the meat providers. Obviously he was in debt, and the debts grew and grew. He was like a gambler who has to take one last chance, risking everything on some stupid scheme. Sometimes he would be successful and be so happy that he had made an extra ten pounds. This would prompt him to buy another Jaguar. Frances figured they had had every second-hand Jaguar that had ever been manufactured.

She and the children lived in fear of the Sunday morning wake-up call, when Joseph would get up at five o'clock and force them to go with him to London to try out a car. Seat belts were not compulsory at that time and the M1 motorway was a novelty to someone like Joseph. Frances would wrap the children in warm clothes and sit terrified in a dodgy car, travelling at speeds in excess of one hundred miles an hour down the motorway to London, just to turn round and drive back to Halten before twelve o'clock for the Sunday lunchtime session in the pub, where he could boast of how he had been to London and back before everyone else had got out of their beds.

Frances and the children had to sit in the car outside the pub until closing time when Joseph would throw the keys at Frances, telling her to drive him home. Very often she refused when she knew the car was unsafe or she was not covered by insurance, but Joseph would not listen, and if she objected, repeatedly hit her in the face with his fist whilst she was driving.

Friday evenings became party nights for Joseph and all his followers. They would congregate after the pub in Frances's home. She always slept with the children on these nights and lay listening to the antics of Joseph and his crazy mates. Their favourite pastime was egg throwing, arming themselves with trays of eggs from the shop. They would stand on each side of the road and throw eggs at each other. Joseph would go too far just to show how powerful he was. He would smear eggs over the neighbours' cars and shop windows, which had to be cleaned before the customers arrived next day.

When Frances got up at three the next morning to start baking bread, the mess that confronted her was appalling. These overgrown hooligans could have raided the bake house, and all her preparations for the next days work would be ruined.

On one occasion when Frances had a contract for a twenty-first birthday party and most of the baking had been done and waiting to be delivered, she awoke to find individual trifles upside down on the wall light fittings and cream cakes smeared all over the shop windows.

Joseph always saved himself with grovelling. He could grovel for England. "I am so sorry. It will never happen again." That saying should be inscribed on his gravestone.

Frances had not seen her dad for two years, but she could not bear the thought of him living alone in a flat with very few possessions. She visited once a week and cleaned his house and took his laundry. One Sunday morning, Frances drove from Doncaster to Halten to return her Dad's clean laundry. Sunday was the only day she had free from the bake house. She walked into the flat and immediately stopped in her tracks. She could smell perfume—cheap perfume. There standing nervously in the living room was Beryl.

Frances panicked and putting the laundry in the hallway. She turned and fled with Jimmy running after her and shouting after the meat van that she was driving. "Frances, please don't go away, again. I need to talk to you."

But Frances could not bear that he had another woman. She decided not to go to Halten again ever.

Jimmy married the woman and left Halten to live in Staffordshire, and to make things worse, he married her on her mam's wedding anniversary, Christmas Eve.

Frances felt so alone. She only had her Auntie Kisaiya left, and she felt responsible for her ill health. In her depressed state of mind, Frances began to think that she was the cause of everything that went wrong.

First her mam dying, then her dad marrying this awful woman and moving to Staffordshire, and poor Auntie Kisaiya who would be well if she hadn't travelled all the way from Halten to look after her. Frances was not capable of making a rational decision about anything and refused to speak to any of her family for a long time.

Chapter 29

1966

The butcher shop was close to the racecourse. In Doncaster, Romanies spent quite a lot of time buying and selling horses and the women folk duckered around the racecourse doors.

Frances would often take the children along the free course in their pram on the Town Moor where the gypsies parked their caravans during Ledger Week.

The gypsies scared her a little, but she would not go home until she had had a good look around for the dark-eyed cousin who had so mysteriously vanished just as she had mysteriously turned up on her doorstep.

One of Joseph's customers was a well-known local artist. He asked Joseph if Frances could sit, fully clothed, for the art club. Joseph laughed.

He could not think why anyone would want to paint Frances. "She is as thin as a lat," he told the man. "You won't need much paint. She can sit if she gets paid."

Five shillings an hour is what she got, and Frances found it quite restful just sitting doing nothing and getting paid for it.

Joseph's violence got worse, and eventually, after a particularly bad night, she packed a few belongings, not forgetting her mam's hunting horn, and took the children to live with Tommy who had married but had no children. She hoped to get a council house and put the children into school in Halten. Joseph had taken Richard out of the private school that Frances enrolled him in when he was three, telling her he was not working to waste it on posh schools. She realised that the future of her children was in her hands. Having worked hard to help build up the business, she could walk away and start again.

Joseph obviously had a mental problem. His doctor told Frances she was in danger after he held her at gunpoint one night when he could not pay his debts. He admitted he had decided to kill them all. She was hell-bent on getting the children away.

Tommy and his wife soon got scared of the threats from Joseph. Eventually Frances went back to Doncaster after Joseph had renovated the house and promised that he would sell the shop and get them a real home. She hoped he would stop getting into debt, which he blamed for his violence. He always had an excuse for hitting Frances. When he hit Richard in the same bullying way, Frances went a little crazy. She knew that she would kill him one day if she did not get away. He always had hangers-on and frequented the same pub in Halten every night. On the nights that he took Frances out, he expected her to refrain from looking at another man or have an opinion of her own. She always had to agree with him in an argument or would suffer on the journey back to Doncaster.

Frances's hands shook constantly, and she very often could not hold a glass in her hand long enough to take a drink from it. Joseph, after a few pints, would point this out to his mates who would make crude remarks and ridicule her.

One of these hangers-on felt very sorry for Frances. He was a decent man and took to singling her out, trying to make her feel at ease. Before very long he was telling her he had fallen in love with her and would take her away if she would go with him. She liked this man but knew he just felt sorry for her. If he only realized how dangerous it was for him to even think such a thing, he would run. This man's attention very nearly pushed Frances over the top. After Joseph's friend started telling her of Joseph's exploits with other women, Frances did not know what to believe. She was thin and tired and began to bargain with Joseph. If he sold the shop and bought a house, she would stay. If not, she would leave.

She had the doctor's and psychiatrist's reports, both telling her to get away from him. The psychiatrist's report said that he had a hatred of women and would never change. Frances made it clear she would not stay in that environment any longer.

Joseph sold the shop and made a decent profit. Excited because he had a pocket full of money, he wanted to change the world. His so- called friend was told to stop calling her, and after some time, he did stop and moved away. Frances would never know if he was serious or not, as she did not trust any man ever in her life again. She was unsure whether or not she had used this nice man to discover the truth about Joseph's evenings out, but of course, she had no idea if he was telling her the truth or not. She was starting a new life in a house without a shop attached, and maybe she could build a home like the one she had lost when Sarah died.

Frances and the children started to look for a new home. Joseph agreed but he wanted to buy some pigs to fatten up. He found a farmer who agreed to rent him some land and bought one hundred piglets. This proved to be a huge mistake. Joseph did not have the expertise to rear livestock. He only knew how to kill it. The pig venture failed miserably.

After moving into a lovely house, which Frances thought had been paid for from the equity from the butcher shop, life seemed to settle down. She was appalled to learn that there was a large mortgage on the house. Joseph had lost all the money. He had accrued large debts and got work here and there, but did not pay any household bills.

Frances went to work in a factory during the day—the same factory in which she had been so miserable in her teens. But this did not pay enough to get them out of debt. She found a fish and chip shop to rent and worked every hour that God sent. In the factory during the day, then home to cook a meal for the children, and off to the fish and chip shop in the evening.

Jimmy had written to Frances asking if he could visit her, as he was very unhappy. She replied saying she would love for her dad to come and stay. He arrived and told Frances that he had a miserable life with Beryl who spent all her time and money on her adopted son. Jimmy thought that Beryl might be jealous of his previous life. He was not allowed to speak of Sarah.

Frances was sorry for her dad but did not know how she could help. He asked if he could come and stay sometimes, just to be near his family. She was only too happy to have him stay, and they went out to buy a bed for Granddad Wiseman, which he used very often during the next few years.

Eventually the family fortunes turned around when she masterminded a plan that culminated in her winning large amounts of money. The local Newspaper ran a weekly competition to Spot the Ball in a football photograph. She studied the picture carefully, having no experience of football whatsoever. After several weeks of losing her money she eventually won the jackpot. Joseph was beside himself with joy. He bought more and more newspapers for Frances to work on, although she could have won the money on just ten newspapers per week.

Word soon got out that Frances was a whiz at Spot the Ball, and every one wanted her to fill in their coupon. She said she would take on the task if they paid her half of their winnings.

More and more newspapers were ordered. Frances approached two local newsagents and bartered the price of the papers. The more papers she bought, the less she had to pay for them. She paid a friend to cut out the coupons and write in all the names and addresses. Eventually she was buying fifteen hundred newspapers a week and spending six days a week crossing the coupons. She never let anyone see the coupons after she had crossed them and insisted that they were all perfectly neat and tidy before they were posted in the door of the newspaper office.

Clean newssheet piled up at the house of Frances's friend and was becoming a problem. She decided to try to sell it off, and after some negotiating on the telephone, she struck a deal with the newspaper to buy back the clean news sheet for ten pounds a ton.

When she reflected on what she was doing, Frances thought it ironic that she was buying fifteen hundred newspapers for a penny each, and after winning sixty percent of the prize money, she was selling the newspapers back to the same newspaper company for ten pounds a ton. She felt quite pleased with herself. When the chips were down, Frances always found a way out. During a two-year period, Frances won twenty-seven coloured televisions, a house full of furniture, and approximately one hundred thousand pounds.

They purchased a beautiful bungalow and set Joseph up with a superb modern butcher shop. He began to don the mantle of a successful businessman, or rather his perception of a successful businessman. Wine, women, song, and, of course, flashy cars were the order of the day. He became involved with the most crooked people who found the most hilarious business schemes through which he could lose his money. He began to get tired of Frances. Why should he discuss business with a woman? The violence started again.

Jimmy Wiseman had made some mistakes in his life, but the biggest was leaving Halten and his family. He hated his life in Staffordshire and looked forward to getting Frances's letters. She had been winning some money and putting his name on the coupons. What a surprise when he won a television and two hundred pounds. He had no idea she had entered him into the competition. She would learn that he had been lonely after Sarah died and that he knew he had handled it badly. Frances had been so hurt. Jimmy thought he would go and visit her after she came back from her holiday. She had written to tell him she was going to Spain for two weeks. Whilst Frances was in Spain, Beryl died.

Jimmy organised her funeral, and Tommy and Amelia attended. He knew Frances would not attend even if she had been at home. She was so stubborn. After the funeral he decided to pack an overnight bag and go to Yorkshire, hoping Frances was back. He needed some family. When he arrived, Frances had just returned from Spain and was only too happy to have her dad for a couple of weeks.

He said he did not want to live in Staffordshire on his own. He wanted to come home. Frances asked him if Beryl had left him the house, but Jimmy said he thought everything had gone to her son. He went back to sort things out, but when he arrived in Staffordshire, Beryl's son had emptied the house and there was a for sale notice on the gate. All Jimmy's belongings—his clothes and his furniture, his beloved piano—everything had gone, and the son had disappeared. He returned to Frances who made him welcome. He was happy. He walked the dog and looked after the garden and soon made friends in and around Frances's home.

After some months, Joseph gave Frances a bad time about Jimmy. He said Jimmy was watching the television when he wanted to watch it and getting better treatment than he did.

Frances had a chat with Jimmy regarding finding him a bungalow of his own. She knew he was hurt, but she was having a bad time with Joseph. They decided to contact the RAF Benevolent Association. They were wonderful. Jimmy was offered a place in a retired officers' home. Jimmy didn't want that. He wanted to stay near his family. He explained that he had spent the last years away from them and needed to make up for the time.

A bungalow was found near to Frances, and Jimmy happily settled in. Frances sued Beryl's son and enough money was raised to furnish a home including a piano. Jimmy was happy he was back with his own family in his own home. He had longed for this day. Now he could rest easy.

Chapter 30

July 1974

F rances had packed the suitcases, and the children were in bed. They had gone to bed early, very excited. The next day she was taking them with Joseph's mother to Malta. They were to travel to London and catch taxi to Heathrow. Frances had spent her last winnings on a holiday. She had intended it to be a holiday of a lifetime for Joseph and the kids. The plan was to go to Cyprus, but unfortunately the five-star hotel that she had chosen, was fully booked.

Joseph had been in Cyprus for two years in the fifties, and he often said he would like to return when the fighting was over. Frances had planned this trip as a surprise. She had booked first class accommodation in the five-star Phoenicia Hotel in Valetta. Three weeks before they were due to travel, Joseph decided he did not want to go. After giving many stupid reasons, he eventually came up with the most ridiculous. He said, "The shop could not manage without him."

The shop had not seen him for weeks except when he collected the money, and God only knew what he did with that. The manager usually ran the whole affair. Frances decided to ask his mother to accompany them on the holiday. Nannan was delighted at the prospect of a holiday abroad. Frances had taken her to Mallorca several years earlier, and she still talked about it.

Soon after his decision to pull out of the holiday, Joseph rang Frances one afternoon in July saying, "I will pick you up in half an hour, be ready!"

"What for?" Frances asked.

"I have bought you a surprise," he said.

Frances got into the back seat of the Jaguar. The front seat was occupied buy one of his layabout friends. She was suspicious. Joseph often brought someone along when he was doing something underhanded. It gave him power to have these men running around after him, but where did she fit into this scheme? They drove out toward Derbyshire. Joseph kept an eye on Frances's face in the rear-view mirror. He was making silly quips about her nervousness when he drove above one hundred miles per hour. Eventually, they arrived at a beautiful little village called Baslow.

He stopped the car and shouted, "Come on then!"

She was very dubious now. He had never in their marriage bought her anything that did not have strings attached. So what was he up to now? They walked through the village with Joseph looking at a screwed up piece of paper he had pulled from his pocket.

"Here it is," he called out to the hanger-on.

The friend probably could not understand why the wife of the butcher was not enjoying being brought out here to be given a present. He knew what the present was of course and had been told that it was for Frances's birthday. Her birthday was two months earlier, and Joseph had forgotten all about it. Still he could find birthdays when he needed an excuse to spend her money on something he knew she would not agree to. Frances stood at the gate of the pretty little cottage while Joseph and the hanger-on knocked on the door.

The door was opened by a very distinguished-looking man in his late fifties. He was obviously expecting Joseph. "Mr. O'Brian, you have found us. I was beginning to think you had changed your mind," he said shaking hands with Joseph. "Come this way, please." He led Joseph and his friend to the garage.

Frances stood at the gate, beginning to understand what was happening. The garage door was opened and there stood a Daimler. Frances was angry, thinking she would explode if she did not get away from there. Turning, she fled along the road they had just walked down. He must have gotten his hands on her money somehow. She had been so careful not to let him find her second bank account. He must have cleared both it and the joint account. A car like this was financial suicide. They had just bought the bungalow, and she had paid the deposit on an acre of land with building permission in an area that had just been taken off the green belt. They were planning to build a beautiful home with stables.

This would be the end. He thought he was a millionaire that had lost more money than she could win. He had harebrained road-laying scheme when he had purchased a JCB earthmover and dug up her lovingly-planted garden whilst learning how to use it. After he demolished a school wall, and had to pay compensation, he decided to sell the JCB, but of course nobody wanted a beat up broken-down JCB. He finally decided to abandon it in the field with five horses he had bought, including a lame racehorse.

The Daimler was the last straw. In tears, she walked through Baslow. They would never recover from this. She had not won anything for eight weeks. The shop was very successful, but Joseph had spent the money before it touched the bank. She had been putting money into an account in anticipation of a huge tax bill in April and hoped he had not found that account. He was a complete and utter fool, believing he was so successful when in reality he had not earned one penny of the money he was spending. She had been a fool to let him have the accolade for the winnings from the "spot the ball" competitions. She had won almost one hundred thousand pounds now, but it did not look like she was going to be able to win anymore.

Although the newspaper wanted to sell all the papers she purchased, management was very nervous of the fact that she was running a successful syndicate. Frances thought that they had been tipped off about how she did it. Although it was perfectly legal, they were getting embarrassed at the amount of times Frances was winning.

Joseph's step sister Agnes Longbottom, and her husband had boasted about how rich they were and just how she did it. Agnes and her husband had won so much money that he had left his job to concentrate on helping Frances run the syndicate. Frances had not wanted any help. She was capable of looking after her own financial affairs, but Joseph had brought his sister along to show off how rich he was becoming. Frances strongly objected. She only wanted people who had been involved from the start to see the coupons.

Joseph and his army of friends collected the money, and these hangers-on were growing in number daily. The more money she won the more she had to contend with.

Now there was an expensive Daimler. Well, he would not have hangers-on for long. If he had used all the money she thought he had, financial ruin was just around the corner.

The Jaguar slowed down and trawled alongside her as she walked along the pavement. Joseph was grinning all over his stupid face, shouting through the open window and pretending she was a street woman. Frances got into the car and sat silently in the back until they arrived home.

Joseph did not take the hanger-on home first. He did not want to be left alone with Frances. He had been down this road before. Frances was saving it for when they got home. He knew the signs. It was too late now. He had applied for a loan and had also emptied her bank accounts even though she was clever bugger, hiding money away that way. Anyhow, she was off on one of her bloody holidays in two weeks, and he would have a free hand then.

After he had dropped Frances off, the passenger said to Joseph, "I have never seen anybody turn their nose up at any present, let alone a bloody Roller, Joe!"

"Well, that's what thanks you get when you treat women too well," Joseph boasted.

Life was strained during the next few weeks. Frances had tried to find out how much he had paid for the Daimler. Joseph said he earned it, and it had nothing to do with her. She refused to be seen in the car and preferred to travel in the Jaguar when she went out. The Jaguar was Frances's car, bought and paid for with her money and taxed and insured in her name, but only she and Joseph knew that.

Joseph was on a high. It was like a drug. He drank gin and tonics in half-pint glasses and became impossible to live with. The children hated the atmosphere. He would not sit in the dining room for his meals because he wanted to watch television. They were not allowed to speak if he was watching television. After he had eaten, he would snap his fingers once for tea and twice for coffee. This would be taken to him. He was usually asleep when his coffee arrived, and the drink would be placed on a side table. This happened each evening before he went out to wherever he went. Frances did not bother to ask about it anymore. It was peaceful when he was out. She wished he would go out and not come back. When he awoke from his sleep, he would take a sip of the now cold drink and throw the cup at the wall because it was cold.

One day I shall get away from him if it is the last thing I do, she thought.

Chapter 31

Summer 1974

F riday August 7th. Frances and the children rose at five in the morning. The luggage was in the car. Frances went back into the house to
give a cuddle to Sooty and Caesar, her dogs. She was looking forward to this holiday. Life had become like a battlefield since she had
moved into the bungalow. When she came home, she would have to
make some decision about sorting him out.

Air Malta looked after them like VIPs. Frances had travelled on package tours in the past, but this was very relaxing, and the children were so
excited. She had a couple of gin and tonics during the four-hour flight
and began to feel better. At the Airport, a representative from the hotel
met them. They travelled in a limousine to The Phoenicia in Valletta. The
hotel was magnificent with views over Valletta harbour. August was a fes-
tival time, and each evening fireworks lit the sky above the harbour.
Frances was at peace. When she had relaxed a little, her hands stopped
shaking and she had a little more confidence to speak to people—not
afraid of being ridiculed if she had an opinion on any subject.

Too soon, the holiday was over, and they were travelling home.
Frances was relaxed and looking forward to sorting out the mess at
home. The children were really happy. Catherine was beginning a new
school when the term started. They chatted happily about buying her a
uniform. The train pulled into Sheffield station but Joseph was not there
to meet them. She called a taxi, and after taking Nan home, went straight
to the bungalow. She and the children arrived at the bungalow, and the
children chatting excitedly about the things they had done and the people they had met.

Frances was first into the bungalow looking for Sooty, the black poodle Joseph had given her before they married. Sooty was almost blind but

could find Frances. She always had a welcome from Sooty and Caesar, the Pyrenean, was in the yard barking his welcome.

Joseph came out to greet them. While Joseph was bringing in the luggage, Frances and the kids looked around. "Where is Sooty?" Frances asked Joseph, when he carried the bags in.

"Dead!" he said cruelly.

"What!" Frances cried. "How did she die?"

"I had her put down. She had had her day. It was cruel to keep her alive," Joseph shouted at her. "Don't start blubbering. It won't bring her back."

Catherine ran into the garage to see her rabbits. She came running back crying, "Daddy, where have my rabbits gone?" She was carrying Sooty's bowl and crying and sobbing.

"I gave them away," he said, turning his back to her so he did not have to see her face.

"Why, Daddy, why?" Catherine wailed.

"Because there was nobody to look after them. When you have animals you should stay here and look after them." Joseph glared at her.

"But Granddad Wiseman was going to look after them," she cried.

"Well, Granddad Wiseman didn't bloody look after them, did he? I gave them away." He was losing his temper now.

She went into her room heartbroken. Richard was outside hugging Caesar. When he came in, he could hear Catherine sobbing in the bedroom. He went down to her room and after looking through the door, he saw the fish tank full of dead fish, floating on their backs. The room smelt foul from the dead fish and the dirty water.

"Did Granddad forget to feed the fish as well?" he sarcastically asked his father.

"Don't get cocky with me," Joseph answered. "I'll knock your bloody head off."

Frances put her arms around Richard and walked back into Catherine's room where they all huddled together on the bed and cried and cried for Sooty, the rabbits, and the fish.

Joseph had gone to bed although it was only four in the afternoon. Frances went into the kitchen to see what was left in the freezer. The freezer door had been left open. Everything was frozen together in one huge ball of ice. Ice cream had melted from the top shelf. This had run into the meat and fish. There was no food in the house, and the whole place stank to high heaven.

Frances looked around for the car keys. She would have to go out and do a shop. The kids were hungry. She quietly went into Joseph's bedroom, trying not to wake him, but he was wide-awake just lying there staring into space.

"What you looking for?" he asked. "Evidence?"

"Car keys," Frances answered. "There is no food in the house. I do not know what the hell has been going on in this house, but it is in a hell of a mess."

Joseph jumped up from the bed, and holding her by the throat, he said, "You suspicious cow—if you don't stop accusing me, I'll get somebody else."

Richard came into the room. "Look what I found in my bed," he said holding up a pair of earrings. Frances looked at Joseph.

"So! I had Bill and Kathy stay one night. I am allowed that while you're off sunning yourselves," he said snatching the earrings out of Richard's hand. "Get in the car. I'll take you out for a meal. That should make you happy, you stuck-up bitch."

"I do not want to go out for a meal. Just give me the keys to my car, and I will do some shopping," Frances shouted at him angrily.

"I don't have your car here. I loaned it out to Josie Brootle," he said, laughing.

"You loaned my car to a mucky little barmaid. How dare you?" Frances screamed at him.

"I dare. I do as I damn well please," he shouted at her.

"She walked out of the room so inflamed with rage that she was shaking from head to foot. It was not because she was afraid of him. She knew he was capable of beating her to pulp, but as long as he left the kids alone he could do as he pleased.

She searched for the phonebook, and after finding Josie Brootle's phone number, she dialled and waited for a reply. "Oh please be in," she prayed.

"Hello?" a female voice answered.

"I understand you have my car. I would like it returned immediately!" Frances shouted down the line.

The voice said "Joseph said I could use it as long as I needed it."

"Well, it does not belong to Joseph. Bring it back here or I shall report it to the police as stolen," Frances said.

"Okay," came the reply, and Josie rang off.

Frances turned away from the phone so angry she could hardly breathe. She wiped the tears from her eyes just as the first blow hit her on her ear. She reeled from the force and fell to the ground. The second blow landed on the wall. This caused Joseph to wince in pain and probable saved her from further punishment. He spat obscenities at her. He felt humiliated that she had rung Josie and demanded the return of the Jaguar. Who did she think she was? He was the man in this family. Everything belonged to him. She had won a piddling bit of money and thought she could rule the roost. He would show her, the bitch. Joseph left the house banging the door so hard that the beautiful glass insert cracked. Frances waited for some time before she rang Josie, reminding her that she had exactly fifteen minutes to return the Jaguar or the police would be informed.

"Joseph has just called to say I can keep the car, and he will bring me the log book. He says that you are a drunken soak and not fit to drive a pram let alone a Jaguar," Josie said, laughing.

Frances was shaking with rage now shouting "I repeat, if that car is not returned to me in fifteen minutes, I shall report it stolen and then you will find out who owns it!" She slammed the phone into the cradle so hard it fell apart. She waited, looking through the dining-room window trying to put the phone back together. Just as she was about to ring the police, the Jaguar came into view followed by Josie's brother driving a broken down old wreck. The Jaguar was left on the road with the engine still running and the door wide open.

Frances went out looked at the inside of the car and felt sick. Some child had obviously been left to do just as he pleased on the back seat. The beautiful leather seats were sticky from sweets. Milk had been spilt on the floor, and the smell pervading from inside of the vehicle was putrid. She returned to the house, collected a bucket of hot water and disinfectant and scrubbed the car until her temper had subsided.

She was feeling quite exhausted now. She and the children had been travelling since early morning and desperately needed some food. After taking the children to a local restaurant, they returned home with Frances who was intent on making a new start in her life. She could not take any more part in this stupid man's life, but she had to be careful to get out with a home. Eventually, Joseph would meet his match. Frances had decided to have all this so-called wealth for herself.

Joseph had met another woman who was very gullible. She offered Joseph sex morning, noon, and night, which turned his head, poor man.

He could not think straight. He knew Frances would take everything if she found out but could not avoid it.

The women in question was married but thought her prospects were better with Joseph. She could only see the big cars, horses and the magnificent home with a wife who just sat at home playing the guitar. She was told Frances O'Brian was a stuck-up bitch, and Joseph O'Brian needed an exciting younger woman. Piece of cake!

After the most dreadful six months of her life, when Joseph tried to get rid of her by any means possible, Frances was at the breaking point. Violence reigned. Frances was very nearly unconscious one night after he had repeatedly hit her in frustration due to his inability to get her to leave. Her life was saved by one of the children, pleading with Joseph to stop hitting Mummy.

"Why don't you get out?" he shouted at her. "We've been married for fifteen years. That's long enough. I'll give you enough to rent a house and keep the kids."

She just kept repeating that if he wanted to go then he should go. This was her house. She even wished him happiness. Eventually, after pulling Frances's arm out of its socket and badly beating her, Joseph left. He was worried that she would call a doctor who would inform the police, and this time there would be sufficient evidence to convict him of grievous bodily harm. He already had a conviction and could not afford another, especially on a woman.

After a two year battle, she had beaten him and was left with the house and a car. There was of course, the problem of an income. She tried to get the butcher shop that had been bought with the money Frances had won. Frances gave her story, pleading that she worked hard to keep the family together and spent hour after hour and day after day for two years carefully measuring photographs of football matches and crossing coupons.

The judge, in his wisdom, refused saying, "A man has to be given his business to be able to pay maintenance for his wife and children."

The maintenance order would give Frances a very good life style. She knew Joseph could never sustain a business without someone watching over the accounts. There would be no maintenance. Three weeks after the settlement, after having run up massive debts, he sold the shop for a meagre amount in cash and vanished.

Life changed for the better. Frances switched back to her maiden name, Wiseman. Her dad helped with the kids and walked the dog. He helped Frances pay bills when she was desperate. She managed to keep a car on the road with the Jimmy's help, and between them they forged a good life out of the mess left by Joseph.

Chapter 32

Life and peace after divorce

F rances had had no peace for seventeen years, and after a messy divorce, she could look forward to a better life. When she had recovered from the humiliation and the adjustments to her new lifestyle, she focused all her attention on educating her children and became an avid reader. She was frustrated at her lack of education and decided to go to college. At this point she studied languages. The next few years were very happy, but Frances could not trust anyone—indeed she would never trust anyone in her life again.

The cottage that Frances had won in the divorce settlement became a focal point for the family, not only for her happy little unit but also for Joseph and his succession of wives and children.

As the years rolled by, Frances tried many times to re-adjust her life. After meeting a famous knitwear designer whilst on a visit to London in 1982, she borrowed money from the bank using the cottage as collateral to finance a small boutique. Unfortunately the supply of knitwear vanished when the designer developed lung cancer and stopped trading. Catherine became a travel agent, and she and Frances had many foreign holidays.

After a short spell selling cars from home, Frances decided to sign-on for work at the local employment agency. On her first visit the agency, the scene was amazing. There were so many people out of work, after the collapse of heavy industry the employment office could not cope with the volume of people trying to claim benefits. After queuing for hours at an old church that had been hired to deal with two thousand unemployed people trying to sign-on in just on one day, Frances was told not to try to for a job for six months. Benefits were paid to her during this time and it gave her a window of time to find some other way of earning an income.

After Richard had obtained a degree in Economics and Computational Science, he worked for six months in a long established computer company in Slough. But this was not what he wanted to do for the rest of his life. He started to look around, and after several moves, met some other like-minded people who decided to start a computer dealership together. He needed ten thousand pounds. The cottage was mortgaged for this amount plus nine thousand pounds to allow Frances to do essential repairs to the cottage and find Richard suitable accommodation in London. Richard took part ownership of the cottage and proceeded to pay the mortgage.

He called his mother one evening, "Mum, do you think you could sell computers over the phone?" he asked.

"I do not know what a computer looks like, Richard," Frances answered.

"If I send you on a course in London, would you do it?" Richard asked, laughing.

"How much would I get paid?" Frances asked.

"I would pay you on commission, Mum," he said.

"I think I can go on a scheme with the employment office allowing me to start a small business," Frances replied, getting quite excited about the idea.

"Okay. You do that, and I will sort out the course," he said. "This course is very expensive. Do not screw up or I will be in trouble. It will be tough, and you will need to come to London for five days and stay in St. Margaret's with me."

Three weeks later, Frances found herself on the railway station in St. Margaret's at five in the morning. People were cramming the platforms, waiting to catch trains into London. She was amazed that so many people spent so much of their lives travelling to work. What a waste of precious young lives. Her London commuter education continued when she eventually caught a train to Waterloo. She was so squashed against these robotic-type people with their dark pinstripe suits and briefcases, she could only just breathe.

The train trundled along very slowly, and she began to panic. Richard had said she should make sure she was not late, or he would lose his money. One of the stipulations required to get into the course was punctuality. Frances had to be at the venue in the centre of London by nine in the morning. One minute late, and she would not be allowed in.

She thought he must be exaggerating, but she would get there if she could through this damned crowd. Why did they not move? She only had ten more minutes. She was queuing to get on an escalator with what seemed like millions of people who all had blank resigned-looks on their faces.

Coming down, the escalator was empty, and Frances made a decision. She held tight to her bag and ran like the wind up the down escalator. She emerged at the top triumphant. She straightened her hair and set off to find the hotel where the course was being run.

She arrived, breathing heavily. To her dismay all the other students were young executives straight out of college, and an exam had to be passed before the course could begin. Frances had never sat an exam in her life. She began to panic. She took the paper with trembling hands and disappeared into the ladies room. After washing her face in cold water she pushed her shoulders back and went out to give it her best shot. She could not let Richard down. She must get in. She was quite heartened to see most of the executive-types making mistakes and being allowed several chances to answer the mainly general knowledge questions. Well, Frances did not have a degree in computational science, but she had lived considerably longer than everyone else in this room and had an extremely sharp memory. There was just a chance that she could pass an exam on general knowledge. After a couple of false starts she was in.

The class started the day with forty students. The teachers consisted of five lecturers who worked together with one at the front of the class and the remaining four standing behind the students. Each student had a telephone on his desk and was asked in turn to speak into it. The four lecturers at the back of the room ridiculed the voices of the students as they tried in vain to convince the guy at the front that they could sell on the phone. Frances was constantly criticized for her Yorkshire accent.

After lunch on the first day, eight students had walked out. Frances would never walk out. Richard had paid a lot of money for this course, and she would show these southerners that they could not break her. She arrived home at ten in the evening, after catching the wrong train and finding herself in Teddington.

Richard was waiting for her. He laughed when she told him how awful the teachers were. "You have four days to go yet, Mum. That is only the start," he said.

Frances was hurt that he found it so funny. He did not seem to understand that she had not had the benefit of the education that he had. She would not give in and was up and on the train every morning.

Friday morning, and Frances was one of only eighteen students left in the course. She had learned quite a lot about people during the past week and felt sure she could sell anything that anyone else in the course could sell. When her turn came to sell a computer to the teachers, she was demoralised, everyone laughed so much.

The teachers changed places moving from front to back, and Frances was singled out to demonstrate how to change the register of the voice. She was told to pretend to be a Gorilla for the rest of the morning and not speak except with a grunt, thereby bringing her high nervous voice down to a deep throaty growl. She was picked on for every vestige of Yorkshire accent she had left.

After lunch the final tests began. Most people had southern accents when they started, and Frances thought that she would never buy anything from someone with such a cultured voice. It sounded phoney. When her turn came she was damned sure she was not going to go out with them laughing at her accent. The tape was replayed, and she was stunned to hear herself speaking so clearly with a perfect English accent. Her voice sounded so confident and sexy.

The whole class applauded her effort, and she was given a certificate stating that she was a woman of steel. To add insult to injury the head lecturer asked her why she had let them take her Yorkshire accent away, telling her that they had enjoyed watching her hang on to her accent knowing that a Yorkshire accent gets you through to the customer much easier than a cultured one. Frances travelled back to St. Margaret's jubilant and ready to push the certificate in Richard's face.

After Richard had paid so much money to train her, she was obligated to him and of course needed to prove herself. She had to try to sell computers on the phone. Her first job was to call accountants in the South East London. She was cold, selling computers to accountants who were sure they did not need technology at that moment in time. The world had not been educated into technology in 1984, especially accountants.

Frances sat looking at the phone for what seemed like hours. She had decided to start at the back of the directories she had been given containing names and addresses of accountants in the South East London. The names started with "z." She had to start somewhere so why not with "z?" *Here goes,* she thought. *Nothing ventured nothing gained.*

THE CALL OF THE HUNTSMAN

Accountants listened intently to Frances's low clear voice. The telephone number she gave them in London was the dealership in which Richard had a partnership. She learned much over the next months about computers and how to sell on the phone. She was very successful and enjoying herself when Richard announced that the company was to be bought by a larger dealership, and she would not be needed anymore.

Chapter 33

Running a Bed and Breakfast

During this time, Joseph flitted from woman to woman, not having much input into the lives of his children. He had never paid maintenance for them and certainly did not want the responsibility. He had a good job as a car salesman and had purchased himself a house in which he lived in a small self-contained area whilst he rented out the other rooms to unemployed homeless people.

He persuaded Richard to buy a house in Yorkshire, promising to collect the rents and pay the mortgage. Richard thought this would give his father a business opportunity and of course the property would eventually increase in value.

The chosen house was in need of repair and had belonged to one of Joseph's crooked friends, but Richard did not know this. Six months later Joseph disappeared.

Richard was living and working in London and asked his mother to take a look at the house. He needed someone to collect the rents and pay the mortgage. He obviously believed that she would be able to ask nicely for the rent, and then trot along to the bank with the all the money. But in the real world, this proved to be very far from the truth.

Frances asked Richard's friends in a local boxing club to accompany her when she checked the house. The sight that met her was dreadful. Graffiti had been scrawled on the walls, and the house had eleven occupants, most of whom were drug addicts with the exception of one who was a drug pusher. Frances told the police of her fears, but she was told to watch her back and not to upset too many people if she knew what was good for her.

With the help of the minder from the boxing club, she started the daunting task of clearing the house of the filth that surrounded the renters. She had never seen the results of drugs before, except on the television. But the anguish of these young men and women was difficult to deal with. Frances decided to sell the property, hoping to recover enough money to repay the mortgage. The estate agent valued the stinking place several thousand less than the amount that Richard had mortgaged it for and told Frances that she would never be able to sell the place in such disrepair.

After studying the situation, Frances decided that she should run the house as a bed and breakfast establishment and try to pay the mortgage from the money she was able to collect from the current residents.

She borrowed enough cash from the bank to clean and decorate the house, replacing beds and bedding and clearing the arrears of the existing tenants and giving them a fresh start without the worry of unpaid rent debts. The rooms were cleaned, decorated, and refurbished. This way, Frances hoped to build the house with a reputation as a place to sleep and recover from life's traumas.

Unfortunately Frances had no idea how bad life's traumas could be and learning to deal with these tenants became a challenge. Some renters had to go when they could not be persuaded to part with the rent money that social security had paid directly to them. The drug- pusher was the most difficult to deal with. He was smart and never gave Frances any reason to terminate his tenancy. He had the money to pay the rent on time because his customers lived around him and were unable to lay off what he sold.

Most of Frances's tenants were young people who had for whatever reason spent most of their lives in local authority care. Some had been removed from homes after they had suffered abuse from their families, both physical and sexual. These young people were very disturbed and found it difficult to trust anyone. Her heart went out to them. They had nothing in this world except the few meagre bits and bobs, which they carried in plastic bags from one bed and breakfast establishment to another.

Sometimes she would sit with them and listen to the stories of abuse in the council care homes. Unfortunately the practice of abuse seemed to be an accepted one. She asked if she could do anything to help the poor kids who were still suffering the abuse in these places, but she was always dismayed when they laughed and asked her who she would tell. Frances suggested that she should tell the police or the social workers but everyone said she should not waste her time because nobody cared. Frances began to poke around, trying to find someone to help, but was always met with the same response, which was a stock response to any problem put to the police or to the social workers regarding young kids just out of council care.

"Mrs Wiseman, don't make waves," she was told. "These kids are winding you up. If we investigate this, they will not back up these claims and court time will be wasted."

When she told the kids this, they assured her that it was happening. After several kids reported the abuse, they were left in the same council homes about which they were complaining whilst waiting for the assault cases to go to court. If you blabbed, the treatment you received in a council home seemed to be worse than the original abuse. She tried to gain the young people's trust, and gradually the house became quite a happy house. Whenever she could afford it, she made repairs to the house, although she was heavily in debt to the bank. Still, she felt she was doing a worthwhile job.

In the late eighties, the government decided to remove the housing benefit from the unemployed homeless under the age of twenty-six years old. Most of Frances's tenants were in this category, and after many hours on the telephone, trying to find someone to explain to her why this vulnerable age group had been singled out, she was informed that the best place for a young person to be brought up was at home with their parents. It was thought that by removing the benefit they would drift back home where they should be. Frances argued that eighty-five percent of her tenants either had no parents or had been removed from their parents because of parental cruelty. In her estimation only fifteen percent fit the description as a good reason to remove the benefit. Her efforts were ignored, and the young people had to move. Frances was heart broken. She had to pay the mortgage on the house and needed the house to be full in order to do that.

After informing the local social services that she was willing to take psychiatric patients if someone from the agency supported her on a regular visiting basis, Francis set about making a home for the homeless psychiatric patients who were victims of the care in the community bill which had recently come into force. If Frances had found the kids from children's homes a daunting task then the psychiatrics would prove to be a lesson in life that she would rather not have learned.

She soon discovered that social workers would offer her the moon when they looked for accommodation for patients being discharged from hospital. The staff were over-stretched and forced to move patients quickly. If the patient was violent, he could be sectioned, but the hospital staff did not want to cope with violent patients they would discharge them at every opportunity. Poor ignorant Frances offered her home to these sick people who needed medical help. She truly believed all the social workers when they promised help her with any problems day or night. Of course support from social services was virtually non-existent, and these dangerous people were out in the community without supervision or any type of structure to help them to adjust to everyday life in the outside world.

Life for Frances became a struggle of day to day survival. If she managed to get the rent from the tenants, she would rush to the bank to pay it. She had to pay the mortgage on her cottage along with the mortgage on the bed and breakfast house, and juggling the books was becoming unbearable.

Chapter 34

1987

One cold December night in 1987, Frances received a call from the local hospital where her dad had been taken. She drove there immediately. Jimmy was so pleased to see her he told the doctor that everything would be alright now because his daughter was there. She would know what to do.

Watching her dad struggle for breath, Frances thought her heart would break. She sat with him well into the night. The ward sister came in and beckoned Frances to follow her outside.

The sister said, "Your daughter is just being admitted as in emergency on the floor below. You go. I'll sit with your dad for a while."

Frances ran down the hospital corridor, her heart pumping so fast it seemed that it would jump out of her chest at any moment. When she arrived, there was a commotion as medics ran alongside trolley at breakneck speed. She caught up with them, trying to see who was on the trolley. It was Catherine, writhing in pain. The trolley moved so fast she could hardly keep up with it. She tried to question the ambulance attendants, telling them she was the girl's mother and demanding to know what was happening.

Catherine was rushed into a waiting operating room with doctors and nurses gowned up ready for her arrival. Frances was terrified. Somebody took hold of her arms and ushered her away from her terrified daughter who was obviously in desperate need of an emergency caesarean. This was Catherine's second child. She had been due for some time. Something must be very wrong.

The need to know what was happening overruled any hospital regulations. Frances found a small window that overlooked a corridor outside the operating theatre. She leaned out of the window as far as she could, watching the comings and goings of doctors and nurses in and out of the operating theatre. Her eyes streamed with tears. She did not know what to do next. Feeling she should be with her dad but unable to leave her daughter, Frances began to sob uncontrollably. A young female doctor came out of the operating theatre, and seeing Frances hanging out of the window, stopped and called out to her.

"What on earth are you doing in there?" she asked.

Frances gabbled out the story about her dad and her daughter through tears and sobbing. The doctor took hold of her and ushered her into a side room were she gowned her in a green robe and asked her to put covers over her shoes.

The doctor led Frances into the recovery room next to the operating theatre, and a baby was put into her arms. The most beautiful little girl she had ever seen was wrapped in a rough hospital blanket, gazing at the world in wonder. The child was staring at her own fingers with a wondrous look, watching them move around in the unaccustomed brightness of the world into which she had suddenly been brought. Catherine was beginning to wake up, and Frances turned the baby for her to see the child. When she was satisfied that Catherine and the child were no longer in danger, she ran back along the corridor and up the stairs to her dad.

"Catherine has just had baby girl, Dad," she whispered into his ear.

Jimmy smiled weakly and whispered, "Thank God."

She felt exhausted her emotions were running the gamut of high and just as suddenly plunged into the depths. Where would this end? She could not take much more.

Later in the same day that the child was born, Jimmy died. Frances had just left his side and stepped out to get some food. She could not believe that God would do this to her—a birth and a death on the same day was unbearable.

During the next week, Frances had to organise a funeral and bring home her daughter and the baby girl. She really did not know where to start. One minute she was crying and the next she was happy, gazing at the child. She had to find strength from somewhere. She had been the one to look after her dad so she had to deal with the business that always goes hand in hand with a funeral.

Catherine had married a very irresponsible man and was about to realise her mistake. Soon after the birth of her second child she had to return to work, leaving the children with her mother to care for along with running the bed and breakfast for Richard. Catherine's husband was causing so many problems at this time. He refused look after the child and certainly would not go to work. Frances thought she would need to hold everybody together until after the funeral. Then she could give vent to her feelings.

Frances would obviously not see her daughter and grandchildren without food, spending large amounts of money on groceries and children's necessities. Joseph left his last lover and asked Frances if she could borrow money on the cottage again to buy a terraced house which he had got involved in with one of the women who had bore him a child.

Frances thought about it and made the big decision to buy the house and run it along with the bed and breakfast. The social services would easily fill the house with tenants but the workload would be hard on her. She cared for her grandchild during the day, and along with cooking breakfast for two establishments and feeding and caring for a baby, life was unbearably tiring.

Collecting the rent was not such a big problem. The state paid the landlord directly, but the tenants were like ticking time bombs. After Frances had been threatened with a carving knife by a little old lady who no one would have guessed had the strength to walk upstairs, Frances decided enough was enough and called in an estate agent to value the property. She was delighted to find the property was now worth ten thousand pounds more and excitedly told Richard. He decided to give Frances the house as repayment of the ten thousand pounds he had borrowed from her to buy into the computer dealership in 1982, but of course, she had to keep paying the mortgages or the houses would be repossessed. She decided to try to keep the house running for another year but was very frightened of some of the psychiatric patients who stayed there. If the voices in their heads told them that she was bad, she was treated to abuse the likes of which she had never heard before.

Sometimes she was an angel and sometimes she was a devil in the eyes of these very sick people. Traps would be set on the stairs to trip her, or excrement would be smeared on door handles to deter her from entering rooms. Life was becoming a nightmare but the nightmare would soon be over.

Of course Richard had no idea that his mother was in danger. Frances only told him what she thought he should know. He would have sold the houses immediately had he known the truth.

The housing market was beginning to move up and up around this time. For some reason people in the south of England believed that houses in the grim North were about to rise steeply. This notion started a rise in the property market so great that hordes of prospective buyers headed north, looking to buy rental property. For Frances this was the best news ever. The buyers wanted rental property, and she had two well-kept properties, which she could not sell fast enough.

She decided to put the houses to auction including the tenants and five years of books showing the profits made and the moneys invested back into the houses. She just wanted to get enough cash to pay off the mortgages and clear the bank debt, but she had to act fast, before the bubble burst and the property market in the north sank to the bottom again.

On the day of the auction, she was so nervous she had a reserve on the properties, which would, if she was lucky, bring enough to pay off all her debts. Then she would be able to find a regular job. To her astonishment when the auctioneer banged down his hammer. her houses sold for two hundred and fifty thousand pounds. Frances was stunned. She could pay off everyone and retain a nice little nest egg for her retirement.

It took three months to finalise the house transition and turn them over to the new owners after which Frances took a long holiday with Catherine and the children. Whilst she was lying on a beach in the sun, she began to plan and make decisions for the future. She needed to find a good investment for a pension fund and enrol at a college. She knew she could not sit at home. She wanted to know more about computers.

Frances spent a year studying basic computing skills passing classes in Accounting, Word processing, Database management, and Spreadsheets. She thought this ought to be sufficient to work a computer.

With a very little knowledge of stocks and shares but with a feeling of excitement about technology, she started to look for a technology stock to buy. She decided on technology security stock and got so carried away that she bought one hundred thousand pounds worth of shares in the stock. After she had done this she began to panic, thinking she had made a big mistake. But eventually she told herself that she had started with nothing so what the hell if she lost it. They could not shoot her. She would just pretend that she never had it in the first place.

Fear of dying

After paying for private medical insurance, she had a routine medical just as a precaution. Whilst she was with the doctor she mentioned that she thought she had a lump underneath her arm. It was not very noticeable, but she would like it checked.

The doctor agreed that she had a lump and made an appointment for the next day for her to see a breast surgeon who took a fine needle aspiration to send to the pathology lab. He told Frances to have a mammogram the next day. Two days later, Frances was working at home when the phone rang.

"Mrs. Wiseman?" the voice inquired.

"Yes," Frances answered.

After introducing himself, the surgeon asked Frances to come to his clinic immediately. She was scared and drove to the clinic in a daze. The surgeon called her into his surgery, and after dropping his papers on the floor several times, he spat out cruelly. "You've got cancer, Mrs. Wiseman. Now when shall we get it out?"

Frances stared at this man in horror. "You mean I have breast cancer?" she asked him, still not believing.

"Yes, it is cancer," he replied. "I can do the operation next weekend, if that suits you. I will remove your ovaries to stop your body from producing oestrogen and reconstruct your breast after surgery."

Just like that, Frances thought. It never crossed her mind to question the diagnosis. This eminent breast surgeon had to know something was bad to want to operate the next week. Her mind was unable to grasp any of the facts that the doctor was telling her. She could not believe that she might die. This man was in a hurry. He kept looking at his watch. She found herself apologising to the man for keeping him. *My God, what is happening to me? I must be dreaming*, she thought.

Asking her to return the following day for blood tests, she was ushered out the door into the cold night. After walking for what seemed like hours, she found herself standing on a bridge overlooking a very dirty river. If she closed her eyes and jumped this nightmare would be over, and she would never have to break the news that she probably only had three years left to live. She thought of the patronising sympathy she would most likely get. She may as well be dead now and get it over with. Her mind was in turmoil. How could she go home and pretend that everything was all right when her whole world was turned upside down? She moved away from the bridge and walked slowly back toward the hospital.

It was November 5th. Frances had parked her car in a road next to a park. She did not get into the car immediately but walked over to a group of people standing around a bonfire. The children's faces were a picture. Someone gave her a sparkler to hold, and the stars from the sparkler mesmerised her.

Suddenly she became aware of a woman watching her with piercing eyes as black as coal and long black hair tied back with colourful ribbons.

Those eyes reminded Frances of the eyes of the gypsy cousin who had sent her and Joseph to Doncaster many years earlier. She turned to walk away from the happy group and back to the car. The women strode over to her, and putting her hands on Frances's shoulders, said in a gravely voice, "It's never as bad as you think, lass, no matter what it is." Then the odd woman turned and walked away, leaving Frances staring after her.

Frances was on autopilot and did not listen to anyone when they spoke to her. She was completely traumatised. The only person to understand how traumatised was her general practitioner who did seem to care that she was in this trance. He taught Frances how to hypnotise herself. She spent hours the next week letting her mind tell her body how to correct whatever was going wrong with her breast. This Frances did religiously. Day and night she put herself into in a trance, believing all that she had been taught regarding the immune system. She visualised the tumour shrinking day by day until she was convinced it was not there at all.

Through the self-hypnosis, Frances was able to prepare herself for the operation. When she entered the hospital, her mind was clear of worry. She would just go to this place in her head whenever she needed to get away from reality.

She awoke from the operation in some pain after the massive surgery she had undergone. The surgeon sat at her bedside. He was apologising to her, saying someone has made a mistake the tumour was not there. Frances was too ill to listen, but she did have a dreadful feeling that maybe it was so bad that they had just sewed her up and left it.

The next time she awoke she felt for her breast; there was a large plaster but it was still there. She still had her doubts about what had happened but discovered that he had removed her ovaries, womb and fallopian tubes, which all proved to be healthy. In fact, the whole operation, along with the trauma and dreadful shock to her body, was unnecessary.

Slowly, she recovered and picked up her life again. But the trauma left her feeling angry that patients were treated so matter-of-factly when they needed someone more like her general practitioner to soften the blow and allow them to take control over the situation.

One day Frances called to see her Auntie Kisaiya who still lived in the same house on Devonshire Street, which Sarah and Jimmy had lived in when they were first wed. She walked through the garden and felt so close to her family in this house. Poor Kisaiya was failing in health now at eighty-eight. Her brother, Kenneth, had died at the age of seventy-two from a chest disease. Kenneth had been buried with Mam, and Dad, and Jean and Lorna, of course, and Frances was feeling very sad and lonely. Kenneth had been the eldest of the Wiseman family and his death was a signal that the winter of her life was approaching.

She talked to Auntie Kisaiya about Sarah and Auntie Alice, who had died sometime before, and asked her if she remembered living on Osborne Street.

Kisaiya replied, "I remember me mam going out in her black hat with poppies on and coming back married."

They laughed, after all, you could laugh seventy-eight years later, but how could anyone understand the shock for poor Kisaiya when she was ten-years-old and her mam went out and came back married to some old man she had never heard of?

"I can remember me mam making me take a gold watch to leave at Mrs. Marsh's house every time she knew our William was coming to visit, because he used look all over the house for it," Kisaiya said. "Me mam always pawned that watch when she wanted some money, but our William said his dad had left it for him. I dared not say where I had taken it. Me mam would have hit me if I had."

Frances asked, "Auntie Kisaiya, you know when you used to put me in the snug in the Catholic Club?"

Kisaiya said. "You didn't like it in there, did you."

"No, I did not. I was scared and it smelt funny," Frances said, wrinkling her nose.

Kisaiya laughed saying, "No wonder you were scared. The undertaker's shed was next door to the club and it was only a small place so when he had made a few coffins he would store 'em in the snug until he needed 'em."

Frances was horrified. "But why did it smell funny?" she asked.

"Well sometimes if a lot of folk had died at same time and when their families didn't have room for the bodies to be laid out at home, the undertaker would put a couple in the snug. Not for long. Not more than a day, but it smelled of that stuff that they washed 'em in to keep 'em fresh."

"Formaldehyde," Frances said, feeling sick at the thought of a four-year-old being shut in a room with dead bodies.

"Those were hard times, Frances. We had to do a lot of things that we would not do now, lass," Kisaiya said sadly.

243

Frances cuddled her Auntie Kisaiya saying, "I know that Auntie, but it has always puzzled me."

Kisaiya died three months later, and Frances knew she would never forget how kind her auntie had been and how hard she had worked in the Doncaster house. Make no mistake, Kisaiya was a true lady.

Chapter 35

The gypsy curse misses a generation 1998

The world had gone mad. Millions were being made overnight on Internet companies that were building a virtual reality world in cyber space.

Frances thought about the terrible risks she had taken with the cottage and the money she had invested very rashly into stock that she knew absolutely nothing about. It would be just her luck for her stock to be in the wrong area of this cyber world.

In the summer of 1996, she had a call from the stockbroker who had handled her business when she had purchased the technology stock. He said that the company was considering an acquisition offer, and a meeting of investors would be held in San Francisco in two weeks time when a vote would be taken on this possible acquisition.

"What is an acquisition, Mr Babbington?" she asked.

"Well, Mrs. Wiseman, an acquisition of a company means just that. A company is acquired by another one, usually a competitor who can then have monopoly over the market place."

"And what other options are there, Mr Babbington?" she asked.

"A company can prepare to IPO which means they are preparing to go to the stock market with their shares," he answered. "In this case, I believe the board is split on which way to vote. Acquisition could ensure that you receive a return of all your investment and maybe a little profit but IPO may make you extremely rich if the shares do well. It is all a bit of a gamble. I am afraid this is why we have to go and listen to what the board has to say. We can then make our decision on how far we want to gamble with the company."

"Which is the best option for this company?" Frances questioned. She was confused and had no idea how this type of business worked.

"We shall not know that for sure, my dear," he said patronisingly, "until we get there."

Poor Frances was not in any position to fly to San Francisco. She was living on benefits and barely able to eat let alone fly halfway around the world to an investor's meeting. She really wanted to go to this event and had several sleepless nights trying to plot a way of raising the money for the fare. Her credit card would cover it but what if she could not pay it back. *What a conundrum*, she thought. Anyhow they could not shoot you so she rang the stockbroker and said she would be travelling to San Francisco with all the other investors.

Charles Babbington called her back to ask if she would be travelling first class. First class! She would be lucky to be travelling in the hold, but she assured him that she would make her own arrangements and would meet up with his party in San Francisco if he would let her know which hotel the meeting was to be held in.

Babbington was quite shocked to hear this but insisted that she travel with the rest of the investors in the limo from the airport to San Jose, where the company was based. Frances let out a sigh of relief and agreed. She would have no idea how to get to San Jose or anywhere outside of the airport for that matter.

"Mrs Wiseman," Babbington added. "Our group will be staying in a small hotel in Santa Clara. You will be joining us there I hope."

"Oh of course," Frances babbled. "I look forward to meeting my fellow investors."

Frances settled down in her window seat, fastened her seat belt, and quietly reflected on what was happening to her. In the last two weeks she had gone from being a depressed single middle-aged woman with little or no prospects of anything changing in the foreseeable future to this a well-dressed educated looking middle-aged woman sitting on the Virgin 19 flight from Heathrow to San Francisco. On her knee was the book she had bought in the airport titled *Zero-to-IPO*. She probably would not understand a word of it but she had spent some time searching for a book that would give her some idea what IPO meant.

The flight left Heathrow at eleven in the morning and landed in San Francisco at one-thirty in the afternoon with an eight-hour time difference. This gave Frances almost ten hours to read *Zero-to-IPO*. She smiled to herself as she packed the book away and prepared for landing. When she had boarded this plane she had very little idea what she was in for on this adventure, but after reading this book, she was quite looking forward to hearing what the board had to say regarding how they had spent her money.

Frances stood in the immigration line and smiled at Mr. Babbington, who had travelled first class with all the other investors. He, of course, had left the plane first. The line was very long and Frances was late joining the intrepid first-class travellers who were to be her companions for the next seven days.

Mr. Babbington ushered her into the limo which was parked as close to the arrivals hall as possible, and they drove away. The driver gave a running commentary on the fifty mile drive through Silicon Valley. The scenery was spectacular. Frances had just read about most of the companies in her *Zero-to-IPO* book and sounded very knowledgeable when she could give a brief history of some of the companies that had sprung out of this valley. Charles Babbington was puzzled by just how much she knew. He had thought that she was not very bright and that he would have to lead her to the right decision when it came to the board meeting. He secretly thought she had just come for a holiday.

The hotel was comfortable, and the food was good. Frances said good night to her companions and was in bed by seven o'clock. Not a wise thing to do when you have just travelled half way around the world. Her companions tried to tell her to stay awake until at least ten o'clock to avoid the dreaded jet lag, but poor Frances could not keep her eyes open.

The limo picked them up the next morning and drove them to San Jose, a bustling city full of technology start-up companies all hoping to make a fortune on the internet. As they left the limo, they were each given a badge with their name on it and asked to pin it to their lapel. They were welcomed warmly by the CEO of the company and taken to the board room for drinks. In the board room, they were greeted by a robot that hugged them with large metal arms and introduced them to the board members by name. Frances was intrigued to find that the robot was actually manipulated by a man with a microphone, hiding behind a screen. His job was to read the name on everyone's lapel and introduce each investor through the robot. This broke the ice and got everyone chatting happily.

Frances did not drink alcohol and was offered coffee. She did not drink any coffee either and settled for a bottle of water. They were given a tour of the offices and shown how the technology worked. Frances was very impressed with how they all knew just what was happening on the web and how to block inappropriate content from sifting through. This is what the company had done with her money—built this wonderful browser to keep children safe on the web. The board meeting was arranged for the next morning at eleven, and the group left to spend the rest of the day sightseeing.

Quite close to the hotel was the theme park, Great America, and Frances decided to spend her leisure time there, watching the families have fun. She decided to have her lunch there and just sit and think for a while. She had asked quite a few questions whilst she was at the company offices and had come to the conclusion that the acquiring company just wanted to break up the company and only use pieces of the engineering that had been developed over the past few years. This did not seem right to Frances. She knew that she would lose all her money if she got it wrong but knew which way she was going to vote at the meeting. She would vote for the company to carry on as they were and prepare for IPO.

When the group was having dinner that evening at the hotel the conversation was buzzing about how they would like the company to go forward. Frances suggested that they would not go forward if they voted for the acquisition. It would go backwards and not exist. She left the table after some heated arguments began. Some of these investors had several million pounds they had invested. She only had a paltry one hundred thousand pounds to lose. She was out of her depth and knew it.

She smiled to herself and repeated, *Only a paltry one hundred thousand pounds*. She could soon make that amount up. Maybe she could get a job at the big department store, ASDA.

Anyway, no need for her to worry. They all knew what was happening in that company. She was not so naive to believe that there were no secret telephone calls taking place between the big investors. If the company had a good chance of going to the stock market sooner rather than later, they would turn down this acquisition.

The boardroom was full, and they all sat around a very large oval table. It reminded Frances of King Arthur and his knights. She hoped these Knights of the Round Table would do the right thing. The vote was to be secret, and the room went silent while the papers were being counted. It was rather an anticlimax, really. The CEO read out the result and only one vote had been cast for the acquisition so the adventure was over.

On her return to the UK, Frances decided to try to forget all about her one hundred thousand pound shares. In fact, she started to call it her "one hundred thousand pound folly." She regularly received updated information from the company and she often had to refer to her IPO book as she called it. It seemed to her that the company was doing very well but she would not count her chickens just yet.

Frances parted company with her fellow investors at the airport. After they had checked in, they were escorted to the upper class lounge to comfortably await their flight. The passengers travelling in coach were not so lucky, but Frances searched the bookshop for something to occupy her mind on the long flight home.

Surviving Breast Cancer almost jumped off the shelf at her, and after reading the synopsis, she decided to buy it. She began to read in the airport and that is where the first thoughts started to haunt her regarding her breast cancer diagnosis. The flight took forever. It really seemed to take longer to fly back to the UK than it did to fly out to the US, but of course, she was flying through the night and needed to sleep and could not get comfortable. During that long night, she began to plan to see a lawyer when she got home and find out what really happened when her extremely healthy body had been operated on. Was it as her general practitioner believed that she had cured herself with hypnosis, or had she never had cancer in the first place. She really wanted to know. If she had had cancer, her descendants should know if there was a dangerous gene in the family.

The first lawyer Frances approached was very sympathetic but informed her that her case would be statute barred because it was over the three-year time limit for investigations to take place, and the defendant would be at a disadvantage. Frances decided to visit the local Citizens Advice Bureau. They listened to her story with great interest, and after taking advice from a medical negligence lawyer, gave her a list of law firms who offered Legal Aid.

Of course Frances had no money whatsoever to live on. Her pension was not enough for her to be able to afford to pay for an investigation. The first lawyer she saw from the Citizen's Advice Bureau list spent two hours questioning Frances about every aspect of the case, and after conferring with his colleagues confidently told Frances that he thought she had a good case to put before the Legal Aid Board. But first things first—

if she could get funding to do the investigations, then he would take on the case.

Funding was granted but just for the investigations. These investigations took years to complete. The first result was from a breast cancer specialist in London that confirmed that Frances had never had breast cancer, and the fine needle aspiration showed no sign of malignancy. She was so relieved. This is what she needed to know. The Legal Aid certificate had to be renewed every six months, and with this confirmation it was just a matter of renewing and renewing until all the evidence was collated. The next big news was when a gynaecologist from Edinburgh confirmed that her ovaries and uterus were perfectly healthy at the time.

Frances was sent to psychiatrist for his opinion on her state of mind. Was she suffering from post-traumatic stress? He was the most ignorant man that Frances had ever met, and she had met a few. She remembered the poor psychiatric patients in the bed and breakfast house and how terrified they were of psychiatrists. She would not like to think that this man who sat with his feet up on the table eating a bacon sandwich had her future in his hands. The psychiatrist sent a report to the lawyer claiming she was an erratic irrational menopausal woman. Well perhaps she was. After all, they removed all the bits and bobs that made her a woman, plunging her into menopause overnight. But that was not the point either. Was she or was she not in this state because she had had the dodgy surgery?

All the evidence was collated against the doctor who had made this decision to rob her of her womanhood. Frances wondered how he would feel if some doctor had irresponsibly removed his testicles. The case was put to a judge in chambers who wanted to meet Frances and the doctor to decide for himself if there was a case to answer. Or was it, as the doctor claimed, that he had informed Frances immediately after the operation that she did not have cancer and that she now was just after compensation. Nothing could be further from the truth. Frances had when she began these investigations only wanted to know why he had made the decision to operate on her before following proper standard guidelines where all the investigations had to be positive before a cancer diagnosis was given. In this case, the fine needle aspiration, the mammogram, the blood tests and the physical examination showed no signs of being positive. In fact, she only had a small fatty tissue under her right arm so why all the surgery?

A date was arranged to meet the judge. Frances was really looking forward to this meeting. She needed to ask this doctor why he had made that drastic decision and to ask these questions in front of a judge would satisfy her nagging doubts about the whole mess. Three days before the arranged meeting the lawyer rang to say they had done a deal with the doctor's lawyers. Frances would get five thousand pounds in cash, and the lawyer would get his fees paid, approximately twenty thousand pounds. The Legal Aid Board would not stand to lose any money, and she would have a tidy sum to put into the bank.

A businessman and friend of the family was brought in to mediate and informed them in no uncertain terms that she did not want five thousand pounds. She wanted to go in front of a judge with the doctor and have her questions answered. The lawyer was not happy at all. He had had enough of this. If they went to trial the Legal Aid Board may not be happy about the possibility of losing twenty thousand pounds plus the trial fees. The other lawyer rang the mediator, saying the best he could do was eight thousand pounds, and if she did not take it, he could not guarantee that the barrister would represent her in court if indeed she did get a trial.

Frances went back to the CAB office for some unbiased advice. They spent most of the day working on the case, but because Frances could not pay for a trial herself and the lawyer was committed to using Legal Aid on a case that a judge may decide, was statute barred because of the time limit on prosecution. Although he admitted to the CAB representative that they had all the evidence to prove that the doctor had committed medical negligence, nothing could be done. Frances took the eight thousand pounds and never trusted the law again.

Millionairess

In the days after her disappointment with the lawyers Frances became quite despondent. The eight thousand pound pay-off had helped a little and paid off the debt incurred when she had travelled to San Francisco, but she still had no prospects of earning more than the very meagre state pension to live on.

One morning when she had not bothered to dress or plan her day, Frances opened the post-box and ploughed her way through the bills and junk mail. She found a letter from Charles Babbington. She ripped it open and read the first line then the last line then the middle bit and then stopped her hands shaking. She started again and read the whole letter aloud.

THE CALL OF THE HUNTSMAN

Dear Mrs. Wiseman:

I have the greatest pleasure in informing you that your technology shares are very much sought after at the moment I have had £3 per share offered and would like to know if you want to sell.

Frances searched the house for her IPO book. She had read somewhere that if the whisper had gone out that the company was going to IPO the shares would become very valuable but three pounds a share would only mean three hundred thousand pounds, and with forty percent tax, she would be better off waiting. After all, she had decided that she had lost this money so she would ring Mr. Babbington and tell him she had no intention of selling her shares until the company reached Wall Street. Charles Babbington was shocked to hear this. He had been sure she would sell and even had a customer waiting to buy. Frances jokingly said to contact her when she was a millionairess.

Ten days later she got the call. "Mrs. Wiseman," the caller said. "Mr. Babbington asked me to call you. He is in a meeting at the moment. He said to tell you that you are a millionairess."

Frances screamed, "You are joking! This is not funny. I could have a heart attack. Who is this?"

The caller confirmed the name and position in the company and left Frances to recover. After the dust had died down and her shares had been sold, which took several months, Frances's one hundred thousand pound investment made a cool twenty million dollars after taxes.

After a wonderful family holiday with her children and grandchildren in the Bahamas, Frances travelled home with the idea that was filling her thoughts and taking over her every waking hour. She had to get back home and start her search for Lambecote Grange. She thought the gypsy curse must have run its course but touched wood and crossed her fingers when she said it.

If only she had received all this money when she was a little younger, she could have made everyone's life so different. She would try to find Lambecote Grange and put the huntsman's family where they belonged. She was past sixty years old and had been struggling for most of her life. If she could find Lambecote Grange, the picture would be complete.

Chapter 36

Lambecote Grange 1999

A lex Campbell was now concerned with Frances's strange behaviour. He called to her, "Mrs. Wiseman, please come back to the house. We still have to view the stables and the old servant's quarters."

"I have seen all I need for the time being, Mr. Campbell," she replied. "Perhaps I could take a look at the history whilst you drive me back to Nottingham."

"Yes certainly, Mrs. Wiseman," Alex answered. He was a little scared of this crazy woman and would like to get back in time to play golf before it got too dark.

When they arrived at the estate agents, Frances insisted on following Campbell into his office.

"Now, Mr. Campbell!" she exclaimed. "Let us get down to business." She sat down, taking a small palm held computer from her bag. She immediately began to take notes. "First and foremost, I would like to know how long the property has been derelict," she said.

"Oh, it is not derelict, Mrs. Wiseman," Campbell stated sharply.

"Well, the property which I have just viewed with you, Mr. Campbell, is definitely derelict. The house has been empty for a very long time, and the land has not been farmed properly for years. I think that describes derelict, don't you?" she asked looking directly into his eyes, which she decided were very shifty.

Alex stuttered and stammered a little. He had lost his grip on reality, and she was reacting in a very business-like way. He would have expected her to bring in some other party before she pinned him down to answering questions like this. Lambecote Grange was on the market for nearly eight million, and decisions involving that sum of money usually had to be considered with mortgage companies and a whole host of other parties before they got down to brass tacks like this.

"Mr. Campbell, I do not have all night I have to drive back to Sheffield and would prefer to go in daylight, so if you would not mind answering these questions, I could be on my way," Frances said, slightly agitated.

"Well the farm was bankrupt eighteen months ago, Mrs. Wiseman," he answered.

"Who are the official receivers, Mr. Campbell?" she asked.

"Bryce and Coombes are the receivers, but the main creditor is Henderson's Bank," Alex replied

"Surely there is more than one creditor, Mr Campbell," Frances said curiously.

"Yes, yes, Mrs. Wiseman. There are quite a few I believe, but of course you would have to speak to the receiver regarding what sums are owed to whom," Alex explained, thinking Peter White, the manager of Henderson's Bank, who was certain he could pick up this property for less than two million, had met his match here. "Mrs. Wiseman, this property is for sale for eight million pounds. That is a very large sum to find. I hope you realise that the possibility of getting this farm working again is almost nil since the mad cow scare."

"Has the land been taken off the green belt?" she asked.

"No this is prime farming land Madam." He answered patronisingly.

"Then I think the farm is grossly over priced." Frances said indignantly.

"Oh you misunderstand Mrs Wiseman." He stuttered. "We have to value land at a rate covering all possible uses."

"Are you trying to sell this farm, Mr. Campbell, or are you keeping it for someone else?" Frances asked, straight to the point and no messing about with protocol.

"Of course I want to sell the farm, Mrs. Wiseman," Alex waffled. "I am just a little shocked at the speed of your interest. It is usual for purchasers to go home and give it some thought before I am asked for all the details."

"I want to know every detail regarding Lambecote Grange. Who owned it? Why did they lose it? How many bids have been made, if any? Who stands to gain most from the sale? And have any applications for 'change of use' been made in the last six months? Now if you can give me all this information, I can then go home and make my next move," Frances said.

"I can't give you all that information, Mrs. Wiseman. I would have to have a meeting with the bank who hold the deeds before I could give you those details." Alex answered, now in a panic. He did not want to upset White or the business fraternity who were hoping to develop Lambecote Grange. But this damned woman had him over a barrel.

"In that case," Frances said moving her chair back ready to stand up. "I shall not waste anymore of your time, Mr. Campbell. Good day to you." Frances picked up her bag and walked toward the door.

"Please, Mrs. Wiseman, you must understand my position," Alex pleaded with her.

"I understand your position completely, Mr. Campbell, and I shall not discuss it with you any further," she said, walking out of the building.

Outside in the car park, she stepped into her sleek black BMW with tinted windows. As she reversed out of the parking lot, she caught a glimpse of Alex Campbell watching her from his window.

It was four in the afternoon as she drove into Nottingham and found a parking spot. After making several phone calls with enquiries regarding the official receiver she rang Bryce and Coombes. Fortunately Mr. Coombes was still in his office and agreed to see Frances straightaway, after she explained to the secretary that she was interested in Lambecote Grange.

Mr. Coombes was much more forthcoming regarding the situation with the offers made on behalf of the businessmen who were trying to purchase Lambecote Grange for much less than the asking price. "You have to understand, Mrs. Wiseman, that I have to do what is best for the creditors and the largest creditor is Henderson's Bank," Mr. Coombes explained to Frances adding, "The problem that I have there is that Mr. White, the local manager of Henderson's Bank, is one of the businessmen trying to have Lambecote Grange removed from the green belt, thereby allowing any purchaser to develop the land and probably demolish the house and stables."

"No, Mr. Coombes. I want Lambecote Grange. It is my heritage. I have perused copies of the deeds, looking back over the last four hundred years and am convinced that George Bingham was my grandfather," Frances said, sitting on the edge of her chair with a worried look on her face. She had found Lambecote Grange and would not allow someone to steal it from her at this stage. It was unthinkable.

"Mrs. Wiseman, my family was related to the Bingham family by marriage and indeed this firm handled all the legal business for Lambecote Grange before Harold Sutton got his hands on it after the death of George Bingham. I know quite a lot about the happenings around that time. I believe there was a son who should have taken over but vanished without trace. What is your connection to the family?" Coombes asked, looking very interested now.

"My mother was Sarah Bingham, daughter of George and Rosina Bingham," Frances replied.

"It is wonderful to meet you, Mrs. Wiseman. This has been a mystery for many years," he said excitedly. "I do hope you can secure the finance for this deal. I would love to have the Bingham family back on Lambecote Grange land."

"Oh, the finance will not be a problem, Mr. Coombes," Frances said smugly. "But the transaction will have to be handled with the utmost secrecy if Mr. Campbell at the estate agents' is anything to go by. I was definitely being given the cold shoulder. I would go as far as to say he was trying to stop me from making a bid on the property," she said, clasping her hands together nervously.

"I suspected as much, Mrs. Wiseman," he said. "May I make a suggestion?"

"Please do," Frances replied.

"Well, you could open an account at Henderson's Bank immediately with a substantial amount of money. At the same time, do not let Peter White realise who you are. We can get the ball rolling without Campbell or White knowing they have an opponent," he said, standing up and pacing up and down. "Not so much money that he will suspect. If you were to deposit a vast amount with the bank, his staff would inform him of the transaction. Do you understand, Mrs. Wiseman?"

"Yes, up to a point, Mr. Coombes, but why use Henderson's Bank at all when I have a perfectly good bank of my own?" she asked, puzzled.

"My dear lady, I must ask you how much money you can raise before we go any further with this conversation."

"If the offer from the businessmen is less than two million, Mr. Coombes, then I shall top that with whatever you think will clinch the deal," Frances replied.

"Mrs. Wiseman, do you have two million pounds?" he asked, looking at her in complete disbelief.

"Of course I do. I would not be wasting your time if I was not in a position to buy Lambecote Grange," she replied angrily. "Would you be so kind to explain to me why Lambecote is on the market for almost eight million pounds when it can be purchased for just over two million?" she asked.

Coombes pushed his chair back and began to explain. "The bank loaned one million pounds to the previous owner who unfortunately could not pay. There are several small amounts owing to creditors, but with all the interest, the total figure I believe is two million. It is my job to secure as much as possible for the land, but in this case, the reason the land has been so highly valued is its prospects for development. Peter White has tried in vain several times to get the land removed from green belt and was hoping that as the place became derelict and overgrown, he would eventually succeed at having it removed. We have to give as much time as we can for a buyer to come up with the full value, but no farmer would want to pay so much for the land when farming is such a low-earning business at the moment."

"So eight million is too high for most buyers," Frances said.

"I am sorry, Mrs. Wiseman, I certainly do not want you to think that I doubt you, but it is most unusual for a woman to come into my office late in the afternoon with an offer to buy a two million pound property. I have to ask you these pertinent questions," he said. "May I ask you how long it would take for you to get your hands on this money?"

"I do understand, Mr. Coombes, but I have no intention of being swindled out of one penny piece in this transaction either by you, the bank, or by Mr. Campbell," Frances answered. "I can have the money in the length of time it takes to wire it from the US, and in the meantime, I will provide you with a note of credit from my bankers. Now, Mr. Coombes, can we proceed?"

"Certainly we can," Coombes said. He was getting excited now. This could prove to be his finest hour—beating the establishment at its own game.

"Now Mr. Coombes perhaps you can explain to me why I need an account at Hendersons bank?" she asked.

"Mrs Wiseman if you use an account with Whites branch you are in control of the whole proceedings". Coombes explained. "If you have a current account with a substantial amount of money in credit. Plus a dollar account set up at the same time ready to transfer direct into this account a very, very large amount of money. White cannot hold up the proceedings without incriminating himself. You can visit the bank and prove that the funds are indeed ready for the transaction."

"I think I shall stay overnight in Nottingham," Frances said. "Tomorrow I will open an account at Henderson's Bank, and at the appropriate time, shall transfer the funds for the completion of the sale. I have my laptop in the car and will e-mail my solicitor in Sheffield with my instructions to start the work tomorrow first thing. If you could fax to him all the relevant paperwork before I leave the office tonight, then I can't see how we could lose this sale. Is there a good five star hotel in Nottingham, Mr Coombes? Shall I need to make a reservation?"

Coombes was very impressed, but he had his doubts regarding Peter White and that gang of crooks. They had been so sure that they would pickup the land at a very low price and had already sold shares in anticipation. They would not go away quietly, he was sure of that. This woman did seem to know her business but was certainly up against strong opposition.

Frances rose early and ordered a light breakfast to be served in her room. She had decided to stay at the Crown Hotel when she remembered her mother telling her how her great grandparents held the Hunt Ball there in the last century. She was really enjoying herself. After depositing two thousand pounds in an account at Henderson's Bank and setting up a dollar account, she smugly drove back to Sheffield for a meeting with her solicitor.

Peter White was in shock when he arrived at the estate agents' office. "Who the hell is this buyer, Alex? You know I want that land. This will not auger well for you if we lose this deal, Campbell. I warn you. Do something about it now."

"I have tried, Peter, but she went straight to the receiver. I personally think she is not a full shilling, but Coombes has accepted her offer," Alex answered nervously. He needed to keep on the right side of Peter White if he expected to trade in Nottingham in the future.

"How much has she bid?" White asked.

"Two point two million," Campbell replied.

Bloody hell I can only raise one point nine million, Alex, and that's stretching everyone involved. White moaned. "How long will it take her to raise it?"

"I can't say, Peter. Coombes will not let on. He has gone very quiet," Alex answered.

"Perhaps it's a scam, Alex. You don't think he is trying to get me to raise my bid, do you?" White asked.

"I don't know this woman, Peter. I have asked colleagues in Sheffield to verify her, but no one has heard of her. Her solicitor is very well-respected and quite accustomed to handling large sums of money. He has refused to speak to me, saying he will communicate only with the receiver," Alex said miserably.

"Who is her banker?" White asked.

"You are, according to the paperwork I have received," Alex replied.

"Well, I shall find out if it is the last thing I do!" White said angrily. "Can I use your phone?"

"Sure, be my guest," Alex said, passing him the phone.

"White here, put Neville on quick!" Peter White shouted, irritated. "Nev, have a look see if that Wiseman woman has an account with us." After a long drawn-out silence, he said smugly, "I knew it, the crafty bugger, how much has she got in there? Only two thousand. Are you sure? What type of account is it? Current and a dollar account! How much is in the dollar account? Why has she opened a dollar account, do you know?" he demanded.

"Well, Alex, she has an account waiting for funds to be transferred from the US. That gives me time to work on old Coombes."

Frances was at home in Sheffield one week later. She answered the phone. "Hello Mr. Coombes is everything all right? I transferred five million dollars days ago. I could give you a check as soon as my solicitor has finalised the contract of sale. I can't move any faster than that. I will drive to Nottingham today. Thank you for telling me."

When she arrived at Henderson's Bank in Nottingham later that afternoon Frances was very angry. She politely announced who she was and asked to see Mr. White.

Peter White was taken by surprise. He had not expected her to visit the bank. "Good afternoon," he said, offering his hand to Frances who shook hands, but very lightly, not wanting to convey any friendliness toward this man.

"Mr. White," she began. "Three days ago, I transferred a considerable amount of money from my American bankers to my account with this bank. I have a dollar account in this bank, and I understand that you have not received this money yet."

White had Frances's account on the screen. "No, I am afraid we have not, Mrs. Wiseman," he said in a condescending way. "I believe these transactions take rather a long time to complete."

"This transaction should not have taken longer than forty eight hours, Mr. White, and the money left my bank on the 10th of April. It is now the 13th of April. Perhaps you could tell me where it is," Frances said.

"I wish that I could," White said leaning back in his chair and smiling a sickly smile.

"You had better start trying, Mr. White, as I will not leave this office until I am satisfied with your explanation," she said.

"Take a look at the screen, Mrs. Wiseman. You have the sum total of two thousand pounds in your account. I do not think you could buy much of a house with that, do you?" he said, laughing.

Frances opened her laptop computer and asked if she could use the phone jack plug. She proceeded to give White a lesson in using the Internet. After she had brought up her bank account in her American bank, she showed White how five million dollars had left the account on the 10th and arrived at Henderson's holding bank on the 11th, moving to the Nottingham bank on the 12th.

"Now, where is my money, Mr. White? What is more, where is my interest? I need answers now please or I shall be calling in the fraud squad," Frances threatened.

"I think there must have been a mistake, Mrs. Wiseman. This has never happened before, believe m-me," he stuttered.

"Do you have lots of customers moving millions of dollars, Mr. White, or are you just incompetent?" she asked, sitting back smiling smugly. The shoe was on the other foot now. "I intend to purchase Lambecote Grange, Mr. White, and I shall not allow a small-time bank manager to stop me."

White and his business buddies tried in vain to raise more money, but he knew he could not match this woman who was single-minded in her quest to own Lambecote Grange.

Chapter 37

Sheffield 1999

rances's lawyer, Richard Basildon, poured the champagne and passed a glass to Frances saying, "Congratulations, Frances, you are now the new owner of Lambecote Grange. I have received the deeds and land registry documents today. The contract is signed and sealed. I wish you well. What are you going to do with it?"

"I have plans, Richard—plans to use it for helping sick people who need a place like Lambecote Grange to rest in and come to terms with what time they have left of life. I have decided to split the land into manageable amounts and offer it for rent to small farmers passionate about growing organic food. I shall renovate the house, taking great care to search for original pictures and bring Lambecote Grange back to its former glory. It is far too big for me to live in, but I could not contemplate selling it.

Frances enjoyed being involved in business and began to work on a plan to offer a peaceful retreat for terminally ill people who needed the skills of doctors trained in psychoneuroimmunology. This was something close to Frances's heart. She believed that what had been taught to her, after the breast surgeon had diagnosed breast cancer, should be offered to anyone who wanted or needed it and to their families who had to survive the trauma of watching their loved ones die a painful death.

"Well, I congratulate you, Frances. This has been a long arduous search, and I am proud to be a part of this achievement.

The Grange was to be a hospice where it was possible to meet someone who believed that one could live even after the medical world had stamped one for the undertaker. The house itself was turned into a retreat for cancer patients recovering from chemotherapy. The patients would be given all the holistic and alternative advice available whilst living in the peace and tranquillity of three thousand acres of land and country walks. The farmland would be restored to complete organic farming, the products of which could help them to recover and build their strength. The rent from the land would pay most of the running costs of the house, and the trust could be registered as a charity. Being considered as part of the living world and not part of the cancer world of surgeons and hospital wards was so very important to recovery. The project would be called the "Lambecote Grange Trust" and would be run by a board of directors that consisted of Frances and Coombes at the head, with an Accountant, and an Administrator taking care of the smooth running of the project.

After a visit to Normandy, she bought a lovely cottage and spent some time there furnishing it in true Normandy style, Frances enjoyed many happy times there. She had had a charmed life and had had the imagination to see further than the present. She had lived with a past full of traumas now put to rest and the ghost of the huntsman could ride on Lambecote Grange land in the knowledge that the dreadful injustice done to his family had been resolved.

Of course, Frances had only invested in property and the land. Internet stock would be here today and gone tomorrow, but houses and land would stay just where they were—sometimes winning a little and sometimes losing a little but never disappearing overnight.

She thanked God for the opportunity given to her, when she had the finance to take advantage of that window of time when millions could be made on the internet. Without this opportunity arising at the right time just when she had sold the bed and breakfast properties, Lambecote Grange would be lost for ever. All the hard work and worry that she suffered when she was trying to make enough money to pay the mortgages on the bed and breakfasts was reaping its own rewards. It was very strange how things planned out in the fullness of time, but it seemed that if you keep your head, do not panic, and always listen to your better judgement, you will get there in the end.

Chapter 38

Lambecote Grange 2000 - Romany cousins

One afternoon, Frances set out to walk around the farm. The sun was shining, God was in his heaven, and all was well with the world. She had had little time over the past months to follow her heart and look for the places her mother had described. Beckett's Wood was where she was heading today. Walking at a brisk pace. She hoped she would not be disappointed. It was late autumn, and the blackberries were ripe in the hedgerows. The leaves fell from the trees, and the air smelled so fresh with a slight nip of frost. This reminded Frances of her childhood when she and Tommy played in the pit woods behind the Woodlands in Halten. She remembered that at this time of year all the children in the woodlands would go into the woods after they returned from school.

November 5th was Guy Fawkes night and each gang of children would collect wood to build a bonfire. They started collecting weeks before the event and the competition to build the biggest bonfire was serious business. The pit village kids would sneak around after dark, ready to steal any good-sized logs that were not carefully guarded. The organisation involved in keeping this wood safe was incredible. A rota system would be used and a sophisticated system of whistles and warning sounds was devised to raise the alarm when an attack was imminent. After school all the kids would hurry home make bread and jam sandwiches if the family could afford such a luxury. If not, they ate raw cabbages or turnips which they stole from the pitmen's allotments. When November 4th arrived, the excitement was so great. This was the night that Guy Fawkes planned his mischief when he tried to blow up the houses of Parliament. On this night the Halten kids played mischievous tricks on the neighbours. Dust bins would be knocked over, or one end of a length of string would be tied to a dustbin lid and the other end tied to the door handle. When all had been set in place, the door knocker was wrapped loudly, and the kids would hide to watch the frightened house-holder's face when he opened his door to a dreadful clatter, caused when his or her dust bin fell over.

Mischief night was especially dangerous for the gang's bonfire. If the pit village kids could reach the woodlands bonfire they would set it alight early, leaving them without a fire for the November 5th celebrations. Extra guards had to be on duty on November 4th..

Frances laughed out loud when she remembered the happy times she and Tommy had had guarding the bonfire. Frances would fight to the death to protect some small piece of wood from going to the pit village. Tommy was just a baby, and Frances would send him off to raise the alarm.

Suddenly she was aware of being watched.

"What yer doin' out here on thee own?" a deep-throated voice bel-lowed at her.

Frances stopped in her tracks startled. "I, err, was looking for Beckett's Wood," she answered timidly.

"Well yer'll not find it around here," the voice answered as a dusky man stepped out from the bushes and blocked her path.

"Let me pass," Frances said nervously.

"What are yer lookin' for?" the man asked.

"I told you I am looking for Beckett's Wood," she said pushing her shoulders back defiantly. "Who are you?"

The man stood, refusing to move out of her way, his eyes screwed up into his wizened weather-beaten face. "I ask again, lady, what are yer lookin' for?"

Frances began to stammer. She was in an impossible position. How stupid she had been to walk out all this way without telling anyone where she was going? She had to try to humour this man or she could be in great danger. "I am looking for a thicket that my mother told me stories about when I was child," she said, feeling stupid telling a tale like that to a vagabond. "I do not suppose you know of it, do you?"

"I know of Beckett's Wood all right, but it's not a place for a woman to find on her own. Yer that woman from the farm, are yer?"

"Yes I am," Frances said, beginning to understand the situation. "Who are you?"

"'Never mind who I am. It's yer what interests me," he said. "what are yer up to at Lambecote Grange?"

"Well I am Frances Wiseman, and I have bought Lambecote Grange just in time to rescue it from developers. I intend to keep everything just as it is, if that is possible. Now what are you doing on my land threatening me like this?" she asked, looking him straight in the eye.

"I live here most of the time," he answered.

"What, here in the woods?" she asked.

"Follow me." he ordered.

Frances followed the man through rough bushes, pushing aside brambles and gorse in an effort to keep up with the him. She knew she was foolish but this was so intriguing. She had to find out how this man knew of her owning Lambecote Grange. After quite a long trek, they eventually came upon a clearing, and sitting in the centre, was a beautifully kept caravan with clean wash hanging around the door. A piebald pony grazed at the front, and an old woman sat in a chair made up of straw and old crochet blankets. She puffed on a clay pipe and watched the man. Frances walked toward her. She did not move a muscle—just sat watching Frances intently. She wore no expression on her wizened face. The man walked up to the door and climbed inside the caravan closing the curtain behind him.

"Just a minute," Frances called to him. "I thought you were taking me to Beckett's Wood." She walked toward the caravan intent on moving the curtain and speaking directly to the man.

"Hold!" the woman spat at her. "What yer think yer doin', eh?"

"I am sorry to bother you," Frances answered, but your husband said he would show me the way to Beckett's Wood."

"I never said owt of the sort," the throaty voice bellowed out of the caravan.

"Sit thee down, lass. Thee are safe enough here. Stop shakin' like a leaf in autumn." The old woman laughed with an equally gravely voice. "Here, get this down thee. It'll do thee good," she said, passing Frances a cup of something hot.

Frances sipped the liquid and recoiled from the taste.

The old woman laughed a raucous laugh. "What's up with yer? It's good herbal stuff. This is what happens when families go bad. They get soft—can't drink good herbal stuff."

Frances sipped the sweet liquid slowly and began to calm down. She had the feeling of complete safety sitting amongst the peace and quiet of these trees. She looked around her, trying to work out just where she was.

"What yer want with Beckett's Wood?" the old woman asked.

Frances found herself telling her story to this woman. The gypsy listened intently, her dark eyes that never blinked or wavered staring straight into Frances's.

"Well yer has found it," the old woman said, laughing at Frances. "So what yer gonna do with it—build a house?"

"Is this Beckett's Wood?" Frances asked, standing up and walking around.

"It is that," the gypsy woman answered. "It's the only place we have left in these parts when we travel down for the Goose Fair. Old Sutton would get the police if he found us here. But Billy Bingham started us comin' here years ago when me ma was with us and we've been campin' here ever since. But we can't make a fire in daylight or we gets moved on."

Frances was dumbstruck. She had never expected to meet up with her gypsy relatives. She thought she must be dreaming.

The old woman stood up and walked straight up to Frances, staring into her eyes as if she could see straight into her soul. "Who are yer? Yer say yer a Bingham, but I have me doubts, they must all be dead and gone by now. So what yer want? What yer doin' here? Yer old enough to be settled down with a family, so what yer doin' round here?" she asked.

"I had hoped to find the stream in Beckett's Wood. My mam told me about it, but this place is dry as a bone. I can't hear water running, and the atmosphere is eerie. It feels like a graveyard," Frances said with a shiver.

"Jack!" the old woman shouted into the back of the wagon. "Come here, will yer?"

The man climbed down from the wagon and moved toward Frances, mumbling something about the ditches needing cleaning. Then she would hear running water.

"Are you saying that this is where the beck used to be?" she asked.

"That's right, missus. Yer standin' in the middle of the beck. When it rains heavy the water gets through them ditches but not like it should. If yer are thinkin' about runnin' that farm up there than yer had better get them ditches cleaned out.

"Oh I see," Frances said, smiling to herself. So this is where her grandmother fell in love with her grandfather right here in this wood.

"Lee, Narrilla. Lee was your relation. She was kicked out for marrying a cart driver. That's the story in the family. Then her daughter goes and marries a squire up at big house. And after he died, she lost everything to old Sutton. What a mean old bugger he was. He stopped all us gypsies travellin' on his land. Some said it was 'cos Billy Bingham should have been squire, and old Sutton were scared stiff he would claim is inheritance and kick him off one day."

"Billy Bingham was my uncle," Frances said quietly, not knowing what response she would receive from these people who had to be her blood relatives.

"So thee is the daughter of Billy's sister—the one that went to live in Bingley, are yer?" the gypsy woman asked.

"Yes I am and I have brought Lambecote Grange back into the Bingham family. I had no idea where to find it but thank God I found it in time to stop it being developed for housing," Frances replied.

"Well yer better get sorted out before there's nowt left to sort out," the gypsy man shouted at her.

"How do you earn your living?" Frances asked. "If you can't let anyone know that you are here then you can't sell goods door to door as you did when my mam was a girl."

"We sell a horse or two and manage. We live off the land, doin' work when we can," the man answered.

Frances had a plan working in her head. She said, "Would you consider a regular wage working for me?"

"We don't want your charity," the woman spat at her.

"It won't be charity, believe me," Frances said. "I really want to keep the land and farm in good order and have no idea what work will be needed on the land. I have rented out several plots to organic farmers, but managing the main part of the land is my job. I desperately need someone I can trust looking around, informing me of jobs needing attention like the ditches that are stopping the beck running through here. I would never have found this place if I had not bumped into you this morning."

"Ha! Yer didn't bump into him. He's been watchin' yer for weeks." The old woman cackled.

"So we have a deal then?" Frances asked. "I shall pay the going rate, and you can stay in Beckett's Wood whenever you need to. I do not want the place taken over with caravans and rubbish. Lambecote Grange is a refuge for very sick people, and I do not need to have them upset by feuding travellers. What do you say, Jack?" she asked looking straight at the man. "By the way what is your name, is it Lee?"

"Boswell, Jack Boswell that's me. Me ma is Shuri Lee. We'll give it a try, missus, and if its like yer say, I'll start today. It's still light. I can get a good bit a work in before nightfall."

267

"Thank you, Mr. Boswell," Frances said, holding out her hand to seal the deal with a handshake.

Jack Boswell spit on his hand and proffered it to Frances who spat on her own hand and shook his, smiling happily at being considered worthy of this Romany custom.

"Before I go on my way, I understand a curse was put on my great grandmother and all issue of that union when she married Len Morton. How long is this curse going to last?" she asked.

"A curse lasts through generation after generation until it gets weakened by time. But if a wrong is put right it's possible for it to pass a generation. It could take hundreds of years to pass away," the old woman said. "I can't remove a curse. Only the one who puts it on can remove it, and she's long gone. We don't curse people for marryin' out now, 'cos we were losin' to many good Romanies when we need to keep up the numbers. But we still look after our own."

Frances set off on her journey back to Lambecote Grange. Jack Boswell rode up beside her on the old piebald used to pull the gypsy wagon. "Where will you start the work, Jack?" Frances asked.

"Oh, I know just where the trouble starts, missus" he replied.

"Jack, will you call at the farm tomorrow and take a look at the stables?" Frances asked. "I was thinking of offering livery to the local hunt members but I have no idea what horses need. The stables have been neglected for some time, but after we clear the rubbish away, I think we could do something with them."

"Them stables used to be the best in the county, missus," Jack said. "I would love to clear 'em out and see good horses in 'em again."

Chapter 39

Romany funeral

Autumn at Lambecote Grange was very hard work for Frances. Having a dream was quite different to actually doing a project as vast as this. She and Jack Boswell had cleaned and scrubbed the stables. Jack had bought four horses from Appleby. He groomed the horses every day and taught Frances how to sit a horse. She was very nervous but soon began to look forward to her riding lessons. She and Jack rode around the farm with Jack pointing out areas that needed urgent repair. Frances's life had changed completely.

Shuri died the following very cold winter. Jack asked Frances if she would allow him to give his ma a true Romany funeral. This entailed all the family gathering together and saying farewell to the departed. The high spot of this gathering was burning the dead woman with her wagon and all her possessions. Frances had to fight to get permission from the local council, but they eventually relented, and Shuri Lee was sent on her way to the afterlife in true Romany style. Families in twelve Romany wagons from around the country attended the funeral. Frances had allowed them to camp in Beckett's Wood for one week only. This was the deal she had struck with the local council. She had also agreed to pay any damages caused by the wagons. The council official thought she had gone out of her mind, but this was very important to Frances. This one last privilege given to this Romany *bori rani*, a truly great lady.

26 December 2002

The frost-covered fields glistened like diamonds, and sitting in the centre of this diamond-studded land, was Lambecote Grange, the winter

269

sunshine bringing the building to life. Milling around at the front of the house were horses and riders, beautifully turned out in readiness for the Boxing Day hunt.

The local hunt club had jumped at the chance to use the stables at Lambecote Grange, and in return, had raised many thousands of pounds for the Lambecote Grange Trust.

The house had become very successful in the care of people who had been given no hope in their fight for life. After treatment with conventional methods had failed, Lambecote Grange offered another chance with alternative therapy, beginning with relaxing the body with reflexology, reiki massage, and Indian head massage with ear candling. This was very successful in relaxing the patient when their muscles had grown taut around the face and head causing so much pain and discomfort. Also, aromatherapy was given and food allergy testing, helping the body to rebuild its immune system with a complete dietary change, including eating only organic food grown on Lambecote land by small holders who were passionate about keeping soil free from chemicals. Grange land produced delicious foods. Most important was a resident doctor who administered psychoneuroimmunology that persuaded the brain to correct the production of rogue cells and using the ductal drainage system of the body to remove the dead rogue cells.

The house was always full and had a waiting list of patients. Frances found it very upsetting when she had to turn people away, but to be successful, the trust had to offer accommodation to relatives, especially children. This was imperative to their recovery. All stress and worry had to be removed from their lives if the therapy was to succeed.

Jack brought Frances's horse around to the front of the house, and after helping her mount, he led her to the front of the assembled riders. They had planned this yesterday when Frances told him about her father's hunting horn and the importance it had on her life. She had very nearly lost it when her dad left to live with the widow. But she had recovered it, and now was the time to use it.

The hunt leader in his red jacket saw Frances being led in his direction, and knowing that she was not an accomplished rider, he made his way toward her.

Jack handed her the gleaming silver hunting horn with all its inscriptions of past hunt leaders, and she held it out to the hunt leader asking him if he would use it in the day's hunting. He was amazed to read the inscription covering almost two hundred years of hunt leaders. After pinning it to his jacket he raised it to his lips and the cry rang out.

NINA WHITEHOUSE

TALLY HO!

The scene brought tears to Frances's eyes as she watched the hunt leave Lambecote Grange in all its splendour. She watched the riders disappear into the distance and could see way out in the front of the pack, a lone rider, riding like the wind over Lambecote Grange land as far as the eye could see.

The Binghams were home again after almost a century. Frances had realised her mother's dream and Rosina's last wish. This was their home, but what a journey it had been for the family.

Frances gazed down at Jack Boswell. He looked so handsome in his new riding gear, not bought by Frances but from his own earnings. He had been instrumental in getting the farm working, and his knowledge of not only the land but the horses and even how and where to purchase stock had been invaluable. What a waste it would have been to lose all that knowledge if Frances had not had the courage to take risks. Lambecote Grange would have been lost forever and this land could have been covered in modern little boxes making Peter White and his cronies very rich.

Jack looked up at Frances with soft admiring eyes and the feeling she had for him welled up inside her. Gypsies had their own marriage arrangements, and Frances hoped both her gentry and gypsy ancestors would have approved of Jack Boswell and Sarah Bingham's daughter, Frances Wiseman, running Lambecote Grange together.

271

Printed in the United Kingdom
by Lightning Source UK Ltd.
113500UKS00001B/232-276